Darkness Bound

J.T. GEISSINGER

DARKNESS BOUND

A NIGHT PROWLER NOVEL

Published by Montlake Romance, Seattle

www.apub.com

ISBN-13: 9781477820100
ISBN-10: 1477820108

Library of Congress Control Number: 2013954788

Printed in the United States of America

To Jay,
for proving that love at first sight and happily-ever-afters
are things that happen in real life, too.

Being deeply loved by someone gives you strength,
while loving someone deeply gives you courage.

—Lao Tzu

PROLOGUE

Excerpt from the New York Times, *Sunday, May 17, 20—*

THE ENEMY AMONG US

By Senior War Correspondent Jack Dolan

. . . indeed, not only is it the duty of every citizen of this great country to fight back against such insidious evil, but also it is the duty of all mankind. For if we allow our fear to weaken our resolve, if we allow misguided empathy for these avowed human-haters to turn us away from the righteous path of self-defense, we will quickly find ourselves facing the plight of so many other species who have walked this Earth before us:

Extinction.

We are at war. To deny this fact is to deny the obvious. We are at war with a cunning, ruthless enemy, whose numbers are far fewer but whose resolve—and capacity for cruelty—is far greater than our own. But even more dangerous than our enemy is the war we fight among ourselves. If we cannot come together as a race to protect our way of life and our continued existence on this Earth, the family of Man will be lost, devoured not only by our enemy, but by our own cowardice.

It is time to put rhetoric aside. It is time for the divisiveness to end. It is time to *act*. If we are to survive this plague that has befallen us, this pestilence of unholy predators who care nothing for our cultures or our history, least of all our lives, we must put aside any sentimental feeling and push back. We must treat the Shifter plague like a newly discovered strain of bacteria that is sweeping the earth, killing us mercilessly. For that is what these predators are: a plague. And like a plague, they will devour everything in their path unless we find a cure.

I know the cure.

It lies in courage and cohesiveness, in the knowledge that human life is sacred, in the willingness to do whatever it takes to survive. *As a species*, we must be willing to do whatever it takes. We cannot allow the majesty of Bach and Beethoven, Michelangelo and Mozart, Shakespeare and Shubert, and even the simple beauty of a Starbucks Frappuccino to be wiped out for all time by the single-minded, devastating hunger of a bacterium. Nor can we allow a few dissenting voices among us to make us shrink from our right and duty to defend ourselves.

I call on you now—as an American, as a citizen of this planet, and as a member of the human race—to join me in supporting our President in his efforts to protect this great nation and our way of life. Write to your congressperson and urge him or her to sign into law the amendments strengthening the Alien and Sedition Acts, and to reconsider the Violent Radicalization and Homegrown Terrorism Prevention Act of 2007 that failed to become law during the 110th Congress.

Let us join hands as a nation and a people, and walk forward together to face this dire threat to humanity. The time for discourse is over.

Now, my fellow patriots, it's time to fight.

ONE

Fire and Ice

Something was blocking her shot. Something *big*.

Squatting on the trash-littered street with her back braced against the smoking metal skeleton of a burned-out delivery truck outside the sprawling, gothic Mercado Municipal building in downtown Manaus, Jacqueline "Jack" Dolan glanced up from her camera and squinted against the brilliant scarlet rays of the setting sun.

The thing blocking the shot was a man. A tall, broad-shouldered hulk of a man, unmoving, silhouetted in black against the light.

Christ. He was ruining her picture!

Irritation stabbed through her gut, sharp as knives. She had to have pictures to accompany the article, and she was in prime position to get some amazing shots of the mayhem occurring inside the popular market, which on any given day saw tens of thousands of visitors flood the massive structure that housed row upon row of food vendors. Meat and fish, olives and wine, poultry and fruit, and every kind of exotic spice—everything and anything could be found there. Covering over twelve thousand square meters of the city, it was the main wholesale distribution center for thousands of restaurants in central Brazil, and a popular destination for tourists and locals alike.

It was also currently engulfed in flames. From within, irregular bursts of gunfire from automatic weapons echoed like cannon fire.

With a muttered curse, Jack waved an impatient hand overhead, indicating he should move.

He didn't. In fact, he stood so still he didn't even seem to be breathing.

She lowered the camera and shaded her eyes from the glare of the setting sun to inspect this unmoving hulk more closely.

He was about twenty yards away on the opposite side of the street, directly in front of the market's entrance. A steady stream of people screaming in panic were shoving and pushing their way out of the market from the open double doors behind him, but he stood as unperturbed as a rock in a riverbed, immovable, ignoring everything around him.

What the hell is he doing?

Her eyes focused on his face, and Jack realized what he was doing was staring straight back at her.

From years of habit, she mentally catalogued the pertinent details for later recall. Dark hair curling down to the collar of his shirt, sun-darkened skin, a hard, unshaven jaw. Lips overfull for a man, a nose that was once straight but had obviously been broken and carelessly repaired. And huge, as she first noticed—six foot five, six foot six, broad-shouldered, and muscular.

But Jesus—what a pair of searing eyes this hulk had. Brilliant yellow-green, heart-stoppingly piercing, as if he could see straight down into her soul. Staring out from that glowering, handsome face, his eyes glowed hot and translucent, like an emerald backlit by the sun. They telegraphed anger. Anger, intelligence, and dangerous intent.

A jolt of something sharp and electric sizzled through her, straight down to her toes.

Her first thought was: *Holy shit, that is one scary-beautiful man.*

Her next, a millisecond later: *Get the hell out of my shot, asshole!*

She waved her hand in another frantic "move it" gesture, this time more aggressively. It also helpfully featured her middle finger, the international sign for "you, sir, are a douche."

It didn't work. Jack groaned in exasperation and shot to her feet. Time to change vantage points.

Just as she was about to turn away, an odd noise arrested her. Over the din of screams and shattering glass and gunfire, she heard a high-pitched roar, a rumbling that accelerated and grew louder, echoing off the buildings. It came from behind her—

Jack turned the opposite direction and didn't even have time to gasp in horror as a Humvee, mere yards away, barreled down the narrow street toward her.

I'm going to kill that guy.

Stupid. So damn stupid. Almost ten years of being embedded with military units all over the world in the most dangerous war zones and she was going to get flattened by a Humvee because she was too busy staring at some hot guy. Her entire body tensed—

Then she was flying through the air, hit hard from the side.

She landed on her back on the sidewalk with such force all the breath was knocked from her lungs. Her head cracked against the cement. She saw stars. Pain flared throughout her body, and everything went black.

When she opened her eyes again, the hulk was bending over her with his hands flattened on the ground on either side of her head, glaring down into her face.

"Are you oblivious, or just plain stupid?" he snapped. It was more of a growl, pitched low and rumbly, his English tinged with the lilting accent of Portuguese. Normally Jack would have found this kind of voice incredibly sexy. At the moment, she found it—and him—infuriating.

"You're the one who's oblivious! What the hell were you doing just standing there in the middle of everything?" She attempted to sit up, and fireworks erupted in her vision. Wincing, she pushed him aside, and brought a hand to her forehead.

"Just sit here for a minute and breathe. You hit your head pretty hard."

The hulk crouched in front of her with his big hand spread in a determined "stay" gesture, looking at her in that strange way he'd been before. She had an odd, fleeting feeling that he knew her somehow . . . and didn't like her. She pushed that aside because if they'd met somewhere before, she'd *definitely* remember.

He wasn't the kind of man a woman would forget.

"I'm perfectly fine," she said through gritted teeth, willing it to be true. Even though she felt bruises already forming on her shoulders, back, and behind, and there was a worrisome buzzing in her ears and a metallic taste on her tongue, she wasn't about to let on, especially to the Incredible Irritating Hulk. Who just happened to appear by her side . . .

"How did you . . ." Jack glanced back across the street to the spot where he'd been standing moments ago, and shook her head to clear it. "What just happened?"

He jerked a thumb over his shoulder. "You got clipped by that Humvee."

Across the street the massive dun-colored military vehicle was parked in front of the market, flanked by two more that had just arrived. Uniformed personnel in flak jackets and helmets, with rifles slung over their shoulders, had taken up positions around the cars and were attempting to direct the fleeing crowd. A line of city police vehicles roared up the other end of the street, lights flashing, sirens screaming, and Jack realized she and the hulk were probably about to get caught right in the middle of a firefight with the hoodlums inside the market who'd started the fire.

The question of how she'd landed relatively unscathed in her present spot on the hard sidewalk after being hit by a five-thousand-pound, seven-foot-wide vehicle became instantly insignificant because it was showtime.

Jack *lived* for showtime.

She grinned, sat up straight, grabbed her Canon—which thankfully had remained in one piece on its strap around her neck—and, as the police cars screeched to a stop and disgorged dozens of armed officers who swarmed the entrance to the market, started shooting.

Then she was flying through the air again, but this time she was being carried. By the Incredible Irritating Hulk, no less.

"What the—put me *down!*" she shouted, just as a deafening volley of gunfire burst overhead. The stone façade of the building behind them erupted in a spray of pulverized cement as bullets tore through the brick, and she was pelted in the face with glass from the picture window beside it that exploded into a million tiny, jagged shards. Cursing, she turned her head and hid in the hulk's neck.

The hulk tightened his arms around her and shot forward in a burst of speed so fast it left her head spinning, her stomach far behind.

In a few seconds it was over and she was being lowered to the ground. In the distance lingered the sound of gunfire and shouting. An acrid haze of smoke tainted the twilight sky, first yellow, then shifting, charcoal gray.

Breathless, her legs not altogether onboard with the task of supporting her weight, Jack looked around. It took a moment before the world settled and she regained her bearings. They were in an alley, deserted except for a skinny orange cat nosing through a pile of garbage beside a Dumpster. At the end of the alley were a fire escape and three unmarked doors. The air smelled like urine and rotting trash and the soft, ripe decay of the tropics.

The hulk snapped, "You have a death wish or something?"

"No, I have a *job to do*." Jack shoved her hair out of her eyes and glared at him. The bangs she was trying to grow out had escaped from her ponytail and were fluttering everywhere. "And you just interfered with that!"

"Actually, I just saved your life!"

He didn't look too happy about that. In fact, he looked as if he was very much regretting it. A muscle worked in his hard jaw as those green eyes flashed and burned.

"Nobody asked for your help! I'm not some damsel in distress; I've been in a hell of a lot worse spots than that and lived." Just because her head was still spinning, and she was still pissed about the Humvee, she added a surly, "Prince Charming."

He crossed his arms over his broad chest and stood there scowling at her. Dressed all in black—boots, jeans, tight T-shirt, leather cuff around one wrist—with those bulging muscles and that bad attitude, he looked exactly like the type of man a normal woman wouldn't want to be alone with in a deserted alley of a dangerous city as the sun went down and the shadows crawled hungrily up the walls.

But Jack wasn't a "normal" woman. She refused to be intimidated, refused to be prey. If this guy wanted to tussle, he'd be in for a big surprise because she had a license to carry a concealed weapon. What she had tucked into the waistband of her pants at the small of her back would pretty much guarantee she'd win if they went toe to toe.

She put her hands on her hips and stared right back at him.

You want a piece of me, big boy? Bring it!

For some strange reason, he looked as if he was going to laugh. He pressed his lips together, causing a dimple to flash in his cheek. His eyes grew amused. He cocked his head and gave her a swift, assessing once-over, his gaze equal parts heated and shrewd, then announced, "You're bleeding . . . Snow White."

In spite of herself, Jack's lips twisted, threatening to turn to a smile.

Who is *this guy?*

To cover her amusement, she said coolly, "Skin jokes. Nice."

Because she was a redhead, and Irish on both parents' sides, Jack had skin the color of milk. She detested it, in part because even casual sun exposure made her burn and her job demanded she was out in the sun regularly, which in turn meant she spent a good portion of her life either peeling or covered in a thick layer of sunblock, and in part because she thought it made her look delicate and fragile, and those were two of the last things she wanted to look like, or was.

If she looked like what she felt like inside, Jack would be a weird transgender hybrid of Xena Warrior Princess, John Wayne, Lisbeth Salander, and Elmer Fudd.

In his sandpaper voice, the hulk said, "You're right, that was rude. How 'bout I make it up to you by buying you a drink?" and Jack wasn't sure if she should cut and run, or just brandish her weapon and tell him to get the hell out of her face. Judging by his dizzying mood swings, he was a little off in the head.

But a tiny little part of her—a forgotten, neglected part— wanted to sit next to him on a barstool and drink in all that masculine sexiness, in addition to drinking a few shots of vodka, which might do wonders for her throbbing cheek and her still slightly spinning head.

She debated longer than she should have. Eventually logic won.

"Thanks, but I'll pass. I've got to get back to work."

She wondered briefly how he'd run so fast so far, then wondered if she had a mild concussion from her head versus the cement. Which would explain a lot, including the urge to have a drink with a big, growly stranger who exuded equal doses of danger and sex appeal, and had all the charm of an open grave.

"You're a reporter," he said flatly, glancing down at her camera and the laminated press badge clipped to the strap. Something in his tone telegraphed his disapproval.

"Yeah, so?"

His gaze found hers again, and it was dark. "This is no place for you. It's too dangerous."

She bristled. "Why, because I'm a girl?"

He regarded her with pinched lips, looking as if he was trying not to say something nasty. He drew in a measured breath, then said, "No, because Brazil is one of the most dangerous places in the world for reporters. They get killed here regularly, men and women equally. Especially now, with all the unrest. Or hadn't you heard?"

There was a kind of dare in the question, and Jack found herself more and more irritated by and interested in the hulk. Whose name she didn't know.

She stood there looking at him a moment, sticky from the humidity, acutely aware of the way the material of her damp T-shirt was clinging to her breasts.

Why was she aware of her *breasts*?

She asked, "What's your name?"

His brows lifted. He hadn't been expecting that.

"It's a journalist thing. Who, what, where, when . . . you know."

He just kept looking at her, brows cocked, but once Jack decided she wanted an answer to a question, she didn't relent until she had it.

"So? What is it?"

He paused for a beat, and she realized he had a habit of that, as if he carefully deliberated each and every word.

Interesting. She knew several people with the same habit, all of whom had warehouses of skeletons they were trying to hide.

Finally, he relented and gave her his name in a clipped monosyllable.

"Hawk."

It was Jack's turn to raise her brows and pause. "*Hawk*? As in, a bird?"

For the first time, he smiled at her. It was carnal and lazy, a sensual upward curve of his lips that transformed his entire face and made her heart skip a beat from the sheer, unexpected beauty of it. The smile softened all the hard lines of his face and brought out that dimple in his cheek again, and she felt its effects in some very sensitive places in her body. She swallowed, surprised at herself, and none too pleased.

Hawk drawled, "As in, eyes like a."

Oh Christ. It's a nickname. Of course he'd have a nickname. He probably thought it up himself.

Because she was still a little off-balance from his smile, she said, "Funny, I would've guessed something more along the lines of . . ." She cocked her head and gave him the same assessing once-over he'd given her. "Rock. As in, head like a."

"You mean, *body* like a," he responded, and had the nerve to wink.

That's when it occurred to her that one, the hulk was flirting with her, two, she liked it, and three, she wanted that drink more than she wanted to get back to the Mercado Municipal and finish the story.

Jack was an expert at compartmentalizing, so she filed that disturbing fact away under her mental What the Hell? drawer for later examination. She never, *never* was more interested in men than work. Except for right this second. With this man with a silly bird nickname, sizzling eyes, and body to match.

Sky out, as her father would say, which in military parlance meant "time to go."

"Okay, Hawk," she said stiffly, "great meeting you. Have a nice life."

Jack turned and began to walk toward the end of the alley, back out to the street.

From behind her he called, "You're welcome for saving yours!"

Without looking back or answering, she lifted her hand in salute, then kept right on going.

She couldn't get back to the Mercado because the police had cordoned off the area and blocked the surrounding streets. No press was being allowed in, so she made do with interviewing a few bystanders and getting some long-distance shots of the smoke billowing into the sky from the burning building.

By the time she made it back to her hotel, it was fully dark, she was exhausted, and she'd finally stopped thinking about her encounter with the hulk. Taxi service had been curtailed to daylight hours because of the recent unrest and she'd had to walk back because the hotel shuttle had dropped her off early in the morning before the outbreak at the Mercado Municipal.

She was lucky to be right there when the riot started. Her intuition had told her to go downtown this morning, and it had been right.

To say that Brazil was in a state of turmoil would be a gross understatement. The country had fallen into total chaos. In Manaus—a bustling, cosmopolitan city situated in the center of the country at the confluence of the Rio Negro and Solimões rivers—stores were being looted, fires were being set, government buildings had been vandalized . . . things were a mess. There were daily marches by a public outraged over the corrupt government and the hike in bus fares in advance of the World Cup that would help to pay for ten additional stadiums.

She'd been sent here on assignment from the *Times* without her usual photographer. Dwindling readership had sent the cash-strapped newspaper into conservation mode, so anything deemed an unnecessary luxury had been axed. Jack was competent with a camera and never minded working alone, so she hadn't been as disgruntled as many of her colleagues had been over the cutbacks. She'd been raised to soldier on without whining, so that's what she did.

The hotel room was more luxurious than she'd expected, with a king-sized bed and an enormous bathtub set against a wall of blue and saffron Moroccan tiles. While the bath was filling, Jack stripped out of her dirty jeans and T-shirt and stood in front of the mirror at the sink in her underwear, delicately picking bits of glass from her cheek with a pair of tweezers.

When she was done, she inspected her work. Not bad, she decided. No stitches needed. She'd been lucky this time.

She wasn't always quite so lucky; the three puckered, round scars on her abdomen proved it.

After she'd soaked in the tub, washed the smoke and glass fragments from her hair, and shaved her legs and everything else that needed shaving, Jack wrapped herself in a towel, wound another around her hair, turned on her laptop, and dashed off a seven-hundred-word article about the day's events. She downloaded the shots from her Canon for her editor to choose from, then uploaded all the files to the paper's encrypted server. It would go live on the web as soon as her editor reviewed it, and would also run in tomorrow's morning edition.

Then she sat staring at the four walls.

This was always the worst moment, when the job was done and she was left alone in another anonymous hotel room with only her thoughts for company.

Thinking was dangerous.

Jack much preferred action to thinking. When you were engaged in some kind of action, you didn't have time to wallow in the quicksand of memory.

She debated going straight to bed, but felt too restless, and knew she wouldn't sleep. So she threw on a clean pair of jeans, a light sweater, a leather jacket as soft as butter, and low-heeled boots. The concierge in the lobby gave her directions to a nearby pub, a raucous place where only the locals went, but the food was good and inexpensive, and there was live music. That all sounded perfect, not only because her per diem wouldn't cover anything fancier, but also because she loved live music and she loved to sit in a crowded spot and just watch people, alone but not *alone*.

The walk was short, along a quiet, well-lighted street, and by the time she arrived and pulled open the heavy wood door to the pub, Jack was famished. But as the hostess led her to a table near the back, her restless stomach turned sour.

Because there, sitting on a stool at the long oak bar that ran the entire length of one wall, was Hawk, just as hulking and handsome as the first time she'd seen him. Once again, he was glowering.

Once again, he was staring straight back at her.

TWO

Simple Creatures

Hawk watched Jacqueline Dolan stride through the door, watched her look around, watched as she caught sight of him and stiffened.

He didn't miss the way her lips thinned. Or the way her heartbeat doubled in the space of five seconds.

That little tidbit should have given him a grim bit of satisfaction at least, but it didn't. She was a job he had to do, a task he had to complete, and nothing more. Forget about the fact that she had incredible hair the color of persimmons, and bright-blue eyes as clear as the Caribbean Sea, and a slender dancer's body meant for—

No. Forget about that, too. *Especially* that.

This bitch needs to be taught a lesson she'll never forget.

Not his words, but he echoed the sentiment. Jacqueline Dolan had almost single-handedly rallied the American public behind her campaign of bigotry, intolerance, and hatred with the despicable—and admittedly brilliant—opinion piece she'd written for the *Times*. She'd played every nerve with the skill of a virtuoso: patriotism, xenophobia, sentimentality for better times past, fear of change, fear of the unknown—*fear* in general. She manipulated people's fears like a puppeteer manipulates the puppet strings.

And she'd been nominated for a goddamn Pulitzer for it, no less.

Voltaire said, "Those who can make you believe absurdities can make you commit atrocities," and Jacqueline Dolan had been incredibly effective at making a lot of people believe her personal brand of absurdity. The sky is falling! she warned, and pretty much everyone listened.

Once the nation was behind the President's anti-Shifter agenda, thanks to Dolan's brilliant rhetoric, he had pushed it all the way to the UN and convinced all the member states that Shifters were the worst threat to mankind since . . . well, since *ever*. Now, in addition to an ancient order of religious assassins that wanted to wipe his kind off the face of the Earth, a greedy multinational corporation that wanted to trap them, conduct experiments, and ultimately use them for profit, they also had the Elimination Campaign, a group of leaders from all around the world who wanted nothing more than to see every single *Ikati* on Earth burned at the stake.

Thanks to you, Red, Hawk thought, watching Jacqueline narrow her eyes at him from across the room. He forced a pleasant smile to his face and was rewarded as her eyes, just for a moment, softened.

And that, ultimately, was why he'd been chosen for the task.

"They drop at your feet like flies," said Xander during the last Assembly meeting, to a chorus of murmured agreement. His wife, Morgan, sat beside him, and sent her husband a warm, heavy-lidded glance.

"Not all of them," she said softly, reaching over to squeeze his thigh.

Hawk had rolled his eyes at that. Xander and Morgan were deeply in love, overtly physical with one another, and rarely apart. Xander had brought her back to his home colony in Brazil only three months back, but after only three days Hawk had seen enough of their constant mooning at each other. If he hadn't known from personal experience that his half brother was the best killer the entire tribe had, Hawk would have thought him weak, hopelessly whipped, and not to be trusted.

Because how could you trust a man who looked at his woman like . . . *that*? There were little red hearts where his pupils were supposed to be, for God's sake.

Though he'd enjoyed many women and the pleasures their bodies could bring, Hawk had never been in love. And he liked it that way. If he ever caught himself staring at a woman the way Xander stared at Morgan, he'd have to slit his wrists in shame.

On a raised platform in a corner of the bar, the band opened with an Argentine tango, languid and sensual. Jacqueline raised her chin and turned away from him, following the hostess to a booth on the opposite side of the pub. She slid onto the red leather seat, grabbed the menu the hostess handed her, and didn't look up again.

Oh, Red, Hawk thought, the smile on his face now genuine, *this is gonna be so much fun.*

Hawk knew three things for sure. One, humans couldn't be trusted. Two, power had to be proven. And three, a woman's love was an easy thing to earn.

He knew all the mysteries of women, all the ways they could and could not be moved, all the secrets of their bodies, all the tangled yearnings of their hearts. He could discern in a glance which ones needed praise and which needed punishment, which were power hungry and which money hungry, which were shy or brazen or mean or cold. He knew if you gave a woman your undivided attention, accompanied by a compliment specifically tailored to an area of deep insecurity—her competence or intelligence or the amount of fat on her ass—she would tell you anything. She would open like a flower to the sun and spill even her darkest cravings, her deepest hungers and longings and needs. And when that happened, if you listened and you didn't judge, a woman would fall in love with you with no more effort than it takes to put a key in the ignition and start a car.

Women were simple creatures.

Jacqueline Dolan was a simple creature.

Though undoubtedly she thought herself quite complex and urbane, with her degree from Columbia University, her career, her accomplishments, her apartment in an expensive high-rise in the middle of Manhattan. He knew from a file they'd compiled on her that she was highly intelligent, competitive, and driven; knew she'd been brought up by her father after the sudden death of her mother when she was just a little girl. But from his short interaction with her, he knew the secret she guarded so closely, the one her pride would defend with her life.

She was lonely. Lonely with a capital L.

Those were the ones who always fell the hardest.

Smart and capable and strong, Jacqueline was at her core a motherless little girl, still struggling to believe she deserved the love she so desperately craved.

Most likely she didn't have enough self-awareness to grasp that fact, Hawk thought, watching her as she ordered something from the waitress at her tableside, pointedly not looking in his direction. Usually only the ones who had extensive therapy were anything close to self-aware—and those enlightened *cadelas* bored him to tears.

He motioned for the waitress. She sprang into action without a moment's hesitation, hightailing it across the crowded dance floor. She arrived a little breathless, blinking rapidly, shifting her weight in her high heels from foot to foot. Judging by the way her ankles were slightly swollen, the shoes were a size too small, and she'd been on her feet a long time.

He said to her gently in Portuguese, "You're working hard tonight."

She blushed. "One of the other girls called in sick. It's my third double shift this week."

She was pretty, if a little worn around the edges. Brunette and busty and not particularly young, she gave him a tentative smile.

Hot little subbie, you'd like me to tie you up and tell you what a good girl you are as I spank that nice plump ass, wouldn't you?

Pretending the music was a little too loud to be heard over, Hawk lightly grasped her wrist and drew her closer. He savored the little gasp she gave as he bent his head to her ear.

"I'd like to send a drink to someone. The redhead in the booth over there."

The waitress held her breath, listening to his voice with every cell in her body. Beneath his fingers, her arm trembled.

"Um . . . uh . . . okay," she breathed, frozen stiff. "What-what kind?"

Hawk thought about it a moment, absentmindedly rubbing his thumb back and forth across her wrist. The waitress exhaled, leaning closer.

"Tequila," he decided, listening to her heart hammer, feeling her blood rush through the ulnar artery on the inside of her wrist. "Whatever's your best." He gave her wrist a firm squeeze and smiled to himself as she let out the faintest of moans.

"Yes," she said almost inaudibly, and he knew she wasn't talking about the drink.

He withdrew and gazed down at her, his eyes half-lidded. She stared up at him in something like awe. "Good girl," he murmured, and the poor waitress actually swayed on her feet.

"Off you go," he said, holding her gaze. She nodded, swallowed, turned, and walked unsteadily away.

Hawk glanced at Jacqueline's table, and found her staring at the retreating waitress with a furrow between her brows. Her gaze came back to him, and he was surprised when she didn't look away. Instead the look deepened . . . as did the furrow between her brows.

Strangely, because he never cared about things like that, Hawk wondered what she was thinking.

Her food arrived, plopped down on the tabletop in front of her by a busboy with the grace of a gorilla. Startled, she broke eye contact and glanced down at her plate. They exchanged a few low words before the busboy stalked away. Above the strains of the violins and guitars and the sounds of feet sliding along the dance floor and a hundred different conversations, Hawk heard Jacqueline mutter to herself, "Fucking moody men."

Interesting . . . and telling. He sensed a lifetime of disappointment behind those words. And something else. Anger or bitterness or maybe even fear, he couldn't tell which.

He cocked his head, studying her as she looked down in obvious disgust at her plate. It contained a cheeseburger and a pile of greasy fries, absolutely normal pub food, but judging by the way she glared at it, the plate might as well have contained the severed head of her arch enemy. She pushed it away, slumped down in her seat, closed her eyes, and sighed.

The busty brunette waitress appeared at her side with a shot of tequila. "The, uh, handsome gentleman at the bar sent this over for you."

Jacqueline sent Hawk a long, stony look. Then she said to the waitress, "Tell the handsome gentleman it's going to take a hell of a lot more than a shot of tequila." Still holding his gaze, she grabbed the shot and downed it in one swallow.

The animal inside him growled in pleasure.

Red wanted to play . . . and she hated herself for it. Nothing like a little ambivalence to spice things up.

He crooked a finger at her. *Come here.* Jacqueline responded by chuffing a short, derisive laugh. She handed the shot glass back to the waitress, folded her arms across her chest, and pretended to study the hideous oil painting of a gaucho on horseback that was hanging on the wall above her booth.

The waitress turned and looked at him uncertainly. He nodded, letting her know it was okay, then gave a small jerk of his chin to summon her. She was there in an instant, breathlessly waiting for him to speak.

When he didn't, she stammered, "The um . . . the girl . . . the lady said to tell you that she . . . uh . . . it was going to . . . "

"I got the gist of it," he reassured her, "but thank you."

The waitress glanced over at Jacqueline, then the band, which had segued into another number. "You heard that? Her table's all the way over—"

"I'm just good at reading body language." He leaned forward, stroking a finger up her arm. "Send two more shots over to her table, will you, beautiful? And keep them coming. She's my boss, and I royally screwed up on the job today. I'm trying to get her drunk so she doesn't have the energy to fire me."

Hawk sent the waitress a conspiratorial smile, which she melted under.

"Oh—your boss!" Relief flashed in her eyes, followed quickly by shy self-consciousness. Then he couldn't see her eyes at all because she lowered her lashes as a bloom of color spread across her cheeks.

Hawk felt a sudden rush of pity for this sweet, overworked waitress, past her prime and ignored by the men here because of it. She was lovely in her own way, maternal and a little old-fashioned, not flashy and brittle-hard like most of the women in the bar. If he didn't have a job to do, he'd take her to bed and give her something to remember.

He reached into his wallet and pulled out a stack of bills. Her eyes widened as he pressed it into her hand.

"No, please, that's too much—"

"It's not even a drop in the ocean of what you're worth, beautiful, but it's all the cash I have on me." He stood, leaned in, and brushed his lips across her cheek. Cupping the back of her neck in one hand, he said into her ear, "You're sexy as hell, and don't ever let any jerk tell you otherwise." He pulled back and stared down into her wide eyes. Her mouth fell open. He said, "Do you understand me?"

Speechless, she nodded.

"Say it."

She said faintly, "I understand."

His brows lifted. Face flaming, she added, "Sir."

He nodded, said, "Good girl," and left her standing in shock at the bar, a wad of cash in one hand, the other braced for support on the stool he'd just deserted.

THREE

An Ache and a Fever

Jack watched him approach with equal parts dread and fascination.

She'd never seen anyone so primal. So magnetic. Like some elemental force, his presence dimmed everything around him as if he drew all the life and color from the room and absorbed it, appearing more vivid, more real and substantial in contrast. He wasn't pretty, over-groomed and polished like so many of the men she knew in New York who had massages and mani-pedis and three-hundred-dollar haircuts. He was masculine in the best sense of the word, rugged and beautiful in his raw, unapologetic *maleness*.

This stranger named Hawk was, simply, devastating.

Unfortunately, he knew it.

He made his way through the crowded, smoky bar, seemingly oblivious to the craned necks, stares, and whispers that followed in his wake. He moved like wind over water, with a grace and lightness that was startling in one so large, and gave the impression he might at any moment shirk the bounds of gravity altogether and float above the floor. Even the men were affected by him, puffing out their chests and raising their chins, posing and strutting like peacocks, trying to compete.

As if a single one could. The instant she thought it, their eyes met. Another of his slow, lazy smiles lit his face.

To her horror, a flood of heat and moisture throbbed between her legs.

The urge to run away became almost overwhelming, but she steeled herself against it, because there was no way she was going to allow him—or her own traitorous body—to intimidate her.

He slid into the booth, taking a seat across from her, and stretched his long legs out and crossed them at the ankle, resting them on her side. This effectively blocked her exit. They stared at one another for a long moment in silence, sizing each other up.

As the band shifted into another song, Jack asked without an ounce of warmth, "You following me?"

Hawk's lazy smile deepened. "I was here first, remember? Maybe you're following *me*."

"Don't flatter yourself. You're not my type."

He leaned across the table, clasped his big hands together on the scarred wood tabletop, stared deep into her eyes, and murmured, "Tell that to your wet panties."

Jack had never wanted to hit someone so much in her entire life. The urge was violent and total, and she had to curl her hands into fists in her lap to keep them from clawing his eyes out.

Because he was right. Goddammit, he was *right*.

Blood rushed to her face. She sat there, counting to ten, staring back at him in silence while a storm of withering heat exploded inside her body. Somehow she knew he sensed it. His gaze dropped to the pulse fluttering wildly in her neck, and when he looked back into her eyes, his own were hot and dark.

Danger! her mind screamed.

Oh, hell, YES! was her body's awful reply.

The surly waiter arrived with her food.

"*Veggie* burger, *no* cheese." He removed the plate on the table and replaced it with the one in his hand, then stalked away again, exuding contempt.

Feeling as if she'd just been flattened by a truck, Jack sagged against the unyielding booth, taking comfort in its rigidity. She wished her self-control would take note and follow suit.

Staring at her plate, she started another count of ten.

Hawk leaned back, mercifully releasing her from his sex-appeal tractor beam.

"Problem with your food?" he asked, his tone solicitous.

This was a much safer course of conversation, but she still avoided his gaze, afraid of what he might find in her eyes. "Not anymore."

There was a pause as he waited for more, silently watching her as she picked up the burger and began to eat.

"Are you always this charming, or am I just getting special treatment because I saved your life and you're too much of a feminist to admit it?"

Jack swallowed. The food slid down her throat in a solid lump. "Try not to break your arm patting yourself on the back about that, Ace. Wasn't the first time I've dodged a few bullets. Won't be the last."

She felt him looking her over, felt his gaze on her face, her hair, her hands, a gaze so heavy it was almost *touch*. A rush of adrenaline made her heart pound. She marveled that she'd been in mortal danger in countless war zones all over the world, yet just sitting there in a booth with this man, not even speaking or looking at him, she felt a thrill unlike anything she'd ever known.

She closed her eyes, unable to resist savoring the sweet sting of exhilaration. She knew she was an adrenaline junkie, and at moments like this, with fear and electricity and anticipation winging through her like a million tiny starbursts, she felt as if she was conducting fire through her veins.

This was her drug. This was what she lived for. Because she was dead inside in so many ways, this was the only thing that made her feel alive.

She breathed into it, a satisfied little smile curling the corners of her lips.

Hawk said, "First time I've seen you smile."

Her eyes snapped open. He was staring at her with the strangest look on his face, a combination of intense concentration and slight confusion, as if he was taken aback by something that didn't fit.

Jack was vaguely aware of her heartbeat, of the pulse of the music, the sway of people on the dance floor, but she was acutely aware of *him*, as if there were an invisible Tesla coil connecting their bodies.

Channeling an ache and a fever of static electricity, the space between them felt charged.

Truly curious, her intuition screaming that she was on the verge of something big, hazardous, and possibly life altering, Jack whispered, "Who *are* you?"

Something in her voice or her face made him falter. He swallowed, that façade of perfect, arrogant self-confidence cracked. His voice barely audible above the music, he said, "Lucas Eduardo Tavares Castelo Luna. But my friends call me Hawk."

His eyes burned. The tension between them was palpable, thick as molasses. Jack was at a loss as to why.

"Why do I feel like I know you?" she pressed. "Or I'm supposed to know you? Or I'm missing something here?"

This trio of questions was met with a brief, telling flicker of what looked like surprise in his eyes—maybe alarm—which was quickly smothered.

In a flash of comprehension that was like a floodlight flipped on, Jack understood.

Her laugh was loud and relieved. "Oh, you're *good*!" she managed between the laughter that wouldn't seem to stop coming. "Damn! She has amazing taste, I'll give her that, but I am going to *kill* her!"

Hawk stared at her in silence as she groaned and passed a hand over her eyes, embarrassed at herself that she thought there was anything else going on between her and this impossibly big, beautiful man with the ridiculous nickname.

Jack had girlfriends, most of them childless career girls like her, but only one best friend with whom she shared everything. They'd met in college, and though total opposites in almost every way, had formed an unbreakable bond of friendship when they'd discovered they had something terrible in common, a horror they'd survived in childhood that had left them scarred in exactly the same ways.

Inola Hart was a full-blooded Cherokee Indian, raised on a reservation, striking and statuesque and whip smart, with a devilish sense of humor that often took the form of practical jokes. She now worked as an attorney at the UN, and the last time they'd seen each other, when Jack had gone to DC for a reception hosted by the President in celebration of getting his anti-Shifter agenda pushed through Congress several months back, Nola had threatened Jack with a surprise for her thirtieth birthday. A birthday that was, in fact, this very day.

The surprise was supposed to be a male escort, so Jack, for the first time in years, could get laid. At the time, it had just seemed like a casual conversation; but obviously Nola took it a little more seriously . . . Jack thought back on their conversation.

"If I just didn't ever have to see him again, you know?" Jack mused as she and Nola stood together in one corner of the grand East ballroom at the White House, scanning the crowd for familiar faces, nursing cocktails and discussing, for the umpteenth time, the problem of their barren sex lives. Neither wanted a relationship, but neither wanted to be celibate either.

"I hear you," replied Nola, neatly downing the rest of her pomegranate martini. "My last time was supposed to be a one-nighter with this junior attorney I met at a charity function, but he turned out to be a friggin' stalker. That guy would not *leave me alone. Do you know I came home one night and he was hiding in the bushes by my front door? I literally had to beat him with my purse to get him to go away."*

At that point Jack turned a critical eye to her friend, giving her tall, elegant figure, nut-brown skin, upswept black hair, and aristocratic features a swift once-over. "Can you blame him? If I were a guy I'd go all stalker on you, too, lady. You look like one of those Indian Disney princesses."

"Please," Nola scoffed, "don't insult my intelligence! Those Indian Disney princesses are just white girls painted brown. Tell me I look like Beyoncé instead. She's beautiful and she isn't sitting around waiting for some dim-witted prince to come along and save her incompetent ass."

"Girlfriend, I hate to break it to you, but you look nothing like Beyoncé."

Nola pretended outrage. "I so do! Okay, Halle Berry then." She stood waiting for Jack's response with her head tilted back as though for inspection.

Jack asked, "Are you operating under the mistaken impression that you're black, crazy person?"

She answered in all seriousness, "I'm just talking general chocolate hotness here." At which point Jack laughed so hard vodka sprayed out of her nose.

"You see—that." Nola watched in amusement as Jack mopped her face and chin with a cocktail napkin. "That right there should be enough for any sane man to fall in love with you."

"No love," Jack emphatically replied. "Remember? No complications. No relationships. Just a little . . . relief every once in a while would be perfect."

Nola brightened. "What about an escort?"

"Uh, no, thanks. I'm as liberated as the next girl, but that's kinda weird."

"What if he was JFK Jr. hot? Like that guy?" She pointed out the tall figure of a man crossing the ballroom. Dark-haired and lean, he was unexpectedly good-looking in the dull crowd of attorneys, pundits, and politicians.

Jack pondered it, then shrugged. "Doesn't matter, anyway. That phone call is not something I could ever see myself making. 'Oh, hi, is this the man-whore agency? Great, please send over your best, pronto.' So not going to happen."

"Maybe I'll surprise you with one for your birthday," Nola countered with a smile, and the two of them laughed and moved on to another topic.

Jack thought Nola had been joking. Clearly she hadn't been. And if anyone could arrange for a hot male escort to wine and dine her in Brazil, it was Nola. The rescue bit was a little over the top . . . God, he must have followed her to the market, too! Unbelievable planning. Touché, girlfriend. Touché.

"You're going to kill who, exactly?" Hawk's voice was gruff, his expression puzzled.

Boy, he was good at this!

"Okay, then, I'll play your little game. *Hawk.*" She had to stifle another laugh as she said his name. He pretended to scowl at her, which made her laugh even harder. The forty-something, busty waitress she'd seen him talking to on the other side of the bar arrived with two shots of tequila and set them on the table, one in front of Jack, the other in front of Hawk. His came complete with batted lashes and a simper.

"Oh, thank you!" Jack smiled broadly at the waitress. She reluctantly dragged her attention away from Hawk to scrutinize Jack in obvious disapproval, lips pursed.

"You're welcome." After a pause and a glance in Hawk's direction, she added, "He's really great, you know."

Ah. This bar was Hawk's normal hunting grounds. Jack wondered if Nola had even gone so far as to instruct the concierge at the hotel where to send her, and decided it was completely within the realm of possibility. Her best friend had wanted to make it seem as realistic and coincidental as possible. This was getting better and better.

"Oh, *totally.*" Jack nodded emphatically and leaned over the table. "I can totally see that. I mean, *look* at him, right?"

Hawk's jaw was clenched so hard she thought all his teeth might shatter. The waitress glanced back and forth between the two of them, and hesitantly said, "It's not my place to say this, but . . . but you shouldn't fire him. He's . . . there aren't many men like him out there."

"Fire him!" Jack scoffed. "Oh, no way! I'm getting my money's worth! Well, Nola's money's worth, anyway." When both the waitress and Hawk stared at her as if she'd lost her mind, Jack said happily, "Oh, never mind, it's all good. Thanks for the tequila, I'm probably going to need it!"

Jack downed the shot in one gulp, savored the burn, set the glass back on the table, and smiled broadly at both of them.

31

A male escort! This was going to be so much *fun*! No strings, no attachments; he'd leave afterward without all that awkward *Uh, I'll call you* BS. As long as he had condoms—plenty of them—she was good to go.

The waitress turned and fled. Jack happily watched her go, then said to Hawk, "So how exactly does this work? Do I need to tip you afterward or anything, or is that all taken care of?"

That lazy, seductive smile from before had turned to a mean-looking scowl, which Jack decided was utterly adorable. God, she couldn't wait to get her hands on him. Just look at those arms! Those abs! That bulge in his jeans! She almost hopped up and down in her seat with excitement.

This way, she could be absolutely free. She could let herself go. There would be no consequences, no ugly recriminations, no relationship whatsoever. She hadn't a single hesitation about the ethics of bedding a male prostitute—it was called the oldest profession in the world for a good reason, and they were both consenting adults, and he was *beautiful*—she wasn't worried about the possible dangers of having a strange man in her hotel room because Nola would have paid a high price to ensure the quality of the merchandise, and the safety and total anonymity of the transaction. In fact, she'd probably had an extensive background check run on him and made him sign a nondisclosure.

The cherry on top of this delightful sundae of sin: there would be exactly zero emotional entanglements. She'd wake up tomorrow morning and he'd be gone, never to be seen again, and she'd be on a plane on her way back to the States.

Her glee was only briefly marred by the cold pinch of anxiety she felt every time she thought about having sex. With an efficiency born of years of practice, Jack ruthlessly squashed that feeling before it had a chance to flower into fear.

Hawk growled, "What the hell are you talking about? And who's Nola?"

"You're right: we should stay to the script. Stay in character, I *love* it." She grinned at him, more excited than she'd been in years.

"Are you drunk?" He enunciated every word, glaring daggers at her all the while.

She sighed and rested her chin on her threaded fingertips. Looking him right in the eye, she softly asked, "How are you going to fuck me first, Hawk?"

All the blood drained from his face.

It rushed back in with a speed that left blotches of red high on his sculpted cheekbones. He stood abruptly, looking angry, hot, and scary, and pulled her just as abruptly out of the booth with a hand wrapped firmly around her upper arm. He leaned down and hissed into her ear, "All right. You wanna play? *Let's play.*"

Then in a very caveman move that made her squeal in delight, Hawk picked her up, threw her over his shoulder, and headed for the front door.

FOUR

Epic Downfall

This broad was seriously deranged.

He'd never seen a woman do a one-hundred-and-eighty-degree turn the way this one had. One second she was glaring at him as if he was a carrier of the plague, the next she was asking him how he was going to fuck her.

Still hanging over his shoulder as he made his way down the corridor to her hotel room, her thighs grasped firmly under his arm and her little feet kicking out in front of him, she chuckled to herself and said happily, "And just look at this *ass*!"

Then she actually spread both her hands across his rear end and squeezed.

What the hell?

He didn't know how he'd lost control of the situation, but he had. And now he was about to take it back.

"Key," he snapped as he stopped in front of room 204.

"Back pocket of my jeans," she whispered, sounding all sexy and breathless with anticipation.

Had that waitress put something in her drink? Had she been roofied? That would certainly account for her strange behavior . . . or maybe she was bipolar. Though he hadn't read that in her file. Not that he'd paid much attention to the file's contents; a cursory skim had told him all he'd needed to know.

Or so he'd thought.

He dug the key from the pocket of her jeans, turned it in the door handle, entered the room, and kicked the door shut behind him. Then he flipped Jacqueline off his shoulder, set her on her feet, and backed her up against the wall.

Her eyes widened as she stared up at him. Her lips parted, and for a brief moment, he thought she might be afraid of him.

She blew that thought from his head when she moistened her lips and said, "Okay. Here's the deal: I want the full monty, Hawk. I want every trick you've got. Don't hold back on me, now. This doesn't happen to me often, so make it memorable. Make it . . . *dirty.*"

Then she rose up on her toes, wound her arms around his neck, and put her mouth on his.

Sweet mother of—she tasted like tequila and green apples and a sweet, delicious ripeness that was just *her.* He lost himself almost instantly, pulled into her taste and scent like a swimmer pulled into a riptide. He allowed himself to just luxuriate in the kiss, in the soft heat of her body pressed against his, in the low, small sound she made deep in her throat.

She mewled as he crushed her tighter against him, and again as he slid his hand up her body and squeezed her breast. Small and firm and perfect, they were the breasts of an athlete, and he longed to take a nipple into his mouth. He wanted to drift on this current of pleasure forever. He wanted to drown in it—

Hawk broke the kiss and pulled back, startled by the force of his reaction to her. He never wanted to drift, or *drown*, in a woman. He never let himself get close. But if she could drag him under with just a kiss . . .

No more kissing, he told himself firmly as he stared down at her. She was breathing heavily, her eyes were soft and drowsy, and he smelled the fragrance of her arousal like perfume in the air, delicious hot readiness that made every part of his body ache with want.

"Damn," she whispered, leaning into him, "you taste like Christmas morning."

He hadn't had a woman so completely ready and unabashedly carnal in, well . . . how long? She wasn't second-guessing herself or him; she wasn't holding back, that was abundantly clear; she was ready for anything he wanted to give her. *Anything.*

God, that was sexy.

She's an evil wench, he reminded himself. When a spike of anger shot through him as he remembered the part she'd played in getting those anti-Shifter laws passed, he pulled her head back with his hand fisted in her hair.

She looked at him with big, enthralled blue eyes, her fingers twisting into the front of his shirt. "Oh—are you going to be rough? That. Is. So. *Hot.*"

"You like it rough?" he growled, staring down at her with what he hoped was a murderous glare, digging his fingers into her bottom.

She responded with a soft, happy sigh. "I like *you*, however I get you."

She *liked* him. That did something strange to his stomach. Before he could spend too much time pondering why he cared that this cold-hearted, bigoted, despicable excuse for a human being liked him, she was talking again.

"Let's get you naked, stud muffin. I want to see my birthday present." She tugged his shirt from the waistband of his jeans and flattened her hands over his stomach.

Stud muffin? Present?

Several things clicked into place, and he had to bite down on his tongue to keep from laughing.

Oh, this was too, too good. This was better than he could have ever expected.

His gaze fell on the Canon with the telephoto lens on the nightstand beside the bed, and with a thrill of victory he realized that *now* it was better than he could have ever expected.

Because the downfall of *New York Times* senior war correspondent Jacqueline Dolan was going to be *epic*—

And caught entirely on film.

FIVE

Old-Fashioned Courtesy

The noise she made was loud, animal, and incoherent. It tore from her throat as her back bowed into an arch against the bed and every single muscle in her body clenched.

"You like that, don't you, Red?" Hawk said in a throaty murmur. When she moaned her approval, he added a second finger to the first.

It had taken him all of ten seconds to get both of them undressed and on the bed, and her into a very compromising position that involved his hot, demanding mouth and fingers, and her spread legs.

"Please!" she gasped, writhing against his hand. "Don't stop! Don't stop!"

She was too close for him to stop. If he stopped now, she'd have to kill him.

He chuckled. "So bossy. If you want me to keep going, you have to tell me what you want, Red. I want to hear you say it."

Her hips bucked as his fingers pressed deeper inside her. "Mouth—please—lick me—suck me—oh God!"

Her gasped plea ended as he lowered his head and took that most sensitive little nub of nerve endings into his mouth again, and sucked, hard. Then with both hands spread under her bottom, he lifted her up and ground his mouth against her. She came in an explosion that felt nuclear.

She sobbed his name, clenched her fingers into his hair, and came again.

Time spun away. The room faded out. All her awareness shrank to the space of a few inches, to his tongue and teeth and lips, the low, approving growl that rose in the back of his throat as her hips undulated uncontrollably in his hands.

Worth every goddamn penny! she thought, delirious with pleasure.

Jack collapsed back against the mattress, twitching with aftershocks, her thighs trembling, dragging air into her lungs in deep, ragged gulps. Hawk looked up at her from between her spread thighs, sent her that beautiful, lazy, self-satisfied smile, and said, "I think someone needed that."

Someone did. Someone *so* did.

Still panting, her limbs liquid and her body covered in a sheen of sweat, Jack laughed weakly and coaxed him up her body with her hands tugging on his broad shoulders. He crawled up the mattress to her until they were face to face and he was looking down at her in smug satisfaction like a big game hunter who'd just bagged an elephant.

She said, "Don't get too cocky, yet, tiger. We're just getting started."

In a lightning-fast move she'd practiced a thousand times, over years of self-defense classes, Jack threw her weight to the side and pushed him over with her hands spread on his chest, using his size to her advantage to throw him off balance. He flopped back against the bed and bounced once. The look of shock on his face was absolutely priceless.

Straddling him, Jack tossed her hair to the side, leaned down, and kissed him.

His reaction was so strange.

First he dug his fingers into her hips. He inhaled sharply, leaned up into her, and kissed her back as if he were starving and she were a ten-course meal, but then broke away just as the kiss deepened in intensity. He stared at the bedside table as if he couldn't bear to meet her eyes.

Jack turned his face to hers with a gentle finger on his jaw. They stared at each other silently for a moment, and his gaze was wary, strangely conflicted. With a little twist of bittersweet recognition, Jack understood.

"It's too personal," she whispered. "Right?"

She'd shocked him again. She saw it in the sudden, unmistakable darkness in his eyes, in the way his entire body tensed beneath her.

An unexpected rush of tenderness filled the normally hollow space inside her chest. Tenderness for him and for humankind in general, for all the ways people had to compromise themselves to survive because life was such a cruel, cold bitch. What terrible circumstance would drive such a beautiful man—an obviously intelligent man—to sell himself like this? He could probably be a supermodel if he'd wanted to, but here he was, in bed with a total stranger for some undisclosed sum, whoring himself out for a buck.

Really, all jokes aside, how *sad* was that?

Jack abruptly felt dirty, and ashamed. She spread her hand over his cheek, seeing him in a totally new light. He wasn't just a hot piece of man ass. He was a *person*.

A person she'd just used.

Hating that her sense of morality had chosen this particular moment to make an appearance, she muttered, "Well, shit."

Jack swung her leg over and awkwardly climbed off him. She sat facing away from him on the edge of the bed, her arms wrapped around her waist, wanting nothing more than to take a shower, get dressed, and run out of this room, never to return.

Looking at the wall, she said, "It's okay. I understand. In fact, we can just . . . this was great, but you don't have to finish the whole . . . you know. We can stop now."

Silence. His gaze on her back, tangible as touch. Then he said, "Wait—are you feeling *sorry* for me?"

Like she thought: smart. Or at least not totally dense.

But she didn't have time to ponder that because she found herself flat on her back on the bed again with a furious Hawk staring down at her, both her wrists clamped in his hands and pressed down to the pillows, his body heavy and hard atop hers, pinning her down.

"Don't you *dare* feel sorry for me!" he snarled, his voice and face filled with barely leashed fury.

Her stomach tightened with the simultaneous realizations that he was a lot bigger than her, he was dangerously angry, and this had the potential to get ugly, fast.

She glanced over at her snub-nosed revolver on the dresser near the door, where Hawk had tossed it with a laugh when he'd discovered it tucked into the waistband of her pants. He'd murmured an amused, "Annie Oakley, hmm?" and tore off the rest of her clothes, and she hadn't bothered to think it might be wiser to keep it somewhere within reach—

"Forget about the damn gun, Red! I'm talking, and you're gonna pay attention. If you still want to shoot me after I've said my piece, I won't try and stop you."

Despite the strangeness of that statement, it made her feel a
little better. She bit her lower lip and stared up at him, waiting.

He spat, "I wasn't some neglected child of alcoholics who grew
into an adult with no self-esteem and a drug problem, or whatever
other stupid idea you *assume* must be the reason I'm in this room
with you right now. I know exactly what I'm doing—I always have
and I always will. I only do something if I *want* to do it, and this
is what I wanted, or it wouldn't have happened. No matter what
circumstances brought us together, *I'm. In. Control.* And I don't
want your pity! Do you understand me?"

Scary-beautiful. Her first impression of him had been exactly
right. And he was definitely right about being in control, because
at that moment it was impossible for her to move with his bulk
pressing down against her and her hands bound by his.

That thought made her hyperaware of their nakedness, of all
the tiny details of his body against hers. Her breasts crushed
beneath the hard expanse of his chest, his heart pounding against
hers, little tickles from the hairs on his legs, his strength, and the
hardness of his body . . .

The hardness between his legs, throbbing hot against her
thigh even as he glared bloody murder down at her.

"I'm sorry. I didn't mean to offend you. I've never done this
before and I felt . . . I felt like it wasn't fair to you. It seemed like . . .
when you kissed me . . ." She moistened her lips, cursing the heat in
her face and the hitch in her voice. "Like it upset you. I hated that,
and I thought . . . I thought maybe—"

"I know exactly what you thought," he interrupted, still angry
but calmer, his tone more even than before. "But you're forgetting
something important."

Jack swallowed, waiting for the proverbial hammer to drop.

A hint of a smile curved his lips. "I'm a guy. For a guy, this is pretty much the dream job. I get *paid* to do the thing I love most; it doesn't get better than that."

Relieved that he seemed mollified by her apology and appeared to be letting the moment pass, and simultaneously amused at his deadpan joke, Jack pressed the smile from her own lips and asked him seriously, "If this is a job, that means I'm your boss, at least for tonight . . . right?"

His brows quirked. He shifted his weight atop her, pressing his pelvis down with added pressure so that his erection dug deeper into her thigh.

In a voice more breathless than she would have liked, Jack said, "Well, I have a few *tasks* I'd like you to complete," and squirmed beneath him.

"Oh no." His small smile grew wider, his eyes grew dark. "You tore up your boss-lady card when you were attacked by a case of conscience. I'll be calling the shots from here on out."

Before she could scream or move or even breathe, Hawk had flipped them both over and was perched on the edge of the bed with her body spread over his bent knees and her behind in the air, as she stared down in shock at shag carpet the color of the inside of a rancid avocado.

He said, "You might want to find something to hold onto," and slapped her on the ass so hard she couldn't even scream.

The second blow remedied that.

She shrieked and bucked, desperate to get away from the stinging pain that kept raining down as he continued to spank her mercilessly, his forearm pressed against her back and his hand fisted in her hair so she was utterly helpless.

"The more you struggle, the longer this lasts. Your choice."

It went far, far beyond sexy or playful; this was serious. This *hurt*. Her toes clenched into the carpet, she grabbed onto the edge of the nightstand and tried to drag herself away, but he was much too strong. Nothing worked. He spanked her again, and again, rhythmically, striking one side of her bottom, then the other, then down her thighs, then back to the starting point.

"Stop!" she gasped between cries of pain. "Please—Hawk—no—I don't like this!"

"Stop struggling, then," he calmly replied, and she knew with absolute certainty that that was the only way this was going to end. She stilled, squeezed her eyes shut, and bit back the sob that wanted to rise in her throat.

The moment she stopped moving, he stopped the torture and began to gently rub her behind, soothing her flaming flesh with feather-light strokes. "Good girl."

Jack was abruptly furious.

"What the *fuck*!" she yelled, craning her neck over her shoulder to look at him.

"Another thing." His other hand tightened even more in her hair so her head was immobilized. "You have a dirty mouth, and I don't like it. If I hear one more curse out of you, you'll get spanked again, but this time I won't hold back. Understood?"

Hold back? He'd been *holding back*? Jesus Christ. But he was staring at her with hard eyes and a clenched jaw, awaiting an answer; because she couldn't move her head to nod, she tried to communicate with her eyes that she hoped he rotted in hell while she said between gritted teeth, "Yes."

He slid his palm across her burning behind and lightly stroked her between the legs. She jerked and gasped as he slid two fingers inside her.

"And don't tell me you didn't like that, little liar. You're soaking wet." His voice dropped as he pressed his fingers deeper and she unsuccessfully tried to smother a moan. "You wanted it dirty, remember?"

"Hawk—please—"

"On your knees, Red." He deposited her on the floor directly in front of him so she was kneeling, staring directly into his spread legs and the enormous erection standing at attention between them.

Holy cow—the *size*—

He grasped her head between his hands and forced her to look up at him.

"You're going to make it up to me for your little pity party," he said, gazing at her hotly. His face was flushed, his eyes were bright with unmistakable lust. "Aren't you?"

Staring up into his eyes, something inside her just melted.

Yes, she was still pissed about the spanking because she wasn't into pain and this was her birthday dammit, but also, yes, she did want to make it up to him. She knew she'd insulted him, and she couldn't exactly figure out why it should matter that she'd hurt this cocky gigolo's feelings, but guessed it was just a little old-fashioned courtesy, a vestige from her mother's long-ago teachings about manners and the right way to treat others.

Even if he was your paid whore.

Perhaps especially if he was your paid whore.

Holding his gaze, Jack nodded an emphatic *yes*.

He nodded back, gently stroked her hair off her face, and smiled at her with an oddly contented look in his eyes, as if she'd just made him very proud.

She didn't pause long enough to examine why his approval should send such a wash of warmth through her veins. She just leaned forward, grasped the hard length of him in her hand, and slid the engorged head of his erection into her mouth.

When he moaned and his entire body was wracked by a violent shudder, Jack also didn't bother to examine more closely the high, sweet thrill that sang through her, pure as sunshine. She just applied herself vigorously to making it up to him, and let the questions of ethics and manners and her own uncharacteristic, wanton reaction to this beautiful stranger fade from her mind.

She knew tomorrow she'd suffer for this. Tomorrow the self-loathing would begin.

Tonight she was just a woman who needed a man, and a soft place to fall, if only for a little while. So she allowed herself to fall, and pushed that old, familiar burn of shame down into darkness.

SIX

Uncomfortable Feelings

Jacqueline Dolan wasn't at all what he'd expected.

Snoring aside—soft and girly snoring, but still snoring none-theless—she might be the most feminine woman he'd ever met, in spite of the tough-chick bravado she wore like a suit of armor. She was tender and passionate and surprisingly intuitive, guessing correctly that the feeling he got when kissing her was a little too . . . much. Though she was operating under a false idea of who and what he was, she still managed to recognize emotion in a stranger, and feel compassion for him.

Compassion. Wasn't that a laugh, coming from her?

Lying beside her on the bed, with the sheets tangled between their legs and the first, faint pink rays of dawn creeping beneath the drawn curtains of her hotel windows, Hawk stared down at her, lost in thought. He'd seen pictures of her before, of course, staring vehemently into the camera as if she wanted to strangle the photographer, or on assignment in some hellhole with her hair in a messy ponytail, mirrored aviators on her stern, unsmiling face, wearing khakis and combat boots, gazing off into the distance. In those photos, the unmistakable impression was one of a woman who was *hard*. Hard, cold, and an utter bitch.

The woman snoring gently beside him now was anything but that. She was actually quite sweet.

He wondered why she tried so hard to hide it.

In sleep, her features lost all their rigid tension, the sharp, wary edges that lent her that standoffish vibe that telegraphed she'd rather kill you than say hello. She had a dusting of freckles across her nose, fine as a sifting of cinnamon, and her lower lip was slightly more full than the top one, giving her mouth an alluring *kiss me* pout. She was bright and sexy and shockingly vulnerable beneath that icy façade, and she was also quite possibly the best lay of his life.

God, was she.

He'd never known a woman with such hunger. Most women were shy or hesitant, especially the first time with someone new, but Jacqueline Dolan had been ravenous, nearly insatiable, despite hours of his best efforts. It was as if she'd been storing up every one of her sexual needs for years, and unleashed them all last night. And, if he was being entirely honest with himself . . . he liked it.

He liked it a lot.

Jacqueline shifted beside him, exhaled a small, restless sigh. Her lids drifted open. She blinked up at him in hazy recognition, her blue eyes soft and warm.

"Lucas Eduardo Tavares Castelo Luna," she whispered, smiling drowsily up at him, "you are a beautiful man. I hope you have a beautiful life. Will you please put the 'Do Not Disturb' sign on the door when you leave?"

Just as quickly as she'd awoken, she closed her eyes and fell back asleep, leaving Hawk staring down at her in shock.

She remembered his name. No one ever called him by his real name.

And no one—ever—had called him beautiful.

An unfamiliar, uncomfortable feeling crept over him, starting in the deepest pit of his stomach and going everywhere at once.

Weak, whispered his father's voice into his mind. *Weak and worthless, like I always said.*

Yes, he had always said that. And despite being dead for over fifteen years, his father still lurked in the darkest corners of his psyche, waiting to pounce on the slightest show of softness or emotion.

Hawk sat up and shook his head to clear it.

"Job to do. Playtime's over," he muttered, gazing at her camera on the night table beside the bed.

He rose silently from the bed and just as silently dressed, all the while willing himself not to take one last look at the sleeping form of Jacqueline. Then he removed the memory card from the camera, and swiftly crossed to the door.

He hung the "Do Not Disturb" sign on the handle as he left.

SEVEN

Goblin Memories

Jack awoke tired, hungry, and deliciously sore.

She stretched, reveling in the way her muscles protested, unused to the kind of vigorous workout they'd had last night. She lay there smiling up at the white popcorn ceiling, thinking one word over and over:

Wow.

Last night had been, hands down, the single most sexy/dirty/ amazing night of her life. They'd tried every position, on every piece of furniture. If there had been a chandelier on the ceiling, they'd have hung from it.

And pictures. Christ, she'd let him take *pictures* of her.

She glanced at the camera still beside the bed, and decided she'd look at them only once before deleting them all and destroying the memory card. He'd been playful when he'd suggested it, coyly asking if she wanted to have a little something to remember her birthday present by, and she'd been so caught up in the moment she'd agreed. Then he'd given her pleasure again and again, the camera shutter clicking furiously, until finally they were both so exhausted they fell into sleep near dawn.

She closed her eyes and remembered the details, savoring them, because she knew it would most likely be another few years before she'd be making new ones with anyone else.

His mouth. His hands. The glowing dark burn of his eyes—

You little whore.

With that, the fun was abruptly over.

She sat up and passed a trembling hand over her face. The accusations didn't stop coming, rushing up from that dark part of herself she kept locked so tightly away, always managing to escape, especially at moments like this.

The most powerful emotion Jack had experienced in her thirty years was shame. She carried it around with her like a demon on her back, a spiteful fiend that hissed into her ear, twisting even the most benign things into elaborate sculptures of ugliness. If a man passing by on the street smiled at her, it was because he could tell she was easy. If she got a promotion at work, it was because her boss expected a little something in return. If anything remotely good happened in her life at all, it was because the universe had a sick sense of humor. She went around all day every day with a thundercloud overhead, waiting for the other shoe to drop, until finally through chance or her own gift for self-destruction, it did.

Other people had emotional baggage. Jack had cargo.

Her stomach lurched. She ran to the bathroom and leaned over the toilet just in time for the first violent heaves to begin.

When it was over, she sat there on the cold tile with her legs curled up beneath her, naked and shaking, bowed over the toilet bowl with her eyes streaming and her heart pounding frantically in her chest.

"I hate you," Jack whispered hoarsely to the empty bathroom. "I hate you and I wish you were dead."

Mercifully, the buzz of the overhead light didn't require her to clarify whom she had meant.

The flight back to New York was long, with a layover in Miami, so by the time Jack arrived at LaGuardia Airport she was physically and mentally exhausted. She hadn't been able to work on the plane; she'd instead alternated between downing tiny bottles of vodka and staring out the window. She knew from hard experience it could take anywhere from a few hours to a few days for the malaise and self-recriminations to wear themselves out. In the meantime she'd be relatively useless, and no fun to be around.

Which meant that stopping off at her father's house in Queens on the way back to Manhattan was a bad idea.

She almost didn't go. But when she checked her voice mail as she waited in the stuffy cabin to disembark, she found her father had left her a message.

"It's your father. Hope your trip was good. I've got cake here; don't forget."

Just as he always ended every call without saying goodbye, he always prefaced every message with a polite, "It's your father," as if she wouldn't recognize his voice, or might have blocked the memory of him altogether. That was depressing, but visiting the house she grew up in was depressing to a multiple of one thousand.

But she didn't want to disappoint him, and knew there would be too many questions if she cancelled. Questions she just wasn't up for answering, and for which he wouldn't relent until he had answers. A trait she'd inherited from him.

In the cab on the way from the airport, Jack chewed every one of her fingernails down to a nub.

"Jackie," her father said gruffly when he opened the door. He looked older than when she'd last seen him—on her last birthday—more grizzled somehow, his formerly gunmetal-gray crew cut now almost completely white. They shared the same clear blue eyes, and his stared out of a weathered face, which was angular and imposing. Though he'd retired from the military years ago, he was a Marine down to the marrow of his bones, with that ruler-straight posture, legs braced apart as if prepared for a hit. He wore his usual: a spotless white dress shirt buttoned up to his Adam's apple, a pair of navy-blue Dockers, black leather shoes polished to a mirror gleam.

Her mother had always tried to get him into something else, add a little variety to his wardrobe, but her father steadfastly refused. *Some things never change*, her mother had said in that particular way she had, laughing and light but angry at the same time, vibrating with a dark undertone that Jack's childhood self never understood, but was afraid of nonetheless.

She swallowed around the lump in her throat. "Dad. Hi. You're looking good."

He cracked a lopsided smile and pushed open the screen door. "Not bad for an old-timer," he agreed, and pulled her into a hard, one-armed hug.

He released her almost immediately. They stood there in awkward silence for a moment, avoiding each other's eyes.

"Well, don't just stand there on the porch gathering dust," he said, sounding even more gruff. "Come on in."

He picked up her duffel bag, then went inside. Jack followed him, letting the screen door bang shut behind her, feeling as if gravity had exponentially intensified and every step she took inside pressed her down harder and harder against the Earth.

Along with her father's wardrobe, the house hadn't changed. The downstairs rooms were bisected at waist level by dark wood wainscoting; flowery wallpaper climbed to the ceiling in a haphazard sprawl; and somber wood and tasteful, understated floral-print furniture had been selected to match. The house had two stories, narrow and dimly lit, with a ragged garden out back and a white picket fence that enclosed the yard in an ironic sham of hominess.

Jack followed her father into the kitchen with the odd sensation she was traveling back in time to one of those fifties black-and-white TV shows. *Father Knows Best* transplanted to modern day Queens. She'd never realized how self-consciously retro the place was, how hard it tried to be individual and colorful, with its checkerboard tiles and sparkly Formica countertops, the cupboards painted turquoise and the appliances that matched.

This room had been her mother's domain, and the eclectic décor reflected it. Gazing around it now, it occurred to Jack for the first time that this room was a big middle finger to the rest of the house . . . the house her pushy, iron-willed grandmother had decorated when the family had first moved in and her new daughter-in-law was away spending some quality time in a room with padded walls.

Jack's father set her bag down near the back kitchen door, almost as if to reassure her she could make a quick getaway if needed.

How well he knew her.

Like a pair of cats warily circling, they cautiously took seats opposite each other at the small table. Each waited for the other to speak first.

Finally, after playing with the salt shaker for a few excruciatingly silent moments, her father said, "You look thin. You eating?"

"I'm fine, Dad. Just . . ." She shrugged. "You know. Working hard."

Because work was the altar at which he'd worshipped his entire life, he nodded in approval. The second-most worthless type of human being on the planet to Thomas "Tank" Dolan was one who was lazy. First place went to—

"Garrett called yesterday. For your birthday."

Everything liquid inside Jack's body froze to arctic ice. She whispered, "Don't."

He sighed and ran a hand over his crew cut. "Jackie—"

"I just walked in the fucking door!"

She jumped to her feet. The chair skittered back over the checkerboard tiles with a nerve-jarring screech. She stood there staring down at him with her hands balled, breathing hard, heat spreading up her neck and ears. Her heart reared up in her throat, threatening to choke her.

He sat back in his chair and spread his hands open in a wordless gesture of surrender.

"I mean it," she warned.

He said softly, "Roger that," and gave her a look of such sad understanding she had to close her eyes for a moment to contain the moisture in them.

She walked to the kitchen sink and leaned against it with her arms folded tightly over her chest, staring out the window to the yard beyond, knowing there were trees and clouds and sunshine, seeing nothing at all.

Her father cleared his throat. "Those wetbacks treat you okay down in Brazil?"

"Jesus, Dad, really?" she said in disgust, not turning.

Her father was many wonderful things, but tolerant wasn't one of them. All "brown" people were wetbacks, Asians were zipper-heads, homosexuals were fags, Middle Easterners were a two-word combination so vile it went beyond the pale. His bigotry was an ugly flaw in a character she otherwise admired, and it pained her deeply to know that someone she loved, who had raised her and protected her and unfailingly cared for her, who had literally once saved her life, was so profoundly deficient.

It was a lesson Jack had learned young, the way good people could also be bad. Things were never black or white, right or wrong, true or false, up or down. There were a million shades of gray in between, a million ways your heart could be broken by not understanding that one essential fact. When you loved someone, you risked overlooking his myriad darker colors to only focus on the bright and shiny whites, until one day the basic black of his nature made a stunning, horrible appearance, and you were knocked on your ass, wondering how you could've been so blind.

Her father's basic black took the form of intolerance for all things "other."

Just another reason to stay away. She knew she couldn't change him. So she simply avoided the toxicity as much as she could, and got on with her life.

After another long, uncomfortable silence, he asked, "You up for some cake?" Without waiting for a response, he rose and opened the refrigerator.

She listened to him move around the kitchen, getting plates and silverware, pouring liquid into glasses, then turned to find him standing at the table over two mugs of milk and a sheet cake large enough to feed a party of two dozen.

White frosting and sugar flowers and candles, and right smack in the middle a huge "Congrats!" scrawled in pink script. She looked up at him with a question in her eyes. For just a moment, his rugged face looked sheepish.

"It's a combination birthday and congratulations cake."

"Congratulations? For what?"

"The Pulitzer, Jackie. I haven't seen you since before you were nominated, remember?"

The faintest hint of recrimination colored his voice. For a moment, she felt guilty that she could only bear being in this house, with all its lurking goblin memories, once a year. Flaws and all, he was still her father, but every time she saw his face all she saw was . . . *him.*

She couldn't even think her brother's name. Her mind flinched away from it like a battered dog expecting a kick.

"Right. Well, that's really nice of you, Dad. Thanks."

"Anything for my little girl."

The layer of rage simmering beneath his light, conversational tone reminded her exactly of how her mother sometimes used to sound: brittle and bottled up, ready to blow.

Jack's father lit the candles. She blew them out. Then they ate their pink and white squares of cake at the table in the cool, weighted silence of her dead mother's kitchen, the air all around them thick with the presence of ghosts.

EIGHT

Blackmail

Sixty percent of the Amazon rainforest exists within the country of Brazil.

Vast, lush, and ancient, it's a place where beauty and savagery exist in equal supply. Scarlet macaws perch preening on the boughs of moss-draped emerald branches while electric eels and green-and-black-banded anaconda slither silently through languid, piranha-rich waters below. There are vampire bats and squirrel monkeys and poison frogs that excrete toxins through their flesh; there are 150-pound rodents called capybara that are hunted by caiman, a reptile that can reach twelve feet in length. High up in the dense, leafy canopy, where the tropical sun filters through in brilliant shafts of emerald green, toucans call with a sound like the croak of a frog, while down on the perfumed beds of fallen leaves and bracken that cover the muffled twilight of the forest floor, leaf-cutter ants and rhinoceros beetles that can carry 850 times their own body weight scuttle about in endless pursuit of mates and food.

Another animal lives in this verdant paradise of jeweled leaves and pristine sky, of towering trees wreathed in mist and the constant musical chatter of the birds that inhabit them. Like many of the animals of the rainforest, this one is a predator.

A predator with that most important of animal survival skills: camouflage.

A muscular, four-legged killing machine with a coat so glossy black it shone midnight blue, and eyesight so sharp it could cut through the dense forest gloom like a scythe, Hawk carried the thumb-size memory card from Jack's camera carefully in his mouth, in a small pouch he'd made from a folded plastic baggie and a few pieces of tape. This part of the rainforest wasn't accessible by foot—human feet, to be precise—and the going was slow. Over the tangled gnarl of buttress roots and the mossed bulk of fallen trunks, around dark pools of standing water and the swift, snaking fingers of murmuring streams, he made his way primarily using his sense of smell. Though he knew the jungle where he'd been born and raised almost by rote, he took a different path home every time he returned from the city, and it was his nose that led the way.

It wouldn't be long now. The scent of a large group of carnivores told him he was close.

A cry from high above pierced the late afternoon humidity of the forest, and Hawk paused in mid stride, lifting his gaze to the sky, visible through a small break in the towering canopy. In the uppermost layer of the rainforest known as the emergent, a harpy eagle soared briefly into view. Falling still, Hawk closed his eyes and concentrated.

As abruptly as he'd frozen, he was flying. Seeing through

another pair of eyes, breathing through another set of lungs, his body left behind in suspended animation on the forest floor.

He felt a lurch in his stomach as his mind adjusted, then the familiar sensation of wind on his face, streaming warm through his tail feathers.

He made a slow, looping turn, scanning the emergent for signs of anything amiss. Glistening green treetops carpeted the landscape for miles, interrupted only by the serpentine black channel of the Rio Negro far to the west, the river he'd traveled up in a rented boat from Manaus before he'd abandoned it and continued on foot deeper into the forest. He spotted the sheared tip of the giant kapok tree that marked the edge of his colony, and pumped his outstretched wings twice, turning his beak to the wind and letting an updraft of heated air lift and cradle him as he crested the rise of a hill. Riding the wind for a moment, he luxuriated in the freedom, delaying for one last, lovely moment the inevitable return to "real" life.

Then with a simple exhalation, he released the eagle and came rushing back into himself, still standing motionless on the forest floor.

Hanging upside down from a nearby branch by his tail, his wise old-man face scrunched up in concentration, an adult male howler monkey was staring at him in curiosity.

Hawk snarled an unmistakable warning, and the monkey went screaming away into the trees. He flattened his ears against his head in a vain effort to soften the piercing shrieks; the primates were named "howlers" for good reason.

He headed off once again, trotting with easy agility over the tangled, thorny floor of the forest.

"Ah, the lone wolf returns," said the Alpha Alejandro with an unconcealed sneer. He lifted an overfull wineglass in contemptuous salute as Hawk entered the Assembly gathering place.

Cold and sharp as an icicle, a spike of hatred stabbed through Hawk's heart.

Cocktail hour already, you degenerate?

Aloud, he said mildly, "Yup," and gave the shortest, stiffest bow that protocol allowed. This amounted to not much more than a jerk of his head.

Eyes narrowed, lips thinned, his expression as sour as if he held a fresh pile of tapir dung in his mouth, Alejandro stared at Hawk from his opulent chair on a raised dais. Tall, lean, and acutely self-conscious, he was the only unmated Alpha in the colonies and also unfortunately happened to be Hawk's younger brother.

Half brother. Same father, different mothers, entirely different life.

On the large wooden platform constructed between the confluence of four massive trees, Hawk stood before the Alpha's throne, his hands loose at his sides, chest back, chin held high. Though in many ways rustic, the Assembly room was also suffused with understated luxury. A hand-carved sideboard of burlwood held crystal decanters of spirits, colorful silk pillows were strewn in artful disarray on white linen divans. Hammered brass vases overflowed with masses of fuchsia orchids and yellow bromeliads, sticks of burning incense scented the air with coriander and orange blossom. In the branches high above hung ironwork lanterns at varying heights that threw fractured prisms of light, and thick swaths of purple fabric, the color of royalty, were draped and gathered to create a ceiling and four permeable walls. The fabric drifted down in gossamer waves that lifted and fluttered in the late afternoon breeze, teasing the floor, casting the platform into restless amethyst shadows.

It was a space fit for a jungle king to meet his council.

Hawk waited with the usual burning, gut-deep anger at being forced to wait for a command, like a puppy awaiting a treat, before he could speak.

Fucking hierarchy. Fucking etiquette. Bloody fucking hell.

Though he never cursed aloud, some days his mind rebelled.

Some days it was all he could do not to tear his hair out and scream.

After passing the security detail that patrolled the perimeter of the colony in a slinking, silent line, Hawk had Shifted back to human form and ascended the rope that hung from the underside of his home, a bi-level wood bungalow with a thatched roof and a shaded patio that encircled the second floor. Set high into the spreading branches of a seven-hundred-year-old kapok tree, it was accessible only by the one rope. Most of the other bungalows in the colony were linked by suspended bridges or zip lines through the dense network of trees, but Hawk liked to be a little more separate than that.

In fact, if he had his own way, he'd live by himself in the caves hidden behind the waterfall.

The only reason he didn't just Shift to Vapor, rise in a shimmering plume from the forest floor, and slip in over the wooden porch railing was because he still had the memory card in his mouth, and he could carry nothing as Vapor. A fact that had proven inconvenient on many occasions.

No sooner had he dressed than a runner was whistling from the ground below, with a summons from the Alpha, who'd obviously been notified the moment Hawk had returned, and was wasting no time in getting an update on the mission. A mission the Alpha himself had devised.

In a characteristic show of defiance, Hawk didn't bring the memory card with him when he went to the Assembly room. He hid it in a place even the most dedicated of the Alpha's minions wouldn't look: under the rim of the toilet bowl.

"Well, go on then," Alejandro drawled. "Tell me what happened."

This line was delivered with cool derision, as if Hawk were the village idiot coming in front of the king to bleat about his lost goat. Fury advanced up his spinal column like an army of hungry fire ants.

"It went according to plan." Even to his own ears, his voice sounded strained. He willed himself to relax as his hands itched to curl into fighting fists.

"Of course it did," said Xander in a conciliatory tone.

Along with the twenty other members of the Assembly, Hawk's other half brother sat beside his wife at the curved tables that flanked both sides of the Alpha's dais. Xander and Morgan shared a look, and Morgan—even in human form, the sleekest, most feral woman of the entire tribe—leaned forward to speak.

"Well done." She held his gaze with a look that said, *Don't let him get under your skin. Don't let him win.*

Of all the colony members, Hawk and Morgan were the ones who chafed most tightly against the cloistered restrictions of their existence. In spite of the fact that she'd turned the colony's most efficient and feared killer to putty in her lovely hands, Hawk had a grudging respect for Morgan's spirit. She was a rebel. She was a fighter. Like him.

Like Jacqueline Dolan.

That thought startled him so much he didn't bother to take offense when Alejandro snapped, "Let's not get ahead of ourselves with the praise, Morgan. I'd like to hear the details before I'm satisfied."

"The details?" Hawk repeated, still musing about his unexpected revelation. He pictured Jacqueline Dolan in his mind's eye, stretched out beneath him on the hotel bed, wearing nothing but a Cheshire Cat smile. He'd had dozens—hundreds?—of other women, and felt nothing for any of them.

So why did that image send such a rush of warmth through his veins?

"Well, let's see. About five eight, a hundred and thirty pounds, hair the color of a sunset, skin like fresh churned cream—"

"How poetic," Alejandro interrupted acidly. He leaned forward, wineglass in hand, eyes burning. "But I'm not interested in hearing about her looks—"

"Oh, you'd like the *sordid* details, then. Well, she's a screamer, I can tell you that—"

"Enough!" Alejandro slammed the wineglass down on the arm of his opulent chair with such force the stem shattered and fell tinkling to the polished wood floor. His face had turned the same color as the wine that was now splashed across his white linen trousers.

The room fell silent. The air went static. Morgan was trying desperately to keep a straight face.

"I'm sorry, did I say something wrong?" Hawk inquired with faux, blinking innocence, and someone on the Assembly actually had the nerve to snicker.

Alejandro was universally disliked. Though he was Alpha by grant of his Bloodline, and he was Gifted with Vapor, which only the most powerful were, Alejandro had failed to earn the respect that was due his position. Not only had he proved himself to be a narcissist, a hedonist, and a debauched gambler who often visited the city for the express purposes of whoring and frittering away his inheritance, he was not the eldest son.

In fact, Xander was the eldest son of the former Alpha. But Xander, like Hawk, hated politics. He'd refused the opportunity to ascend to his father's position. He'd only recently—begrudgingly—consented to join the Assembly at his wife's insistent behest. So Alejandro sat in the Alpha's chair instead of Xander, and the entire colony suffered for it.

As for Hawk, he was the product of the former Alpha's unfortunate liaison with an unmated young girl during a brief period between his marriages to the two wives who produced Hawk's half brothers. Hawk had royal Blood, but was the only illegitimate child the tribe had seen in generations. To the tribe, he was *Salsu Maru*, the Least Son.

The Bastard.

An object of equal parts desire—females seemed to love his air of brooding rebelliousness—and derision, Hawk was an outsider among his own people. He never had, and he never would, belong.

A fact which Alejandro took every opportunity to remind him.

"Where are the pictures?" Alejandro slowly enunciated each word, staring at Hawk as if he wished to drive a stake through his heart. Which he undoubtedly did—the vain hate being mocked.

Before he could answer, Morgan interjected, "I was actually thinking we might go in another direction with those pictures."

Alejandro stared at her with a look that would have made a serial killer quake, but she simply amended it politely, without an ounce of fear, "With your permission, My Lord, of course."

Alejandro might have missed the faint laughter in her voice, but Hawk didn't.

What's she up to?

"May I speak, Sire?"

She rose, leaning forward so a profusion of ample, creamy cleavage pressed in open invitation against the low neckline of her blouse. Most members of the colony wore as little as possible when in human form to circumvent the clinging jungle heat, but Morgan had a clothes fetish. Her wardrobe choices were made independent of the weather. When she'd first come to live in the jungle with Xander, she'd mourned the shoe collection she'd left behind in her far more sophisticated colony in England like a child mourns a pet run over by the neighbor's car.

Foolish fetishes aside, the woman had a body made to be showcased in designer clothes.

Alejandro's gaze flickered to the irresistible siren's call of the top swell of Morgan's breasts. Beside her, Xander stiffened in anger.

Women had to use every weapon available to them, and Morgan was a veritable arsenal of sex appeal. "Sire" this and "My Lord" that and a cruise missile of va-va-voom aimed straight in Alejandro's direction—whatever she had in mind, the Alpha didn't stand a chance.

Hawk felt no pity for Xander, sitting red-faced and livid beside her. *Allow yourself to fall for a bombshell like her, make her your wife, what did you expect? Your life would get easier?*

Still staring at her breasts, Alejandro gave Morgan permission to speak with an imperious wave of his hand.

"Thank you, My Lord." She inclined her head and dipped an elegant curtsy in a show of deference that visibly mollified the flustered Alpha. He sat back into his overstuffed chair with a sniff, snapping his fingers for more wine. A young attendant leapt to his side, removed the broken glass from between his stiff fingers, and replaced it with another, already full.

"As we all know, this reporter has caused us irreparable damage. Things were bad before, with the murders of the twenty-six politicians and religious leaders on Easter that Caesar coordinated, but they got even worse after she wrote that article and rallied humans behind her agenda of hate."

Murmurs of assent swirled around the room. Looking at Alejandro, but including the entire Assembly, Morgan continued.

"It occurred to me that, although your plan for revenge was excellent—as always, Sire—perhaps we might take it one step further. Perhaps we might look at it in a larger context, one that would benefit us beyond just ruining her career and reputation."

She paused, and the room held a collective breath.

This was a dangerous thing she attempted. The line she walked was paper thin. If the Alpha decided her tone or expression or even her posture weren't to his liking, if he detected even a hint of disrespect, it would be within his rights to punish her in any way he saw fit.

Including stringing her up to a tree and leaving her there until her corpse was picked clean by the birds.

It had been dangerous for him, too, but he honestly didn't care. Irritating Alejandro was the closest thing to fun Hawk ever had. He suffered canings on nearly a weekly basis, but he was a quick healer, and thought it a small price to pay for what little amusement he had available.

But for a female to challenge the Alpha, it was more than dangerous. It was downright crazy.

It was suicide.

Jesus. The balls on this broad. He glanced at Xander, wondering how on Earth he handled a firecracker like that. Xander looked as if he were wondering the exact same thing.

Slowly, Alejandro's brows lifted. Clearly relishing his power to hold them in thrall, he let them all stew in uncertainty for a moment until giving her permission to continue with the barest grudging nod.

Morgan said simply, "Blackmail."

"She has nothing we want," the Alpha countered.

"Forgive me, Sire, but she most certainly does," Morgan demurred with a shake of her head that sent her glossy dark hair swinging around her shoulders.

"Which is?" Alejandro drawled. Staring down Morgan's shirt, he moistened his lips.

"Influence."

Hawk understood her immediately. He also knew by the expression on Alejandro's face that he'd rather piss himself in public than take a suggestion from a woman, no matter how brilliant that suggestion might be.

Hawk had to play it carefully. Knowing Alejandro as he did, he felt confident of his hand.

"I think we should just stick to the Alpha's plan." He tried to convey a casual tone of both slight disapproval and amusement, as if he thought her a ridiculous creature who should stay in her place.

Oddly, his dismissal made Morgan smile.

"Let her speak," snapped Alejandro, right on cue.

Nothing if not predictable. Though his lips wanted to curl as Morgan's had, Hawk kept his expression disapproving, his unblinking gaze trained on her face.

Morgan said, "If this woman is powerful enough to turn public opinion one way, she's powerful enough to turn it the other. If, instead of using the pictures simply to discredit her and ruin her career, we used them as motivation for her to write another article—"

"Ah," said Alejandro, the light of understanding dawning in his eyes. "I see."

He seemed intrigued, but it wasn't enough. He needed a little help.

"Morgan, I'm sure the Alpha already thought of that," Hawk scoffed. "We don't need to spend any more time on this; we've already got what we need from her. Leaking those pictures will guarantee she won't be in a position to write any more high-profile opinion pieces—"

"Of course I thought of it," Alejandro interrupted, right on schedule. He sent Hawk a condescending stare. "But I may have been too hasty in disregarding this possible course of action."

So that his eyes didn't roll in his head like a pair of tossed marbles, Hawk stared straight back at Alejandro, concentrating his energy on keeping his expression perfectly neutral.

Alejandro turned his attention back to Morgan. He brushed an invisible piece of lint from one of his pristine linen sleeves and said with supreme indifference, "Naturally, I had a few ideas regarding how we might proceed in this area, but you may continue and share yours."

Her voice, dripping with what could be interpreted either as sarcasm or abject groveling, depending on where you stood, Morgan said, "*Thank* you, Sire." She dipped another curtsy, just as ironic as the first.

Alejandro beamed, Xander scowled, and Hawk had the startling thought that Morgan might be the smartest person in the room.

Had she foreseen this entire scenario? Alejandro's reactions, and his own? Were the two of them playing right into her hands?

She adopted a brisk, businesslike tone. "What I propose is this. Let's make this woman aware of our intention to expose the evidence of her, ah . . ." she floundered, but recovered quickly, "*exploits*, and offer her a chance to avoid public humiliation. If she writes another article denouncing the first, we can destroy the photos. If she refuses, we simply proceed as planned. But if she agrees, we have the opportunity of a lifetime. A highly respected reporter who reconsidered her position and now fully supports Shifters will, if nothing else, grow doubts in the minds of those who agreed with her in the first place. We could even insist she call for a repeal of the anti-Shifter laws, speak in front of the UN. If it doesn't work we've lost nothing either way."

Judging by Alejandro's frown, he was seriously considering the merits of her argument. Hawk gave him another little shove in the right direction just to be sure.

He sighed and shook his head, looking at the Alpha with fraternal scorn as if to say, *This broad is a real piece of work, right?*

Alejandro's lips thinned. Looking directly at Hawk, he said coolly, "Your logic is impeccable, Morgan. Well done."

Hawk tried hard to look crestfallen, but guessed he probably just looked constipated because Alejandro stared at him with venomous intensity like a cobra just before a strike.

But it was Morgan who went in for the kill.

"And I think to add credence to her sudden change of opinion, this reporter should be brought here to live with us. To observe us. So when she tells the world how wonderful we really are, she has a response when they ask, 'How do you know?'"

Hawk's mouth wasn't the only one that dropped open. All around the room, mouths gaped. Eyes rounded. Faces stared back at her in disbelief. There were a few low, horrified gasps, some nervous chuckles, a lone curse from one of the older Assembly members, whose astonished face had blanched white.

"Live with us?" Hawk blurted, dropping his feigned scorn for true incredulity. Was she *insane?* "Morgan, that's just crazy. We can't have a *human* come live with us—"

"Why not?" She turned to gaze at him in steady self-confidence.

"We'll be completely exposed, that's why not! I mean, consider for a minute what could happen. Even if she does agree to it and comes here, there's no guarantee she won't tell anyone our location. In fact, why *wouldn't* she? Blackmailed and kidnapped—I assume she'd have to be kidnapped; she's not gonna come waltzing through the jungle on her own—and held against her will, forced to write something she doesn't believe. You think this woman is just going to keep our location a secret? And even if, for some unfathomable reason, she *did* keep our location a secret after we released her, there's a few people I can think of who would have absolutely no problem getting it out of her! In some pretty nasty ways! Don't forget, there's a huge bounty on all of our heads! We *can't* live with humans."

That's when Morgan played her trump card. "The Queen thinks we can."

Hawk's jaw closed with an audible *snap*. The room fell into crackling silence.

Ah yes, the Queen. Their powerful, liberal, half-human Queen, the mere mention of whom had the entire room sitting up straighter in their chairs, soiling their underwear.

Including the Alpha.

Aside from Morgan and Xander, Alejandro was the only one present who'd ever met the Queen. To hear it told, she was so stunning and powerful he fell at her feet and sniveled like a teething baby.

In a quiet, menacing voice, Alejandro said, "The Queen is not here."

"She will be. Soon," said Thiago, the young man in charge of building the new compound that would house the Queen and her family. She'd given birth to twins a few months back, and hadn't been able to relocate to Brazil until the babies were old enough. They were expected within weeks.

Morgan nodded. "And I daresay, it would reflect so well on you, Sire, that you had the foresight and compassion to bring this reporter here in the hopes of giving humans a better understanding of our kind. I know the Queen well. This is exactly the kind of thing that would please her."

With an air of virgin innocence as false as a pair of wooden teeth, Morgan folded her hands together at her waist, smiled at the Alpha—gazing up at him demurely from beneath a fringe of black lashes—and stood waiting for him to speak.

And Hawk saw the genius in her plan.

Alejandro was now in a pickle of epic proportion.

If he agreed to Morgan's plan, he'd look weak. Weakness was the one thing an Alpha could *never* show, because it would call his entire rule into question. But if he disregarded the plan, he risked the Queen's displeasure. And a creature who could turn not only to panther and Vapor, but also to any animal she wished, to any element, to any *thing*—including her currently favored form of a fire-breathing, enormous white dragon—was not a creature you wanted to piss off.

Hawk watched Alejandro squirm over the conundrum with a glee he hadn't felt in years.

"The colony is stretched to capacity as it is," the Alpha began slowly, thoughts churning behind his glittering eyes. "We've already had to assimilate the members of the Nepal, Quebec, and Sommerley colonies because of the threats against us. Not only are we overcrowded, but we are the last bastion of safety for our kind. We're the only colony that hasn't been discovered by the Expurgari. And, as far as we know, the only one Caesar hasn't discovered as well. If we bring this human woman here, we risk not only discovery . . . we risk the extinction of our entire species. If this colony falls, we all fall. Forever."

Morgan's reply came in a voice clear and strong. "The risk of extinction is upon us no matter how we proceed with this reporter, Sire. There's no going back to the old ways of hiding and pretending that kept us safe for so long. The world has shrunk far too small for us to hide any longer. Even the rainforest is disappearing, eaten up by logging and agriculture, by human development. How long will it be before they find us simply because the forest has been devoured by their civilization? How long can we reasonably expect to survive here like this—one generation longer? Two?"

Men moved their weight uncomfortably in their seats. It was the unspoken, gnawing fear among them, the question of what would happen when there were no longer any wild places left to hide. How would they survive as they had been for millennia, in secrecy and silence? What would become of them once Man consumed all the shadowed, untouched places, breached the dark heart of the rainforest that had shielded them for so long?

"Our discovery is inevitable," Morgan continued. "Even if we move from here, there are few places left on the planet where we can hide. Humans already know we exist; they have the most terrible proof. Caesar—the traitor, the murderer—is who they think we all are. Let's give them reason to believe we shouldn't be judged by the worst among us. Let's give them reason to step back from their hate and hysteria, and consider us not as enemies, but as equals. Let's give them something more powerful than hate. Something even more powerful, possibly, than love."

Morgan glanced away from Alejandro. Her gaze rested on Xander's anxious face, and she looked at him with such unconcealed adoration that a pang of something akin to jealousy twisted Hawk's heart.

What would it be like to have a woman like her look at you like that?

"And what might that be?" Alejandro prompted.

Morgan turned her eyes back to the Alpha. She said simply, "Hope."

Silence, loud as thunder. Off in the distance a bird screeched. The cry was cut off abruptly, as if it had been swallowed.

Morgan continued, softer than before. "Humans aren't so different from us. They want better lives for themselves. They want better lives for their children. They want a better world. They *hope* for all these things, just like we do, and that's what makes us the same. That's why we have to show them we're better as friends than enemies. That the world can be a better place if we can learn to coexist. But they can't know about us unless we take the risk and show them. And we have no better opportunity than with this reporter. Here, in a controlled environment, she can see us . . . and she can testify to the rest of the world what she saw."

Morgan stepped forward from her place at the table, her hands clasped against her chest, her face full of fervent emotion. Every eye in the room was trained on her.

"My Lord," she entreated in a low voice that throbbed with emotion, "let us lead the revolution. Let us be the ones who finally have the courage to step into the light. Let us be the bringers of hope to a world that so desperately needs it."

Hearing these words, Hawk was moved to the core of his soul.

He was moved by Morgan's bravery and her eloquence, by her passion and idealism, but most of all by the inescapable realization that she had indeed planned this entire scenario, right down to the words she would speak.

She was risking everything, including her life, for the cause of peace. For people who misunderstood her, who because of the actions of a madman actually *hated* her, Morgan was risking death.

This might have been the most blatant display of sheer courage he'd ever seen. It was a small thing, just standing there alone, but colossal in scope in the effect it might have.

It was genius.

"Alexander," said Alejandro in a flat tone, without looking away from Morgan, "your wife continually surprises me. What a warrior she would have made had she been born male."

In exactly the same tone Xander replied, "She's twice the warrior of any male I've ever met." He added a curt, "Brother."

Alejandro cut his gaze to Xander. "I'm sure you meant 'Sire,'" he said, deadly soft, his fingers white around the stem of his wineglass.

The smile that spread over Xander's mouth was grim. He inclined his head and said nothing, the muscles in his broad shoulders rippling with tension.

Morgan, sensing an impending disaster, intervened. "My Lord, please forgive me if I've overstepped my—"

"No." Alejandro's voice rang out through the open-air space. "You've done the right thing. There's nothing to forgive. From *you.*" His icy gaze swept over the gathered men, who'd frozen at the anger ringing in his voice. "I expected more, however, from the rest of you. How is it that Morgan—a new addition to our colony, I might add—has my best interests at heart, and shares my exact thoughts on the proper way to proceed with this Dolan woman, yet the rest of you do not?"

The silence that echoed throughout the Assembly room was cavernous and fraught. Everyone present knew there was no correct answer to this question. Judging by the way tension ebbed from Xander's shoulders, however, Hawk realized that Morgan was out of imminent danger.

Alejandro had decided to pretend the entire thing was his idea, his earlier disagreement only for show.

"My apologies for my short-sightedness. You're right."

Alejandro's eyes raked over Hawk with a fury that was palpable. "Of *course* I'm right," he hissed. "I. Am. The. Alpha!"

"Yes. You are." Hawk kept his voice devoid of emotion or inflection. "And I'm sure you've already thought of how we should next proceed."

The Alpha paused just long enough so the tension in the room rose to a new high. He said, "Naturally." Then he smiled with such malevolence it sent a tingle of sinister premonition down Hawk's spine.

Whatever he was going to say next wouldn't be good.

"You're going to get this Dolan woman. You're going to bring her back here—unharmed, mind you—and she'll stay with us for a period of time that I'll determine." His ugly smile grew wider, and so did Hawk's certainty of impending doom.

The Alpha proved him right with his next words. "And during her time here . . . she'll be living with *you.*"

Hawk's heart screeched to a stop inside his chest. The thought of sharing his home—his sanctuary—with a woman was about as appealing as having all of his teeth pulled out with a pair of pliers, one by one. Without anesthesia.

Which Alejandro undoubtedly knew. Everyone knew it: Hawk was a loner. He hated petty conversation almost as much as he hated any kind of obligation, and women were chock-full of both. Of all the females he'd wooed since he was a young man, not a single one had ever been inside his home. He went to theirs or they met in the forest or, in the cases of the human females he met in the city on the procurement trips he was regularly assigned to, at hotels with rooms rentable by the hour. Anywhere he could make a quick, clean getaway once the fun had been had.

And after what he'd done to her, Jacqueline Dolan would, no doubt, make regular efforts to kill him in his sleep.

Disaster.

Morgan was blinking in surprise. Beside her, Xander gazed at him in sympathy. The other Assembly members looked as if they might break into hysterical laughter.

The loner, the outsider, the infamous Bastard, forced to share his own personal space with a *human* female who despised him as much as he despised her, for an indeterminate amount of time, under the watchful eyes of the entire tribe.

Hawk couldn't think of a worse fate.

But Alejandro wasn't done. "You'll be in charge of making sure everything goes according to plan, and that this reporter forms a more favorable opinion of us. You'll be in charge of ensuring that article is written—"

"And in return?" he interrupted, seething. "If I successfully bring her here and convince her that not only should she not *kill* me because of how I used her, but that she should also produce an article in direct contradiction to the one that won her such fame, what do I get?"

Alejandro grinned. "You get to keep your head attached to your body."

Morgan went white, Xander turned red, and Hawk wished, for not the first time, he'd been born anyone else, in any other time, in any other place than this.

"Run along now, Hawk," said Alejandro, still grinning. "And try not to cock it up."

NINE

A Proposition

Having survived the dreaded annual birthday pilgrimage to her father's house, Jack returned to her apartment in the city. Exhausted and in dire need of a shower, she greeted the stark stillness of her empty apartment with the same level of enthusiasm one approaches a trip to the gynecologist.

Standing in the dark foyer—the overhead light had burned out again—she looked around, weighing the silence.

High ceilings. Tall, uncovered windows across the length of two walls. Yawning space, devoid of furniture or even rugs to muffle the walnut floors that echoed with every step. Hoping a home of her own would help fill the gaping hole inside her chest that seemed to grow larger with every passing year, Jack had purchased the loft three years ago with the idea of putting down roots, of making a welcoming space she could return to from her travels, a spot uniquely her own.

The roots she hoped to grow had failed to flourish. She'd never had the time—more honestly the inclination—to decorate beyond the mere basics. Bed. Desk. Chest of drawers. She didn't even have a dining room table. After three years the place was almost as bare as the day she'd moved in.

It fits though, Jack thought wryly. Unembellished and unwelcoming, the space was undoubtedly hers.

She dropped her duffel bag on the floor just inside the door, and stripped off her jacket and T-shirt. She left them both atop the bag, kicked off her shoes, and headed to the kitchen in her bra and jeans. The fridge revealed its usual array of barren shelves and empty drawers, with the exception of a single bottle of Stella Artois.

"Hello, beautiful," Jack said, reaching for the beer. She made quick work of popping the top, and leaned against the counter to drink it, swallowing in long, greedy gulps.

Thank you, God, for getting me through today. The bickering of car horns in traffic drifted up from the street twenty stories below, and Jack enjoyed a moment's peace.

Until the phone rang.

"Not home," she said aloud, hearing her voice echo through the loft as if through the walls of a canyon. "Leave a message."

When the machine on the kitchen counter clicked on—she still kept the bulky answering machine she'd had since her freshman year in college—Nola's voice broke the silence.

"Your cell is off. Just checking to make sure you didn't get shot in Brazil. Because, you know, with you that's always a possibility."

Smiling, Jack picked up the phone.

"Shot with a sex pistol," she drawled, her smile growing wider.

Hearing her friend's voice, and thinking about the handsome stranger named Hawk, both managed to lift Jack's spirits.

"Hey! You're home! When did you get in?"

"Literally right this second." Jack looked at the half-empty bottle in her hand. "I was just getting something to eat."

"Let me guess. Beer and veggie pizza."

Jack laughed. "Minus the pizza. You know me too well, lady. How are you?"

"Just making sure you're not dead in some jungle somewhere, like I said. And calling to wish you a happy belated birthday. Did you think I forgot?"

"Oh, you *obviously* didn't forget! I gotta hand it to you, No, that was one hell of a birthday present. I don't know how I'll ever be able to repay you. The guy was like some supermodel assassin rock-star sex god. Unbelievable. I won't ask you how much you had to shell out for that kind of quality, but whatever you paid, he was worth it. I think I'll be sore for a week."

A beat of silence. The siren from a police car several blocks over screamed loud in pursuit, then faded away. Then Nola asked, "What are you talking about?"

Hearing those words, spoken in the flat, interrogating law-yerly tone Nola used when she wasn't kidding around, Jack's stomach dove toward her feet.

"You didn't buy me a guy for my birthday."

It was a statement, not a question, spoken in a tone to match her friend's. A movie began to play in Jack's mind. Images flashed by with lightning speed, and unforgiving clarity.

Sweat soaked sheets, naked bodies, tangled limbs, hunger.

Camera flashes.

Pictures.

"Buy you a guy for your birthday?" Nola echoed with a snort.

Then she gasped. "Oh God, Jack, don't tell me you hooked up with some guy you . . . you thought I . . ."

At Jack's answering silence, Nola began to laugh. "You did! You so did! I need details, right now!"

Do you want something to remember me by? Hawk, beautiful and coy, holding up the camera. *Jack's* camera.

Her gaze flashed to the duffel bag, discarded by the front door. "No, I've gotta call you back."

Jack hung up before Nola could reply. She launched herself across the room, fell to her knees, and ripped open the bag, panting with panic.

The Canon was there, in its hard leather case.

The memory card, however, wasn't.

As she stared down the empty slot in the side of the camera, horror—cold, slimy, and total, like being submerged in a tank of eels—washed over Jack. She broke out in a sweat. Her hands began to shake. Her heart started to race as if she'd been injected with adrenaline.

Set up. Jesus Christ, I've been set up!

But by who? And why? She sagged against the wall, hardly feeling the cold plaster against her bare shoulders, and stared down at the Canon in her hands.

She knew she'd made enemies over the years; she'd never shied away from controversy in her career. It could be a politician, angry about one of her scathing op-ed pieces, or one of the many military leaders she'd met during an assignment, and pissed off with her attitude or refusal to listen to orders. It could be a colleague; she knew she wasn't particularly liked among her peers, for a whole host of reasons, which mainly boiled down to her inability to trust anyone.

It could even be one of the more vocal critics of her anti-Shifter article. Not everyone was on board with the idea that Shifters were mankind's enemy.

Who was it who'd warned her someone might try to retaliate if she took such a strong stance against the newly discovered threat of Shifters? Who had said to her, "You're just putting a big bull's-eye on your back, missy. You see what those crazy animal rights activists do to celebrities who wear fur coats—what they'll do to you will probably be a lot worse than throwing some red paint."

It came to her in a blinding flash: old Mrs. Weingarden on the third floor. They'd ridden up the elevator together just after the article had come out a few months back, and the elderly woman had clucked her tongue and shaken her head, wondering why Jack needed to get on a soap box and rant and rave about patriotism and the American way of life. "Warmongering" she'd called it.

Jack understood in a bitter, wish-it-wasn't-so way that the urge to fly her patriotic flag was tied to her loyalty to her father. He was her only remaining parent, her only remaining link to the time before she was the hollow shell she was now. He'd paid for the best therapists, and put her in private schools, and got her involved in sports, though none of it served his hoped-for purpose of making her forget what had happened.

But he'd tried. He'd tried everything he could. So she did her damndest to make him proud of her, even though she knew it was only a futile attempt to remake a past that had died long ago, and taken her heart with it.

Denial set in.

Jack began to rummage frantically through the duffel, tossing out clothes, feeling all around the bottom, scavenging through the smaller bag of toothpaste and tampons and ChapStick, ripping the whole thing apart.

Finally, the bag was empty. There was no memory card.

She sat staring in shock into the gaping opening. *It can't be. This can't be happening.*

In response to her voice in her head came her mother's, sneering and quite decidedly filled with glee.

Serves you right. You little whore.

Jack shook her head, shoved away from the wall, jumped to her feet. "Think. Just *think*," she said, beginning to pace. "When those pictures get out—because of course they're going to get out, don't kid yourself—what am I going to say? How can I spin this? I was drunk? Taken advantage of?"

She paused, considering it. Remembering the total abandon with which she'd participated in the best sex of her life, the brazen way she'd posed, clearly enjoying herself, clearly lucid, she began pacing anew. "Okay, you obviously weren't taken advantage of. You just had a lapse in judgment. Stress of the job, that sort of thing. I mean, I was shot at yesterday! Of course I wasn't in my right mind! This kind of stress reaction happens to men all the time, right?"

Even to her own ears, this argument sounded lame. Women were held to a different sexual standard than men, that was the harsh reality. It didn't matter that she was single and had every right to sleep with whomever she wanted; the press would crucify her. Her judgment, morals, and entire character would be excoriated. A sexy romp with a total stranger while on assignment in a foreign country, with graphic pictorial evidence that she loved every minute of it to boot?

She would be fired. Her career would be over. She would lose everything she'd worked for so long to build. If she were lucky, in six months she'd be working at a fast-food drive-through.

If she were lucky, in a few years everyone would have forgotten that the woman who pushed the President's anti-Shifter agenda through Congress was a total slut.

Jack's gaze fell on her laptop. Her heart throbbed inside her chest.

She crawled on her knees to the computer, flipped it open, and turned it on. With a whir it was awake, awaiting her command. With trembling hands, anticipating the worst, she Googled her name.

Nothing new. No headline news, no breaking scandal.

The relief was so palpable she felt as if someone had showered her in cool water. But anxiety quickly rose again as she realized the lack of news might mean nothing at all. It might mean the pictures were just sitting on her editor's desk, at this very moment, but she just hadn't gotten the call yet. It might, in fact, mean any one of a million different things, all of them bad.

Because whatever had prompted Hawk to take those pictures and steal the memory card had to be bad. There were no two ways about it.

Jack got her first glimpse of exactly how bad it was when an electronic chime notified her that she had a new email message.

With clammy, trembling hands, she opened the email. A timer popped up, along with a notice, "This email will be deleted in ten seconds."

She read the sender's message, saw the picture attached, and let out a scream of anger so primal and raw the overhead light in the foyer flickered on.

Above a photo of Jack kneeling between a man's legs with his huge, jutting member shoved straight down the back of her throat, her cheeks hollowed, her upturned eyes glazed with lust, were the words, "This one's my favorite."

It was simply signed, "Yours, Rock. As in, head like a . . ."

But that wasn't the worst of it. Oh no, the worst was just about to rear its ugly head.

Another email arrived from the same anonymous address. She clicked on it, her hands now shaking so badly they looked palsied. It was a video file, again with a self-destruct notice, this time set to one minute. When she opened the video, Jack felt simultaneously urges to vomit, faint, and beat something bloody.

Hawk, clothed all in white, beautiful and somber, stared straight into the camera. Behind him it was dark, but she could make out the vague outline of furniture, some kind of gauzy curtain, the branches of a tree. For a moment he did nothing, just stood unmoving with his hands hanging loose at his sides.

Then—unbelievably, horribly—he began to change.

First it appeared to be a trick of the light. There was a shimmer, a glow appeared around him as if emanating from within. The glow grew brighter, the shimmer more distinct, until all at once the flesh-and-bone man that was Hawk dissolved into a floating plume of glittering gray mist, ethereal and insubstantial, floating halfway between the floor and the ceiling like a disembodied spirit.

His clothes fell with a soft rustle of fabric to the floor.

Jack made a strangled sound. She went hot then cold, and found it increasingly difficult to breathe.

Breathing became next to impossible when the floating gray plume of mist gathered in on itself, and coalesced into the largest, most beautiful black panther Jack had ever seen.

It padded toward the camera. It paused, sat back on muscled haunches, staring into the camera with those eyes of vivid yellow-green, and let out a low, rumbling growl that stood all the tiny hairs on the back of her neck on end.

Oh God, oh God, oh God . . .

She'd been set up and used by . . . by one of *them*.

Bile rose in her throat. She clapped both hands over her mouth. Memories again swirled in a Technicolor tangle in her mind, vivid images of the two of them in every possible sexual position. Memories of his words, both harsh and tender, as he pushed himself inside her and brought her to orgasm, over and over again.

Jack didn't have time to linger on those terrible memories, however, because again the image on the screen was changing shape. The panther changed back to mist, the mist changed back to man—naked, glorious—and the man came close to the camera, so close she saw the stubble shadowing his jaw.

Those cat eyes still burning lucent green, Hawk said into the camera, "I have a proposition for you, Jacqueline Dolan."

He continued to speak in a low, cold monotone, as the bottom fell out of Jack's world.

TEN

Dust and Domination

Aside from the sand that insinuates itself into every crack and crevice, the main problem with living in a desert is the heat.

Suffocating, relentless, palpable as a hand pressing on the crown of your head, the heat of the northern Sahara is particularly trying. Especially for a group of predators who originated from the lush, tropical heart of the African rainforest, a place where it rains at least once a day.

"If someone doesn't figure out how to get me some ice," muttered Caesar Cardinalis, sprawled in a high-backed rattan chair with one long leg flung over the wooden arm and a tepid glass of water in hand, "someone is going to die." He stared around the arid, dusty room, eyeing each of his guards in turn. All of them had their hands clasped behind their backs, their gazes trained on some invisible point in the distance, a solid row of weapon-heavy soldiers as unnecessary to their lord and master's continued health as snowshoes in the tropics.

Caesar added with languid ill humor, "And when I say someone, I mean *everyone*."

The guards—knowing all too well this wasn't an idle threat—shifted their weight from foot to foot, and sent each another quick, anxious glances.

One of them stepped forward. Larger than the rest, he was a cool, efficient killer with a withering stare and the impressive musculature of an elite athlete. Like the others, born and bred in darkness in the catacombs below Rome, he had eyes the color of polished obsidian, but unlike the others, he didn't tremble when he addressed their leader.

He was, however, smart enough to keep his gaze lowered deferentially to Caesar's bare, tanned feet. Before speaking, he bowed.

"I took the liberty of ordering a diesel-powered generator, Sire, the day we arrived. It's being delivered soon to the market at Jamaa el Fna. With your permission, I'll take Nico with me to pick it up when it arrives."

Marcell waited patiently for Caesar to assess this and pass judgment. This kind of independent thinking was not something Caesar normally appreciated, but knowing their luxury-loving leader as Marcell did, he'd taken the risk with full confidence of reward.

A reward that was ensured when Caesar replied, "Thank Horus *one* of you has a brain."

Careful to keep the self-satisfied smirk from his face, Marcell bowed a little lower, then returned to his place at the wall.

The kasbah in Morocco that Caesar and his followers had settled in after their abrupt departure from Spain was vast and crumbling and echoing empty, one of the hundreds of abandoned sandcastle palaces left to bake in the sun by a clan of long-ago Berber warriors. Situated in an unexpected oasis along the former route of the caravans over the Atlas mountains to Marrakech, the stronghold built of earth was isolated from any human settlements, and steadily collapsing.

In spite of its decay, it was spectacular.

An austere, sprawling maze of red clay and stone, it still held the echoes of its former glory and conspicuous wealth. Elaborate stucco pillars, brilliant mosaics, soaring Moorish doorways, and intricately carved woodwork had survived the harsh desert climate, as had a store of handwoven wool rugs, stashed in rolls of dust-covered canvas in the dungeon below. Along with a few pieces of mismatched furniture bought from a local bazaar, the rugs were now scattered about Caesar's rooms on the uppermost floor of the palace.

The view from Caesar's bed chamber revealed an abandoned cobweb village below, surrounded by multilevel towers and a series of crooked, interlinked alleyways. When he had looked down on the deserted dwellings for the first time, Caesar had felt a thrill of delight as he imagined all the generations of humans who had died within those walls.

Because the only good human was a dead one.

The kasbah's dusty beauty was matched by its eerie stillness. An incessant hot breeze was the only thing that stirred in the smothering heat of the day. The only thing that broke the yawning silence was the occasional flapping of a vulture's wings as it peered from the tower ramparts with avid black eyes for anything freshly dead.

More often than not, the vulture found what it was looking for. Caesar tired quickly of the playthings he kept chained to the dark dungeon wall.

"All right." Caesar pulled himself to an upright position in the chair. "What's the current count?"

Again it was Marcell who spoke. "Eight hundred sixty-two, Sire."

Caesar was pleased. Their little colony was growing quickly.

After a brief pause, Marcell added, "Not including the females, of course."

Caesar waved a hand dismissively. Naturally the females wouldn't be counted—unless they were pregnant, that is. Then they actually had value. Speaking of which—

"How many females are near whelping?"

Marcell didn't have to consult a written ledger or any notes to correctly answer Caesar's inquiry. He knew all the important details of his master's plan by heart. He was intelligent, ambitious, and knew that pleasing Caesar was the only way he'd ever get the things he wanted for himself, so he made it his business to anticipate his master's needs.

"Ninety-two. Another two dozen have been recently confirmed pregnant."

When Caesar blinked in surprise, Marcell allowed himself to smile. "You've been quite prolific, Sire."

Caesar chuckled, a sound as dry and humorless as the striking of a match.

Ikati females only went into heat—called the Fever—once per year, and many times did not get pregnant, a fact which aggravated the *Ikati*'s already dwindling numbers. Human females, on the other hand, bred like rabbits. A single female could potentially birth upward of a dozen children during her fertile years. More if assisted with drugs.

As the son of a king who regularly mated with human women to increase his own half-Blood army, Caesar had no qualms about following in his father's footsteps. Like his father, he'd rid himself of the human mothers when they were no longer useful.

The vultures around here are going to be getting very, very fat, he thought, smiling.

He rose from the chair and stretched. "Well, we're going to have to finish the addition to the nursery much sooner than we thought, aren't we?"

Marcell inclined his head. "It's near completion, Sire. I've been overseeing the construction myself. If you like, I can take you on a tour today."

In an uncharacteristic display of camaraderie, Caesar walked over to Marcell and clapped him on the shoulder, beaming. "You, my friend, are worth your weight in gold." He studied Marcell's face for a moment. "Why don't you choose from the stock in the dungeon and take the rest of the day off. Enjoy yourself. You deserve it. You can show me the nursery tomorrow."

Marcell bowed. It was deep and respectful, and not at all ironic.

The "stock" in the dungeon was of the highest quality, chosen carefully from cities near and far to satisfy Caesar's highly refined aesthetics. The females were young, busty, and universally pretty, a veritable smorgasbord of pleasure from which to choose. Marcell had his eye on one particularly lovely specimen who'd been snatched from a public market not three days ago, whom not even Caesar had had the chance to sample. A dusky, delicious brunette by all appearances not yet out of her teens.

"Sire," said Marcell, gratitude ringing in his tone.

Caesar's gaze, cooler, swept over the other guards. "As for the rest of you, get back to digging the trenches for the aqueduct. I want running water within the week. Do I make myself clear?"

Judging by the chorus of "Yes, Sire!" that rang out, he had.

Caesar left the room, whistling, on his way to make an important call on his satellite phone.

Time for stage two in his plan for world domination to be set into play.

ELEVEN

Arch Enemies

The moment the black hood was pulled over her head from behind and the line of bobbing boats moored at Pier 61 at the Chelsea docks vanished from sight, Jack experienced a terror so bone deep and incapacitating she wasn't able to move her legs when a hand placed at the small of her back gave her a firm push forward.

She'd tried to mentally prepare herself for death, but that's like trying to mentally prepare yourself for childbirth, or being cheated on by the love of your life. No matter how well you think you can handle it, reality is a bitch with a twisted sense of humor.

In such situations, dignity is the first thing that flies out the window.

Jack's frozen legs refused to bend. She pitched forward with a strangled gasp, sucking cold night air into her mouth through the scratchy cloth of her new headwear.

The hand that had pushed her grabbed her arm before she could hit the ground face first. It was joined by another hand—big, with a vice-like grip—and Jack was pulled back to her feet and steadied.

"Better get your legs working, Red," said a gruff male voice into her ear. He was so close she felt his warm breath slide down her neck. "You're gonna need 'em where we're going."

Beyond the thundering of her heart and the roar of the blood rushing through her veins, Jack recognized that silk/sandpaper voice, though she hadn't yet glimpsed its owner. Terror morphed instantly to rage, an emotion she was far more comfortable with.

She hissed, "If I were you I'd be more worried about how well my hands are working. Because the minute they get the chance, they're going to claw out your eyes, asshole!"

A low chuckle. The musical *chink* of metal sliding against metal. Then his voice, now amused. "Glad to see we're still on the same page."

"We were *never* on the same page, you lying, scheming, underhanded, son of a—"

The cold bite of metal encircled her left wrist, then her right. A snap and a tug, and both her hands had been pulled behind her back. It happened so quickly it was over before she could react, before she could even draw in a breath.

Handcuffs.

The rage grew. Burning hot, engulfing, it felt as if she were standing on the surface of the sun. Her entire body vibrated with the urge to kick and hit and scream and claw and hurt him, hurt him, *hurt him*.

Beside her, Hawk exhaled a slow, ragged breath. "Yeah. The feeling's mutual, believe me."

Trying to regain a shred of her lost dignity, though her emotions were evident from the way her voice shook, Jack said, "This cloak-and-dagger routine is unnecessary. Just kill me now. Just get it over with."

Jack felt Hawk's surprise. There was a beat of silence as he processed that. He answered ominously, "If I wanted you dead, woman, you already would be." Then his big hand curled around her bicep, and he propelled her forward.

He walked quickly, with purpose, his strides even and long. She had to hurry to keep up, but it was difficult, due to his pace, her blindness, and the way he kept her so close beside him, dragging her along. She muttered a curse as she lost her footing on an uneven patch of ground.

Hawk's fingers tightened around her arm. "What did I tell you about that mouth?"

Judging by his tone, she'd found a sore spot . . . which she intended to ruthlessly leverage. In the darkness behind the hood, her lips formed a bitter smile.

If I'm going to die, I'm going to piss you off as much as possible before I do.

She didn't believe for one moment that Hawk wasn't going to kill her, probably in the most gruesome of ways. She'd seen the violence his kind was capable of. She knew the nature of these Shifters who called themselves *Ikati* was bloodthirsty, and utterly merciless. Their leader, Caesar, had slaughtered the Pope on live television during his Christmas Day speech, for God's sake! Then on Easter, he'd murdered every important religious and political leader across the globe. The US, French, and Russian presidents; the UK, Israeli, Canadian, Japanese, and Italian prime ministers; the chancellor of Germany; the chairman of the US Joint Chiefs of Staff; the Supreme Leaders of Iran and North Korea; the two Chief Rabbis of Israel; archbishops and cardinals from various countries; Grand Imams . . . it had been a highly coordinated, perfectly planned, chillingly effective declaration of war that screamed in big, bold letters: WE HATE HUMANS.

The entire massacre illustrated with chilling clarity the *Ikati*'s ability to bypass with ease even the most sophisticated of human security measures.

So Jack had no illusions she would be treated well, or would be alive when the sun rose tomorrow morning. This was her final night on Earth, of that she was sure.

What she wasn't so sure of was the reason he'd wanted to meet at the docks.

The "proposition" he'd offered in his emailed video had been ambiguous at best. In return for not releasing the photos of the two of them in *flagrante delicto*, she would be required to come to the docks at midnight three days' hence, with nothing other than the clothes on her back. No handbag, no cell phone, no camera, no questions asked. She was to tell no one about him or their agreement, and he assured her all her communications were being carefully monitored, including her cell phone, email, work phone, and house phone, so he'd know if she talked.

That was all bad, but what finally cinched the deal was the threat to her father.

Hawk was oblique about it. The casual mention of "your father will suffer if you don't comply," was enough. He didn't need to catalogue in detail what would happen if she didn't show. She imagined her father's body eviscerated as those others had been, the unfortunate twenty-six who had met their maker with their entrails arranged in a gruesome, glistening pink tangle on the floor around their heads.

So she'd put her mail on a vacation hold. She'd paid her mortgage and bills in advance for three months. She'd run her daily route through Central Park six times in three days, trying to clear her mind and steel herself for the worst. Finally she'd taken a taxi in the middle of the night to the marina on the Hudson River.

And now she was here, stumbling along blindly beside the man—creature—who had been the best sex of her life and would unfortunately also be the one to gut her like a fish.

Hawk stopped. She bumped against him, sucking in a breath of surprise at the full body contact. He flinched away as if he'd been burned. "Step up," he said curtly.

"How high?" was her arctic response.

There was a beat of what she imagined furious silence, then he put his hands under her armpits and lifted her from behind— easily, as if she weighed no more than a child—and deposited her unceremoniously to a surface that was, just slightly, rocking.

A boat. They were on a boat. Dear God, he was going to dump her body out at sea.

Would she still be alive when she went in the water? The thought of drowning, handcuffed, in a hood, made her shudder.

She hoped he killed her before he threw her overboard.

"Do us both a favor and stop thinking," Hawk snapped, taking her firmly by the arm. He guided her around a few turns, down three steps, then pressed her down into a soft seat with his hands on her shoulders. Jack sat there rigid as a plank, hands clammy, sightless and helpless and hating the scared-dog trembling that wracked her body in spite of the long, slow breaths she pulled into her lungs in an effort to calm herself.

Hawk stood too near. She imagined he was, at that very moment, withdrawing a knife from his boot.

"The hood will come off as soon as we're far enough away from land. The handcuffs . . . well, that's going to depend entirely on how you behave." His voice lowered. "And you should know, before you go trying anything stupid, you can't get away from me. You can't overpower me. And you can't hide anything from me.

I'll know what you're thinking of doing before you do it, so again—don't try anything stupid. I don't want to have to hurt you, but I will if you make it necessary. Submit yourself to this, and in a few weeks you'll be back home, no worse for wear."

Submit? A few weeks? *I'll know what you're thinking?* She needed answers.

"You're taking me somewhere."

She knew she'd guessed correctly when he remained silent. Relief flooded her body, a flower of hope blossoming in the hardpan of her terror. "Where? Why?"

He made a small sound, quieter than a chuckle, and she wished she could see the expression on his face. Was he laughing at her?

"Because there's a story you need to write, that's why. And it requires a little . . . research."

A story? Was this a ruse? Some kind of sick game to give her hope before he slit her throat and tossed her into the ocean?

"How do I know you're not just going to release those pictures, even if I do 'submit,' or write this story? How do I know my father—"

"One thing you'll very quickly learn about me," he interrupted, his voice like granite, "is that I keep my word. Remember that. And remember what I've told you."

I don't want to have to hurt you, but I will if you make it necessary.

She remembered with cheek-burning shame how he'd spanked her in the hotel room, how badly it had hurt, and knew without doubt he was entirely capable of hurting her. She guessed the bastard would probably enjoy it.

Swallowing around the tightness in her throat, Jack remained silent.

"Surprise, surprise," Hawk said, moving away. "The viper *can* keep her venomous mouth shut."

His footsteps moved out of hearing range, and Jack was left
alone in a room she couldn't see, breathing in her own recycled
breath beneath the uncomfortable hood, listening to the sound of
big engines shudder to life as a foghorn sang a mournful bass note
somewhere far off in the night.

She wasn't a whiner, he'd give her that much.

Jacqueline Dolan was where he'd left her over an hour ago,
sitting soldier straight and silent on the small beige leather sofa
along the starboard wall in the quiet comfort of the cabin. The
Pegasus was a beautifully restored forty-six-foot motorsailer he
kept in the marina in Santarem for the monthly procurement trips
he made for supplies, and she purred at a swift nine knots through
the black Atlantic waters. He was seated astern at the helm, feeling
the sea breeze sting his cheeks and snap through his hair, watching Jack through the small windows near his feet that provided
an excellent view into the main cabin and galley.

He glanced behind him. As far as the eye could see, there was
only starlight reflecting off dark water. They'd left New York far
behind.

Time to remove her hood.

He set the boat to autopilot, stepped out from behind the
wheel, and ducked into the cabin.

And Jacqueline stiffened and inhaled sharply as if someone
had lanced her with a pin.

She was afraid of him. Even if she hadn't moved an inch,
Hawk smelled it all over her. He knew her fear was justified—he'd
told her he'd hurt her if he had to—but the knowledge irritated
him nonetheless. He'd never intentionally hurt a woman before.
He hoped that remained the case.

Though if anyone deserves it, it's her.

Pushing aside his disjointed thoughts, he stepped in front of Jacqueline, and pulled the hood from her head.

Blinking, she squinted into the light and turned her face away, but not before giving him a murderous glare. She breathed deeply, nostrils flared, lips flattened, and he simply stood and watched her, waiting for her to speak.

As he'd instructed, she was dressed in sturdy, lightweight clothing: jeans, black T-shirt, long-sleeved cotton jacket that matched the tee, hiking boots. *Looks a lot better naked*, he thought, unable to press the smile from his mouth.

"I have to use the toilet," she said, looking away.

"Be my guest."

She glanced up at him. Twisting slightly to the side to show him her handcuffed wrists, she said with barely repressed fury, "And how exactly am I supposed to manage that?"

"Would you like me to take off your pants for you?" He smirked. "It's not like I haven't already seen everything you've got."

Jacqueline turned away, biting her lip. Crimson crept up her neck and spread across her cheeks. She whispered, "You're despicable."

"And you, Red, are a bigot."

Her head whipped around. She stared at him open-mouthed, horrified. "I'm not a *bigot!*"

Hawk crouched down on the glossy teak floor directly in front of her so they were eye level. She leaned back a few inches, caught herself, then lifted her chin and stared back at him in defiance.

"You're prejudiced, intolerant, and full of hate. You despise things you don't understand, simply because you don't understand them, and they're different from you. That's a textbook definition of a bigot."

She had the audacity to look outraged. "I understand you and your kind perfectly well! *You're* the ones who are full of hate! You slaughtered dozens of people, just for sport, just to terrorize us—"

"*We* didn't do that!" He leaned closer to her, his pulse spiking, anger tilting toward fury as her eyes widened in alarm. "*One* of us did that, and believe me when I say I'd like to kill that traitor myself for what he did! He's a rabid dog that needs to be put down, but you judged us all based on the actions of one! Then you convinced everyone else that we were all the same, that all my kind should be exterminated like some kind of rodent infestation!"

Eye to eye, seething, they stared at one another. He didn't realize when it had happened, but he was gripping the sofa cushions on either side of her legs so hard his knuckles were white. He'd never before felt such a strong urge to wring a woman's neck.

"That king of yours, Caesar—"

"He's not our king," he snarled, moving even closer until their noses were an inch apart. "He only *thinks* he is. He thinks he's a god, in fact, but he's nothing more than a moron with a god complex, which are two very different things."

One of her brows arched. With withering disdain, she said, "That must run in the family."

Throttle her? Kiss her? She deserved the first, but he found himself struggling with the second, a magnetic attraction equally as strong as it was repellant.

What the hell is wrong with me?

The smart thing to do was stand, so that's exactly what he did. He looked down at her—pale and livid, watching him in silent fury—and realized how wrong Morgan had been to think they could change this woman's mind. This plan was doomed to failure.

From a safer distance, he said with deadly quiet intensity, "Let me ask you a question, Red. How would you like it if the entire human race was judged by the actions of, oh, say—Adolf Hitler? Or maybe Stalin? Or how about Charles Manson? Why is it you think only *we* must all be exactly the same as our lowest common denominator?"

Her silence throbbed.

"I'll tell you why. Because you're a bigot."

"Stop saying that," she said with a clenched jaw. She shot to her feet, and he thought for a moment she might try to kick him in the crotch.

Interesting. He'd found a sore spot. Which he intended to exploit to its fullest potential.

"I'll stop saying it when it stops being true."

They stood there in a silent stalemate, both breathing hard, until finally Jacqueline gave up. "Are you going to let me use the toilet or not?"

Her hair, disheveled and damp with perspiration, was falling into her face. Her lips were skewed to an I-hate-you twist, slight lavender shadows beneath her eyes belied her fatigue. In spite of himself, Hawk felt a brief, unwelcome pang of sympathy for her.

He reached into his pocket and retrieved the small metal key. "Turn around."

She complied. Hawk turned the key in the lock, unclasped the handcuffs, and pulled them from her wrists.

Then she whirled around and slapped him hard across the face.

For a moment he was too stunned to react.

"That's for using me." Her voice shook. Her eyes glittered vivid, furious blue. "And for threatening me and my family, and for calling me a bigot. And for putting a fucking hood over my head like I'm a prisoner being led to the gallows. And I don't care how big and strong and scary you are, if you ever put your hands on me again, so help me God, I'll kill you."

Hawk regained his composure. He slipped the cuffs into his back pocket and worked his jaw where she'd hit him; it stung. Snow White was stronger than she looked.

He leaned in close to her face. "Okay. I'm reasonable. You get *one*, Red—and that was it. And so help *me* God, if you don't stop cursing, I'm going to take you over my knee again, and this time you won't like it nearly as much as last time. Understood?"

Her only response was to blanch.

Hawk withdrew. He jerked his chin to the companionway that led to her berth. "Head's in there, so's a bed. The whole boat's been cleared of anything you might try to use as a weapon, so forget it. Try to get some sleep. You'll need it."

Then he turned, slammed shut the main cabin door, went topside, and roared his frustration into the wind.

TWELVE
Trouble

"I don't understand."

Standing on the narrow, silty banks of a sluggishly flowing river the color of a strong cup of coffee, Jack stared into the dense green tree line, not five yards ahead. The vegetation was so thick it appeared impenetrable, with visibility reaching only a few feet into the forest. Umbrella-shaped trees draped in moss towered over lower palms and shrubs of an infinite, endless green variety; and off in the distance a line of rolling hills climbed to taller peaks shrouded in thick mist.

Two days on a sailboat, another on a small skiff, half of a fourth in a tiny canoe, and Hawk had brought her to a rainforest?

Did he intend to *camp*?

She turned and looked at Hawk, who was pulling the small canoe they'd arrived in onto the riverbank. He dragged it a few feet into the dense underbrush, covered it with branches, then returned, brushing leaves from his hands.

His shirt was drenched in sweat, clinging to the hard lines and angles of his body. Jack quickly averted her eyes from the sight of flexing muscles beneath wet cotton. She knew all too well what he looked like beneath his clothes, and was doing her damndest to forget it because he was a son of a bitch.

"I don't understand," she repeated, irritated with herself. *Don't look at him. Do. Not. Look.*

"That seems to be an ongoing problem for you," he observed dryly, walking near. Big and male and rugged, with four days' worth of beard and a mane of unkempt dark hair, he seemed perfectly at ease in this emerald wilderness, as he exuded his usual aura of danger and unvarnished sex appeal.

"Where are we?" Jack asked with growing annoyance. Christ, it was so humid you could cut the air with a knife. And what was that hideous screeching off to the left, coming from behind those bushes? A banshee would have trouble being heard over that racket.

You're a long way from home, Dorothy.

Hawk stared off into the forest, his normally bright eyes dulled by some unknown emotion, some unspoken thought that seemed to leech all the vitality from his face and body the longer he remained silent. Finally, in a voice tinged with melancholy, he said, "Home."

Then he strode purposefully toward the wall of green and disappeared into it.

She waited for him to return. When he didn't, her first instinct was to run.

But where? Turning to look in both directions, she calculated her chances for escape, realizing quickly just how poor they were. With no food, no water, and no idea how to guide herself out of this wilderness and back to civilization, she'd most likely die within days.

She glanced at the river, wondering what might be hiding beneath its dark surface, then jumped as the screeching in the bushes grew louder. Something began to snort and paw at the ground.

Panicked, Jack leapt into a run. Crashing through the underbrush in pursuit of Hawk, she stumbled blindly ahead, calling his name.

Was he going to leave her in the jungle? Alone? Was this the plan—some kind of twisted episode of *Survivor*?

"Hawk! Hawk!"

A hand reached out and snatched her just before she went tumbling over the edge of a narrow ravine.

"Careful!" Hawk yanked her to safety and pushed her against the trunk of a moss-covered tree. He held her there with his hand twisted into the front of her shirt, glaring at her as if she were the stupidest creature on Earth, but she didn't respond with her usual acidic retort because behind him was a panorama of such staggering beauty she was stunned into silence.

Every shade of green, from palest celadon to brilliant jade to deepest myrtle, dominated the lush landscape. Sunlight filtered down from high above in diamond shafts that bejeweled gracefully arching ferns and black-barked trees and mossed boulders. Beyond the initial thicket of dense shrubs along the riverbank, the forest opened to a lush, Jurassic woodland that Jack imagined the Garden of Eden had looked like. Verdant. Misted. Teeming with life. Even the air was incredible. Warm and soft and perfumed, it was filled with a symphony of birdsong, the whir and hiss of insects, the echo of other animal calls high in the treetops above.

"Oh," she said in a small voice, unable to produce another coherent thought.

Hawk released her shirt, frowning.

Staring around in awe, Jack tentatively asked, "This is where you live?"

He nodded, once, a curt affirmative.

"It's so beautiful. So . . . untamed." Without thinking, she added, "It suits you."

Their eyes met. Jack colored and looked away. Hawk didn't seem to know what to say to her blurted compliment, so, mercifully, he ignored it. Instead, he launched into a litany of instructions, delivered with the brisk economy of a drill sergeant.

"Stay close to me. Watch your step. Don't touch anything if you can help it; many of the plants have toxins. If I tell you to stop or be quiet, do it. There's a million ways to die in this jungle, all of them unpleasant. We're gonna be walking for several days, and there will be places I'll have to carry you—"

"Days! We're going to be walking for *days*?" Eyes wide, she looked around at the tropical wilderness. "What are we going to eat? Where are we going to sleep? How are we going to—"

"I'll take care of everything. But let's be clear on this: I'm in charge. If you don't want to die in this jungle, you're going to have to listen to me." His eyes darkened at the expression of indignation crossing her face. "Even if you don't like it."

Though she was loath to admit that she needed him, Jack knew she was at his complete mercy. She also knew he could have already killed her, or let her die, if that had been his intention.

"No, I don't like it," she said, "but I'll make you a deal."

His swift reply was, "You're in no position to negotiate."

She ignored that. "If you tell me why I'm here, I'll be more cooperative. I need to know what I'm walking into. I'm not good with surprises—"

"Could've fooled me." His lips curved with a ghost of a smile.

Jack knew he was referring to how they'd met, but she pretended ignorance. Never mind the telling heat in her cheeks that was quickly spreading to her ears.

"I'm not good with surprises," she repeated more firmly, "and I don't do well with mysteries, either. Tell me why you've brought me here and I'll be much more likely to listen to you. Keep me in the dark . . ." She shrugged and folded her arms across her chest. "And I'll make this as difficult for you as I can."

The smile faded from Hawk's face. He stared at her long and hard, his green eyes calculating. In a voice that was low and uncomfortably intimate, he finally asked, "You really hate not being in control, don't you?"

Her blush spread all the way to the roots of her hair.

"I risk my life all the time in my job," she said defensively. "That's not something a control freak would do."

One of his shoulders lifted and fell, a casual gesture that perfectly managed to convey his disregard for that excuse. "So in addition to being a control freak, you have a death wish. The two aren't mutually exclusive."

Hawk's words struck a nerve, sending a cold rush of shame through Jack's body. Something dark and ugly began to unfurl in the pit of her stomach, slithering under her ribcage with reptilian menace. She had to look away from him, and spent the next several silent seconds staring at a brilliant blue-and-black butterfly flitting with bumpy grace over a bed of nodding white flowers.

Eyes stinging, Jack admitted quietly, "It's not a death wish. It's the opposite. It's a way . . . it's a way to feel more alive."

Why? Why the hell would you tell him that, idiot? Him, of all people!

That palpable scrutiny again. Hawk's gaze roved over her face with such searing intensity she felt naked. A cavernous silence stretched between them, raw and aching, as painful as a wound.

"Look at me."

His voice was unexpectedly gentle around the command, and

it was worse than if he'd been harsh. Jack closed her eyes, willing herself calm, willing the sick feeling in her gut to subside—neither of which worked.

She felt fingers on her chin, warm and firm, a soft coercion. He kept that slight pressure in his fingers when he said, "Since you want a deal, I'll give you one."

Jack opened her eyes and looked at him, knowing whatever would come next wouldn't be anything she'd like.

He said, "I'll tell you where we're going if you tell me the last time you were with a man before me."

Oh. Oh God. Her cheeks flamed as if painted with fire. "None of your business!"

"It is if you want me to tell you where we're going."

Exasperation, embarrassment, and anger writhed like a basket full of snakes in her stomach. "Why does it matter?"

"Because you're a puzzle, Red," he answered gruffly, eyes burning, head tilted to one side as he examined her face. "And I can't get any of the pieces to fit." His fingers on her chin tightened. "How long?"

Just do it. Just tell him. What have you got to lose?

Nothing. Everything. She debated with herself a moment, then, feeling as if the ground had turned liquid beneath her feet, feeling as if she could die from shame, she told him the truth. "Five years."

Hawk's gaze dropped to her mouth, then he looked back into her eyes. He nodded, as if what she said had made sense. As if he was pleased by her honesty.

There was that wash of warmth through her limbs again, sweet as sunlit honey, that unexplainable ache of satisfaction that she'd gratified him in some small way.

Insanity.

He'd used her. He'd tricked her. He'd kidnapped her. And she should feel in any way glad that this animal/creature/thing was happy? There was only one explanation for this foolishness.

She was losing her goddamn mind.

With forced coldness, Jack said, "Your turn."

She might have imagined reluctance as he dropped his fingers from her face. He raked a hand through his disheveled dark hair and looked off into the forest, his face closing off as if a door had swung shut. "I'm taking you to my colony."

Adrenaline blasted through her nerves, setting every one ablaze. "Colony" could mean anything from dozens to hundreds to thousands—of *them*.

Her mouth went dry. Her voice rose an octave. "Why? What—what are they planning on doing with me?"

Hawk looked back at her, all the softness from before gone. He smiled, and the threat in it sent a tingle of fear down Jack's spine.

"That's two more questions. You want answers, I get another two questions of my own."

So. A game of cat and mouse. *Hell if I'm going to be the mouse.*

"I'm not answering any more personal questions."

Hawk's smile grew wider. "Well, then I guess you'll just have to wait and see what they're planning on doing with you when you get there."

Without waiting for a response, he turned and walked away.

The first day passed without incident.

Jacqueline kept up with him better than he'd expected, and she stayed mostly silent as well, a fact he was both grateful for and oddly disappointed by. It occurred to him more than once during their silent trek through the rainforest that his curiosity about her was a dangerous thing, a distraction he should be ruthlessly smothering; but for some strange reason, the longer they walked and the more silent she remained, the stronger his urge to uncover the dark secrets beneath that deceptively porcelain façade.

He'd told her the truth when he'd called her a puzzle. With her pale skin and delicate features, she looked as fragile as a doll, but was as fierce as a tigress when threatened. Her eyes held an ocean of sorrows, which was intriguing, but her posture and bearing and even her words said she'd rather slit your throat than admit she was anything but as tough as a rhinoceros hide.

Then there were the odd moments of vulnerability that leaked from her steel-plated armor. Those were the most devastating of all.

"Five years," she'd whispered, an admission he knew cost her greatly, evidenced by the flare of anguish in her eyes. He guessed there was a bottomless well of pain hidden behind all the attitude, guessed it was accompanied by an equal measure of shame. But he didn't know the what, why, or when of it.

He didn't know the reason a woman like her—sexy, smart, incredibly passionate when she let her guard down—would be without a man for five years.

And he wanted to. Damn it all to hell, he really did.

But Jacqueline Dolan was a job, and nothing more. A means to an end. A few more weeks and he'd never have to see her again. He could go back to his life.

His predictable, chafing, restricted life.

Hawk shook off that disturbing thought and stopped in front of an ancient fig tree, the gnarled buttress roots at its base snaking away over the forest floor in mossed confusion. A stream burbled somewhere nearby, which was good; they'd need water.

"We'll sleep here for the night." He set about clearing a space in the fallen leaves and bracken for a makeshift bed. Watching him with wary eyes, Jacqueline lowered herself to the nearby trunk of a fallen tree.

Twilight was spreading green gloom over the floor of the forest. It would be dark soon.

Then he could hunt.

From behind him, she said quietly, "Is it safe?"

He turned to look at her. She was staring intently at the space he was clearing beside the tree.

"On the ground, I mean. Couldn't we . . ." Her eyes lifted, and she gazed into the high branches of the tree.

"You'd feel safer in the tree than on the ground?"

In a guarded voice, she replied, "In my experience, the ground is always where the predators are."

This surprised Hawk for several reasons. First, she was correct. The larger predators—including him—hunted the forest floor. Second, how would she know that? Finally, there was a double meaning behind her words, he was sure of it. The way she gazed longingly into the tree was telling, but of what he didn't know.

Another puzzle piece. Another misshapen clue that didn't fit.

"All right. I'll find a spot, and come and get you. But once we're up, we're up for the night, understand? Whatever business you have to take care of, take care of it now."

Her lips twisted. She nodded, understanding his meaning.

"And, uh, bury it."

Jack stood, looking as if she'd rather be anywhere else on Earth at this moment. "Roger that, Rambo," she said dryly, and ducked under the low, spreading branches of a giant philodendron.

Hawk watched for a moment, stretching his senses. He smelled loamy earth and wet vegetation, felt the scant vibration of a duo of capybaras nosing through bracken several dozen yards away, heard a thousand different bird and insect noises, but sensed nothing dangerous. There were no predators nearby that might leap on her mid-squat.

Satisfied, he leapt with ease onto one of the taller buttress roots that supported the tree and began to climb the trunk.

Ten minutes later, he descended to find Jack anxiously awaiting him, her neck craned up as she watched him climb down, her arms wrapped around her body as if for protection.

"I should have brought my gun," she muttered, glancing around the quickly darkening forest. The night creatures were beginning to stir, and the air was alive with strange, new noises. Bearded pigs, leopard cats, flying fox bats, and the deadly caiman were all emerging from their daytime slumber with a hunger that would only be satisfied by fresh meat.

"You don't need a gun." Hawk jumped down and landed silently beside her. "You have me."

She made a face, the meaning of which he didn't care to decipher.

"You're going to have to hold on tight as we climb, understand? You don't want to fall—"

"Oh, for God's sake, you don't need to give me a safety lecture," Jack interrupted, moving so close to him he felt the heat of her skin. She looked up into his eyes and declared, "Let's do this."

Hawk suppressed a smile. Bossy, brave, fragile, stubborn . . . if she wasn't such a prejudiced pain in the butt he might have actually liked her.

He leapt back onto the tall buttress root and held out a hand. She scrambled up beside him with surprising agility, grabbing his hand for balance, but immediately released it when she steadied. Their eyes met, and she quickly glanced away.

"All right," Hawk said, all business, "arms around my neck.

Try not move too much. And keep your ankles crossed, or your feet might get in the way of my—"

"Wait," Jack interrupted, understanding dawning over her face. "You don't think you're going to *carry* me up this tree, do you?"

His brows arched. He pointed to the branches far above. "How else did you think you'd get up there?"

She looked affronted. "The same as you. Climb."

Hawk knew her well enough by now to realize an argument was imminent. He crossed his arms over his chest and glared down at her, but she wasn't backing down.

"I know. You think you're better than me because you have a dick and I don't. But I'm perfectly capable of climbing this stupid tree, and I'll prove it to you." She tried to brush past him, but he stopped her with a hand on her arm.

"Can't let you do that, Red. I'm responsible for your safety. If you fall and break your neck, it's my head on the chopping block."

Hawk knew he'd made a big mistake when her eyes narrowed and her gaze, sharp as an eagle's, honed in on his face.

"Forget it." Then he reconsidered, and smiled. "Unless you'd like to negotiate."

She chewed the inside of her lip and scowled at him, wondering, no doubt, how she was going to bash in the side of his head. "A question for a question," she pronounced, correctly guessing his terms. He nodded, his smile growing wider.

Jack studied his expression. Then, in a stunning display of honesty that left him reeling, she solemnly said, "I have a lot of experience climbing trees. I did it all the time when I was a kid because I had a lot of things I needed to hide from, and those things were afraid of heights. I know you're bigger than I am, and you're stronger than I am, and no doubt you could force me to go up this tree on your back." She swallowed, hesitating for the briefest of moments before continuing, quieter than before. "But if you do that, I will feel weak, useless, and totally dependent, all of which are things that make me crazy.

"You were right about me hating to not be in control. Feeling in control is the only thing that keeps me sane, because there was a time in my life when I was completely *out* of control, completely helpless, and that's something I can never be again. So, please. Just let me try to climb this fucking tree. If you think I can't handle it, if it looks like I'm about to fall, you have my permission to throw me over your shoulder or drag me up by my goddamn hair if you want. Just . . . please let me try. Before you decide for me."

She stood staring up at him with eyes wide and shining, and Hawk felt as if a giant, invisible fist was squeezing his heart.

He said, "I don't think I'm better than you because I have a dick. And I don't think you do it on purpose, but that mouth of yours makes *me* crazy. Can we agree that if I let you try to climb this tree, you'll try to cut out the cursing?"

She pulled her lower lip between her teeth and chewed it. "Why does that bother you so much?"

A million different memories flooded Hawk's mind, all of them bad. "Because the things *I* needed to hide from when I was a kid just loved to scream curses." His voice hardened. "Right before they beat the hell out of me."

The expression that crossed Jacqueline's face then was indescribable. She looked as if she might throw her arms around him, or burst into tears. But she did neither of those things. She only nodded, then waited, standing perfectly still.

Hawk exhaled a hard breath. "All right, Red. You first. Don't make me regret this."

Still serious, she nodded again, then moved past him. Finding notches in the rough bark of the trunk, she pulled herself up. She paused just before climbing, and turned to look at him.

"Thank you, Lucas." Her voice was quiet in the gathering gloom. Their gazes held just longer than was comfortable, until he jerked his chin, indicating she should climb.

So she did. He watched her with more than a little trepidation and a burgeoning premonition of doom as she quickly and confidently began to scale the trunk of the mammoth tree.

Jacqueline Dolan, he thought, unable to tear his gaze from her as she climbed, *you are trouble with a capital T.*

Hawk shook his head, ran a hand through his hair, then leapt onto the trunk beneath her.

THIRTEEN

A Guarantee

The three men who sat around the oval conference table in silence inside the soundproof office at the elegant townhouse on Sutton Place in Manhattan were so different from each other that an observer might have a difficult time determining why they were meeting at all.

The Secretary-General of the United Nations was a slight, bespectacled man named Min Ji-hoon, formerly the Foreign Minister of the Republic of Korea. His air of humble geniality belied a razor-sharp intelligence, and a fierce competitive streak that drove him like a merciless slave master. To the press he was known as "the slippery eel," due to his ability to deftly avoid questions, a particularly valuable skill for a diplomat.

Directly across from him sat another bespectacled man, this one white-haired and missing one hand and an eye. The hole in his skull was covered by a black patch, giving him the look of a pirate, but the look in the other blue eye that stared out from behind his glasses was anything but piratical. It held the flat, killer gaze of a jihadist, of one who had seen and done things no man ought to have seen and done. He sat perfectly still and straight in his chair, clad in a tailored black suit that hid the unfortunate fact that one of his legs was aluminum from the upper thigh down.

The man was known by several names, including the Doctor and, like all the others in the multinational organization to which he belonged, John Doe. To the gathered group, and the businessman he represented, he was known simply as Thirteen.

The third man at the end of the table was the largest, most imposing, and most arresting of the three. Clad in a simple cloth robe the color of blackest night, with a cowl and hood hiding the pale dome of his bald head, the albino named Jahad sat with his large hands folded peacefully in his lap, gazing at Thirteen with a look in his gray-lavender eyes that could only be described as chilling. There was no love lost between the two men, and though they'd worked together once before to catch the beasts they still pursued, the operation had ended disastrously for both of them, and each bore the scars of their failure.

Jahad's were internal, however. Though unseen, his claustrophobia was nearly crippling.

He had scars aplenty from earlier exploits, including those from the fire that had almost killed him as a boy, leaving him with hideous pocked and puckered flesh on the right side of his face and body, and a hand that was curled to a claw. All in all, he was a most unusual sight. Most people couldn't bear to look at him for more than a few seconds at a time.

The Secretary-General was currently experiencing exactly that problem.

"How can you be sure this tip you received was credible?" Min said to Thirteen, trying hard not to glance at Jahad. It was like trying not to look at a car accident on the freeway. You wanted to see a glimpse of a bloody corpse, yet hoped simultaneously not to.

"Certain details were given that proved credibility beyond a doubt. I wouldn't be here if there was any question of authenticity," replied Thirteen, his one eye glittering icy blue, cold as an arctic sky. His voice held a strong German accent that, in addition to his missing parts and that lone, frigid eye, made him seem like something straight out of a folktale by the brothers Grimm.

"And just to be perfectly clear, your organization is willing to underwrite the entire cost of this operation? If this tip proves accurate, and we move forward with your plan, we're likely looking in the hundreds of millions, including reparations to the Brazilian government, and any affected farmers or indigenous tribes. The cost of reforesting alone will be astronomical. Destroying an entire section of the Amazon rainforest—"

"Money is no object to the Chairman," Thirteen interrupted, sneering. "You of all people should be aware of that."

A flush crept over the Secretary-General's cheeks. The Chairman had given generously to his election campaign. He'd never met the man—he remained an enigma, a faceless entity represented only through third-parties such as Thirteen—but his influence, and bank account, were definitely real.

For the first time, Jahad spoke. His voice was deep and somehow soulless, matching the empty look in his pale eyes. "We're not looking for money. What we want is a guarantee."

The Secretary-General finally looked directly at Jahad. Blinking behind his large glasses, he waited for the albino to continue.

"The UN will not interfere in any way. You will sanction this action, and allow us to proceed in whatever way we see fit."

Min's brows lifted. "I can't give a unilateral guarantee that there won't be a call for some kind of accountability. The Security Council will want to get involved—"

"There will be *no* interference."

The threat in Jahad's tone was obvious. It had Min sitting up straighter in his seat, the flush in his cheeks deepening. His voice went up an octave. "It's my duty to report any matter that threatens the maintenance of international peace and security. Can you imagine what Brazil might have to say about this? Let alone the international conservation communities—"

"You can convince them," Thirteen interrupted, sounding absolutely sure of it.

Min looked back and forth between the albino and Jahad, his outrage growing. Who did these two hooligans think they were, ordering him around? "The General Assembly can override me. They have veto power, regardless of what I recommend. The United Nations isn't a monarchy, gentlemen. There are one hundred ninety-three member states, each of which gets a vote."

Thirteen's lips curved upward, but it was grim and ugly, a mockery of a smile. He set a leather briefcase on the table, clicked it open, and withdrew five manila folders, each with a name neatly typed in the upper right-hand corner.

"The five permanent members of the Security Council who hold veto power are the only ones who really matter. In these folders you will find information about those five members that might . . . *motivate* them to agree with whatever you suggest."

Min was almost afraid to touch the folders Thirteen pushed across the table toward him. He glanced at Jahad, who sat stone-faced and shark-eyed at the end of the table, then back at Thirteen. He lifted the flap on one of the envelopes and withdrew a black-and-white photograph from within.

With a sick twist in his stomach, he shoved the photo roughly back into the folder.

In a tone so hissed it was nearly reptilian, Thirteen said, "Our friend Mr. Drake certainly does enjoy those underage boys."

The Secretary-General said stiffly, "This is not the way to go about convincing people your plan is correct, gentlemen."

"*Im gegenteil*," said Thirteen. "On the contrary, this is exactly the way to convince them. Self-preservation is the strongest basic human motivation, even beyond that of procreation or the need for food or shelter. Every man has a flaw, a secret, or a regret he will go to any length to hide. Uncover it, exploit it, and there's nothing he won't do for you. This is the key to politics, Mr. Secretary-General. This is the key to gaining consensus. Surely you must know that by now."

The satisfied smirk Thirteen sent him told Min he had underestimated the lengths these two men would go to get what they wanted. It also told him he'd made a terrible miscalculation when he'd accepted money from the Chairman.

He sat stiffly back into his plush leather chair and gazed at Thirteen with new respect, and new animosity. He chose his next words carefully. "Blackmail will not be necessary, gentlemen. These creatures slaughtered twenty-six of the world's most important religious and political leaders in a coordinated attack that left no question about their disposition toward the human race. Or their ability to bypass our defenses. Public opinion is already on your side. A few well-timed words are all that will be needed to ensure your operation moves forward without incident."

"But backups are always good, too," said Jahad, smiling like Thirteen. On him it looked even more unnerving, the grin of a crocodile as its jaws snapped closed over your head.

The Secretary-General abruptly stood, signaling the end of the meeting. "My housekeeper will show you out. If you need to contact me again, I suggest you do so on a secure line, and not at the UN where a record of all calls are kept. My private cellular is off-grid. Use that."

Thirteen and Jahad stood as well, acknowledging the instructions with matching expressions of disdain.

No one shook hands. The Secretary-General turned and hurried from the room.

FOURTEEN

Silent Agreement

Like a rat nibbling the toes of a drunkard lying unconscious in a dark alley, something was worrying the edges of Jack's sleep.

It was a slipping, sliding, ambiguous sort of unease, a presence that took a shadowy form beneath and behind the surface of things, ghostly and teasing and altogether unwelcome.

What was it?

Or who?

It was just out of reach, this maddening specter, but still it had weight. It had heft, and . . . warmth. Yes, warmth, and a sinister sort of gravity, so that she felt pinned beneath an invisible entity, unable to free herself from its grip.

No—she had to get free. She had to get away. She had to save herself from this unwanted pressure, slowly threading its way down through her pores into the meat of her cells.

In her dream, Jack began to run.

It was the horrible, sticky-syrup run of nightmares, where even the strongest push of muscle gained only the most meager effect. She pumped her legs, desperate for escape, desperate to gain traction, but felt glued to the ground. The warmth turned suffocating. The weight bore down harder and harder, until finally Jack knew she would be crushed beneath it like a bug beneath a shoe.

No . . . no . . . not again!

A scream tore from her throat. She jerked upright, blinking into humid darkness.

Then there were hands on her shoulders, a gentle shake, a low voice, urgent beside her ear. "Jacqueline! Wake up! Wake up—it's me! It's Hawk!"

Trembling, breathless, frozen in fear, Jack stared up into Hawk's face—handsome and shadowed, his brow crumpled into a frown—and let out a sob of despair.

She buried her face into her hands.

"Hey. Take it easy. Just breathe, all right?" Hawk's big hand settled on the small of her back, tentative and calming.

Safe. She was safe. It had only been Hawk's warmth she felt in the dream, Hawk's presence. Hawk's weight.

Not . . . *his.* The one who could never be banished, no matter how hard she tried.

Exquisitely aware of Hawk's hand on her back, Jack exhaled a long, shuddering breath. "Sorry."

"It's okay." His voice was gravelly with sleep. "I think you were just having a bad dream."

A recurring nightmare, more like.

"Yeah."

Avoiding Hawk's penetrating gaze, she looked around, seeing nothing but endless, restless green. It was still dark in the forest, but far above in the treetops, a faint sheen of lavender glimmered, the promise of morning.

It would be daybreak soon. Even now, the first notes of birdsong were echoing through the trees, trills and warbles of a million varieties that flavored the air like so many exotic spices.

They'd climbed high into the spreading boughs, and Hawk had made an ingenious bed at the junction of the trunk and two wide branches. After gathering smaller limbs—that he ripped away from their moorings with such ease it looked as though he were pulling weeds instead of the thick, leafy offshoots they were—he'd lashed them together to form a hammock of sorts, secured with strong, rope-like vines, overlaid with a thick weave of palm fronds and the moss that draped from the tallest branches, feather light and downy soft. It was a snug, effective resting place, and to top it all off, it was safe.

Safe being a relative term. She wouldn't have to deal with any forest floor predators, but there was an even more dangerous one sleeping right beside her.

Much different from the first night we spent together, that's for sure.

Hawk quietly asked, "So, who's Garrett?"

It became almost impossible to breathe.

She found his gaze in the dark, looked into those glittering, preternatural green eyes, and shivered in horror. "What did you say?"

He absently brushed away a strand of hair that had fallen into her eyes. "You were screaming that name. That and . . . other things."

Jack squeezed shut her eyes, blocking the sight of his face. "Please don't tell me what other things. Please don't. And don't ever say that name to me again."

There was silence for a moment, then she heard his deep inhalation. His hand on the small of her back flexed slightly, his fingers spreading father apart, as if trying to impart more comfort.

Hawk said, *"Você está seguro comigo."*

Without opening her eyes, Jack whispered, "What does that mean?"

He removed his hand from her back. When she finally looked at him, he was staring back at her with something like compassion in his intense gaze. But Jack knew that had to be wrong, because he'd made it perfectly clear he felt nothing for her but disgust.

"It means . . . okay."

They both knew it meant far more than that, but they both pretended it didn't. Since she was an expert at pretending, this suited her just fine.

With swift grace, Hawk stood. For the first time, Jack noticed he wasn't wearing a shirt, and the knowledge that he'd been sleeping right beside her half naked for the entire night made heat rush to her face. She glanced away, heartbeat fluttering, mouth dry.

"I'll get some food, and then we'll get going again. I'll only be a few minutes."

As swiftly and silently as he'd arisen, Hawk disappeared over the side of the suspended boughs. She heard the slight rustle of leaves, then nothing more.

When she was certain he was gone, she lay back down into the leafy comfort of their makeshift bed, put a hand over her face, and cried.

Hawk took longer than necessary gathering food for their breakfast, for two main reasons. One, he sensed she needed to be alone. Two—

He was having a tremendously difficult time marshaling his fragmented emotions.

This wasn't like him at all, this nurturing stranger who felt things like pity and understanding and the urge to offer comfort. Especially to someone like her!

She's your enemy, he reminded himself every time she pinned him with the raw force of that blue, blue gaze. *She's evil. She's a danger to us all.*

Only she didn't *feel* evil. Or dangerous. Or like an enemy. She irritated him, yes, she angered him, yes—he thought she had a long way to go in the open-mindedness department—but she also sparked an emotion he'd never felt before in his life. Not for a woman, not for anyone.

Protectiveness.

In a show of completely irrational, testosterone-driven idiocy, he felt protective of this walking contradiction under his charge, and he was supremely pissed off at himself for it.

When she'd awakened—screaming and thrashing out of her dream—his guarding instincts had gone into overdrive. If he'd had a sword in hand at that moment, he was sure he'd have chopped the tree in half before coming back to his senses. As it was, he'd barely restrained himself from leaping from the hammock, Shifting into panther, and snarling bloody murder into the darkness to keep the proverbial wolves at bay.

But there were no wolves. There was only Jacqueline, wild-eyed, pale, and shivering, looking as if what she really needed was a hug.

He'd had to restrain himself from that, too.

"*Você está seguro comigo,*" he'd told her in a moment of foolishness. *You're safe with me.* What had he been thinking? *Was* he thinking? No, he decided, he wasn't thinking. At least not with the head atop his neck.

Violently yanking the plum-shaped yellow fruit from the low-hanging boughs of a camu camu tree as if it had personally offended him, Hawk mused over what his strategy should be. Obviously he needed a plan to move forward; he couldn't just march ahead blindly, allowing his emotions to take charge. What he needed was distance, but that was an impossibility in their current circumstances.

Physical distance is an impossibility. But emotional distance . . .

Right. Emotional distance. Keep the walls up. Don't talk about anything personal. Stop wondering what was going on in that mind of hers. *Don't look at her, either,* he chastised himself. Every time his gaze lingered too long on that incredible mouth, that fiery hair he'd gripped fistfuls of as he'd shoved himself deep inside her—

Hawk stilled, closed his eyes, and hissed an aggravated breath through his teeth.

This was going to be harder than he thought.

By the time Hawk returned half an hour later, Jack was in much better control of herself. She'd dried her face, combed her fingers through her hair, and smoothed her wrinkled clothing; and she was sitting with her back against the trunk, legs crossed, with what she hoped was a cool, unreadable expression on her face.

Hawk was carrying an enormous, glossy monstera leaf, the scalloped edges gathered in one fist, center bulging. He set it in her lap.

"Eat as much as you can," he said curtly. "You'll need the energy. We won't be stopping for another break until late tonight."

Jack looked down at the big leaf unfurling between her legs, and gasped in surprise.

Orange and red and green and yellow, smooth skinned and freckled and shiny and rough, the variety of fruit and berries he'd gathered was astonishing. There were passion fruit, figs, mangoes, and prickly pear; there were bananas, Brazil nuts, and purple-blue acai berries still on the vine. There was a dozen more varieties she'd never seen before, all of them unblemished, as if he'd selected only the most perfect specimens and left the rest to the birds.

"This is amazing!" Jack inspected the bumpy skin of a canary-yellow star fruit with awe. "Do you know how much this stuff costs in a grocery store? What's that one? And that?"

Hawk took a seat across from her. "There are more than three thousand different kinds of fruit in the rainforest. The vast majority of them are unknown in the Western world." He pointed to each in turn. "That's chirimoya, and the small red ones that look like cherries are capulin."

Jack's mouth began to water. Her stomach grumbled its discontent.

"Okay, well . . . here." Eager to dig in, she lifted the leaf and its contents from her lap, spread it on the hammock between them, and picked up a fig. "I'm a good eater, so you better dig in before it's all gone."

"No."

Surprised, she glanced up at him. He shook his head and gestured to the food.

"That's all for you. I already ate."

"Oh." They stared at one another. "What did you eat?"

One corner of his mouth quirked. "I doubt you'd want to know."

Of course. He was a carnivore. Her appetite vanished when she pictured the poor little animal that had been his breakfast, and was now being digested inside his stomach.

"Well." She cleared her throat. "Thank you for not making me have what you had."

"I knew you wouldn't be interested. Even if I'd cooked it."

When she looked up at him, laughter glimmered in the depth of his emerald eyes.

He'd eaten it—whatever it was—raw? Ugh. Nasty times one thousand.

"How do you know I wouldn't have been interested in . . ." Her nose wrinkled. "Meat?"

He lifted one dark brow. "Generally vegetarians aren't."

She frowned at him and asked, "How did you know I'm a vegetarian?"

Hawk looked away and for a moment Jack thought he wouldn't answer. He stared off into the canopy of trees, a muscle in his jaw jumping. "Veggie burger," he said, his voice empty. "No cheese."

How he'd remembered that small detail from the night they'd met became insignificant compared to the grating realization that this macho, George of the Jungle carnivore probably thought her an idiot for choosing not to eat meat.

Something he had in common with her father.

Anger began its familiar march across her nerve endings, advancing with breakneck speed.

Jack said acidly, "Yes, I think it's unethical to consume sentient beings. Especially when there are so many other choices that don't involve the systematic torture and murder of millions of animals every year. But I can see how someone like you wouldn't get that, what with your big *fangs* and all."

Hawk turned his attention back to her, and it was so focused and menacing it was like being caught in the crosshairs of a sniper's rifle.

"*You're* lecturing *me* about ethics? Hypocrite."

Blood rushed to Jack's face, but before she could respond, Hawk continued.

"I happen to agree with you that the way *your* species deals with feeding itself is disgusting. *My* species, on the other hand—the one you so despise—has no need for slaughterhouses and meat-packing factories and fast-food restaurants that serve poison packaged as food. We consume what we need, and no more. We hunt when we're hungry, not for sport or entertainment, and we respect the lives we take—lives, I might add, that were spent the way Nature intended. Outdoors. Not in a cage, awaiting a painful, horrible death. So don't talk to me about ethics, Red. Your entire *race* is unethical."

He shot to his feet, turned his back on her, and went to stand at the far edge of the hammock of boughs he'd constructed using nothing but his bare hands. He raked those strong hands through his hair, and stood there like that for several long moments, fingers clenched, back rigid, silent, and quite perceptibly seething.

Jack watched him with the sinking feeling she wasn't on the right side of this argument.

Her anger fizzling, she looked down at the food he'd brought her, and sighed.

What did it matter if she'd offended him? *He'd* tricked *her*. *He'd* used *her*. She should be the one filled with righteous outrage, but somehow it had gotten so turned around that she felt . . . what? Sorry? Guilty? Why should she feel guilty for upsetting him? She hated him!

Jack stared at the muscled, rigid lines of his back. *I do hate him . . . right?*

She pinched the bridge of her nose between two fingers, realizing that what she felt for him wasn't what could accurately be called hate, and that was unacceptable.

When did all her convictions go squishy in the middle? Why did this man/not-man continue to confuse and confound her?

More important: Why on Earth did she care?

Too many questions, not enough answers. Jack supposed she could go round and round with herself like this for days, without getting anywhere. In the interim, it seemed there was only one right thing to do.

"Hawk," she said softly. When he didn't turn or respond, she said his name again.

"What?" The word was hard, wintry cold.

"I apologize."

Slowly, he lowered his hands to his hips. His head turned a fraction, and he stood there in silent profile, waiting, a breeze ruffling his dark hair. The rising light gleamed soft off his bare back and broad shoulders, and she thought he looked like a pagan god in a sky kingdom of green and gold and sapphire blue.

"That wasn't nice of me. That comment about your . . . um . . . fangs."

Wishing he'd put his shirt back on so she wouldn't have to wrestle with the compelling desire to ogle his spectacular physique, Jack dropped her gaze to the fruit. "My dad always ridiculed me for not eating meat, and it sort of felt like . . . like you were doing the same thing."

After a moment, in a voice slightly less frigid than before, Hawk said, "I wasn't."

For some reason, Jack actually believed him. She said, "Okay," and sat there with her shoulders rounded in a posture of defeat, wondering if the world would ever make sense again.

She heard a low, vexed exhalation, the sound of feet brushing leaves. Then he was standing before her once more. He crouched down and put a knuckle under her chin, forcing her to meet his eyes.

He said solemnly, "We're not all like Caesar. We're not all bad. Most of us just want to be left alone to live our lives in peace."

Jack whispered, "Ditto."

Hawk dropped his hand from her face and nodded, and in the span of one moment to the next, it felt as if they'd come to some sort of silent agreement. A subtle change took place; there was a tacit understanding that they were no longer enemies . . . but neither were they friends.

What exactly they *were* was a subject Jack wasn't inclined to investigate.

Turning her attention to the lovely array of fruit presented to her by this maddening, confusing, beautiful predator she was so determined to hate but unfortunately didn't, Jack selected a dusky fig, pear-shaped and perfect, and began to eat.

FIFTEEN
Strange Revelations

They made better time through the verdant maze of the rainforest than Hawk had anticipated, primarily because Jacqueline was in incredible shape. Her endurance was remarkable, matched by surprising sure-footedness and that stoic resistance to uttering anything resembling a complaint.

To be fair, she wasn't saying much of anything at all.

After she'd shocked him—again—by apologizing for her snide remark about his fangs, there had been a moment when Hawk had felt certain they'd reached some sort of new understanding. But she'd retreated from it like a snail curling back into its shell, and had barely spoken a word to him in the two days since.

Considering his conviction to keep his emotional distance in spite of their forced proximity, he should've been grateful. But gratitude wasn't the word he'd use to describe his feelings about the silence that stretched between them. No. It was closer to raw discomfort, paired with a gnawing compulsion to ask her again who Garrett was.

He guessed therein lay the key that would unlock the thousand closed doors she kept around her heart. Though he knew he should let them stay closed, finding out what made her tick was like an itch he needed to scratch.

Maybe when he had all the pieces to her puzzle, the itch would be satisfied, and he could finally leave it be.

So when she started asking him questions—tentatively posed, as if both fearing and needing the answers—Hawk abandoned his prior game of tit for tat and simply gave her straightforward answers.

"How many of . . . you . . . are there, where we're going?"

He held a thick, low-hanging branch aside for her, waiting as she passed beneath it. They were deep in the ancient heart of the forest now; everything was a tangle of roots and trees and fast-running streams, cloaked in humidity, teeming with an opus of birdsong. The occasional low rumble of thunder shivered the canopy high above, and, as it did most afternoons at this time, it had begun softly to rain.

"I couldn't give you an exact number, but it's probably quadrupled over the last three months."

"Why's that?"

He released the branch and moved ahead of her, careful to point out a log, on which she might twist an ankle, half buried in leaf litter. She fell into step behind him as he led them up a gently sloping hill, the trees above dripping water onto their heads.

"The other colonies have been evacuated here."

"*Other* colonies?"

He stopped abruptly and turned to her. She halted and stood eagerly awaiting his answer while brushing tendrils of hair, mermaid damp and curling, off her forehead.

"Who, what, when, where, and why," he said, debating. "Ever the reporter, aren't you?"

A wry quirk of her lips. "Don't forget 'how.'"

Ah yes, as in, how much should he tell her? He wondered what Alejandro would have to say about him divulging this kind of detailed information to a woman who wrote for one of the world's largest newspapers, then decided that Alejandro could go straight to hell. If he didn't want humans knowing *Ikati* business, he shouldn't have come up with this stupid plan in the first place.

"Five total, including mine. But only three of the other four have relocated here." He turned and began to trudge ahead. She followed, right on his heels.

"Why hasn't the fourth one relocated?"

"Because they're ruled by a group of unusually stubborn males, that's why."

"So you—your kind—are ruled by groups of males?"

He chuckled. "No. Until recently, as a matter of fact, each colony was ruled by a single Alpha, chosen by Bloodline or the winner of a ritual power challenge. The males of the—" Hawk almost blurted out "Roman colony," but caught himself in time. It would be sheer stupidity to give away specific locations. "The colony ruled by the group of stubborn males is an anomaly. Their Alpha was killed, and his personal retinue of guards decided to rule as a united council instead of selecting a new Alpha. But that's not the norm for the *Ikati*. We're very hierarchical. Something like your military, with everyone having specific positions and orders coming down from the top. We're not a species prone to democracy," he added sourly.

"You said 'until recently.' What happened recently?"

Sharp as a tack. No wonder she made a good reporter.

"Recently," Hawk drawled, ducking under a tangle of vines hanging down from the thick stand of trees that flanked them, "we crowned a half-Blood Queen with a fondness for more . . . progressive ideals."

"What's a half-Blood?"

"A crossbreed. Half human, half *Ikati*."

Jack stopped dead in her tracks.

He turned to look at her, and she was staring at him in utter astonishment, her eyes popped so wide he could see white all around her irises.

"Yes, we can breed with you," he said in response to her obvious shock. "And to answer to your next question: no. There aren't many half-Bloods. It's forbidden for us to mate with humans, as a matter of fact, but it does occasionally happen. Doing so is punishable by death, however. Actually, strike that," he amended, thinking of the Roman colony who had an entire caste of half-Blood soldiers bred by the murdered Alpha. "The one colony I mentioned that's ruled by the stubborn males?"

Her head bobbed.

"Their dead Alpha didn't see any problem with mating with humans." Hawk's voice turned dry. "He didn't see any problem doing a lot of forbidden things. Then again, he didn't know they were forbidden. Not that he'd have cared," he added as an afterthought, and turned and began walking again, knowing Jacqueline would follow, which she did.

"Why didn't he know? Why wouldn't he have cared? Can the half-Bloods do what you do? You know, turn into a . . . a . . ."

"Panther?" he supplied when she faltered into silence.

At her small, hesitant sound of acknowledgment, Hawk smiled. He'd have loved to have seen the look on her face when she viewed the video of him Shifting. "The ones who survive the Transition can."

They walked in silence for a moment, listening to the rain pattering on the leaves and the calls of the birds high up in the canopy. Then Jacqueline said, "You don't really need me to ask, do you?"

I just like hearing your voice.

Startled by the thought, he didn't answer for a moment. He held the words in his mind, turning them over and over like an interesting artifact he'd unearthed from some ancient tomb.

What a strange revelation: he liked the sound of her voice. He liked her northeastern American accent, the broad *a*'s and tensed *o*'s and taut pronunciation, the way she said "fahrest" instead of "forest," the way "Mary," "merry," and "marry" would all sound alike. It made her seem exotic to him, like a rare species of bird, China white and crimson red and freckled.

He tried to remember ever noticing or caring about the particular cadence or tone of a woman's voice, but couldn't.

"The Transition is a do-or-die event for half-Bloods that occurs at the age of twenty-five. No one knows exactly why, but human and *Ikati* blood is ultimately incompatible. They survive for a while, but just like a clock ticking down to zero hour, there's an expiration date for those of mixed Blood. Which is one of the many reasons it's forbidden: having a halfling child is basically condemning that child to an early death. Only every once in a great while, it isn't. The half-Bloods survive their Transition— their first Shift—and they go on to lead a normal life with their Shifting abilities intact."

Hawk didn't add that the dead Alpha of the Roman colony— a brilliant geneticist in spite of being a homicidal maniac—had developed a serum that allowed all half-Bloods to survive the Transition. Which even at this moment, his insane, immortal son was using to develop a half-Blood army with which to wipe out the entire human race.

He didn't think it would be prudent to mention that particular detail.

"Why didn't the Alpha know it was forbidden?"

Hawk shrugged. "We only just discovered this colony a few years ago. The four confederate colonies have known about each other's existence since our ancestors were hunted to near extinction in Egypt under Caesar Augustus. The remaining few fled and settled in small, isolated communities around the world—"

"Hunted? Egypt? Caesar Augustus?"

They came to a clearing in the thick underbrush. Through the trees, Hawk saw the waterfall he'd been able to hear during the past twenty minutes of their ascent up the hill. In spite of her ability to keep up with him, Jacqueline was tiring, evidenced by her breathing, which had become labored the higher they climbed. He gestured to a large rock several feet away, shaded by a corozo palm.

"Let's rest a while."

She sat with a groan, unlaced her boots, pulled them off, and began to massage her feet.

"So—you were saying?" she prompted, wincing as she pressed on the arch of her left foot. "Hunted?"

"This isn't the first time you've wanted to wipe us off the face of the planet," Hawk said wearily, stretching his neck. "Even before Cleopatra, our interactions with humans were . . . treacherous, at best. One of you is always trying to exterminate us."

Jacqueline had stilled. Holding her foot in hand, she stared at him with a look of incredulity. "Cleopatra? You're saying Cleopatra was one of *you*?"

He smiled. "One of *you*, too."

"Another half-Blood Queen?"

He nodded. "Clever and cunning, and extraordinarily powerful. Like all the Queens, including the new one. An *Ikati* Queen doesn't come along often, but when she does, great changes swallow us." He added darkly, "No doubt this time will be the same."

"Why?"

Jacqueline stared at him with such laser-like intensity, Hawk felt as if he were a fly trapped in a web. A fly who almost—almost—didn't want to escape.

Stupid, self-destructive fly. Serves you right if the spider eats your dumb ass.

"A Queen is always the most powerful of all of us, even more powerful than the Alphas. Because of that, she's above the Law. She can do whatever she likes, without consequence. Combine all that power with complete freedom . . . let's just say it's never gone well."

She sat a little straighter, her expression avid. "Would I know any of the others?"

Hawk debated for only a moment before deciding to be truthful. "Marie Antoinette."

Jacqueline gasped. "No!"

"Yes. And you see how well that ended. Aside from those two and the new one, there hasn't been a Queen in millennia. But you'd probably recognize a few others of our kind who've successfully lived among you."

Jacqueline waited, unblinking, attuned to his every word. Hawk began to tick a list off his fingers.

"Sir Charles Darwin, Sir Isaac Newton, Michelangelo di Lodovico Buonarroti Simoni—"

"No!" Jacqueline exclaimed, louder.

He sent her a sardonic smile. "Yes. Michelangelo. One of your lauded examples of humanity in that lovely article you wrote."

In a voice so hollow it sounded as if it emanated from the depths of a well, Jacqueline asked, "Michelangelo wasn't human?"

"That doesn't devalue his accomplishments. In fact, considering he lived with all the pressures and complications of successfully managing a secret life, I think it makes him even more impressive, don't you?"

Jack looked at him for several long moments, examining his face. Her expression wavered somewhere between defeat and despair. "You're telling me the truth."

"The truth stings, doesn't it?"

The sorrow in her eyes welled up again as if his words had summoned it. "Almost always." In a haunted whisper, she added, "You'd think I'd know that by now."

She stared off into the trees, lost in thought, and Hawk felt again that odd compulsion to know what she was thinking. The compulsion that seemed to be quickly turning into need.

He knew himself well enough to understand that this dangerous desire to get inside her head went hand in hand with the equally dangerous desire to protect her. He didn't like either, but he wouldn't deny these urges existed . . . nor would he pretend both these urges weren't linked to an intense physical attraction he felt for her. An attraction that grew stronger the more time he spent by her side.

He just didn't know what, if anything, to do about any of it.

She confused him, which made him feel helpless and off balance, feelings to which he was unaccustomed, and ill-equipped to handle.

She turned her head and pierced him with a look. She blurted, "Was it your idea—the setup? The blackmail?"

Something in her eyes told him this was important to her. So when he answered, it was with a twinge of pride that he could deny it. "No."

Hawk sensed her relief, which flooded him with guilt, and the terrible compulsion to tell her the complete truth.

"But . . ."

She looked at him sharply.

"The pictures." He cleared his throat, willing himself not to look away. "Using your camera was a little . . . improvisation on my part. I had a small camera of my own available, but when I saw your camera on the nightstand . . . I knew you'd be more likely to play because it would seem so much more natural. And using your own camera against you would make our revenge all the sweeter . . ."

He couldn't take her fraught look any longer. He glanced away, ashamed.

In a small, horrified voice, she asked, "Where we're going . . . your colony . . . have they all seen the pictures? Has everyone seen me . . . us?"

Self-serving bastard that he was, Hawk saw an opportunity, and pounced on it.

"I've already told you more than I should. So if I answer your question truthfully, I get an answer of my own. Even if you don't like mine."

Panic flickered across her face. She began to twist a strand of her hair between her fingers, over and over, chewing the inside of her lip as she debated. After a moment of silence, she dropped her head and threaded her hands into her hair, staring at her feet.

Then she stood and faced him. "Agreed."

Courage, he thought. How much courage did it take to walk into this situation, to go where she knew she wasn't safe or particularly welcome, to entrust a man who'd already betrayed her, to get an answer that may or may not be devastating, and in return answer a question she probably already knew the content of, and would be loath to respond truthfully to, if her last reaction was an indication.

As if from a distance, Hawk heard himself say, "I know this isn't easy for you. And if it's any consolation . . . I admire your courage."

Her throat worked. She looked at him, her eyes fierce. "I'm not courageous, Hawk. I'm a coward. I've been afraid every single day of my life. I'm afraid right now. Most likely, I'll be afraid until the day I die."

Had she told him she was in love with him, he wouldn't have been more astonished. Her honesty felt like a sucker punch to the gut.

As if pulled by an invisible lure, Hawk took a step toward her. "That's exactly why you *are* courageous. That's what courage is: moving forward in spite of your fear. Not letting fear make the decisions for you, no matter how hard it tries. Walking toward danger when everything inside you is screaming at you to run away."

He took another step toward her, then another. She didn't move as he approached, she just watched his progress with vivid blue eyes.

He stopped a foot away. Rain glimmered in her hair, a fairy crown of shimmering drops atop the sunglow red, and he had to resist the violent urge to plunge his hands into all that beautiful hair, tug her against his body, and cover her mouth with his.

"Tell me," she said, a whispered demand that may as well have been, "Kiss me," the way his body reacted, the tightening he felt in his groin as he stared down at her. The sudden heat flooding his veins.

"No one has seen the pictures but me."

Her lids fluttered shut. She exhaled a quiet breath, then nodded.

She believed him. Why that should make him so happy, he didn't know.

She opened her eyes and gazed at him. Without waiting for the question she knew he would ask, she said, "Garrett is my older brother. It's his fault I'm so fu—" She stopped herself, and began again. "It's his fault I'm so messed up. He's the reason I'm always so afraid. He's the one who broke me. And I'm not saying this to make you angry or play games, but I can't talk about him. I can't talk about him without wanting to put a gun to my head and pull the trigger, to be free of this ocean of fear I've been drowning in for so long."

Her eyes filled with moisture. A lone tear tracked a zigzag path down her cheek, and before he knew what he was doing, Hawk had lifted his hand and brushed it away with his thumb.

"No one could break you," he said vehemently. "You're too goddamn strong."

She blinked. "You cursed," she whispered, staring at him wide-eyed.

"And you didn't," he replied, his voice strangely hoarse. In fact, he realized, she hadn't cursed at all in the last two days.

Since he'd asked her not to.

They stood there like that in silence, his hand on her face, her gaze locked to his, until the sudden screech of a howler monkey brought them both abruptly back to Earth.

Jack took a step away, and dropped her gaze to the ground. She sat back down on the mossy rock, shoved her feet into her boots, then rose and walked away.

"Waterfall," she said stiffly over her shoulder. "Bath."

She disappeared into the trees, leaving Hawk alone in the clearing, his heart twisting like a wild animal inside his chest.

SIXTEEN

Off to See the Wizard

If pressed, Viscount Weymouth would have to say he first began to hate the Queen the day she stopped him from killing Morgan Montgomery.

It was several years ago, but the memory of it still rankled him, doubly so because Morgan was supposed to be executed for plotting to kill *him*.

He was Keeper of the Bloodlines of the Sommerley colony, and prior to the Queen's arrival, he'd been an important member of the tribe. He might even go so far as to say *revered*. His position wasn't only ancient and respected, it was necessary to the continued survival of their species. Without him and the Matchmaker, couples would woo and wed willy-nilly, and what would become of them then?

Nothing, that's what. The purity of their Bloodlines would be lost, and so, most likely, would their Gifts. Eventually they'd be no better than humans.

And now that the new half-Blood Queen had decided to abolish the Law of arranged matches and allow young couples to let "love" be their guide, Viscount Weymouth had been effectively neutered, and hated the Queen even more.

Love. Such quaint, plebeian folly.

Though he shouldn't be surprised; the Queen's own father had been executed for falling prey to its grasp. As for himself, he'd never been touched by love's dangerous whims. His own wife of thirty years was an outlet for the base urges of his body and a valued breeder—she'd given him two strong sons—but nothing more. It was a peculiarity of *Ikati* nature that they mated for life, but that didn't always mean they mated for love. In fact, Viscount Weymouth was convinced love was a concept some long-ago female had devised during the throes of a forbidden passion in order to feel absolved from guilt.

Females, he thought with contempt, staring at his reflection in the floor standing mirror as he adjusted his mustard velvet cravat beneath his florid jowls. *Always more trouble than they're worth.*

Satisfied his old-fashioned neckwear was in perfect order, the viscount patted the lapels of his matching silk vest and turned to and fro before the mirror. He sucked in his paunch, for a brief moment envisioning the slender young man he'd once been long ago, then released it with a gusty exhalation that strained the waistband of his custom-made Italian trousers. This was, in all likelihood, the last time he'd admire his formidable figure in the oval polished glass of his bedroom, and he was in no great hurry to move along.

God only knew what those savages in the rainforest in Brazil would be wearing. The thought of himself clad in a loincloth made him shudder.

"They're ready for you, My Lord," his valet said, bowing from the bedroom door.

"Yes, I imagine they are," replied the viscount absently, donning his jacket. He didn't move from the mirror.

Behind him, his valet raised his brows, but the viscount only smiled.

Let the Queen and her lapdog Alpha wait a while longer. He was in no rush to comply. Though outwardly he remained a loyal servant, inwardly he'd stopped complying long ago.

Case in point: the Plan.

Devised by that madman Caesar Cardinalis—a creature as equally devious as he was insane, neither of which, in the viscount's opinion, negated the soundness of his stance on the correct way to handle both humans and the liberal new Queen—the Plan was simple. The rewards he'd reap if he carried it off successfully, however, would be extravagant indeed.

Deliver the message to the Brazilian colony that their destruction was imminent and they could either join Caesar or die. Lead everyone to Morocco. Kill the Queen.

Not necessarily in that order, of course.

He'd already been quietly assisting the more vocally dissatisfied members of the colonies to join Caesar for months. He had only to read the weekly reports of the names of the attempted deserters to know where to look. It was an unfortunate fact of colony life that some couldn't bear the weight of their burden to stay secret and silent from the rest of the world, and tried to run. They were always caught, always severely punished—oftentimes put to death—but that didn't stop the random attempt.

Only now that Caesar had decided to fast-track his plan for *Ikati* world domination and had spread the word that all deserters were welcome with him, the attempts were no longer quite so random.

His valet cleared his throat. Viscount Weymouth rolled his eyes, and gave himself one final once-over.

"All right," he said, satisfied. "Off we go."

Humming "We're Off to See the Wizard," the viscount followed his valet out of the room.

The Sommerley colony in southern England was the largest of the five *Ikati* colonies spread over the globe, and by far the most opulent. The Alpha who originally settled it had been concerned only with secrecy and the safety of the few with him who'd escaped the deadly clutches of Caesar Augustus after Egypt fell to Rome, but successive generations of his offspring, emboldened over time by the hubris of those who'd outwitted death, proved particularly adept with money.

The tribe began to amass a fortune in textiles and trade.

Spices, incense, precious stones, ebony, silks, rare woods, gold . . . there were few things in which the tribe didn't have a financial interest. By the mid-sixteenth century, they'd grown too wealthy and were comprised of too many to escape notice any longer.

The Crown itself took an interest in the secretive, dark-haired clan living like kings at the black ragged edge of the New Forest. Envoys were sent. Discussions were held. Calculated lies were presented.

Concessions to the visibility their success had brought were made.

Eventually, an earldom was granted, then a viscounty, then a barony, and the tribe that had so long tried to stay hidden found itself included in the ranks of the most visible and documented group in the civilized world: the British peerage.

So the English *Ikati* learned to hide even more effectively by hiding right under their enemies' noses.

Except for the occasional shiver of fear that would tingle the spine if one looked too long into the vivid green eyes of these elegant imposters, nothing seemed amiss. No one was the wiser. Life proceeded smoothly.

Until one day it no longer did.

"Morocco," Leander McLoughlin, current Earl of Normanton and Alpha of Sommerley, said, speaking to the beveled glass panes of the picture windows in the East Library of Sommerley Manor. He snapped the word as if it were sour, as if it tasted bitter on his tongue.

"Hmm," agreed the woman seated in the plush comfort of an antique silk Hepplewhite chair behind him. Absently, she stroked her fingers over the downy pale fluff atop the head of the newborn she held swaddled in her arms.

Only sixteen weeks old, and so tiny. Like her twin sister, Honor, Hope was a solemn baby who rarely smiled, and even more rarely cried. The pair had been born after a difficult pregnancy and a long, excruciating labor, and their somberness seemed to acknowledge the fact that they'd been brought into the world only after a great deal of pain.

Hope looked up at her mother now with a peaceful, even stare, so intent and far-reaching it was as if she saw straight through her into some other landscape. It was at moments like this the Queen felt with absolute certainty her children were creatures born not of her but *through* her, as if they'd existed somewhere else before,

147

whole and infinitely intelligent, and her body had only been the portal to bring them forth into this plane of existence.

Jenna loved them with the voracious, violent adoration of a new mother. Into the darkest, smallest corner of her heart she shoved the unspeakable suspicion that her two daughters were something dangerous, the likes of which had never before been seen.

The night they'd been born, a red-tailed comet had scored the dark sky, vivid as a drop of blood. Jenna had witnessed such signs two other times in her life, and both had been harbingers of disaster.

Of death.

Stop being morbid, they're only babies! She leaned down and placed a gentle kiss on Hope's forehead.

Leander turned from the window. "You're sure Caesar's in Morocco?"

Jenna glanced up at him. Black hair that always looked wind-swept, even after it had been combed; a lean, taut body; the bearing and powerful presence of an emperor. And that snap of connection, every time their eyes met.

It never failed to surprise her, the way her heart took flight when he gazed at her. Still, after being married nearly five years, after two children, after everything. He could still make her pulse race with a mere look.

"He's there. I can See it."

It had been a mystery as to why it had fled in the first place, but as soon as she became pregnant, Jenna could no longer See. Her Gift connected her to all the *Ikati* across the globe. Like stars against the midnight sky, each one appeared to her as a separate, twinkling entity. Even the half-Bloods. The moment she'd gotten pregnant, however, her Sight had fled . . . and so had her ability to read minds with a touch of her hand. So had all her other Gifts. She couldn't even Shift to panther anymore.

But the moment she'd given birth—*voila*. Like a switch had been turned back on. Unfortunately, the mind reading—the one Gift she needed the most—hadn't yet returned.

"It's too far, Jenna. It's too dangerous."

Leander's voice had gone from bitter to forbidding. The way he looked at her was forbidding, too, all knife-blade eyes and thinned lips and smolder. Jenna had to press the smile from her mouth.

It wouldn't do to let him think she was laughing at him. She wasn't, but neither was she going to let her domineering, beloved husband dictate what she would or wouldn't do.

She never had before. No reason to change now.

Jenna stood. Beside her chair was a bassinette, a cocoon of white silk and ruffles in which she laid Hope beside her sleeping sister, tucking her under the blanket.

"Go to sleep, little one."

Obediently, Hope closed her eyes. Jenna shook off the eerie feeling that her four-month-old daughter might have understood what she'd said.

She approached Leander, watching him watch her hips sway as she walked. Once in front of him, she reached up and wound her arms around his neck.

"I won't go too near," she promised, pressing a soft kiss to the space between his throat and shoulder. She nuzzled his neck as his arms came around her back and he pulled her into a crushing tight hug.

"You won't go near at *all*," he corrected gruffly. "And stop trying to manipulate me with feminine wiles. You'll just end up getting thoroughly ravished."

Jenna laughed into Leander's neck, a low, husky laugh that had him tightening his arms even more around her back.

"And we both know how much I *hate* that," she teased.

Leander gently pulled her head back with a hand in her hair, staring intently into her eyes. "No. Just—*no*, Jenna. I won't allow this. It's too dangerous, and we have more to think about than just ourselves." His burning gaze flicked to the bassinette, then back to her. "They need their mother." His voice grew soft. "*I* need their mother. If anything happened to you . . ."

She shushed him with a finger to his lips. "Nothing is going to happen me, love."

His dark brows drew together to a scowl. "You could easily be seen—"

"I'll fly high. Too high to be noticed."

"There's nothing to be gained—"

"Information is power. We have to know what he's doing, what he's planning. That's best done up close and personal."

"You just said you wouldn't go too near!" he all but shouted, tensing.

Jenna sighed, extricated herself from his arms, and went back to gaze down into the bassinette. *So small. So fragile. What kind of world will you grow up in, little ones?*

A better one than she'd grown up in. Of that she was determined.

"It was a figure of speech. I'll get in and out as quickly as possible. They won't even know I'm there—"

"He'll smell you a mile away! He'll *feel* you."

Yes, that was a problem. The *Ikati* could all feel her presence, tangible as a kiss on the cheek.

If she was in physical form, that is.

"I'll go as the west wind." She turned to find him scowling at her, arms folded across his broad chest, anger rolling off him in waves.

She drew near to him once again, gazing up at him with the slight, coy smile she knew he couldn't resist. "A sandstorm. A thundercloud." She spread her hands over his chest. Beneath his pale blue button-down shirt, his heart thudded hard and erratic.

Very angry. Better up the ante.

She leaned in and brushed her mouth against his. Her tongue slid along his lower lip. "I'll go as the rain."

"Jenna!" Leander groaned, but in the frustrated plea she detected the first, faint crumbling of his resistance.

"You know I'm the only one who can do this, Leander. And it has to be done. You and the girls go ahead of me to Brazil. I'll take a quick detour to Morocco, then meet you there. I promise I'll be in Brazil by the time you arrive." She unwound his crossed arms and settled them around her waist. Then she went back to nibbling on his lower lip. She breathed, "And I'll be waiting with bells on."

"You're *evil*," he protested, crushing her body to his once more.

"But you love me," she whispered, and kissed him.

They stood there entwined for a long, breathless moment until a politely cleared throat dragged them abruptly back to reality.

"Your Highnesses." Viscount Weymouth bowed low from the waist. He straightened and beamed at Jenna and Leander, who broke apart but stood with their arms around each other's waists.

"Weymouth." Leander cocked his head, narrowing his eyes. "You're looking rather pleased with yourself this morning."

A faint blush rose in the viscount's cheeks. He glanced at his valet, standing stoically beside him, staring at nothing. "Just . . . er . . . just anxious to begin our journey, My Lord," he stammered, walking stiffly into the opulence of the East Library. Prisms of fractured, golden sunlight reflecting from the crystal chandelier hanging from the gilded ceiling above glinted off his spectacles, and shone from the dome of his balding head. He paused beside the marble fireplace, staring pensively down into the dark hearth for a moment. Then he turned and said briskly, "Is everything in order?"

Leander slanted his wife a look. She blinked up at him, smiling coyly again, and he clenched his jaw, shaking his head. He exhaled hard, raked a hand through his hair, then gave her a gentle kiss on the temple.

He murmured into her ear, "Our discussion isn't over yet." To the viscount, he said, "Yes. We're ready. Aren't we, darling?"

"Ready as we'll ever be." She sent the viscount a long, searching look, under which he squirmed.

The blush in his cheeks deepened, turning them ruddy. "And how are you feeling this morning, Your Highness?" he asked, a little too brightly. "Any sign of the Sight returning?"

Jenna and Leander shared a knowing glance.

They hadn't told anyone her Sight had returned once the children had been born because there was a traitor to be found . . . and nothing brought out the circling wolves like a whiff of weakness. It would be so much more convenient if the mind reading would return—she'd simply line everyone up and shake their hands, and it would be done—but at least they knew where Caesar was hiding. It would have to be enough for now.

"No, not yet." Jenna sighed, pretending dismay and doing her best to look crestfallen. "All the other Gifts are intact, but the Sight . . . we're still hoping, of course."

"Of course!" the viscount enthused, rising up on his toes as if he were going to hop. He lowered himself immediately and nervously cleared his throat. "Er . . . well, then, if there's not anything else, I'll wait outside. My family is already gathered in the motor court, along with the rest of the Assembly."

Jenna's stomach squeezed to a knot. Once they left, Sommerley would be a ghost town. No one knew if they'd ever be able to return. For a woman who as a child had never lived in any one place longer than a few months, Sommerley had become more than a home. It had become a sanctuary.

Her arm tightened around her husband's waist. *Home is with him. Home is wherever he and the girls are. Nothing else matters.*

"Thank you, Edward," said Leander. "We'll be down in a moment."

The viscount and his valet bowed their goodbyes and left, and Jenna and Leander stood looking in silence around the grand, glittering room.

Leander turned to her. "It's twelve hundred miles from here to Morocco—"

"Thirteen hundred sixty-eight," Jenna correctly softly. "I know, love."

He stared at her a beat.

"I looked it up."

His eyes bored into her. "How long have you been planning this?"

She stroked his cheek with her fingertips. "I'm going to be fine, Leander. I promise I won't take any unnecessary risks. Caesar won't even know I'm there . . . you know I can do this."

As he stared down at her, a muscle in his jaw flexed, over and over.

"If I leave soon, I can be there before sunset. A bit of recon, then I'll head toward Brazil."

He shook his head. "You'll be flying over open water on the way back. What is it? Two, three thousand miles from Morocco to Manaus?"

"Four thousand two hundred fifty." Jenna pressed her fingers against that angry muscle in his jaw, willing it to calm.

Leander cupped her face in his hands. "This is insanity! You'll be totally exposed! Over that distance, you'll have to fly without stopping, for . . . how long? Days, likely! There're airplanes, there's radar . . . you don't think someone will notice a huge white dragon flying over the Atlantic Ocean?"

"I can be Vapor," she said gently. "I can be a bird—"

"What if you tire? What about food, water? What if, God forbid, you get injured? Jenna, *think!*"

She removed his hands from her face, and stepped back, out of his reach. She watched his face, his desperate, begging eyes, and steeled herself against them.

"I'm doing this, Leander. You know how much I love you, but I'm not asking your permission. This tribe is my responsibility, our survival is my responsibility, and I'm not just going to sit by helplessly while Caesar tears us apart and makes the world hate us. I'm going to spy on him and his little pack of rats, and find out what their plan is, so we can formulate a plan of our own. I'm sorry you don't approve, but I'm doing it. This isn't a negotiation."

His eyes flashed. "And what about the girls? They're still breast-feeding—"

"Grayson Sutherland's wife is still breast-feeding, too."

Grayson was an Assembly member, one of the few families left at Sommerley who'd be making the trip with them to Manaus. His wife had conveniently given birth the month prior, and had agreed to care for Honor and Hope in Jenna's absence.

Leander's face hardened. "A wet nurse. I see you've thought of everything."

"I have. And everything will be fine, you'll see. Please, just trust me."

They stared at one another while the long-case clock chimed the hour. When the doleful tolls faded into silence, Jenna asked quietly, "Did you think I'd just stand by and let him walk all over us? Did you think when my Gifts returned I wouldn't retaliate?"

Leander blinked. His lips parted. Dread leached the color from his face. "You can't kill him, Jenna. He can't be killed, you know that. Don't even try; you'll only end up getting hurt. Or worse!"

"Everything that can be made can be unmade. We just don't know how Caesar can be unmade yet, but he can. He might be immortal, but he isn't invincible. Even Superman has his Kryptonite—"

"Superman is a comic book character! Caesar is real!"

"He's got a weakness, Leander. I know it. And I'm going to find out what it is."

In a hoarse, disbelieving voice, he asked, "Even if it kills you?"

Yes.

The word was unspoken, but Leander saw it in her eyes. In the way her chin lifted, the way her back straightened, the way her gaze, always so soft when she looked at him, turned steely.

Yes, she would die for them. For her beloved, beautiful husband and her two new babies and this clan of magical, mystical beings who'd accepted her as their own, even though she was only half their world. Only half their Blood.

"It's my responsibility. More than anyone, you understand responsibility. If the roles were reversed, you'd be doing the exact same thing."

He closed his eyes. Jenna knew he knew she spoke the truth, and she also knew he hated to admit it.

"If anything happens to you, it will end me. You do realize that, don't you?" he whispered. He opened his eyes, and they blazed. "I won't go on without you. I can't."

She stepped into the circle of his outstretched arms and rested her cheek against his chest. He buried his face in her hair and they clung to each other, hearts pounding, the dark, uncertain future rushing toward them at the speed of a runaway train.

Jenna gently kissed her love on the cheek. "You'll never be without me. Even when I'm far away, my heart is always with you. My heart will always only be with you."

Then, without waiting for a response, without giving him the opportunity to try to argue her out of what she needed to do, she Shifted to Vapor.

It rose to a burning bright peak within her, effortless as breathing, smooth as silk. From one heartbeat to the next her body transformed from cumbersome flesh and blood and bone to cool, lovely mist, weightless and wonderful. As it always did when she left her physical self behind, a song of joy pierced straight through her, thrilling and impossibly sweet.

Goodbye, my love. Wish me luck; I'm going to need it.

As she surged in a glittering gray plume toward the window that stood ajar at the end of the room, Leander was left holding up her empty dress in the stillness and splendor of the East Library, watching her go with haunted, anguished eyes.

Like an arrow sure of its mark, the half-Blood Queen of the *Ikati* shot out into the morning sky.

SEVENTEEN
Arrival

"Before we do this, Red," Hawk said, his voice low and serious, his face a mask of stone, "there are three things you need to remember if you're going to get back to New York in one piece."

That sounded ominous enough to Jack, but his manner made her even more anxious. She'd never seen him this . . . wired.

After her emotional admission a day and a half ago, before she'd gone to bathe in the pool beneath the waterfall, they'd settled again into silence. He'd politely requested that she let him stand nearby—back turned—to make sure nothing snuck up on her during her swim, and he'd kept his word. Crouched on an outcropping of rock just above the warm, clear waters, he'd never once looked her way . . . and she'd checked repeatedly.

But his gaze had never strayed from some fixed point in the distance, far overhead.

Following her blurted admission about her brother, she found both Hawk's request to stand guard and his respect for her privacy deeply touching.

Even after more than thirty-six hours, she was still raw and bleeding in places inside of her that had been scabbed over for years. He must have sensed it, because he allowed her to retreat into the snug, safe corner of her mind she'd created long ago to cope when things went sideways. He only spoke to her in gentle tones to warn her of some obstacle in their path as they walked, or instruct her on the finer points of forest living, like how to use a handful of foaming berries and a macerated twig to brush her teeth, or how to funnel rainwater from the curved leaves of trees when she was thirsty. Last night, when she'd awoken screaming from another nightmare, he'd only squeezed her into the hard warmth of his chest until she stopped trembling, then released her and stared silently out into the vast emerald darkness, never speaking a word at all.

Now, after a week of sailing the ocean and trudging through wilderness and forging a kind of bizarre, backward alliance based on blurted honesties, silences that should have been uncomfortable but were companionable instead, and the knowledge they'd already forced one another to re-examine some of their sacrosanct beliefs, they stood together in the soft sapphire aftermath of twilight, looking down into the wide, misted bowl of an emerald valley wherein Hawk said his colony lay.

"What are the three things?" Jack's voice was as low and solemn as his.

He was examining the landscape below the hill they were about to descend with eyes so focused and predatory she thought briefly his nickname was exactly apropos. A raptor's gaze held just that kind of piercing, hungry keenness.

"First and most important, the Alpha is always right. No matter what, no questions asked."

"The Alpha," she repeated, unsure. "How will I know which one is the Alpha?"

His lips quirked. "Trust me, you'll know."

Adrenaline threaded along her nerve endings like a barbed, creeping vine, lifting all the tiny hairs on the back of her neck. "Second?"

"Second, you're only here to observe. Opinions won't be welcome, and you might find yourself missing your tongue if you say the wrong thing. Females don't have quite the . . ." He searched for a word, then tried a different tack. "Let's just say the feminist movement hasn't reached the rainforest." His eyes, electric green even in darkness, met hers. "Yet."

"Got it. You're all a bunch of tongue-chopping Archie Bunkers."

His smile soured. "Not all, no. But enough for it turn deadly if, for instance, Gloria Steinem showed up and started burning bras."

Deadly? Her mouth went dry. "Duly noted. Mum's the word. And third?"

The smile vanished. When he again spoke, her heart began to flutter like a hummingbird's at the ominous tone in which they were spoken.

"Don't go anywhere without me. Especially at night."

They stared at each other. Off on the distant horizon, a full moon crested a range of rolling black hills and spread her pallid glow over the treetops.

"Tell me they're not going to hurt me," she said, carefully watching his face. "Tell me I'm going to get out of this alive."

He turned to her and looked down on her from his full, imposing height, his manner as intense as the look in his eyes. "No one is going to hurt you," he insisted with vehemence. "Anyone who's stupid enough to even *look* at you the wrong way will have to deal with me."

That protectiveness again. That freely offered—and unde-served—shielding from harm.

Why would he defend her against his own kind, after what she'd written, after how she'd argued for war against them, after all she'd done? He'd said he was responsible for her safety . . . but was there more to it than that?

Do I want there to be?

After a moment of fraught indecision in which she debated the merits of opening this particular can of worms, Jack said, "I thought you thought I was a bigot."

He answered softly, "I thought you thought I was a lying, scheming, underhanded son of a dung beetle."

The air all around them breathed with the lush music of the rainforest. Frogs croaked. Insects whirred. Mammals chirped or called or howled. Everything smelled of nighttime and wildness, and the space between them was palpably alive. Jack felt on the verge of something vast and bottomless, a weightless, sightless sensation of falling or flying blindfolded, of jumping into impen-etrable blackness and having it swallow her whole.

Why do you make me feel like this?

Why is it when I look into your eyes I feel . . . free?

"I *do* think you're a lying, scheming, underhanded son of a dung beetle," Jack agreed, letting him see the truth of it in her unguarded gaze. "I hate that you tricked me. I hate that you used me." She hesitated, then went on, smaller; emotion constricting her voice. "I hate that I liked it so much."

He said her name, his eyes as soft as his voice.

"I hate that I could have looked back on that night with only good memories—*amazing* memories—and now I can only look back and see one more betrayal."

She'd wounded him. She saw it in the way he stiffened, in the way his glittering eyes reflected back sorrow and shame. For a moment she was brilliantly, blindingly *glad* she'd hurt him. For a moment it was enough that she wasn't the only one in pain.

But then he whispered with searing, startling remorse, "I didn't know you, Jacqueline. I didn't know *you*. If I had, I never would've agreed to it. I never would've hurt you. I thought you were something else, some*one* else, this heartless woman who felt nothing, who only wanted to spread hatred and fear. But you're not. You're . . . unexpected. You're . . ."

He hesitated, but seemed unable to continue, or unsure of what to say.

His gaze dropped to her lips.

Everything honed to a crystalline clarity. His eyes, his face, the space between them, crackling hot. A frenzy of emotion whipped her heartbeat into a thundering gallop, and it became hard to breathe.

A sinister rustling in the underbrush ripped her attention away from him to the dark forest.

Hawk whirled around. He shoved Jack behind him with one hand. From his throat he issued a low, preternatural hiss.

It was answered by more hissing from the darkness.

Jack froze in horror as she peeked around Hawk's shoulder and saw, slinking forward in a solid line from the depths of the jungle, ten monstrously huge black panthers. Their long tails waved in sinuous harmony, their eyes shone with predatory malice, their muzzles full of sharp fangs were bared.

They moved clear of the underbrush, slowly spread apart, and sank into coiled, silent crouches.

Poised to pounce.

EIGHTEEN
The Big Event

"I didn't realize our lord and master would send a welcoming party," Hawk snarled in the Old Language to the gathered animals, feeling Jacqueline's fingers digging into his back. "You're lucky I didn't rip off your heads before I realized who you were!"

A flash of light, a coil of smoke, and there stood Luis Fernando, head of Alejandro's security detail, naked as the day he was born.

Smirking.

"*Su sahapu beleti immaru masku amari sumsu mimma, ahu.*"

Translation: You were too wrapped up in lady white skin to realize much of anything at all, man.

"*Edin na zu*, Nando," Hawk replied, shooting the naked Fernando a murderous glare. *Go to the desert.* It was the equivalent of "go to hell" in the ancient tongue, and was used in the same way.

How much had they heard?

If the smirk on Nando's face was any indication, far too much.

Wonderful. Absolutely wonderful. Already this was proving to be the disaster he'd foreseen, and they hadn't even stepped foot inside the colony.

In a burst of energy that sent a heated blast of air rippling through the small clearing, the nine other panthers Shifted as one. Behind Hawk, Jacqueline squeaked in terror.

"Aren't you going to introduce us?" Nando stepped forward and peered in avid curiosity around Hawk's shoulder. Against his back, her fingers trembled, and before Hawk knew what he was doing, a low warning growl rumbled through his chest.

It brought Nando up short. His brows lifted. "No need to get testy, *ahu*." His lips twitched. He added, "You lying, scheming, underhanded son of a dung beetle."

The other nine burst out laughing, and Hawk's temper snapped.

He stepped forward, lashed out with his fist, and connected with Nando's jaw like a hammer against a mango.

The big male went flying backward in an awkward tangle of naked limbs. He landed on his back in a thicket of underbrush with a thud and the pouf of flying foliage. Shouting a volley of curses, he thrashed around among the low branches until he scrambled to his feet again, while the others howled with laughter, slapping one another on the back.

"The next one who says another word is going down with him," Hawk snarled, eyeing each of them in turn.

"*Somebody* hasn't gotten laid recently," chuckled one of the group.

Another answered, "I'm sure he'll take care of that later tonight; Luiza's so hot for him to get back she's practically in Fever."

Hawk had them both flat on their backs with devastating punches before either of them could make a move in defense.

"Anyone else?" he shouted to the remaining seven.

No one replied.

Cradling his jaw and staggering around in the demolished bushes, Nando snarled, "You won't be able to play with Luiza tonight because you'll be back in the stocks again, *Salsu Maru*! You can't attack the Alpha's guard!"

"We'll see about that," Hawk muttered. He turned, grabbed Jacqueline's hand, and pulled her along behind him as he marched into the trees, not bothering to look and see if the group had followed.

They hadn't yet . . . but they would.

They always did.

After trudging through the dark forest behind a seething Hawk for about five minutes—and regaining her equilibrium after witnessing a group of giant black cats morph into a group of giant naked men—Jack said, "So! That went well."

He spat something in that strange, beautiful language Nando had spoken. His strides were so long and hurried she nearly had to run to keep up with him.

"Just out of curiosity . . . are you that popular with everyone in your colony?"

Still he didn't answer. She heard grumbling and growling over his shoulder, some noises that sounded like a spitting snake, but he didn't answer or even break his stride, seemingly determined to get where they were going as fast as humanly possible.

Humanly. Ha!

Jack was breathing hard, and it wasn't because of their accelerated trek through the jungle. Her nerves were screaming, her heart was pounding: she felt as if she might jump right out of her skin.

This was it. This was what she'd spent nine days of her life sailing and hiking and dreaming about, and getting mentally prepared for.

The Big Event.

Did a bride walking down the aisle feel as nervous as this?

She doubted she'd ever find out.

"Uh . . . Hawk?"

Silence.

Okay. You don't want to talk. Fine. Let's try—

"*Salsu Maru!*"

What a lovely sense of satisfaction that was, watching him freeze mid-step when she spoke those two—admittedly unknown—words.

He whirled around and stared at her with all the geniality of a shark contemplating the fat, luscious form of a seal bobbing in the waves above its open maw.

"You don't even know what you're saying!" he spat, livid.

Jack crossed her arms over her chest. "Whatever it was, it served my purpose. I have your attention now."

His lips thinned. His nostrils flared. His eyes—the darkest, richest emerald—narrowed.

Scary-beautiful. Been there, done that. Moving on.

"I just want to ask you this one thing, and then we can continue our lovely death march down the hill toward my ultimate demise."

He waited, breathing hard, his eyes flashing *Danger!* like neon signs.

Jack drew in a breath and asked, "Are you okay?"

He blinked a few times. His nose twitched. "Am *I* okay."

He'd repeated it flatly as if she'd spoken in a foreign language and he was trying to grasp the meaning of the words.

"Yes. That's the question: Are you okay?"

It seemed to pull the plug on his anger, letting it filter out of his body like water down a drain. He exhaled, passed a hand over his face, and muttered, "You're a real piece of work, you know that?"

Jack frowned at him. "Uh . . . no. Yes? I don't know. What do you mean?"

"Do you have any sense of self-preservation whatsoever?"

It seemed a reasonable query, delivered with a solemn, intent gaze, so Jack answered it honestly. "Yes. My sense of self-preservation is intact, thank you. As is my sense of empathy for other people who might be having a hard time. Which you seem like you might be having. Hence the question."

Bizarrely, Hawk groaned. "You see—*that!*" He pointed an accusing finger at her. "Stop doing that!"

"Doing . . ."

"Being nice!" he shouted. "Being compassionate! Being . . . *you!*"

"Don't be me," Jack repeated, nonplussed. "Right. You'd rather I be . . . ?"

"Someone else! *Anyone* else! Be the cold-hearted bitch I thought you were before I got to know you better!"

That hurt. It also confused the hell out of her. "Why are you mad at me?"

He shouted, "Because you make me *crazy!*"

Jack dropped her arms to her sides. "Hawk—"

"No! Just—no! We're going to keep walking, and you're going to keep quiet, and we're going to go into the colony, and you and I are going to forget anything ever happened between us. You're going to get your story, and get the *hell* out of my life! All right?"

Jack wasn't stupid. She understood men; she'd had plenty of experience with their rage, their possessiveness, and their irrationality when pushed into a corner.

She knew by his words and his tone and the fury in his eyes that she'd triggered all the dark, slinking monsters of his nature, the things he would never admit to himself that he felt or thought or needed, and in doing so, had sealed her own fate.

She'd driven him away.

She'd made him hate her.

She was going to die in this jungle, alone.

The realization sliced through her body, cold as winter wind.

Fine. Hate me. Leave me. Go back on all your promises.

You won't be the first.

Calmly, quietly, looking Hawk dead in the eye, Jack said, "All right." Then she brushed past him, striding ahead into the dark forest.

After she'd gone several paces, Hawk called from behind her, "You have no idea where you're going."

"Yes, I do. This way." Jack shoved a branch out of her face that appeared from the darkness.

She heard his "Argh!" of exasperation, and hoped he choked on his tongue.

"Jacqueline, stop!"

Tch! Like I'm taking orders from you again! She kept marching forward, stumbling over tree roots, flailing her arms in front of her to keep away the vines and branches and something that hovered nearby, whirring ominously close to her head. Was it a bird? An insect? A vampire bat? With her luck, it probably *was* a vampire bat, and she was going to die in the rainforest with a furry, winged rodent attached to her neck, fattened with her blood.

Figures.

Hawk called her name again, angrier this time, and when she didn't respond, he bolted after her. His immense speed brought him in front of her in a heartbeat. She stopped short, glaring daggers at him from only a few feet away.

He said tersely, "You can't see. You'll hurt yourself. You have to follow me."

"I'd rather eat a pile of shit than follow you."

This line was delivered with zero emotion or expression; it was just a stated fact that had the blood rising in his cheeks. He studied her face for several moments.

"You're angry with me."

"Your powers of comprehension are remarkable. Congratulations on your acute grasp of the obvious."

His lips tightened. He folded his arms across his chest.

"Oh, not happy? If I recall, not two minutes ago you told me—*so nicely*, I might add—you'd rather I be the cold-hearted bitch you thought I was. Well—done. Here she is, Bitch of the Century!" Jack spread her arms wide in a "ta-da!" gesture.

He snapped, "Stop it!"

"*You* stop it!"

"You're acting like a child!"

Jack felt as if her eyes would pop out of their sockets. She yelled, "*I'm* acting like a child? You just punched three guys in the face because you thought they were making fun of you!"

He shouted back, "They *were* making fun of me! Because of *you*!"

"What?" she screeched, livid. "How was that possibly *my* fault—"

"It's your fault that I'm here in the first place, babysitting, when I could be doing something a little more useful with my time!"

Jack gasped in outrage. "Well I'm so sorry I'm infringing on your precious *time*! No doubt you'd rather be spending it with *Luiza*—"

"It's your fault for writing that article and pushing us into a corner and forcing our hand!" he shouted over her, stepping closer. He was furious, breathing hard, his eyes blazing green fire. "It's your fault that I'm all upside down and inside out and can't tell my ass from the end of my nose!"

"It must be hard since they both look alike!" Jack yelled, shaking in rage.

Hawk, vibrating rage back at her, stepped even closer and got right up into her face so they were staring at each other like two fighters in a ring waiting for the bell to sound.

He shouted, "And it's your fault for making me feel all these . . . horrible . . . *feelings*!"

Then he reached out, grabbed her, pulled her against his chest, and kissed her.

For a moment there was nothing but cold shock and breathlessness. She was so stunned she didn't even close her eyes. His mouth was hard and unforgiving against hers, a solid pressure without softness, but then he opened his lips and slid his tongue against hers.

Cold shock was replaced with white hot, encompassing heat.

His taste was velvet soft and complex and lovely in the way of pure, natural things, like sunshine and starlight and clear running water, or the sweetness of a summer peach plucked right from the tree. It was the same as the first time she'd tasted him, and she reveled in it the same way, wondering beyond the sudden rush of pleasure how anything could taste quite so delicious.

Her arms wound up around his shoulders. Her lids slid shut. She pressed herself against him, her anger forgotten, and he moaned into her mouth.

The kiss went on and on, rough and deep and greedy and wonderful, until she was so flush with desire she ached.

He had calluses on his hands, she remembered that from when she lay naked beneath him at the hotel and he'd peaked her nipples simply by brushing them with the rough pad of his thumb. Now those hands were cradling her head and bottom, crushing her against him so tightly their bodies were nearly as fused as their mouths, so tightly she felt the straining hardness of his erection, pressed against her lower belly, straight through their clothes.

She broke away first. She opened her eyes and looked up at him. He didn't open his eyes, and he didn't release her. He just held her like that, breath ragged, lips parted, a tremor running through his chest.

She watched as he slowly came back to himself. He swallowed, licked his lips, his lids drifted open. He blinked as if he didn't know where he was, but then his eyes cleared and a new look came into them, replacing the warm haze of only seconds before.

Horror.

"I'm sorry," he rasped, releasing her so quickly the cool night air was a shock against her breasts, so recently pressed into the heated expanse of his hard chest.

He stammered, "I'm sorry . . . I-I don't know . . . it-that won't happen again."

Though he was avoiding her eyes, his expression told her he was mortified. He stepped back and clasped his hands behind his neck, as if to keep them from going anywhere else.

"Okay," Jack whispered, her head still spinning. "That's good." She nodded, confused and off-kilter, but unwilling to admit that it *wasn't* good, especially since he seemed so aghast and ashamed with himself.

She pushed her feeling of disappointment—*stupid, stupid*—down and away, hoping it would never reappear.

Because judging from the way his face had gone white and he was blinking like a baby bird who'd utterly failed his first attempt at flying and now lay stunned and broken on the sidewalk, that wouldn't be happening again.

Without another word, he turned and walked stiffly away, and Jack was forced to decide whether to follow him or stay in the jungle. Alone. In the dark.

She followed him.

After fifteen minutes of silent walking, they broke through the trees and, at long last, Jack got her first glimpse of the colony, filled with supernatural creatures, which would now be her home.

NINETEEN
Hostile Inspection

Magical. Enchanted. Spellbinding. Dazzling. Unreal.

All those words and an onslaught of others passed through Jack's mind in a jumbled blaze as she stood, stunned and open-mouthed, at the edge of the forest, gazing up into the trees.

Because that's where the colony was:

Up.

Above her head for as far as her eyes could see stretched a suspended city, hidden cleverly within the network of ancient branches. Hundreds upon hundreds of sculpted wood structures—as organic and natural as the trees themselves, appearing as if they'd sprouted from the very trunks that held them—floated as if on air.

Illumed with thousands of flickering lanterns hung in windows and branches and on the suspension bridges linking one tree and structure to another, it was the most astonishing thing Jack had ever seen in her life.

It was the most beautiful thing Jack had ever seen in her life.

It was an architectural masterpiece.

She felt dwarfed by it, by its beauty and the sheer genius of its creators. She'd been to the Vatican once when she was on assignment in Italy, had stood in the vast, echoing silence of the central nave of St. Peter's Basilica, and had felt exactly these same feelings.

Awe. Reverence. Utter humility in the presence of such grandeur.

The forest floor beneath the suspended city had been cleared of the underbrush that made the trek through the rest of the jungle so difficult, and the base of each tree had been landscaped with orchids and bromeliads and pygmy palms, all the colorful confusion of the jungle tamed and shaped to please the eye. At the base of one of the trees ahead of her, Hawk had stopped and was looking back at her with a flat, empty expression.

His voice matched his face when he spoke. "Come on. They'll be waiting."

They?

With trepidation that equaled her amazement, Jack stepped forward into the beautiful, terrifying unknown.

His dead father was having what could politely be termed a conniption inside the confines of Hawk's skull.

Idiot! Moron! Stupid fucking weakling!

Doing his best to ignore the shrieked hysterics that always echoed in his brain at times like this, Hawk doggedly trudged onward from the edge of the colony, leading Jack to the place he knew the entire tribe would be gathered.

Where they always gathered on nights of the full moon.

Ummum Nanna was the monthly festival of the moon at its apex. His isolated tribe here in the rainforest had kept the old ways of celebrating the Earth and her great magic through the generations, and they had festivals for everything. Full moon and flood season festivals, vernal and autumnal equinox festivals, the winter solstice and midsummer festivals, birth, death, and wedding festivals . . . it went on and on ad nauseum. Hawk pretty much despised the lot, because enforced togetherness featuring singing, dancing, and ritual chest-pounding was his idea of hell on Earth. He already heard the singing, felt the pulse of the drums. He wondered how drunk everyone was . . .

How drunk Alejandro would be.

He should've timed this better. He should've timed their arrival to be any other time but tonight, but they'd made such unexpected good progress through the jungle, and honestly Hawk hadn't been thinking about this particular moment.

He'd been too preoccupied thinking about everything else.

About her.

About those lips. Those eyes. Those pert, perfect—

Ersetu tola'ath! screeched his father.

Earthworm. An oldie but a goodie.

"We're almost there," he growled over his shoulder to Jacqueline, who, when he looked back to ensure she was following, was craning her neck to gape at an empty iron structure the shape of an oversize bird cage, which hung conspicuously from the branches of one of the smaller trees.

"What's that?" she asked, pointing.

Hawk ground his teeth. Might as well get her used to the darker side of tribe life, right off the bat. Maybe it would scare her straight and she'd be quiet, which was everything he could possibly hope for, considering he'd determined he was never going to talk to her again.

"Gibbet."

"A cage you hang people in until they rot? You're fucking kidding me!"

"Not people. Criminals."

"Oh, thanks for the clarification! I'll be sure not commit any crimes! Goddamn brilliant!"

He stopped and turned to glare at her. "We're back to the indiscriminate cursing again?"

She sent him an arch look. "The bitch is back, remember?"

Hawk wondered if this was what it felt like to be poisoned, this slow, acidic blackness creeping through his body that threatened to choke off his oxygen and boil the blood in his veins.

He turned and marched onward.

After a moment, she followed behind.

The scene that greeted Jack when they passed under the natural bridge of rock that spanned a swiftly running stream was something right out of a Hieronymus Bosch painting.

Half-nude bodies, glistening with sweat, bathed in firelight, writhing to the heavy beat of drums. People—beautiful people, unnaturally so—spinning and twirling and dancing, laughing and kissing and drinking, as uninhibited and wild as the untamed forest that ringed the clearing. An enormous bonfire, spitting orange ash and whorls of smoke into the dark sky where it lingered, casting a dreamy haze over everything. Tables to one side of the revelry laden with platters of food, all of it demolished as if pounced on by ravenous predators. A raised dais opposite the tables with a throne of carved wood and purple fabric, upon which sat a heavy-lidded, grinning man—dark-haired and golden-skinned like the rest—holding an elaborate gold chalice and tapping his bare feet to the beat of the drums.

Had she not been quite so flabbergasted, Jack might have laughed.

Two words came immediately to mind:

Erotic derangement.

The dancing bodies were adorned in the most intricate, delicate trinkets, in an array of color that flashed crimson and sapphire and emerald in the firelight. They wore chokers of gold worked with precious stones, bracelets of garnet and onyx and tigereye, hair combs dotted with peridot and freshwater pearls. Some had elaborate feather headdresses; others wore armbands of bronze or headbands of silver or rings on each finger, a pharaoh's fortune in jewels on vivid display against the black velvet backdrop of the night jungle.

Pagan yet refined, carnal yet not at all coarse, they were abandoned and alluring and what "civilized" people might deem wild or debauched, but there was something that elevated their movement and revelry beyond mere wanton, physical expression.

They were wild, yes. They were sensual, yes.

But they were also quite perfectly . . . perfect.

She gaped at them in wide-eyed admiration until Hawk noticed she was no longer following. He stalked up to her, gave her a indecipherable look that might have been either a warning or fury, grabbed her wrist, and dragged her behind him as he headed toward the group.

They were noticed.

All at once, the drums fell silent. The dancing stopped. Everyone turned to watch their approach, and every single hair on Jack's body stood on end.

It was like nothing she'd ever experienced in her life, this feeling of acute, hostile inspection. A thousand pairs of eyes bored into her. A thousand unfriendly faces turned slowly as Hawk guided her through the parting crowd toward the dais. A whisper rippled through the crowd, and Jack caught snippets of conversation from all around her, some of it in Portuguese, some of it in the other language that seemed to be their own, and some of it—unfortunately—in English.

"That's her—"

"It's the human—"

"So pale—"

"That hair—"

"Hope he puts her in the stocks—"

"Deserves whatever she gets!"

Hawk pulled her before the dais and gave a curt nod of his head to the man lounging on the throne, his head tipped back as he inspected them both like something he might like to squash underfoot.

He was handsome in an old-fashioned matinee idol way, with slicked-back black hair, an aquiline nose, and an air of arrogant boredom particular to the wealthy and powerful, who wear their privilege like a ring on their little finger.

The Alpha! Do I bow? Do I smile? Do I go ahead and faint?

The Alpha solved her conundrum of manners when he drawled, "Well, well, well. Lord Bastard returns . . . with his prize in tow."

He'd said "prize" with obvious irony. His feral gaze perused her, uncomfortably keen, and Jack tried with all her might to remain calm and stone-faced while everything inside her was screaming to run.

That, she knew, would be a terrible idea. Nothing brought out the predatory instincts in hunters like seeing the backside of prey darting off in terror into the woods.

All right. Let's do this. Fake it 'til you make it, Jack!

She tried for a respectful tone while looking the Alpha in the eye. "I'm afraid I don't know the proper way to address you, so please forgive me if this is rude."

Beside her, Hawk hissed a low warning. Jack ignored him. She twisted her wrist from his grasp and stepped forward, shoulders back, head held high. In a clear voice that carried over the crowd, she said, "I'm Jacqueline Dolan. It's a pleasure to meet you . . . Mr. . . . . Alpha."

Because her dead mother had been concerned with manners and appearances and enjoyed showing off her only daughter like a blue-ribbon cow when company came to their house when she was a child, Jack knew how to execute a perfect, proper curtsy. In her dirty jeans and jacket, with her hair tangled and her face most likely smudged with dirt, Jack sank into a swift, elegant curtsy, bowed head and bent knees and all. She straightened, beaming at the Alpha as if he were visiting royalty and she were a peasant girl he'd flung coins to on the side of the road.

There was a beat of astonished silence. The tension in the air felt like a wire pulled close to snapping. The only sound was the crackling of the bonfire, and it seemed as if everyone held a collective breath.

Hawk stood behind her, radiating a fury so dangerous it actually had *heft*.

The Alpha burst into laughter.

He threw back his head—displaying an impressive set of long, white teeth—and gave himself over to gales of belly-clenching guffaws until finally he stood, still chuckling and shaking his head, and stepped away from his throne.

He sauntered down the steps of the dais, looking at her down his nose. He took her hand, bent over it, and brushed his lips over her knuckles. "*Encantada*. The pleasure is mine," he purred. "Or at least I hope it will be."

He straightened, still smiling, still holding her hand while gazing at her with those sharp, sharp eyes, and Jack knew that this man literally held her life in his hands. If he wanted to, he could simply kill her now. No one in the outside world would ever know what had happened. This would be the end of her story, the end of her life, the end of the line.

Her bones would be buried in the jungle. No headstone would mark her grave.

It was all up to him.

Would Hawk even try and stop him?

Her hand still resting in the Alpha's, she blurted a sincere, "Thank you."

One of his dark brows quirked. "For what?"

She blinked, realizing her faux pas, but couldn't take it back now. "For . . ." She cleared her throat. "For . . ."

"For not hurting you," he guessed when she faltered. His voice was quiet, his stare fixed.

There was no moisture in her mouth. Jack couldn't speak for a moment, but when she'd recovered her composure, she simply said, "Yes."

His gaze cut to Hawk, standing silently behind her. "And what would make you think I would do a thing like that, my dear?"

The Earth was turning too rapidly beneath her feet. Her equilibrium had tilted, and it seemed the only thing holding her to the ground was the cool weight of his hand grasping hers.

Jack whispered, "Because if I were in your shoes . . . that's what I'd want to do. I'd want revenge."

The Alpha narrowed his eyes, contemplating her expression, mulling the words over. After a moment, he released her hand. A tiny smile crooked one corner of his lips.

"You're quite direct, aren't you?" His eyes began a languid

survey of her body that heated her cheeks. "Though perhaps it's just recklessness."

In a tight voice, Hawk said, "She doesn't mean any disrespect—"

"If I wanted your opinion I'd give it to you!" the Alpha hissed. "Don't try my patience, Hawk, so soon after our new visitor has arrived."

At that moment, Luis Fernando and his cadre of guards arrived, shoving their way through the crowd to get to the front.

They barged toward the dais, hulking and silent, until they stood beside Jack in a row. She kept her eyes focused on Alejandro because Nando and his guards were still unclothed.

No one seemed the least bit concerned with their nudity.

The Alpha took one look at Nando's bruised and bloody face, and his expression hardened to granite. "Ever the rebel," he snarled, lip curled in disdain. "How many lashes do you think it will take before you finally learn to respect the rules? Fifty? One hundred? Perhaps two hun—"

"No need to count to one thousand. I get the picture," Hawk interrupted, sounding bored. The look on his face was anything but bored, however. He glared at the Alpha with unconcealed hatred.

The Alpha glared back with murder in his eyes, and Jack went cold.

Lashes . . . stocks . . . the gibbet. My God, these creatures are barbarians! And judging by the look on the Alpha's face, Hawk was about to be on the receiving end of some very nasty barbarism, indeed.

"It wasn't his fault!" she blurted, and she reached out and seized Alejandro's arm.

The crowd gasped as one, their shock universal.

For a moment there was nothing, just frozen silence and a look of stunned disbelief on Alejandro's face as he looked down at her hand wrapped around his arm. His gaze snapped back to her face and his look told her one thing for certain.

She'd just made a terrible, irreparable mistake.

"I'm sorry," Jack whispered. She released his arm, and took a small step back.

"Well," said the Alpha calmly after a long, horrible moment. He lifted his gaze to the crowd. His voice, clear and strong, carried to the far reaches of the clearing. "It appears we're going to have not one but *two* canings to complete the evening's festivities!"

He clapped his hands. The drums resumed their throbbing beat. The crowd looked on in ominous silence.

And Jack shrank back in terror as two hulking males approached her from either side, while the Alpha watched her, a sinister little smile playing over his face.

TWENTY

The Punishment Tree

The hulking males brushed right past her, however, and grabbed Hawk.

He didn't struggle, comment, or even looked surprised. He simply let the males lead him away through the crowd as Jack watched on in stunned disbelief, too shocked to move.

The Alpha watched Hawk's receding back. "Nando . . . you know the drill."

Beside her, Luis Fernando stiffened in outrage. "Sire! He attacked *me*!"

Alejandro snarled, "And you were either too slow or too distracted to evade him! Either way, he bested the head of my security detail . . . which doesn't make me feel particularly *secure*. Failure isn't an option. You know that. Take your lumps like a man or your second-in-command is getting a promotion."

He didn't mention what would then happen to Nando, but judging by the look on both their faces, it wouldn't be pleasant.

Nando hesitated for only a moment, then followed the path the other guards and Hawk had taken through the crowd.

Jacqueline was left standing beside the dais alone, reeling, her heartbeat arrhythmic, her skin clammy with sweat.

From behind her, Alejandro directed, "Morgan. Accompany our guest to the punishment tree."

He stepped past, sent a sidelong, penetrating look in her direction, then made his way through the parted crowd with the rest of his security detail in tow while the drums throbbed and pounded.

As Jack watched him go, a gentle hand touched her arm. "Whatever happens next, don't let them see you cry," said a woman softly.

Jack turned.

The lady in question was brunette and statuesque, with an angelic face and the body of a Vargas pinup model. In a figure-molding red dress that perfectly showcased all her physical assets, she possessed an air of sophisticated, ladylike chic that was enhanced by her British accent, all of which served to make her even more conspicuous in the atmosphere of pagan decadence.

The expression she wore seemed out of place, too. This bombshell looked at Jack with something like empathy.

And . . . worry?

"If he makes you cry, he wins. Understand? This isn't just punishment for Hawk and Nando . . . he's betting you won't be able to take it and you'll break down in tears," Morgan murmured, curling her fingers around Jack's bicep. "And if you do, you put yourself in grave danger. Here, weakness isn't just a character flaw." Her gaze turned flinty. "It's a death sentence."

Beyond her horror and hammering heart, Jack found her voice. "W-why are you telling me this?"

Morgan's fingers tightened around her arm. Somehow the touch seemed comforting, not at all threatening, and Jack felt the insane urge to trust her, which was only reinforced by her next words.

"Because I need you to stay alive, Jacqueline Dolan. I need you to thrive. And you're only going to do that if you don your big girl knickers and watch what's about to happen without batting an eye. If you get through tonight without showing weakness, all your tomorrows will be much easier." She smiled, a wry twist of her lips. "Trust me on this. I know what I'm talking about."

Using gentle force on Jack's arm, Morgan propelled her forward. Jack allowed herself to be led away, glad for the elegant presence beside her and the hand that felt more and more as if it were the only thing holding her up as they moved through the crowd, faces turning as they passed, the silence almost suffocating.

As it turned out, the punishment tree was aptly named.

It was old and crooked, its branches black and devoid of leaves like a haunted tree in a ghost story, the kind of thing you see silhouetted against a fat orange moon on greeting cards at Halloween. Wound around its thick, gnarled trunk were heavy iron shackles on chains. Dangling gruesomely from the upper limbs like hellish ornaments were dozens of skulls, pale and grinning in the moonlight.

That wasn't the worst part, though. The worst part was the dark stain in the dirt at its base, a sinister, spreading splotch that belied the countless punishments that had taken place beneath its naked boughs.

Hawk stood before it with his head bowed, eyes turned to the ground, hands hanging loose at his sides. Around the tree in a circle hundreds deep, the tribe gathered, still with an eerie silence, to watch. The Alpha stood at the edge of the circle with spread legs and folded arms, smirking.

Jack and Morgan were allowed to pass to the front of the crowd, and Jack's cheeks burned molten hot as they went.

"How bad will it be?" she whispered through stiff lips.

Morgan hesitated a moment before answering. "Depends on how squeamish you are."

Jack swallowed the bile that rose in her throat. Shaking hands, pounding heart, a cold sweat . . . she recognized the signs of panic, and tried to take deep, slow breaths to counteract the impending hyperventilation.

She'd seen many horrible injuries in her career. The human body was fragile, and could be torn apart in a million gruesome ways. She'd become somewhat immune to it, to the sight of blood and the wretched screams of pain from wounded soldiers and civilians in war zones, but the thought of hearing *Hawk* scream . . . the thought of watching *him* bleed . . .

"No. Weakness."

Morgan's voice was barely discernible above the roar of the blood rushing through Jack's veins, but she heard the steel in it nonetheless.

They halted at the front of the ring of silent witnesses. With a final look of warning, Morgan released Jack's arm. She walked with regal grace to the other side of the circle, and grasped the outstretched hand of a man waiting there for her, an enormous, amber-eyed male with dark hair shorn close to his head and a glower that could freeze lava. One of the few others fully clothed, he pulled Morgan against his body in a tight, possessive embrace, and leaned down to murmur something into her ear.

Morgan glanced at Jack, looked over at Hawk, then nodded. She looked back at Jack with that warning still evident in her eyes.

No weakness! Don't cry! Don't let the Alpha win!

Realizing this might be one of the more difficult things she'd had to do in her life, Jack nodded back, determined.

"We'll do this in English for your benefit, my dear," said the Alpha to Jack without taking his gaze from Hawk, who lifted his head and stared straight at her.

That focused look reminded her of his warnings, uttered such a short time ago.

One: the Alpha is always right.

Jack stayed silent, staring back at Hawk while the panic in her body rose to a burning, bright shriek of noise and pressure, painful as if her nerves were being scraped with the blade of a knife.

Was he afraid? Would he be badly hurt? What was that look in his eye?

Was it fear? Resignation?

Was it . . . blame?

Two: opinions won't be welcome.

"Lucas Eduardo Tavares Castelo Luna," the Alpha intoned, "*Salsu Maru* of the House of Air. For your disobedience you will be punished in accordance with the ancient rites, and will receive two hundred"—he glanced at Jack, hesitating only a moment before amending it to—"*one* hundred lashes. What do you have to say before punishment commences?"

Hawk's gaze was so focused on Jack's face, his stare so burning and intent, she felt as if he was trying to slip inside her body using only his eyes.

Three: Don't go anywhere without me. Especially at night.

"The same thing I always have to say. Nothing."

Hawk's voice was empty, so empty and hollow and cold, but those eyes . . .

He'd tried to warn her. He'd tried to tell her to be quiet, to be safe, to let him lead the way, yet she'd ignored all the advice he'd given her simply because she was hurt and confused over his kiss, over the way he'd reacted to it as if putting his mouth against hers had been the biggest mistake of his life.

It's your fault for writing that article and pushing us into a corner and forcing our hand!

God . . . he was right. This was her fault.

This entire situation was *her fault!*

"Then we'll proceed," said the Alpha, sounding smug, flush with anticipation.

As if cued, a man stepped forward from the crowd.

Sinewy, squat, and shirtless, he sported a black hood that covered his head. Only his eyes were visible through the dark cloth. They peered out with a feral, quicksilver flash like a wild thing from a nighttime wood. Two more males approached, stripped Hawk's shirt off his back, turned him around, and shoved him toward the tree.

Oh God—oh God—No!

They chained him to the trunk. He remained mute and as placid as a lamb, allowing them to encircle his wrists in metal and raise them over his head so he stood flush against the dead tree with his legs spread, his broad, naked back exposed, his cheek turned to the black, broken bark.

He was so beautiful it hurt to look at him.

From a small wooden stand beside the tree, the hooded man selected a cane from among perhaps a dozen of different widths and sizes. Long and tan and curved to a handle at one end, it sported small notches along its slender length, breaks that seemed sinister, able to inflict more pain than a solid one. The man in the black hood took the cane, positioned himself behind Hawk, and raised his thickly muscled arm.

The lower half of the cane was stained red.

The storm inside Jack rose to a howling, bright peak.

No! No! No!

"Wait!" Jack screamed.

Hawk stiffened. The Alpha's head snapped around. Across from her, Morgan's mouth opened into a silent O of horror, the same shape as her huge, disbelieving eyes.

The same shape as every eye in the crowd around her, as far as her own could see.

"This was my fault . . . this wasn't Hawk's fault . . . even the reason he hit Nando was my fault!" The words poured out, one over another, as Jack stepped forward into the open heart of the circle, pleading with the Alpha with her eyes, with her voice, with her outstretched hands.

"Please, he shouldn't be punished . . . I should be the one to take the lashings! It should be me! Please, don't hurt him! I'll . . . I'll stand in his place!"

Gasps and cries of disbelief from the crowd.

"No!" roared Hawk. He strained so hard against the chains every muscle in his body flexed taut with the effort. "Jacqueline— *shut up!* You don't know what you're saying!"

"You offer *belu*?" the Alpha breathed, his face gone white.

All around her were astonished, gaping faces. Even the hooded man's eyes were wide and shocked.

She didn't understand the word, but she understood the meaning.

A ritual punishment. A ritual pardon . . . with a price.

"Yes." Jack said it again, louder, to the crowd, lifting her head so her voice could travel over their heads. "Yes. I offer *belu*."

Hawk screamed in outrage. He began thrashing against his binds like a madman, kicking against the trunk of the tree and twisting his body so he could see her over his shoulder.

"She doesn't understand!" he shouted to the Alpha, the cords in his neck standing out. "She doesn't know what she's agreeing to! Don't listen to her! Don't listen!"

A tumult began in the crowd. Whispers became chatter, then shouts. Bodies turned to one another in astonishment, gesturing at her, at Hawk, at the Alpha, the energy mad and electric, until everyone seemed to be talking at once, moving closer, the circle tightening like the invisible noose that squeezed around her neck, cutting off her air.

Voices crested over her in a wave. A flash of heat engulfed her. Jack stood with her heart in her throat, staring at the Alpha in breathless anticipation, awaiting his response.

"A female cannot offer *belu*." He looked around the crowd for confirmation. "This isn't done! This is unprecedented—"

"It *can* be done," countered a firm, raspy voice.

The old man who had spoken stood near the Alpha, slightly behind him, hidden in long shadows cast from the tree.

Alejandro turned. He recognized the old man, and gave a small, respectful bow. All around him, others did the same, until the entire gathering had paid their respects to this diminutive figure. The shouts died back to whispers.

Short and bent, leaning heavily on a cane, he was clothed in a simple cloak of white, his feet bare, his head wreathed in a fluffy halo of snowy hair like a floating ring of clouds. He stepped forward slowly, gazing at Jack with eyes as keen as a freshly sharpened blade. The tiniest of smiles lifted his wrinkled lips.

"It is in accordance with *Ama-gi*. The girl can offer substitution—"

"She's not one of us!" Alejandro protested, shooting Jack a horrified glance. "She's—she's—*human!*"

Quietly, the old man said, "*Ama-gi* does not discriminate based on race, *Sarrum*. The principle of *belu* holds true regardless of the birth—or sex—of those who invoke it." His gaze, brilliant, blazing green, undimmed in spite of his obvious age, rested on Jack. His small smile grew wider, almost challenging. "If she wills it, the human woman may stand in Hawk's stead. She may offer her own pain as a tithe for his."

Jack blurted, "Nando, too! It wasn't his fault, either. This entire situation is my doing . . . it's my fault and I should be held responsible. I-I offer *belu* for Nando, as well!"

The defiant, agonized, sustained scream that emitted from Hawk's throat sent a rash of goose bumps crawling up Jack's spine, but she was undeterred. She straightened her back, lifted her chin, and nodded at Nando, who stood gaping at her on the side of the crowd in shock.

Across the circle, Morgan stood speechless, clutching her giant male, the look on her face one of awed disbelief.

Anyone who's stupid enough to even look at you the wrong way will have to deal with me.

Hawk had offered his protection. He'd gone to his punishment willingly, without complaint.

But it wasn't his fault. It was hers . . . all hers.

Above all things, Jack believed in justice. She believed in an eye for an eye. She believed in "manning" up to mistakes.

She believed in honor.

Because her own childhood had been entirely devoid of fairness, of any semblance of what could reasonably be deemed right and wrong, Jack fervently believed in taking responsibility for those errors one could claim as one's own . . .

And this one was all hers.

Hawk. My strange, maddening, wonderful enemy/protector/betrayer/friend . . . this one isn't on you.

"Mr. Alpha," Jack said quietly, looking at Alejandro, "I will tithe for both of them. I offer *belu* for Hawk and Nando."

The hooded man seemed aghast at the turn in events. He stood dumbly with the cane gripped in his hand, looking back and forth between her and Alejandro, his gaze confounded.

The Alpha stared at her long and hard. He muttered, "So be it," and gestured for Hawk to be released.

It took four men to subdue him once his wrists had been unbound. They wrestled him to the ground, shouting, throwing punches, until finally he lay on his stomach with his arms bent painfully behind his back, a knee between his shoulder blades, pinned but still struggling to get free.

He kept shouting as the Alpha opened his palm toward the hooded man, kept shouting as Jack stepped to the tree, kept shouting as the hooded man instructed her to remove her jacket and shirt. She did, hands shaking, and stood there in only her bra, deeply frightened but understanding this kind of ritual punishment meant there were rules, rules that could be learned and obeyed—or smartly circumvented.

If they meant to kill her, there would be a different kind of ceremony for that, she felt sure.

The hooded man's two assistants encircled her wrists with iron, and chained her to the tree. The rough bark scraped her stomach and breasts. The night air felt cool and soft against the bare skin of her back.

Her heart pounded so frantically she couldn't catch her breath.

"Jacqueline Dolan," said the Alpha, his voice tight and dark. "Reporter for the *New York Times* . . . *human*. You have invoked *belu* in accordance with the ancient rites, and will stand in place for the two you have named. You will receive . . ."

There was a long, terrible pause. Jack closed her eyes and rested her cheek against the tree trunk, waiting.

"Fifty lashes."

Only fifty. She sagged against the chains, grateful for this show of mercy. On the ground, Hawk began screaming.

"No! No! No! Alejandro, please! Don't! I'll take twice my punishment! She can't heal the way we do—she'll be hurt—she'll be *scarred*!"

His screams were ignored.

The Alpha asked her, "Do you have anything to say before punishment commences?"

Jack began to shake so badly the chains rattled. She looked up and found Morgan's face in the crowd, saw her standing with both hands clapped over her mouth, her eyes bright with unshed tears.

It hit her like a wrecking ball. Morgan was going to cry for her.

Witnessing her fear, this woman, this stranger—this creature she'd once argued should be exterminated—was going to *cry*. She was going to engage in that dreaded, deadly show of weakness. And there was Hawk on the ground, screaming he'd take twice what he'd been given, so she could be spared. Even the hooded one didn't want to hurt her. She'd seen it in his eyes. As she looked around the gathered faces—most stunned, some confused, others obviously feeling compassion for her predicament—she had the startling epiphany that Hawk had been right.

She *was* a bigot. She'd judged them all based on the actions of one.

Then came another swift, terrible realization: they lived in isolation like this, here in the darkest heart of the jungle, because of people like her. Because of humans, who'd hunted them near to extinction centuries ago, who were even now trying to do the same thing.

And this Draconian system of punishment she was about to become so familiar with was, in all likelihood, designed in an effort to keep them safe. Hidden.

But it actually kept them oppressed.

In a hoarse, tremulous voice, Jack said, "Yes, I do have something to say." She took several deep breaths, trying to steady her shaking voice and body, but it didn't help. So when she spoke it was with that awful, telling tremor of fear, her voice as loud as it would go. It carried well past the tree and the clearing, into the humid dark of the night.

"I was wrong to judge you. I'm sorry. I didn't know."

There was another silence, broken only by Hawk's continual pleading.

Then Alejandro said simply, "Begin."

TWENTY-ONE
Belu

Four feet long, half an inch thick, soaked in an antiseptic bath made from boiling the roots of the suma plant and the leaves of the flowering herb clavillia, the cane applied with full force to the naked skin of Jacqueline Dolan's back and shoulders was made of a lightweight, flexible wood from the Capirona tree.

Flexibility causes less damage to the underlying tissues. The skin, however, disintegrates.

At the first *crack* of impact, Jacqueline sucked in a loud, hard breath. Her back bowed, her head flew back, and her mouth opened wide, as did her eyes. She pulled hard against the wrist restraints, her fingers wrapped white-knuckled around the chains.

What she didn't do was cry out.

The next strike distorted her face to a grimace of pain. Her eyes clenched shut.

By the fifth horrible, echoing *whack*, all the color had drained from her face and she was shaking uncontrollably, her jaw gritted so hard all the tendons in her neck stood out.

She still didn't make a noise.

Standing beside Morgan, watching with his arm wrapped tightly around her shoulders, Xander muttered, "Damn."

Hawk, still being restrained by the four men on the ground, had turned his head away.

When the count reached ten, someone in the crowd behind Morgan whispered, "Ten."

Whack!

Someone else said, "Eleven."

Whack!

"Twelve." More voices, joining in with the first.

Whack!

"Thirteen."

Now the crowd took up the count in unison, their voices growing stronger with each unforgiving strike of the cane.

Whack!

"Fourteen!"

By the time the count reached twenty, the entire crowd was shouting together. And still Jacqueline was silent, though her body jerked violently with each blow. Nando looked as if he was going to vomit.

A female had never before been caned against this tree.

Their punishments, though handed out liberally, were typically less severe than the males', who were able to withstand more vigorous physical discipline as they tended to heal faster than the females. The punishment tree had seen floggings and canings and beatings of various violence and bloodshed, but never had a woman stood chained to its trunk.

Never had a human stood there.

Never had a female offered *belu* for a male . . . one she wasn't even mated to.

Whack!

"Twenty-one!" roared the multitude.

With every hit, with every vicious stroke that elicited howls of agony from almost all the previous victims under the cane's unforgiving bite, but produced nothing from Jacqueline but that awful, unyielding silence, Morgan felt a growing certainty she was witnessing something holy.

When the count reached twenty-five, Alejandro held up his hand.

"Enough."

Álefe, the tribe's *usmi*—the hooded punisher, literally translated as "he who shows the way"—lowered his arm and stepped back, breathing hard. Jacqueline sagged against the tree, swaying on her feet, her face a mask of agony. From her position, Morgan couldn't see Jacqueline's back, but Hawk's guttural moan when he turned to look at her told her everything.

Alejandro jerked his chin at the *usmi*'s two assistants, who jumped to comply with their master's command. They released Jacqueline's wrists from the shackles and chains, one at a time. When she was free she collapsed into their arms, boneless as a rag doll.

"Let him go," said the Alpha to the four holding Hawk. They did.

He sprang to his feet. He sprinted to her. He shoved the two males aside and gathered her up—gingerly, tenderly, fury and anguish twisting his handsome face—hooked one arm under her knees, pressed her chest to his, and cradled her head with his other hand, leaving her bleeding back untouched. Without a word, he turned and strode swiftly away into the darkness with a semiconscious Jacqueline in his arms. The crowd parted silently for them to pass.

Everyone watched them go.

Xander said under his breath, "I don't understand. I don't understand any of this. What the hell has gotten into Hawk? Why would he care so much about her? Did you see his face? The way he fought? And the human . . . why would she do that for him? For Nando?"

"I don't know," Morgan answered in a whisper, just as the first of the tears crested her lower lids and began to stream down her cheeks. She swiped them angrily away before anyone could see them.

This had been her idea. Though the Alpha had approved it and even pretended he'd not only agreed to it but had also thought it up in the first place, it was Morgan who had wanted this, who had risked this very outcome. She'd brought the woman here, knowing all the dangers, all the ways an outsider could be harmed or worse, and yet she'd hoped they'd somehow navigate the murky waters together to find a common ground, a safe place where they could come to understand each other. A place where they might learn to live peacefully, so they could show the rest of the world it could be done.

Now that hope was as flayed and bloodied as Jacqueline Dolan's skin.

What would she tell the world of them now that she'd been beaten bloody within ten minutes of her arrival, beaten so badly her knees wouldn't even support her own weight?

The old man in white stepped forward into the clearing. He was *kalum*, the priest, Keeper of the Ancient Ways, the oldest, most venerated member of the Manaus tribe. Without speaking, he turned in the direction Hawk and Jacqueline had gone, gazed into the darkness, then bowed low at the waist.

One by one, the crowd began to follow his example, paying their respects in silence, until the only one left upright was Alejandro.

The Alpha gazed impassively at the lowered backs of his subjects, then turned and walked slowly away.

TWENTY-TWO
So Wrong so Quickly

The fury was a thing inside of him, an animal of bloodlust and blackness that wanted to claw its way out of his skin.

Hawk couldn't remember the last time he felt such pure, unbearable rage.

With Jacqueline cradled limp and bleeding in his arms—breathing shallowly, white with shock—Hawk went to his home, his pace just under a run so he wouldn't jostle her. Cursing his lack of a ladder and the proper tools to make a pulley, he entered his home the way he always did when in human form.

He climbed the rope.

With Jacqueline a dead weight over one shoulder, he slowly and carefully pulled them up with both feet twisted around the rope, one hand pulling as his powerful legs pushed, an arm wrapped around her thighs. He navigated them carefully through the circular opening in the floor that opened into the lower level, and, once he had his feet beneath him again, took her upstairs.

He laid her on her stomach on his bed as gently as he could, wincing when she moaned.

She was conscious, but barely. When he straightened and got his first good look at her raw back up close, it was all he could do not to scream at the top of his lungs and break every piece of furniture in the room.

Alejandro would pay for this.

He knelt beside her, brushing the hair gently from her face. "I have to wash you, *namorada* . . . clean the skin to ensure there's no infection. Then there's a salve . . . you're going to be fine, okay? I'm going to take care of you. I'm going to take care of everything."

Her lashes fluttered. He glimpsed her eyes, blue, hazed with pain. She whined, a small, high noise in the back of her throat. Her lids drifted closed.

God, what had he done? How had he let this happen? He'd promised her no one would hurt her; he'd promised her only moments before they came here that he'd protect her and now . . .

Every curse Hawk had ever heard flooded his brain, and he wanted to shout them from the windows. He wanted to kill something with his bare hands. He wanted to make someone bleed.

He rushed to prepare the salve that would help her. Because he so often needed the salve himself, he kept most of the ingredients dried in glass jars in the cupboard. There were a few items that had to be fresh, an antimicrobial herb and a vine whose leaves were an analgesic, so he went into the forest for those, hating to leave her but having no choice. When he had gathered and prepared all the ingredients, he ground them to a paste with a tincture of other medicinal extracts, and returned to her side with clean cloths and a large bowl of cool water.

He saturated the cloth in the water, wrung it out, and caressed Jack's arm. She hadn't moved from how he'd left her, sprawled facedown on his bed.

"Okay, Jacqueline. I'm going to start. I'll wash away the blood first, then apply the salve. I need you to try and stay as still as possible." His voice dropped to a whisper. "I know it hurts. I'll be as gentle as I can."

She made a faint noise of acknowledgment, but didn't open her eyes.

The strap of her bra had broken during the lashings. He cut the elastic around her shoulders but otherwise left it intact so he didn't have to move her to get it out from beneath her body. Then he began.

As soon as he touched the cloth to her naked back, she gasped and jerked as if she'd been electrocuted.

"I know. I'm sorry. I know."

He stroked her arm, trying to soothe her, cooing soft words of encouragement as he gently washed away as much of the blood that had streaked down her lower back and sides as he could. The *usmi* had avoided the delicate kidney area, thank God, but there would be scars.

There would be so many scars.

Twenty-five to be precise.

Her breathing had changed from shallow to ragged, strained. He looked up from his work to find her staring at him, her lips twisted, eyes glazed in agony.

She whispered, "Boy, that was a real barrel of laughs." She cracked a smile. Then her eyes squeezed shut, her face crumpled, and she began to cry.

That was worse than anything yet. Her tears were like a sword thrust straight through his chest, punching the breath from his lungs, leaving him weak-kneed and trembling.

Hawk lowered his forehead to hers. Her skin was hot, burning hot.

"Finish," she pleaded, the barest of whispers. "Please . . . Hawk . . . get it over with."

When he pulled back he had to look away and swallow, trying to gather his wits and his strength, trying to understand how things had gone so wrong so quickly, trying not to give way to tears himself.

Mercifully, his dead father's voice remained silent.

He finished washing the streaked and caked blood from her skin. He applied a thin layer of salve with the lightest touch possible. He laid clean strips of cotton over the ointment, removed her boots and socks, and gave her small sips of water and a tonic to drink that would help the pain and help her rest.

Hawk sat on the floor next to the bed and held her hand until she fell into a still, silent sleep. He stared out the windows through the night, watching over her, keeping vigil until the light rose soft and pink over the tops of the trees.

Then he went downstairs, leaned over the porch railing, threw back his head, and screamed so loudly it sent every bird in the trees within a quarter mile into panicked, shrieking flight.

TWENTY-THREE

The New York Times, *Tuesday, October 1, 20—*

JOURNALIST MISSING, FEARED DEAD

Jacqueline Dolan, veteran reporter and senior war correspondent for the *New York Times*, has been reported missing. Last seen by a neighbor on the afternoon of Wednesday, September 25, Ms. Dolan initially rose to prominence with her coverage of the Iraq war. The first female reporter to be embedded with an infantry regiment on the front lines of a conflict, she was also one of the youngest reporters ever hired by the *New York Times*. Over the past decade, she has reported on hundreds of international military conflicts, and has traveled with US troops to war zones in foreign countries on more than a dozen occasions.

A police search of Ms. Dolan's apartment uncovered no clues into her disappearance, but friends and family speculate she may have been the target of retaliation by the subjects of her Pulitzer-nominated opinion piece, "The Enemy Among Us." A treatise on the duty of the human race to preserve our culture and history in the face of the Shifter invasion, "The Enemy

Among Us" was widely lauded as the driving force behind the adoption of new anti-Shifter legislation both in the United States and abroad, and sparked heated debate on the topic.

For now the investigation is ongoing, but anyone with any information about the current whereabouts of Ms. Dolan are encouraged to contact their local police department . . .

TWENTY-FOUR

Capture and Exterminate

Aside from being a dragon, being a dolphin had to be the most kickass thing in the world.

Slicing through the water at a speed of just over eight knots, Jenna was having the most fun she'd had in a long time. In spite of the seriousness of her mission and the current—awful—outlook for peace between the *Ikati* and humans, the simple pleasure of leaping over and swimming through seventy-two-degree seawater with a group of twelve other dolphins was sublime.

Pod, she corrected herself, glancing at the sleek forms swimming beside her. A family of dolphins was called a pod.

Though she must look odd to them, pure white as she always was in animal form in contrast with their pearl gray, they'd accepted her with the happy, curious ease of Labradors greeting a newcomer in a doggie park. She'd flown most of the way across the Atlantic toward Morocco in dragon form because it was fast-est—skirting the landmass of Spain and evading airplanes where necessary by Shifting to Vapor—but, famished and tired after almost ten straight hours of flying, she decided to rest.

Over the open ocean, there was nowhere else to rest but in the water.

So in she went.

Fish were plentiful, the water was warm, and echolocation proved to be *awesome*. It took a while to get the hang of communicating through her nasal passages, but if the other dolphins thought her clicks and whistles slightly strange, they didn't mention it.

The urge to stay in this form was strong, but Jenna was close to her destination now. She had to focus on the task at hand.

She squeaked a farewell—it sounded a bit like a creaking door—thrust hard with her powerful tail, and sailed high out of the water and into the air, where she promptly Shifted to a gull.

A moment of disorientation and some awkward wing-flapping, and she was off.

The coast loomed wide and desolate ahead of her, a strip of virgin sand with a rocky scrub landscape beyond that opened to the vast Sahara, far in the distance. A stiff headwind hindered her progress, and with her small gull wings working much harder than larger dragon ones, Jenna was exhausted by the time she reached the outskirts of the sprawling, inland city of Marrakech. In the purple-gray dusk, it shimmered beneath her like a mirage.

Scent and noise and heat rose, buffeting her in waves. Roasting meats, kebabs, and couscous from the souks; cumin, coriander, and the warm musk of curry from the spice markets; sweet honey and baked bread from the *chebakia* vendors in the medina, the soft chivvies of women calling their children home for dinner from their play in the dusty streets.

She pushed on, determined to find Caesar's hideaway near the Atlas mountains by nightfall. Perhaps she needed to Shift to something a little bigger beforehand.

The air felt strange.

Though the peculiarity of his Gift of Immortality had the unfortunate side effect of leaving him unable to Shift to panther, or anything else for that matter, Caesar did enjoy the heightened senses of his kind.

Tonight his senses told him something was amiss.

It was like . . . an electric charge in the air. Like a storm descending, only without any physical evidence a storm would produce. He stood at the uppermost point of the kasbah, in the crenellated turret that overlooked the fortress and the desert beyond, eyes scanning the night sky.

No thunderclouds, no wind, no telltale darkening of the stars that foretold the oncoming rush of sand from a sandstorm. Nothing.

And yet . . .

High overhead, a falcon soared, making wide, lazy circles. Caesar narrowed his eyes, watching it turn. He'd never seen a pure white falcon before.

Peregrine. Female.

He knew it was female because they were always larger than the males, and this one had a wingspan to rival a vulture's. That was where the similarity ended, however; this bird was beautiful and regal, nothing at all like the ugly scavengers that looked more like enormous, long-necked vampire bats, some kind of hideous prehistoric carrion eaters.

Strange . . . the falcon seemed to be looking back at him. Watching him with keen, intelligent eyes.

It folded its wings against its body and slanted into a hunting dive.

Which seemed to be aimed straight at the spot he was standing.

Knowing that the peregrine falcon was the fastest member of the animal kingdom, capable of reaching speeds well over two hundred miles per hour in its characteristic dives, Caesar took a step back. Then another, as the bird rocketed toward him, set on what seemed an imminent collision course.

He jumped into the safety of the turret stairwell with a shout of anger as the falcon swooped right down over his head, black talons extended.

"Crazy fucking bird!" he screamed at it as it passed overhead and swept soundlessly out of sight.

When he again chanced a glimpse out of the turret, he spied the tail end of the bird, receding into the distance toward the mountains, jagged as shark's teeth against the sky. It banked right and soared for a moment, then turned back in his direction.

"Nico!" he hollered down the spiral stairwell of the tower. "Get up here with your bow!"

It was probably breeding season. The stupid thing most likely had a nest nearby and was in protective mama bird mode, but he had enough problems—he didn't need an insane predaceous avian to add to them.

As he wanted with anything that annoyed him, Caesar wanted it dead.

And Nico was the best archer he had.

He trotted down the steps, reaching the bottom just as Nico arrived with his bow and quiver of arrows.

Caesar pointed up the staircase. "Bird. Big, white. Kill it. Then bring it to the kitchens; I fancy roasted falcon for dinner tonight."

Nico bowed. "Sire."

Confident Nico would make quick work of the task and he'd soon be dining on fresh bird breasts, Caesar strolled off down the echoing stone hallway.

Before dinner, he had a meeting with Marcell. There were many, many more rooms that would soon be filled aside from those in the nursery.

Very soon.

"We've completed work on the aqueduct. If all goes well with the testing, we should have fresh running water by tomorrow morning."

Caesar shook his head, marveling at the genius of his first-in-command and favorite guard, Marcell. Only yesterday he'd successfully installed the diesel generators that, in conjunction with a freezer, allowed Caesar to have that coveted desert luxury: ice.

Leaning back into his chair in what he thought of as the library, though there were no books, only soaring ceilings and a lot of empty space, he steepled his fingers beneath his chin and smiled.

"Well done, Marcell. Just in time, too. I anticipate we'll need as much fresh water as we can get within the next few weeks."

Standing as he always did whenever Caesar was present, Marcell cocked an eyebrow. "You've had word?"

"I have. They're on the move. Won't be long until Weymouth's part of the Plan is complete. And quite honestly, I think work on the subterranean dig needs to be stepped up. Substantially. Otherwise we simply won't have anywhere to put them all." He watched a long-legged spider crawl over the sill of the window across the room. With no glass to keep the outside out, the empty casements were conduits for the myriad insects, arachnids, and creepy crawlers of the desert.

Spiders gave Caesar the heebie-jeebies. They just looked so . . . evil. And this one was doubly sinister because it was *albino*. Ugh.

"As you wish, Sire. I'll double the crew and accelerate the deadline." He paused. "If I may be so bold as to make a suggestion, Sire?"

Caesar turned his attention back to Marcell.

"I find a little . . . *incentive* always helps motivation. If the men were to have a reward awaiting them if they finish ahead of schedule . . ."

His lips quirked, and Caesar grinned.

"If they finish the tunnels and all the necessary rooms ahead of schedule, they shall each be allowed to choose a female from my own personal stock in the dungeon. How's that?"

Marcell bowed. "Excellent, Sire." He straightened and grinned back at his master. "I guarantee the shovels will be flying."

At the mention of flying, Caesar's look soured. He sat back in his chair, gazing at Marcell with narrowed eyes. "That reminds me of something. Shortly after Weymouth arrives with his group in tow, he needs to have some kind of accident. Make it believable, though. Nothing too exotic. And I can't be anywhere nearby; we don't want to get off on the wrong foot with the new arrivals. But a traitor like him simply can't be trusted. If he'll turn on his own leader—even if she is a female—he's fully capable of turning on me."

Marcell considered it a moment before answering. "Perhaps a fall down a flight of stairs. The stone in this kasbah is crumbling badly; the steps could give way underfoot at any time."

Pleased, Caesar nodded. "I'll leave it to you. Just make sure I'm doing something very visible with the rest of the colony when it happens. Making some kind of kumbaya speech about unity, et cetera."

"Any idea what he has planned for that Queen of theirs?"

Caesar's lip curled. *Queen. As if a woman could ever lead. Ha!*

He rose, crossed to the windows, and gazed out into the starry, arid night. "Poison, I believe. For her and her Alpha. The two little brats I think he means to smother in their crib. Not that I particularly care about the methods. The end result is my only concern."

"And the rainforest colony? The ones Weymouth can't convince to join us?"

Caesar smiled at the stars, a glow of satisfaction spreading through his chest. "I hated my father, you know," he mused, watching the twinkling heavens. The sky was so clear here at the edge of the world, the stars winked like a million coins at the bottom of a wishing well. "Not only because he always favored my sister over me, but also because he always looked at me with such disappointment. I think if he were alive today, however, he'd be very proud of me indeed. After all, I'm carrying on his legacy. Keeping your friends close and your enemies closer, that sort of thing. I've given the hunters enough to go on so they know where to strike. 'Capture and exterminate,' were the exact words used, and I confess I've never heard two more beautiful words in my life. Whoever isn't a friend is an enemy; remember that Marcell. There are no in-betweens for us. In war, everyone must choose a side."

Marcell said with deference, "And how genius of you, Sire, to use one enemy to kill the other."

"Only the first step, that one. Once the *Ikati* are under my rule, I'll strike the final blow. What I have planned for the Expurgari and our new friend Thirteen and his corporate backers will make the Holocaust look like Sunday in the park. After that, we'll take over Marrakech, then infiltrate every major city in the world and begin to impregnate the females, just as I've done here. According to my father's calculations, it will only take a few generations for the entire human species to be wiped from the face of the Earth."

Caesar's smile grew wider, the flush of satisfaction more intense. "Three moves ahead, he always said. You have to stay at least three moves ahead of your opponent. My father loved his ridiculous chess metaphors, but he was right. The pawns will fall, the knights will fall, the Queen will be toppled . . . the whole board will be wiped clean." His voice grew quiet. "And the King will rule, once and for all. Forever."

A movement in the corner of his eye caught his attention. The albino spider, still crouched in all its diminutive creepiness on the sill, had reared up on its hind legs and was crazily waving its front legs in the air.

"Great Horus, that's disgusting," Caesar muttered, and brought his fist down hard atop it.

Nico entered the room. "I couldn't locate the bird, Sire. You must have scared it away."

Caesar sighed. "Well, no matter. If it comes back, you know what to do."

Nico bowed out of the room. Marcell said, "What have you got there, Sire?"

"A dead spider."

But when he opened his hand to scrape away the remains, there was nothing there but a fine grit of sand, blown in by the wind.

TWENTY-FIVE
In a Pickle

Hawk was pressing something to her lips.

Jack cracked her eyes open to find him kneeling beside her, holding a small cup to her mouth. It was morning; sun slanted in brilliant yellow beams across the floor and walls behind him.

"Drink," he said, his gravel voice gentle. "It will make you feel better. It has something special for the pain, and strong healing agents."

Too weak to argue, she opened her lips and swallowed the thick liquid, wrinkling her nose at the pungent stench of burnt sludge. She gagged at the taste. It was a horrid combination of scorched earth and moldy barnyard, tannic and bitter. She coughed, eyes watering.

"That tastes like ass!" she protested, her voice as weak as the rest of her.

"There she is." He smiled a crooked smile. "Little Mary Sunshine with a mouth like the devil's toilet."

"Please, that was tame." Jack spat a wet piece of plant material—bark?—from between her lips. "I never even let you hear the best ones out of respect for your delicate nerves."

Hawk placed the cup on a small table beside the bed and folded his arms across his bent knees. Gazing down at her, his eyes were both relieved and terribly sad. He looked as if he'd just awoken on the wrong side of a three-week bender.

"I'm all ears." His crooked smile widened, flashing a dimple in his cheek.

Jack wondered if there was a word stronger than excruciating that might describe the throbbing, clawing misery in her back, burning fire up and down her nerve endings. Agonizing? Searing? Torturesome?

"Fucktard," she said, through gritted teeth.

Hawk raised a brow. "That wouldn't be aimed at me, would it?"

"Assmuncher."

He wrinkled his nose in exact mimicry of her reaction to the potion he'd just given her. "Hmm. Now there's a lovely visual."

"Cockopolis."

"I think I went there on vacation one year," he mused. "It reminded me a lot of Vegas."

"Dickweasel douchewaffle motherfucker cocksucker bonehead prick."

He pursed his lips, impressed. "Anything that starts with the letters *x*, *y*, or *z*?"

Jack thought about it, then shook her head. "I'll work on it, though."

His gaze went to her back, and he sobered. "I'd ask how you feel, but I already know." Their eyes met again, and his grew tortured. He whispered, "Jacqueline, what on Earth were you thinking?"

Ah, the sixty-four-thousand-dollar question. Or was it the million-dollar question? She was having a wee bit of trouble focusing. The room had taken on a lovely glow, soft and soothing, and the heat in her back had cooled several degrees.

Damn, that nasty sludge was potent.

"Did you know swearing actually helps relieve pain?" When Hawk just stared at her silently, she nodded. "It's true. I read it in *Time* magazine. Some psychologist did a study where people stuck their hands in a bucket of ice water. The ones who were told to curse could leave their hands in the water up to forty seconds longer than the ones who were told they couldn't curse. Apparently swearing activates the brain's endogenous opioids."

"Endogenous opioids," Hawk repeated uncertainly.

"Pain-relieving chemicals similar to drugs like morphine and oxycodone." Jack giggled, liking the sound of the word. Ox-y-co-done. It began to repeat itself in her head, echoing softly in the background as she continued to speak. "The only problem is, the more you curse, the more tolerant you become of the opioids, so you have to curse even more to get the same amount of relief. Isn't that the most ironic thing you've ever heard?"

"Actually," he answered quietly, reaching out to stroke a finger lightly down her cheek, "volunteering for a nasty punishment in place of someone you don't even like and who isn't worthy to wipe your shoes on is the most ironic thing I've ever heard."

Jack considered that, closing one eye to relieve the dizziness caused by the way the room was tilting to one side. "I think we're using the word irony in the wrong way. Like that stupid Alanis Morissette song, "Isn't It Ironic?" None of the things she sang about *were* actually ironic. They were just coincidences or bad timing or total misses. I'm sorry but a black fly in your chardonnay is in no way ironic. It's gross. And a death row pardon two minutes too late is just freaking tragic, not ironic. Right?"

She paused, liking immensely the lovely weightless sensation snaking its way through her body.

I wonder if I could float? I bet I could float . . . I wonder if I could fly?

Hawk was looking at her with a combination of amusement and concern.

"And I do like you," she sighed, smiling as the last of the pain leaked out of her body, replaced by wonderful, spreading pleasure, soft as a cashmere blanket. "You're very . . . what's the word I'm looking for?"

His eyes darkened. The smile fled from his face and he sat staring at her in silence, his brows drawn together, jaw clenched.

"Broody," she pronounced. "You're very broody. You've got that whole James Dean/Mr. Darcy/Marlon Brando thing nailed. And you smell good. And you taste like the lottery. I mean, what I think I'd feel like if I won the lottery. Does that make any sense? Euphoric, that's the word. Or euphoria, maybe? I'm not sure, my brain seems to be taking a little trip to the twilight zone at the moment. Either way, I like you a lot, which is a problem, considering you lied to me, used me, and basically totally screwed me over."

She beamed at him, happy and pain free and just about as relaxed as she'd ever been.

Was it another effect of the nasty barnyard brew that made her think his breathing had changed? His posture had stiffened?

"Although since we're being honest here, I have to admit I understand the motivation. You thought I was a major bitch. Which, let's face it, I gave you good reason for. Plus you sort of apologized—actually you *did*, right? I think you did anyway, which counts. And you were all protect-y of me in the jungle—is that a word?—with Nando and those other guys, and you seemed really freaked out at the punishment tree, like you didn't want to see me get hurt. And you offered to take twice as many lashes if Alejandro would let me go, which is *totally* chivalrous.

"So I don't know. I'm in a pickle. I'm supposed to hate you but instead I think you're interesting and soulful and smart, and probably the most beautiful thing I've ever seen. And that's not even getting into how incredible you are in bed—I mean, I thought we were going to light those sheets on *fire*—or the fact that I know you have just as many skeletons in your closet as I have in mine, and you hate to admit it just like I do, which makes us alike. Also . . . you're the only man I've ever known who makes me forget about my fucked-up past. When you look at me, I feel . . . clean. Free of all the dirt, you know? As for being unworthy to wipe my shoes on, don't sell yourself short. Any woman would be lucky to have you. Hell, any *man* would be lucky to have you! And even though in hindsight it was probably a stupid thing to do, I would do it again, you know. Offer *belu*. For you, I would."

Jack inhaled a breath that felt cool and invigorating, like night air from an alpine woods. She'd never felt as free and careless, even if the room had become fuzzy around the edges and the only thing still sharply in focus was Hawk's face.

For some reason his expression was that of a man fighting hard to remain in control.

"This stuff is *amazing*! What is it? I'm seriously feeling no pain!"

"I suspect it's different than what I thought it was, but I'm glad your pain has gone." His voice was oddly raspy and constricted as if he'd recently spent a good deal of time screaming.

"*So* gone!" Jack whistled. She lifted her head from the pillow, and gingerly stretched the muscles in her back, lifting her arms slowly overhead. Feeling nothing, she tried a tentative roll onto her side, and when that produced no pain, she swung her legs over the side of the bed and sat up.

"Careful!" Hawk barked, shooting to his feet.

Smiling broadly, Jack looked up at him, but he'd averted his gaze and his face had gone red.

"Jacqueline. You need to . . . uh . . . I had to cut your bra away from your shoulders . . ."

Jack looked down at herself, surprised to see her breasts exposed, but unconcerned about it. Somehow being seminude in front of Hawk felt exactly right.

"Right. Thanks." She stood, and the shredded cotton fell to the floor. She announced, "I have to pee. And brush my teeth. And I'm hungry. And what is that pretty thing hovering outside in the tree? It's huge!"

Hawk looked where she was pointing. He turned back to her, alarmed. "That's a dragonfly. It's only two inches long."

"Really?" Jack squinted at it. "Huh!"

"Okay." Hawk took a breath, shook his head, and crossed to a polished wood dresser on the opposite side of the room. He withdrew a gauzy, white chemise, and returned to her side, holding it up between them like a shield. "Turn around. I'll help you put it on."

She complied.

"Hold your arms up."

She did, asking, "Why do you have women's clothing in your drawers?" The stab of jealousy was profoundly unwelcome in her lovely haze of happiness. "Is that Luiza's?"

"No." He threaded her outstretched arms through the the dress. "It's yours. I had it made for you when I found out you'd be staying with me. Everything you need is here." He dropped the dress over her head and she pulled it down around her waist, turning to look at him as she did. She swayed as the whole room turned with her, and Hawk steadied her with his hands on her shoulders, simultaneously frowning and wide-eyed, which made her giggle.

She unzipped her jeans and shucked them off, leaving them on the floor. "Bathroom? Or do I just pee out the window?" The horror on his face made her giggles turn to laughs.

He simply pointed. Jack turned slowly, arms out for balance, and crossed the room. It was open and bright, with spare, streamlined furnishings, the "walls" consisting of a waist-high wooden railing and nothing else. The jungle was dense all around and she had the sensation of flying through green clouds as she walked.

Whatever this stuff is, I'm going to bottle it and bring it back to New York. I'll make a killing. The excruciating pain in her back from when she'd awoken was utterly numbed.

The bathroom was a surprise. She'd been half expecting a hole in the floor, but there was a proper toilet and a beautifully carved wood sink on a pedestal, though no shower. And no mirror. Which she was thankful for when she touched a hand to her hair, as snarled as jungle tree roots atop her head.

She used the toilet, cleaned her teeth with the little foaming berries in a wood dish on the sink, combed her hair with her fingers, and returned to find Hawk leaning against the wood railing near the bed, head bowed, shoulders slumped, attitude utterly defeated.

Jack was overcome with empathy. *He looks so sad. I don't want him to be sad. I want him to be happy.*

Like me!

Smiling through her fuzzy sunshine haze, Jack stepped toward him.

A pair of slender arms slid around his waist and tightened as a cheek rested against his back.

Hawk's head snapped up. He stopped breathing. He clenched his hands around the railing so hard he thought it might splinter.

"Don't be mad. You just looked like you needed a hug is all," Jack said softly from behind him.

Her arms were around his waist. Her face was against his back. Her chest and stomach and legs were pressed against his body—*tight* against his body—and she was making a little satisfied sound in her throat, a sigh of contentment that had his eyes bugging right out of his head.

What in the hell did I give her?

Slowly, he straightened. He turned, breaking her grasp on him, but as soon as he'd faced her, she wound her arms up around his shoulders and buried her face into his neck. She stepped on top of his feet like a child, standing on his toes, and hugged him again.

"You give good hugs," she sighed into his neck. "You're very cozy for such a big bad wolf." She giggled, correcting herself. "Cat. Big bad *cat*."

Hawk had to fight to breathe. He murmured her name, arms out, hands spread wide as if in surrender. He couldn't touch her. If he touched her . . .

"You have to hug me back!" she protested, burrowing closer, and the feel of her body against his—her breasts against his chest, her pelvis pressed to his, her lips against his throat—brought the animal inside him wide awake, hissing in pleasure. Between his legs, an erection charged to life.

Get a hold of yourself, Hawk! She's completely out of it! Whatever that concoction was you got from kalum *this morning was a lot stronger than a mere healing tea!*

Unfortunately his body wasn't on board with that idea. His heart felt like a jackhammer inside his chest, and that erection was threatening to split his pants open. The urge to rip off his clothes and hers and sink himself deep inside her was almost overpowering.

Because he already knew how amazing she felt. He already knew what she could do for him, the pleasure she'd give, and so did the animal writhing inside him.

Slowly, being careful not to touch her back, he rested his hands on her hips. *Maybe if I just wait here like this for a second she'll—*

She made a low noise deep in her throat and flexed her hips against his, and Hawk thought he might lose it completely if she moved against him again. He'd never felt such fierce, intense *need*.

He sunk his fingers into the flesh of her hips, holding her still. He growled, "Jacqueline . . . stop."

She tilted her head back and blinked at him, smiling lazily, her eyes half-lidded and filled with heat. "Stop it because you like it, you mean?"

He swallowed. She fit perfectly against his body, warm and soft against his hardness and angles, and it felt so right he forgot to lie. "Yes."

Victorious, she smiled wider. "No," she whispered, grinning wickedly, and rubbed her pelvis against that straining hardness between his legs.

With a deep warning growl rumbling through his chest, Hawk fisted a hand in her hair and tightened the other around her hipbone, pinning her in place. He glared down at her, fighting the powerful instinct to take her, to make her arch and scream beneath him, to make her *his*.

She wasn't his. She could never be his. They were from two different worlds, and one day soon she'd go back to hers and he'd never see her again.

And the way he felt about her, the confusion and distraction and inability to think about almost anything else when she was near told him that on that day when she left, she'd be taking his heart with him.

Better to stop this insanity now, before she took his soul, too.

"Stop! You're not in your right mind! That drink I gave you, it's making you do this—this isn't *you!*"

She threaded her fingers into his hair, arching against him. Very throaty, she said, "This *is* me, Hawk. This is what I want to do every single time I look at you. This is what I'd do every day for the rest of my life if I could. *This.*"

She kissed him.

Everything else faded to black.

It was the same as the first time he'd kissed her at the hotel, the same as the next time in the jungle, when he was so overcome with emotion all he could do was lash out like a cornered animal because he didn't know what else to do. He didn't know why but she made him feel things he'd never felt before.

Things he was afraid of, because he knew he could never have them.

Things that threatened to swallow him whole.

Of course he kissed her back; he didn't have a choice. Once her lips were on his, instinct and desire took over and pushed his rational mind aside. His hand found the firm roundness of her bottom, and he stroked his fingers over it, pinching and rubbing, the chemise silky soft against his palm. She moaned into his mouth and he shuddered, wanting so badly to hear that while he was inside her and her legs were wrapped around his waist.

"Please, Lucas," she whispered, rubbing her breasts against his chest. Her nipples strained hard and pink through the thin fabric of the chemise. "Please. You know what I need. Please give it to me."

He groaned, closing his eyes. It *killed* him when she called him by his given name. And to ask for *that* . . .

He was going to die. That's all there was to it. She was going to kill him.

"I can't, *namorada* . . . it would be taking advantage of you. I might be a selfish, miserable bastard, but I don't take advantage of women when they're drugged!"

"What if I took advantage of you, then?" She slipped one arm from around his neck to stroke his erection through the front of his pants.

He froze. Another groan escaped his lips as she rubbed her thumb over his swollen head. He gripped her wrist and said through gritted teeth, "Don't. Do. That."

"You like it. You love it. You should see your eyes," she said, still stroking him.

He was throbbing beneath her hand. Twitching. Aching.

He whispered her name, teetering on the razor's edge of restraint, staring down at her in agony. *I can't do this. She'll hate me. This is wrong—she doesn't know what she's doing!*

With a depth of self-control he wouldn't have believed himself capable of, he placed his hands on her shoulders and set her away from him, giving her a hard little shake.

"No!" he shouted hoarsely.

She arched a brow and blinked. "You don't have to be so crabby about it."

Hand shaking, Hawk pointed to the bed. "Go back to bed, lie down, and sleep it off!"

Impossibly, she yawned, not even bothering to cover her mouth. "Maybe you're right. I am kind of sleepy." Then in a totally uncharacteristic show of obedience, she turned around, crawled up on the bed, and lay on her side with her knees pulled up and her hands folded beneath her face, as if in prayer.

She promptly fell asleep.

Hawk stood staring at her in disbelief, panting and sweating as if he'd just run a sprint.

He was going to kill *kalum*.

He went into the bathroom, unzipped his pants, took his swollen cock in hand, and stroked himself until he came with a stifled groan and mighty spurts, the entire time imagining Jacqueline on her knees before him, her cheeks hollowed as she sucked him into ecstasy, her eyes upturned to his, shining blue and lustfully bright.

TWENTY-SIX

Song of Extinction

Kalum, Keeper of the Ancient Ways, lived in a cave that Hawk had always been insanely jealous of, both for its distance from the rest of the tribe and its incredible view.

Situated on a rocky outcropping at the top of a hill beside a roaring waterfall, the cave had been hand dug by one of *kalum*'s ancestors, yet sported perfectly smooth walls and floors that conducted the wind in sighs and groans along its winding corridors. The main room gaped wide yet felt somehow snug. Thick woven rugs interrupted the cold expanse of stone floors, and clusters of candles burned in niches in the walls day and night, casting warmth and wavering light into the echoing spaces.

When Hawk came barging in like an angry bull, *kalum* was busy preparing something in a kettle hanging over a small fire.

"You gave me the wrong thing!" His voice bounced off the stone walls, repeating itself before fading into silence.

The old man glanced up at him, his face impassive as he stirred the gently simmering broth in the pot. "A proper greeting, if you please, *mar sarrim*."

Prince. It was *kalum*'s pet name for Hawk, one that made no sense in the context of his life and which Hawk always supposed the old priest uttered with irony.

The real irony, not the fake Alanis Morissette kind.

Hawk stopped, bowed, blustered, *"Ati me peta babka."* Gatekeeper, open your gate for me. Then he repeated, "You gave me the wrong thing for the girl! The potion—it was wrong!"

Kalum stirred and stirred, unperturbed by Hawk's agitated state. "Did I now? And what makes you say that, *mar sarrim*?"

Hawk began to stalk to and fro before the fire, waving his arms like a madman. "She was . . . intoxicated! Not in her right mind! She was saying crazy things, doing crazy things!"

"Hmm," said *kalum*.

"It was like she was a different person or something—like her body had been taken over by aliens!"

"Hmm." *Kalum* stirred the pot, watching Hawk as he made a fourth pass in front of it.

"I'm telling you, it didn't work, something went wrong—"

"It took the pain away." This was stated as a fact between delicate sniffs of the steam rising from the bubbling mixture in the cauldron.

"Well . . . yes. She didn't seem to be in any pain at all, actually."

"So it worked perfectly." *Kalum* tasted the hot broth, sipping from a long-handled ladle, and nodded in satisfaction. "Almost ready."

Hawk ground to a halt and stared at the old man. *"Kalum,* listen here—I can*not* have her in that condition until she heals!"

"Taxing your self-control, is she?" the old man said, mirth twinkling in his eyes.

"Wait. You knew that would happen? You knew she'd get so . . ." His face turned red.

"No. I did not. Everyone reacts differently to the brew. But judging by that"—his gaze dropped to the bulge in Hawk's trousers, the erection still refusing to diminish even after he'd finished his sad little self-molestation in the bathroom—"your little *Gibil* had her inhibitions stripped away along with her pain."

Gibil meant One of Fire. Knowing *kalum*, it could simply be referring to her red hair . . . or it could mean something else altogether.

Hawk groaned and ran a hand over his head. "You can say that again. And apparently her sense of reality, too. She actually thinks she *likes* me."

"Would that be so hard to believe, in light of what she did for you last night?"

Hawk looked askance at the old man, taking up his pacing again. "She would have done that for anyone. She's very . . . protective."

"As you are protective of her," *kalum* said with a small smile.

"That's different!"

"Is it?"

Hawk was becoming increasingly frustrated by this irritating, circuitous conversation. He didn't want to disrespect the priest, but kalum had given him a potion that was supposed to relieve Jacqueline's pain and instead turned her into some kind of horny beast who blurted nonsensical things like, "Please give me what I need," and "This is what I'd do every day if I could," right before she kissed him.

The woman was clearly not rational. Which was *kalum*'s fault!

"In case you're wondering, *mar sarrim*, anything she might have said was the truth."

Hawk froze in place. The priest was calmly crumbling a handful of dried herbs into the cauldron.

"What?"

The small smile the priest had been wearing seemed to be growing larger. "It's a common side effect. Euphoria and pain reduction are the main effects of the spirit vine, as are the occasional vivid hallucination, but I added a few special things of my own. I customized it, you understand. So if her body reacted to the potion by stripping away her inhibitions along with her pain, it also stripped away her ability to prevaricate."

Hawk stared at him with his mouth hanging open, his face blank.

"She can't lie," added *kalum*, assuming Hawk didn't understand.

But he did. He understood, but he didn't *believe*.

The priest shrugged. "Suit yourself." He ladled some of the bubbling broth into a bowl and held it out to Hawk. "Anteater stew?"

"She can't lie," he repeated, ignoring the offered bowl. "For how long?"

"For as long as it takes for her body to burn through the potion. Two days, possibly three."

"Three days!" Hawk shouted. "I have to live with her like that for *three days*?"

"It's no good shouting at me, *mar sarrim*. The only way to remove her pain was to give her the brew. And you wanted to remove her pain, yes?"

"Well, yes, but not to make her . . . like . . . *that!*"

"Hmm," said *kalum*, dipping into the bowl of stew with a spoon. He swallowed a mouthful and pointed at it. "Oh, that's tasty. You sure you don't want any?"

Hawk cradled his head in his hands, pressing on both temples in an effort to make the sudden throbbing subside. *This isn't happening. This can't be happening!*

The priest said innocently, "Don't get yourself all worked up over this, *mar sarrim*. If she's too much for you, just let Alejandro take care of her. I'm sure he'd be more than happy to take her off your hands . . . did you see how he looked at her when she introduced herself?" He chuckled. "Thought he was going to drool all over his own feet."

A spike of jealousy, scalding and black, shot through Hawk's chest. He lowered his arms to glare at the old man. "I know what you're doing, and it's not going to work!"

Kalum walked over to him with small, unsteady steps. He gazed up into Hawk's face, smiled, gave him a fatherly pat on the cheek, and said, "What you think is down, is up. What you think is up, is down. They are the same, yet they are different. Yes?"

"*Kalum*," said Hawk, jaw tight, "don't speak to me in riddles. What are you saying?"

"I'm saying the way to understand the truth is to stop resisting it. The swan that believes it is an ugly duckling is no less a swan, but for its own perception. The day is also night, the dark is also light, the hunters are also the hunted. Reality is nothing more than a mirror, reflecting back what you shine forth. The truth is a mutable beast, docile or devilish simply depending on where you stand."

Hawk stared at him, seething. "Well. How enlightening. Any clearer and it would be crystal."

The old priest looked pleased by his sarcasm. "It will give you something to think on, then." He clapped his hands together, as if summoning invisible servants. "Now get out of here; I've got two mating ceremonies and a birth blessing to do today, and you're messing up all the good energy in this cave. Scoot!"

He shuffled back to the fire, dismissing Hawk with a wave.

Hawk watched him for a long, silent moment, before turning on his heel and marching back out the way he came.

When Hawk had gone, the priest finished his anteater stew with intent mindfulness, savoring the flavors, knowing this would be the last time it would ever pass his lips.

He made it often, in batches large enough to offer bowlfuls to the many visitors he had each day, hankering after potions or ointments or blessings on babies and unions, after punishments and before cremations, during the Season of the Inundation and at *Akitu*, the beginning of the New Year. Other days he made it with tapir or tamarind or capybara meat, there were a dozen different combinations, but he knew by the time it was due for the anteater to be featured again, he would no longer be here.

None of them would.

He finished it. He rinsed out his bowl and put away the spoon, carefully drying both. Then he went to the beautiful chest at the foot of his sleeping pallet, and opened the lid.

Handed down father to son as the position of *kalum* had been, the fossilized wood chest bore the mark of every priest of the tribe, stretching back over two thousand years. It had arrived with them when they'd fled Egypt, one of the only things to survive the trek. In it were kept the sacred scrolls, called *edubba*. Written in the Old Language, they were copied by hand thrice a generation to ensure the teachings survived when the paper began its inevitable decay, victim to the rainforest's dewy clime.

Kalum knew exactly which scroll to select. His father, like his father before him, had ensured he would recognize the signs when the time came. He unrolled the parchment, gazing solemnly at the lines he already knew by heart.

It was a poem, merely four stanzas long, titled *"Sanu Enzillu."*

Song of Extinction

A prince of Air, a daughter of Fire
A mournful cry and a funeral pyre
A blooded heart, a sacrifice
Foretell the end of Paradise

A diamond Queen, aspect of white
Her two young babes, bereft of light
Augur nigh a time of strife
A battle lost to lower life

A comet red, a moon of blue
A sum of five reduced to two
An evil trickster, wishing well
Looses all the dogs of Hell

These things in all will come to pass
The sand runs out the hourglass
Harken and be not headstrong
To Death's cold arms we soon belong.

Kalum finished reading. He rolled up the scroll, placed it back in the chest atop the stack of others, and closed the lid. He said a prayer to *Ama-gi* in the Old Language, rose from his knees, and went to stare out the mouth of the cave into the vast, green beyond.

He'd known this day would come.

As soon as the new Queen had been crowned—the Diamond Queen they called her, just as beautiful, just as rare—he knew it would be within his lifetime. She had twins on a night a red comet scored the sky, and he knew the time crept closer. Then the four confederate colonies had merged, leaving only the Roman colony outside the arms of the rainforest. "A sum of five reduced to two."

And now the red-haired human, who'd arrived just last night.

Kalum had never seen a redhead before. Actually, the only humans he'd ever seen had been the indigenous tribes of the forest, glimpsed from afar, but the moment he saw her, he knew she was the "daughter of Fire" of the poem. His father had called redheads *Gibil*, "One of Fire."

Hawk, son of an Alpha, born to the House of Air, was the prince in the poem. It was his cold heart that had been awakened—blooded—by the human, her sacrifice at the punishment tree.

A sacrifice that took place on a full moon. The second full moon in a single month.

A blue moon.

As for the rest of it—the funeral pyre, the trickster, the battle—he knew those would come, too. Soon.

"And so begins our end," the old priest murmured, watching a flock of parrots burst from the tree line in a tangle of yellow and blue. They vanished with a quicksilver flash into the misted sky, and *kalum* turned back to the cave and went inside to prepare.

TWENTY-SEVEN
Tiny Buddhas

Edward, Viscount Weymouth, was mad.

Furious was a word more apropos for the emotion scraping his guts like a bowl being hollowed out by a whittler's knife. Since he'd discovered the Queen wouldn't be accompanying him and the rest of the final families of Sommerley on their journey to the rainforest, he'd been so angry he'd given himself a headache from his constant teeth-gnashing.

"Something she has do first," Leander had explained in his oblique, maddening way the day they'd left, and wouldn't be convinced to speak further about it.

Edward had the sneaking suspicion that the "something" Jenna had to do was related to Caesar and Morocco. But he couldn't do anything about it . . . for the time being.

For the time being, the Plan was put on hold.

Leander had kept him close during the flight to Manaus on his private jet, even closer during the boat and canoe rides up the rivers that snaked deeper and deeper into the jungle. There was no opportunity for him to sneak away and make a warning phone call during all the time of their journey, and now they stood in a quiet group of fifteen on the banks of a silty river, staring into the dense jungle undergrowth from which a greeting party of six large black panthers had just emerged.

"It will be a few days from here, depending on how quickly we move," said Leander quietly, nodding a welcome to the silent, watchful animals who'd come to guide their way through the forest to the colony where the rest of them awaited.

Bollocks! Days? Who knew what trouble that wretch of a Queen could stir up by then! Sweating profusely in his formal, fitted vest and cravat, Edward's fury grew.

There was nothing to be done about it, however. He'd just have to keep his fingers crossed that Caesar might discover her and take care of that part of the Plan by himself. If truth be told, Edward was more than a little afraid of the Queen . . . and not entirely sure she was as ignorant of his duplicity as she seemed.

He assured himself that didn't make sense—certainly she would have had him killed immediately if she knew—just as Leander instructed them to remove their clothes.

"I'll Shift last and ensure the saddlebags are in place, and the children are secured. Then we'll begin."

He nodded to Olivia Sutherland, Grayson's young wife, who'd been assigned to care for the twins in their mother's absence. From what Edward had seen, she'd done a thorough job, cooing and clucking over them just as she did with her own small baby, but for some odd reason she was becoming more and more pale since they'd left Sommerley.

Afraid, most likely. She'd never been outside her home colony in her life.

On the sand, the men lined up the specially made nylon bags that would strap around their bodies in animal form, holding the clothing they now wore and the few mementos they'd been allowed to take. Then with the exception of Leander, Olivia, and two other females who held the children in their arms, the gathered group disrobed silently and swiftly, Shifted to panther, and stood waiting.

Edward was last.

He'd long ago decided he preferred his human form to the animal one. He didn't want to *be* human, but he enjoyed fine clothing and fine dining and all the elevated pleasures of the highest of their society, such as eating with a knife and fork, not tearing into steaming, bloody flesh with his fangs. He was *not* looking forward to running around in the jungle like so many primitive beasts.

Which he was, to be sure ... but he was also *British*, for God's sake! He was a viscount! His rainforest kin living in the wilderness were, in all likelihood, no better than savages!

He couldn't wait to get the hell out of here and head on to Morocco, where Caesar, he guessed, knew how to serve a proper meal.

With a sigh of regret and more than a little distaste at being forced to take off his clothes in front of others—more savagery, no doubt the natives went naked all the time where they were headed—he stripped. Then he shed his shape like a snake shedding its skin, and Shifted.

Standing on four paws on the hot riverbank in the blistering tropical sun, he sighed again, only this time it sounded like a hiss.

Leander folded and packed the clothing, while Olivia secured another custom-made satchel around her husband's body that would carry the twins, snug in fur-lined pouches, secure on his back. Their own child went on the back of another male, a sturdy, reliable Assembly member with an equally sturdy wife. Once the bags were packed, Leander strapped them to the waiting animals, careful to make sure the buckles were neither tight nor loose, then removed Hope from Olivia's arms.

"In you go, love," he murmured to the baby, tucking her into one of the pouches. She gazed up at her father, silent and impassive, eyes round and unblinking, and Edward repressed the shudder that always wracked him when he looked too closely at the twins. There was just something . . . *off* about them. He glanced away as Leander repeated the procedure with Honor.

"Ladies," Leander invited. The two other women undressed and Shifted, but Olivia stood frowning, the fingers that she'd been using to unbutton the front of her dress faltering, then freezing in place.

King of the Jungle, thought Edward with a sneer, watching the worry lines on Leander's face deepen. *How far the mighty have fallen!*

"Olivia?"

She glanced up at Leander. Blinking, glancing around in confusion, she said, "I-I'm sorry. I'm not sure what's wrong . . ."

Edward's ears pricked, as did the others'. The calls of the birds and the burbling of the river took on a sinister cast.

"What do you mean? What is it?"

She moistened her lips, obviously panicking. Squeezing her eyes shut for a moment, she concentrated, then released her breath in a rush. "I can't! I can't do it!" she shrieked, shaking her hands as if trying to rid them of crawling spiders.

"Calm down, it's all right!" Leander strode to her side. Several feet away, her husband lifted his huge, wedge-shaped head and stared at her with brilliant yellow eyes, long silver whiskers twitching.

Olivia looked up into Leander's face and whispered in horror, "I can't Shift, Leander. It's . . . it's gone. It's just gone!"

Can't Shift? Tosh! What's she getting on about? Edward stared at her in confusion. Of course she could Shift—they all could. From puberty on, their latent Gifts became realized. Some later than others of course, but *all* eventually discovered their heritage. And their Gifts certainly didn't come and go like some kind of head cold!

Except . . .

Edward's gaze cut to the twins, nestled on Grayson's back. They were both staring at him with inscrutable calm, like tiny Buddhas. Together, they smiled.

All the fur on Edward's neck and haunches stood on end.

Tension gripped the group, palpable as a squeezed fist. The six animals watching from the tree line slunk forward on silent paws, hackles raised, ears upright.

"You must be cut somewhere, Olivia, that's all," Leander reassured her gently.

"Th-this is different. I can feel it—"

"No." Leander interrupted her, his voice flinty cold. He repeated it again as he reached out to squeeze Olivia's arm. She looked up at him, open-mouthed, white-faced, trembling. "You're obviously just slightly injured. A scrape, a small break in the skin—you know it can be anything. There's a cut you can't see somewhere, something you did during our travel. Perhaps in the canoe; it was a bumpy ride. Even a splinter would suffice, you know that."

The Alpha was staring at Olivia in unblinking intensity, radiating authority . . . and something much darker. Something that had Grayson prowling forward, his own hackles raised.

"It's all right, everyone," Leander reassured the group in a controlled voice. "I'll stay behind to travel with Olivia and

Grayson." He broke eye contact with Olivia to regard the group of six guides. "One of you can travel with us, to show us the way. The rest of you can proceed ahead with the remainder of my group. I don't want to delay the majority from reaching the colony and settling in."

There was a moment of indecision, a slight hesitation. But they were accustomed to taking orders, so even though there was an unspoken consensus that something was definitely amiss, Edward and the other refugees from Sommerley followed as five guides turned and vanished back into the lush green landscape from whence they came.

Before stepping into the humid, leafy unknown, Edward glanced back one final time.

Leander still had his hand on Olivia's arm. Grayson, still in animal form, stood beside her, a low growl rumbling through his chest. The lone remaining guide still waited patiently at the edge of the forest for the trio to move.

And the twins were still looking at him.

Smiling.

TWENTY-EIGHT
Gobsmacked

Three days. She can't lie. This is what I'd do every day if I could.

The chaos inside Hawk's skull was composed of howling winds, volcanic eruptions, and those fifteen words, repeating themselves with such vehement, shrieking force he wondered if he'd slipped over the fine line between sanity and insanity, and had finally lost his mind.

It definitely felt like it.

Clumsy and distracted, he trudged blindly down the hill from the priest's cave, bumping into everything as he went, not even bothering to slap away the low-hanging tree branches from his face.

Three days. This couldn't be happening!

She can't lie. That can't be possible! Can it?

This is what I'd do every day if I could.

That one was the worst. That was the clincher, the lighted beacon atop this towering skyscraper of disaster. Combined with the impossibility of numbers one and two, number three was sheer madness. Because oh *Dios mio* . . . what if it were true?

What if it were *all* true?

Groaning aloud, Hawk put his head into his hands, which was why he didn't see what lay on the ground in front of him. He walked right into it, stumbled, and fell flat on his face.

"What the . . . ?"

He leapt to his feet, shook his head, and looked around, hoping no one saw this display of complete idiocy, and realized he'd arrived home far more quickly than he realized, wrapped as tightly as he was in the tumult inside his mind.

But this didn't look like his home.

In a circle all around the base of the large tree he called home were strewn flowers, a riot of orchids, water lilies, and passion flowers that carpeted the ground, thick and fragrant. Atop the flowers were bowls of fruits of every shape and variety, handmade soaps wrapped in squares of fine linen, candies made of boiled sugar and dried fruits, pottery and figurines carved from rare wood and jewelry . . . so much jewelry laid out on swaths of embroidered silk as fine and intricate as a spider's web that the air glittered in fractured rainbow prisms of light.

He stood stunned, uncomprehending, until Morgan appeared, bearing a package in her arms. She came and stood beside him, surveying the scene.

"Well," she said after a short silence, "I can see they beat me to it."

Hawk managed a weak, "Huh?"

"You'll have to preserve most of this fruit, though. There's no way the two of you can eat it all before it spoils."

"Uh . . . uh-huh." He stared at the bounty laid before them, words failing him.

Morgan nudged him with her elbow. He turned to look at her, and she smiled. "You have the exact same look of bewilderment my husband gets when I tell him I love him."

"What is all this?" Hawk gestured to the display.

Morgan regarded him for a moment, dark brows lifted, her expression sympathetic, if slightly amused. "You men. It must be hard to go through life so completely clueless."

Hawk blinked at her. "I'd say 'huh?' again, but that would be redundant." He paused. "It's honestly all I have right now, though."

Morgan patted his arm. "I know, duckie. I have every confidence you'll figure it out eventually, however." She deposited the bundle she carried into his arms. "A little something for our new friend. Tell her it's from me, will you?"

Hawk looked down. Whatever she'd given him was light, wrapped neatly in a soft, soft fabric of indigo blue, and tied with a white silk ribbon. He looked back at Morgan.

"You're not going to tell me what's going on, are you?"

"I could, but watching you flounder is too much fun to resist. I have to take it where I can get it." She winked at him. "I'm sure you understand."

Hawk scowled. He wished he could cross his arms over his chest to look more intimidating, but her bundle wouldn't allow it. He made his voice stern when he demanded, "Morgan, I'm in no mood for games. Tell me what this is!"

She produced a lovely, ladylike laugh, chiming like a bell.

"Oh my! Positively *terrifying*!" she teased, looking up at him. "You forget who I live with, Hawk. Xander makes fire breathing dragons look like bunny rabbits. And if he doesn't scare me, you're certainly not going to!" She looked at him sympathetically.

"Although that was a good attempt. Had I been anyone else I'm sure I would have been very, very afraid." She smiled. "Extremely."

He growled and she laughed again, moving away. "Just don't forget to tell her it's from me," she called over her shoulder with a wave. Then she was gone.

And Hawk was just as confused as he was before she'd come.

He gazed up the trunk, looking at the underside of his home, and wondered what he would find when he climbed the rope.

Only one way to find out.

He carefully picked his way through the sea of gifts and began to ascend.

But Jacqueline was sleeping just as he'd left her, innocent and peaceful as a child. He laid Morgan's gift on the dresser, and checked Jacqueline for fever by pressing the backs of his fingers to her forehead. Her skin felt as it always did: soft, fine, and warm, but a normal temperature, not flush with the heat of fever. His fingers drifted down her temple and caressed her cheek, and she sighed softly in her sleep and pressed her face against his hand.

He froze. His damn traitorous heart began to pound in glee.

Hawk eased slowly away from the bed, trying not to think of those three words that might just be the death of him.

She can't lie.

He turned away, deciding to busy himself with cleaning up the mess.

By the time Jacqueline awoke to the first of the early evening rainfall, Hawk had managed to gather all of the jewelry. He'd laid it out on every available surface, where it glittered on every table and dresser and chair, festooning his home like ornaments on a Christmas tree. Making, trading, and collecting shiny trinkets had been a favorite pastime of the tribe for centuries, and though he'd never had an interest in amassing his own treasure trove, he was now in possession of a substantial collection. He didn't know exactly what to do with it all, but had a vague idea that he'd ask Jacqueline's opinion.

He'd brought up the fruit in the large basket he usually used for foraging, and had left it in an enormous pile in one corner of the living room. He didn't have a kitchen—none of them did—the preparation of food was a communal activity—so he'd no idea how he'd "preserve" the fruit, as Morgan had suggested, but thought he might ask Jacqueline about that, too.

He was just about to make another trip down the rope to gather the rest of the pottery, figurines, and candies when Jacqueline appeared at the top of the stairs, looking sleep addled. Her hair stuck up all over her head like the bristles of a bottle-brush tree.

"Do you have a shower?" she mumbled, rubbing an eye with her fist.

Hawk wondered if she remembered anything she'd said earlier, deciding quickly that he hoped she didn't. Drug-induced amnesia would make it much easier to deal with the situation.

Much easier to deal with than drug-induced nymphomania, that was for sure.

"Yes." Strange that his voice could crack like that over a single-syllable word. He cleared his throat. "I'll show you. It's this way."

She descended the stairs from the second floor and followed him silently, her eyes barely open. Once they passed through the living room and stepped out to the deck that ran along the perimeter of the first floor, she stopped dead.

Hawk turned to look at her. "What is it?"

She blinked drowsily several times. "There's a giant pile of fruit in the corner of the room."

Hawk nodded. "I know."

"What's it doing there?"

"Well . . . beginning to rot, probably."

She blinked a few more times, eyes clearing. "It wasn't there when I came in."

He was surprised she'd noticed anything when she came in last night, considering her condition. And the fact that she had been hanging upside down over his shoulder. "It was here this morning . . . I found it all at the base of the tree." He gestured to the low dresser behind her overflowing with piles of jewelry. "Along with that."

She turned, did a double-take, and stared open-mouthed at the booty. She turned back to stare at him with lifted brows.

He shrugged. "I know. Don't ask me; it just appeared while I was out. There's still a mess outside. Look." He pointed to the round opening in the floor where the rope that acted as the sole means of an entrance and exit hung down; it was bolted to the ceiling above, which was the floor of the second level.

She crossed to it with tentative steps and peered down. She said softly, "Oh. That is so sweet."

"Sweet?" he repeated, confused. "What is, exactly?"

"Well, if I'm not wrong, that looks to me like some kind of . . . offering." She glanced up at him. "Like a ritual thing. You know, when worshippers leave gifts at the temple, like that."

All the breath left Hawk's body in a soundless rush.

Maqlu. The tribe had performed the sacrament of *Maqlu* for Jacqueline, in honor of the sacrifice she'd made.

The sacrifice she'd made for him.

She was looking at him with concern. "Are you all right?"

He hadn't recognized the sacrament for what it was because he'd never seen it before. It had never occurred in his lifetime. And he was so detached from the ancient rites . . . He didn't attend the ceremonies, he didn't listen to the teachings of the priest, he'd even refused to take the bride the Matchmaker had insisted he mate with as a young man because he'd rather take the lashings than marry a female he didn't love. And he *had* taken the lashings. And more, when he refused again several years later; it was a different female this time but it had the same result. After that there were no more proffered matches, and it became sport to the unmated females of the tribe to see who could land him . . . but no one ever had. His heart remained untouched.

Until now. Until her. Until this human woman, so different from him yet so alike.

He was moved. Something shifted inside of him, a cold solidity went liquid soft, and he felt alternatively hot then cold, then broke out in a sweat.

Ama-gi . . . please, not her. Anyone but her.

Jacqueline straightened. "What is it? What's wrong?"

I think I just realized I'm in love with you.

He closed his eyes, swallowed, curled his hands to fists to control their shaking. After a moment, when he regained a semblance of control, he said, "I think you're right, about it being an offering. I think this means . . . they like you."

Her eyes lit up. "Me? Are you sure? Hawk, this is probably for you—"

"No, Jacqueline. It's for you. Trust me, it's for you."

There was a herd of stallions inside him, racing over the open fields of his heart, pounding and snorting and grinding the final shreds of resistance to dust beneath their hooves.

Yes, he was in love with her.

And he couldn't think of anything worse.

"You look a little green," she said, alarmed, coming close. She lifted a hand to touch his face but he caught her wrist and held it suspended between them.

"No." It was all he could manage in his current electrocuted, gobsmacked state.

She asked quietly, "We're back to this again? Me trying to touch you and you saying no?"

Hawk closed his eyes, swallowing a groan. She remembered. God help him.

She said, "Okay. Here's what we're going to do. I'm going to ask you something. Then I'll take a shower, and you're going to sit over there on that chair and think about what I've proposed. After my shower, you can answer me." When he opened his eyes, she was staring at him with unwavering intensity, those Caribbean-blue eyes piercing him to the bottom of his soul. "I want an honest answer, and I want you to mean it, either way."

Hawk was as afraid of the question as he was what his answer might be. He croaked, "What's the question?"

"Let's be lovers until I leave."

The stallions inside his chest reared up en masse, pawing the air and whinnying.

He managed a choked, "That's not a question."

She smiled, stepped closer, lifted her other hand to his chest where she spread her palm flat. "Can we please be lovers until I leave?"

"No." That single word was the hardest thing he'd ever said in his entire life.

"You're supposed to think about it!"

"You're not supposed to be under the influence of mind-altering substances when you ask!"

"Well how long am I going to be under the influence then?"

"I don't know," he groaned, stepping back as she pressed against him. "Two or three days. I'm not sure."

"Oh," she said, brightening. "Okay." She stepped away from him, smiling. "I can do two or three days. But after that you're toast, bird man. Now can you please show me the way to the shower?"

Stunned, barely functioning, Hawk pointed to the porch. "Outside. On the right. Use the pulley to start the flow."

Her smile grew dazzling. "You should see your face right now. God, I wish I had a camera."

Then she turned and made her way to the porch, whistling, while Hawk cursed every deity he'd ever heard of for his miserable bad luck.

Love had finally found him, and so had love's bastard brother. Misery.

TWENTY-NINE
Beautiful Ruins

Jack's sleep had been deep and restful, free of the monsters that usually stalked her dreams.

She'd awoken to the sound of gently falling rain, feeling peaceful, the drug Hawk had given her still numbing the pain and keeping her afloat on cloud nine. He'd been acting weird again, resisting her advances though she knew he wanted her as much as she wanted him. It was sweet, she decided, turning her face up to the spray of water. Sweet and silly, because she wasn't going to stop wanting him when this drug wore off.

She wasn't ever going to stop wanting him. How could she have thought otherwise?

The gravity shower was ingenious. With a bladder somewhere high up in the branches so the stored water was warmed by the sun, it operated with a simple pulley system to turn the spray on and off. There was handmade soap and some kind of citrusy-smelling gel in an unlabeled jar she assumed was shampoo; and she washed her hair and body in dappled sunlight, mindless of the strips of fabric on her back that were slowly peeling off and landing at her feet in sodden blobs. When she was finished, she dried off with a towel and went back inside.

Hawk was sitting with his head in his hands on the bed, looking as if he'd been run over by a truck.

"Did you sleep at all?" she asked.

His head jerked up. He stared at her, emerald eyes bloodshot and wild, and cleared his throat.

He seemed to be doing that a lot.

Jack had wrapped the towel around her body, but unwound it and began to blot her wet hair with it. Hawk turned beet red, shot to his feet, and turned his back, standing with his hands on his hips.

He muttered to himself, "I'm going to *kill* that old man."

"Hey, what's this?" Jack picked up a package wrapped with a white silk ribbon from the dresser.

Without turning, Hawk said, "It's a present. From Morgan. For you."

It sounded as if he were having difficulty getting more than a few words out at a time. "Does nudity bother you?" she asked. Curiously, it no longer bothered her, though she clearly remembered that it used to. Why, she couldn't fathom. It seemed so natural to be naked, especially here in the jungle.

Especially in front of him.

"Let's talk about something other than nudity," he said through clenched teeth.

Jack stood thinking a moment. "Do you think you should take a look at my back before I get dressed? Most of the bandages came off during my shower."

"You got them wet?" he shouted, spinning around. He realized his mistake, clapped his hand over his eyes, and did a quarter turn.

"Oh. Yes. Was that bad?" She was having a little trouble differentiating between what was good and bad. Everything just seemed so *good*.

"Jacqueline. Listen to me carefully. Put the towel back around your body, and come over here and sit on the edge of the bed." He paused. "Can you do that for me? Please?"

She did, and sat waiting. He lowered his hand from his eyes and glared at her. He pointed.

"Turn that way."

She complied again, commenting, "You're really crabby today."

He blew out a hard breath and sat down on the edge of the bed behind her. "Pull your hair over your shoulder."

Once she had, he eased the towel down a few inches past her shoulder blades. Silence.

"How does it look?"

His voice came a little easier. "Better than it should. Stay like that; don't move."

He rose from the bed and was back in a moment. Then he began to spread ointment over her skin.

It was cool and smooth and wonderful, especially with the added warmth from his fingertips. "That feels so good," she whispered, shivering in pleasure.

He froze. Seconds later, he resumed a little more tentatively. She kept quiet because she didn't want him to stop, and she sensed he would if she opened her mouth again.

He worked his way across both shoulders, down her spine, over her ribs on either side, ending just above the small of her back where his fingers lingered just a moment too long.

Then he said quietly, "Done."

She turned to him so quickly he flinched. They stared at one another in silence for a long moment, the only sound the rain drumming softly on the roof above.

"I did something wrong again, didn't I?"

He closed his eyes and breathed slowly in and out through his nose, gripping the small container of ointment so hard his knuckles were white. "No. You didn't do anything wrong."

"Then why are you angry with me?"

He opened his eyes, and they were pained. "I'm not . . . don't think that. I'm not. It's just . . ."

When he didn't go on, Jack said, "I meant what I said before, you know. It's not what you think; it's not the drugs. I know what I'm saying when I say I want you."

His eyes widened.

She leaned forward, repeated softly, "I want you, Lucas."

He crushed the jar of ointment in his fist.

"Oh! Let me see your hand!" He'd hurt himself! Jack peeled his fingers open one by one as he sat there breathing raggedly, his jaw tight, nostrils flared.

"It's. Fine."

"It's not! You're bleeding, Lucas!" The blood was oozing through the mess of clear goo and broken glass in his palm.

"Stop calling me Lucas," he said roughly.

"Stop being such a baby!" she shot back, irritated that her lovely fog in Pleasantville was being invaded by his not-so-lovely mood.

"You stop being—like you're being!" he roared, red-faced. Jack stilled.

She said innocently, "Oh, you mean . . . like this?" and let the towel fall to her waist.

His gaze fell to her naked breasts and his eyes went dark. His expression turned hungry, oh so hungry, but also hard. Emotion was rolling off him in waves, anger and desire and something else, a terrible, heavy thing with depth and midnight blackness.

"You wouldn't offer yourself so lightly if you knew what I really wanted from you," he threatened, deadly soft, his body still as stone. He looked into her eyes and for a moment she almost felt fear.

But then she saw it.

Longing. Loneliness.

Suffering.

She recognized it instantly. She'd glimpsed it on her own face often enough in the mirror to know that look anywhere, that urgent pathos, welling to the surface.

That total lack of hope.

She put her hands on either side of his face. He closed his eyes and turned away, but she forced his head back, forced him to look at her. He allowed it, breathing hard, every muscle taut, every inch of him bristling.

"I don't know what's on the other side of this moment," Jack whispered, feeling her own hands tremble as she cradled his face. "And right now I don't care. All I know for sure is that I'm thousands of miles from home and you're the one who brought me here . . . and I want you, Lucas, no matter how crazy that might be."

He'd begun to shake. "You don't know what you're—"

"I. Want. You." Jack kissed him. Gently, just a brush of her lips against his.

He froze, not responding. Not pulling away.

She tried again, softly stroking her tongue across the seam of his lips. He gasped as she sucked on his lower lip, drawing it between her teeth. He was watching her, his eyes wary, heavy lidded but wolf bright, his breathing erratic, not participating and not touching her, just allowing her to do as she pleased.

She began to explore his mouth with her tongue.

She slipped it between his lips, using gentle suction and gliding, getting a jolt from the connection as his tongue slid against hers. Her hands went around his neck, her fingers threading into his hair, and she pulled him closer, deepening the kiss.

One of his hands closed around her shoulder. His shaking had worsened.

"I took advantage of you once," he said hoarsely, pushing her away. "I can't do it again. I won't."

In answer, she took up the edge of the towel, wiped the broken glass and ointment from his hand, dropped the towel on the floor, and crawled into his lap.

He groaned as she pressed her naked body against his.

Jack wrapped her arms around his broad shoulders and leaned close to his ear so her lips brushed his earlobe as she spoke. "Let me ask you a question, Lucas. Does it feel to you right now that you have some kind of advantage over me? Because if I'm being honest, I really think I happen to have the upper hand at the moment."

He sank both his hands into her damp hair and grabbed fistfuls of it, pulling her head back to stare down at her in agony. "You're drugged! You'll hate me tomorrow!"

"There *is* no tomorrow," she whispered. "Everything we have is right here, right now." She pulled his head down to hers, taking his lips. He moaned, a deep, masculine sound in his throat, and dropped a hand from her head to squeeze her bottom. Needing to feel his hardness at the center of her, where the ache had become a gnawing, burning need, she wriggled around in his arms and straddled him. He was hard and huge between her legs, the material of his pants the only thing between them.

"Jacqueline," he protested, grimacing when she rocked against him, his hands spanning her hips.

"I need you, Lucas," she said, begging softly against his mouth. "Please. *Please!*"

It was that final, soft plea that broke through the last of his tenuous restraint. With a strangled oath, he leaned in and kissed her so ravenously he thought he might draw blood.

She made a little squeal of pleasure when he broke the kiss, panting, to take her breasts into his mouth. First one nipple, then the other, feeling so greedy and out of his mind he was sucking hard, using lips and tongue and teeth to taste her, growling like an animal, unable to restrain himself, kneading her soft flesh as he ran his tongue over and over and around those hard puckered nubs, loving how they grew even harder as he suckled them.

"Yes," she groaned, arching back into his hands, shivering. "God, yes, please, yes!"

He remembered how she was the first time at the hotel, totally unrestrained and uninhibited, and she was the same now, grinding her pelvis into his erection, pulling his hair so hard it was painful, begging him in gasped breaths to taste her, kiss her, be inside her.

And he loved it. He loved every mad, wild, breathless second of it.

He loved it even more this time because he knew her, he knew how strong and brave and wonderful she was . . . and because he knew it had to end.

"I can make you come," he panted, breaking away from her beautiful breasts to stare up at her face. "This doesn't have to be for me. I can give you what you need without . . . I don't want . . . I don't need—"

"Don't you dare!" she said vehemently, grabbing hold of his face and staring at him, going from lusty to livid with whiplash speed. "Don't you say another bullshit word! Don't you ever lie to me again, Lucas, do you understand me? Never!"

He stared back at her, speechless, his body threatening to erupt into flames if he couldn't get inside her.

"That's right," she whispered, gentling, satisfied by whatever she saw on his face. She kissed him again, the most tender kiss he'd ever had in his life. "Your eyes tell me everything, Lucas. Your eyes say, 'I *do* need,' and 'I *do* want,' and 'I *do* care,' no matter how much your mouth says the opposite. So I'm telling your mouth to shut up. Let's let your eyes do the talking from now on, okay?"

She was looking at him, waiting for an answer, her pulse beating hard and fast in the hollow of her throat.

How can you see me? How can you see inside me like this? How can you undo me with a single look?

Hawk was overcome by the wave of emotion that swept over him. He felt bare, naked, like she'd stripped away every layer of steel he'd laid over his heart and it lay there raw and vulnerable inside his chest, beating just for her, just because of the man she made him feel like when she looked at him like this. At that moment he understood with excruciating clarity why a man would kill for or die for a woman, why he would protect her with his own life, why he would lay his soul at her feet and swim through shark-infested waters to get her a lemonade if that's what she asked him to do.

He would do anything, give anything, to have this woman look at him forever the way she was looking at him right now.

For the first time in his life, Hawk felt as if he *belonged*. Here in this room with her in his arms, in deepening twilight with the rain singing a sad, soft melody through the trees, he felt like he was finally home.

Looking into his eyes she whispered, "Me, too, sweetheart. Me, too."

He closed his eyes to hide the moisture welling up, afraid he would drown in this river of insanity.

Gone. She'd be gone in days or weeks . . . and this feeling of beautiful homecoming, of *rightness*, would leave with her.

But then she kissed him, and he forgot about tomorrow, forgot about anything else.

There was only her. There was only the two of them. Together. Alone.

He tore his shirt off over his head, throwing it across the room. They kissed again, frantic, hungry, and he loved the feel of her breasts against his bare chest. He crushed her against him, even in his reckless fever mindful to avoid hurting her, and she stripped off his belt and unzipped his pants, finding the way of it even without breaking the kiss.

She pushed him down on the bed with a hand on his chest, yanked his pants down to his hips, and with both hands wrapped around his swollen shaft, slid his erection into her mouth.

He groaned, loud and broken, his head tipped back into the mattress, body bowed. His eyes slid shut as she stroked him with her tongue, sucking and wanton and wonderful. He slid his hands into her hair and cradled her head, helpless against the pleasure of her mouth, his hips flexing instinctively, thrusting up into all that amazing hot wetness, every muscle in his body straining.

He moaned her name as she took him all the way to the base.

He smelled rain and heard the distant rumble of thunder, felt the crackle of lightning in the air, felt himself on the verge of cracking wide open, the pleasure so intense it threatened to push him into oblivion.

Too soon!

"Jacqueline," he rasped. "Please." He only managed the two words but she understood. Still holding his stiff shaft in one hand, she sat up, crawled atop him, and sank down on top of his erection, until he was fully seated inside her.

God—tight—beautiful! His breath rushed out in a hiss.

She leaned over and kissed him. He sank his fingers into her bottom and thrust up, hard. She cried out and he thrust again, loving her expression of pure pleasure, loving the way her nails dug into his shoulders as she clung to him, gasping, riding him and rubbing her breasts against his chest. She arched back and he sucked a nipple into his mouth, nipping with his teeth, nipping harder when she moaned how good it felt, encouraging him with her hands around his neck and her hips undulating with each of his thrusts.

He sat up, taking her with him. He sank so deep inside her they moaned together, his own husky sounds muffled by her breasts. She wrapped her thighs around his hips and rocked against him, shaking and breathless, her heart pounding against his chest, keeping time with the furious beat of his own.

"*Namorada*," he whispered, gazing up at her face in rapt amazement. "*Namorada minha.*"

She looked down at him, their eyes locked, and Hawk felt as if time itself had stopped, and all of the universe had shrunk down to the few inches between their faces.

"We'll always have this," she whispered back, her voice shaking with emotion, the look in her eyes almost tortured. "No matter what happens in all our tomorrows, we'll always have tonight. Promise me you'll never forget tonight."

Hawk slowly nodded.

He knew in the darkest part of his mind, where he kept all the truths that were too hard to bear, that his life had reached its peak in this moment, and there could be nothing in all those tomorrows to come that would ever compare to this. To her, so fine and fierce in his arms, to the way his soul seemed to have expanded to encompass everything around them, the room and the trees and the forest, the world itself.

He'd never felt so alive, or so humbled. Or so *full*, as if he'd been empty for all eternity, and it had taken this one human woman to breathe life into him until he was real and complete, the Tin Man who'd finally been given his heart.

Jacqueline nodded back. A silent pact was sealed.

Tonight would brand them—for better or for worse—forever.

As gently as he could, Hawk eased her down to the mattress. She told him with her eyes and her smile that it was fine. It didn't hurt. Still inside her, he bent and kissed her and she wrapped her arms around his back, raising her legs and crossing her ankles around his waist to cradle his body with hers. She coaxed him to move with a fluid motion of her hips when all he wanted to do was stare down at her, memorize the pattern of freckles across the bridge of her nose, count each golden eyelash, note every fleck of blue and green and silver in her eyes. But his body was a slave to her, subject to her will, and that motion of her hips coerced him in a primeval, irresistible way.

He began to thrust. Slow, shallow strokes as he watched her face for any signs of pain.

"Deeper," she breathed, running her hands down his back and arching against him.

He complied, flexing his hips, the animal inside him roaring with pleasure when she gasped his name. He thrust again, and again, each time with added force, until she was clawing at his back and crying out, her head tipped back and her hair spread wild around her.

He began to lose himself.

Sensation pummeled him from every direction. The warm, clean scent of her hair and skin, the heat of her, the satiny curve and weight of her breast in his hand. The sound of the rain and her cries and his own, ragged breathing, the feel of the blood rushing through his veins. Pleasure, searing, white-hot, surged up his spine, and just as she opened her eyes and looked up at him and gasped, "Yes, now—please—with me now!" Hawk slid over the edge of reality, utterly abandoning himself to her, to the magic they made together.

He pumped deep. Once, twice. He felt her sex clench around the length of his shaft, felt the rhythmic pulse and throb of her orgasm begin, and he shouted, jerking, as his own orgasm ripped through him and he spilled his seed inside her.

The intensity of it stole his breath.

It went beyond pleasure, closer to pain, a burning that scorched his body and emptied his mind and spun him off into wordless oblivion. He could only make hoarse, haggard cries as he throbbed and twitched, delirious, his head thrown back, every muscle in his body tight.

She whispered his name. He looked down at her. They stayed like that, panting, gazes locked together through the final, furious waves. When their bodies slowly began to relax, still they stared into one another's eyes as the trembling and the tautness eased, rocked by the occasional pulsing aftermath until those too had stopped, and the only thing left was their labored breathing.

He rolled her atop his body, pushing her hair from her face and bringing her head to his chest where he cradled her, and stared up at the shadow-streaked ceiling in wonderment as his heart continued its wild, ragged beat, its song of ecstasy and madness.

"So strong," she whispered, her cheek pressed to his breastbone. "You have such a strong heart."

Hawk gently kissed Jacqueline's forehead. He wanted to say, *It belongs to you. It will belong to you forever,* but he didn't. He couldn't.

He could never let her know how she'd wrecked him for any other woman, or how he knew they were doomed, a modern cross-species Romeo and Juliet, or how badly he suddenly wanted to cry.

All he could do was hold her.

Love her.

Surrender himself to the beautiful ruins of their unhappily-ever-after.

So that's what he did, all night long.

THIRTY
The Chairman

Watching a daddy longlegs pick its way with graceful delibera-
tion up the wall of the conference room in pursuit of an unsus-
pecting fly at Section Thirty headquarters in Luxembourg,
Thirteen idly wondered if there was anything so ridiculous in the
entire world as a religious fanatic.

No, he decided, listening to the man barking like a rabid dog
on the other end of the phone line. *Miley Cyrus is more sensible
than this* dummkopf.

"Jahad," he interrupted patiently, "be reasonable. I understand
your predicament, and the goals of your organization." In Thirteen's mind, the word "organization" had air quotes around it—
Jahad's band of psychopathic brothers who'd hunted the *Ikati*
since the Inquisition were more akin to a serial killer fraternity

than anything else. "But the surest path to success is partnership, even if our objectives seem to be at cross purposes."

"Cross purposes" was putting it lightly. The goals of the Expurgari and the goals of Section Thirty were in total discord.

"They must all be exterminated!" hissed Jahad. "They will escape from any facility you build—you can't contain *mist!*"

Ah, but you could. There were ways.

"We only need a few specimens, Jahad. A dozen at most, you can slaughter the rest—"

"Even one is too many!" Jahad shouted. "They must be purged in the fire of righteousness! They are an abomination unto the Lord!"

Thirteen rolled his eyes.

"I need to call you back, *freund*," he said as a blonde in a tailored black suit holding a cell phone mouthed *the Chairman* at him through the conference room's glass door. Thirteen hung up on Jahad, rose from the table, and took the cell phone. He nodded at the woman—one of two hundred operatives in the facility—and held the phone to his ear.

"Everything is ready," said a man on the other end of the line.

The voice was cultured yet utterly lacked any other discernible quality of individuality: it was neither high nor deep, was devoid of accent or distinctive speech patterns, and always stripped of emotion. To Thirteen, the voice sounded nothing so much as clean, or perhaps empty, and he'd often wondered if it was computer generated, or enhanced by some electronic device.

He'd never before heard a human voice sound quite as soulless.

Not that it bothered him. He quite liked the idea of working for a man with no soul. There were few better ways to advance in this world than to lack any sense of moral compunction, and the Chairman—so called because no one in all his hundreds of multinational corporations knew his real name—had advanced very far indeed.

"I'm having a little trouble convincing our friends at the Vatican of our agenda," admitted Thirteen.

The Chairman chuckled, and even that sounded empty. "We'll give them more money. Money relieves even the most pious man of his scruples. God Himself could be convinced to look the other way if He were given a big enough bribe."

"We'll have to go over Jahad's head. He's not the sort who cares about money."

"Then we'll send the money directly to the pope himself. I've dealt with him before, when he was cardinal. He's a reasonable man." The Chairman paused. "To Jahad we'll send a goat. Or three."

Yes, that would be more apropos. The last time he and Jahad had teamed up to hunt the *Ikati*, Thirteen had unfortunately acquired firsthand experience with Jahad's unnatural . . . fondness for the cloven-hoofed animals.

"And if that doesn't work, we'll cut the Expurgari off altogether," the Chairman added. "We don't need them for this."

"True. But we also don't need them as an enemy. They hold the worst grudges, and their power is still considerable. And if we can use their minions for the bloody work, so much the better. I don't like the idea of putting too many of our people in harms' way." Thirteen had seen what terrible things fangs and claws could do to fragile human flesh. His own mother had been mauled to death by a tiger in a circus when he was a boy. The experience scarred him, left him with a pathological hatred for cats, and a thirst for vengeance, all of which served the Chairman's purposes to a T.

There was a pause, then the Chairman said, "If this operation goes successfully, Thirteen, you'll be promoted to Two."

Everyone in the organization had a number, a straightforward indication of their status within the association. The Chairman himself was One. Thirteen sank slowly into the nearest chair, overcome. "Sir," he whispered.

"I'm counting on you. This is the culmination of my life's work. If we can get even one of these creatures into captivity and conduct the necessary experiments, we can change the course of history. Tell your friends at the Vatican whatever they want to hear, and I'll take care of their compensation." There was a slight pause. "But I want to make myself clear on one point, Thirteen."

"Yes, sir?"

"Failure is not an option."

Though his hollow voice contained not a single inflection of threat or menace, those few words were enough to convey that Thirteen's employ with the Chairman wouldn't be the only thing terminated if anything went awry.

Because he was the kind of man who accepted unpleasant realities and had never held the expectation that his life would end quietly, Thirteen simply answered, "I understand you perfectly, sir."

He knew better than to promise success, however. No matter how well prepared the soldiers were, no matter how the odds might seem stacked in their favor, the outcome of any battle was unforeseeable. To think otherwise was only self-delusion, a mental weakness of which, fortunately, Thirteen was free.

"The op goes live at zero five hundred hours October fifteenth. I need you at the Manaus Air Force Base at eighteen hundred the evening prior for briefing."

"Brazil's military is cooperating?" Thirteen was surprised. He'd thought they were going in with the Circuit, the Chairman's private military company. That was one of the reasons he'd needed to ensure the cooperation of the UN; the hiring of mercenaries was prohibited by the United Nations Mercenary Convention.

The Chairman said, "I'll give you one guess as to why."

Money. All things in life ultimately came down to that. He made a sound of acknowledgment.

"And Thirteen?"

"Yes, sir?"

"If you manage to capture only one of them . . . you know which one I want."

Thirteen smiled, thinking of the anonymous phone call they'd received from someone who'd said he wanted to "serve mankind." The information he'd given had been vast and invaluable, with details only someone who'd lived in close proximity to the creatures would know—abilities, weaknesses, locations—and one particular detail that caused Thirteen to shudder in disgust.

There was one *Ikati* who could Shift not only to an animal, or to a puff of air.

One of them could Shift to *anything*.

"*Verstanden*, Herr Chairman," said Thirteen. Understood. He understood everything, and he felt peace descend on him, the kind of peace only clarity can bring.

In less than a week, he'd capture that Queen of theirs, or he'd die trying.

As would they all.

The Queen in question was, at that very moment, flying southwest at breakneck speed over the Atlantic Ocean.

Capture. Exterminate. Those two words had become the resident demon inside her skull.

She'd meant to stay longer, to spy on Caesar, gain some insight into a weakness they might exploit to end his life, but then she'd heard about Weymouth, about what he planned to do to the colony, to her husband and children . . .

Her muzzle curled back over long, sharp teeth. Fury rose inside her, sharp as knives. At long last, she'd identified the snake in the grass.

If he lays a finger on any of them, I will hunt that bastard to the ends of the Earth.

Skimming the underbellies of the clouds, her will held her aloft when her wings faltered. She was exhausted from her flight from England to Morocco, and hadn't rested nearly long enough. With at least a two-day flight into the heart of the rainforest ahead of her, Jenna knew her will would be put to the greatest of tests.

But failure wasn't a possibility. Not with so many lives at stake.

Sinuous and silent as smoke, the white dragon pumped her wings harder. She pushed upward into the cloud layer, moisture beading her lashes and the ruff along her neck, sliding off pearlescent scales, then punched through it like a bullet through wet cotton, trailing mist behind her barbed tail in long, looping curls. She climbed high, as high in the atmosphere as she could go, where the air was thin and hard to breathe but offered far less resistance, and soared into the heavens, shooting like a star across the sapphire sky.

I will hunt him until the end of time.

THIRTY-ONE
Sharing Stories

As anyone who's ever been in love knows, time isn't a fixed thing. Time is flexible. It bends. It stretches. It even stops, curling back on itself like a cresting wave, so that a single moment can be lived over and over with the suspended weightlessness of infinity.

Propped up on one elbow on the bed, floating in that weightless space where lovers often find themselves, Hawk stared down at Jacqueline. Content, awash in a sensation he thought could most closely be described as bliss—was this what heaven felt like?—he drifted on a current outside the place where clocks tick and watch hands turn and sundials tell their tales with growing shadows.

"Are you hungry?" He was whispering, unwilling to break the spell. Stretched out nude beside him, their legs intertwined, Jacqueline reached up and gently stroked his cheek.

"You've been hand-feeding me fruit and sweets all night. How could I possibly be hungry?" She was whispering, too, and her soft laugh sent a shiver of happiness through him. He leaned down to nuzzle her neck.

"I had to make sure you kept your strength up," he said, and they laughed together.

Hours and hours of lovemaking, beautiful as poetry, raw and tender and altogether unforgettable. How had he ever thought emotionless encounters with females he didn't really know or care for were fulfilling? Those empty couplings seemed now as hollow as seashells at the shore: pretty, lovely trinkets, but ultimately dead.

"Well, it certainly worked." She kissed him, running her foot up the back of his calf. "Why do you call yourself Hawk, anyway?" she said against his mouth. "You're not a bit birdlike, as far as I can tell."

He smiled, gazing down into her soft eyes. "I'll take that as a compliment."

She shrugged, coy, and he swatted her bare bottom.

"Don't you dare start that again!" she squealed, pushing against his chest. It didn't move him, of course. Nothing could move him from his present spot, attached to her side securely as a barnacle.

"You loved it," he said, his voice thick.

"Shut up and tell me about your silly nickname," she demanded, smiling at him, and his heart swelled inside his chest.

"First I want to take a look at your back. Sit up."

Her response was to yawn. A shiver ran through her body. All her muscles pulled tight, then she relaxed back against the mattress with a contented sigh. "Still can't feel anything. I'm sure it's fine."

Fine was something he very much doubted. He needed to inspect it with his own eyes. He'd been careful—as careful as he could be while in an altered state of crazed lust—but now he was beginning to realize he might have unintentionally hurt her, and *kalum*'s spirit vine concoction ensured she was in no state to feel a thing.

I wonder what she'll feel about last night when it wears off.

He pushed aside that thought with ruthless determination. Time was still on his side, and he was going to enjoy every single second of it.

"Up." He righted himself and pulled her along with him.

She grumbled and groused as he gently turned her away and brushed her hair over her shoulders. Then he stared in silence at what he saw.

The skin of her back was no longer raw. It wasn't healed, per se, but neither was it broken. It was striped pink and white in a raised crisscross pattern from her shoulders to six inches above her waist, a pattern that should have still been oozing blood and pus. It wasn't. She would most definitely be scarred, but the healing process was . . . well, it was remarkable.

He owed *kalum* big time.

"I told you it was fine," Jacqueline said, smiling lazily at him over her shoulder. "You should listen to everything I say from now on. Clearly I'm always right."

"Oh, *really*?" Equal parts relieved and amused, he wriggled his fingers into the curve of her waist, and she shrieked.

"No tickling! I hate tickling!" She leapt from the bed, but he was faster. He caught her up in his arms before she could take two steps, and held her tight against his chest.

"I bet it's one of those things you *say* you don't like, but you actually love," he teased, loving her weight and warmth in his arms. "Like spanking."

"Or like you," she said, her head tilted down, gazing up at him from beneath her lashes.

It hit him like a wrecking ball in the chest. He froze. His heart stuttered to a dead stop.

Or like you.

She was toying with him. She was incoherent. She was just teasing.

Right?

She can't lie. She can't lie.

Kalum's words started up a broken-record repetition inside his mind again, and he had to force himself to draw breath into his lungs or he'd pass out cold with her in his arms.

"I want to hear about your nickname!" she insisted, winding her arms around his neck, and resting her head against his shoulder, acting as if nothing had just happened at all. Acting as if his entire universe hadn't slid off the edge of existence and exploded in space.

"Ah . . . I . . . it's not very . . ." Hawk swallowed, blinking past his disbelief and the blind, aching hope that had stunned him like a two-fisted punch.

"Tell me." She pressed a kiss to the hollow of his throat.

He closed his eyes briefly, willing himself calm. Willing the room to stop spinning madly. "It's easier if I show you," he said, then gently set her on her feet.

He pulled on a pair of pants, selected a clean chemise for her from the dresser, and helped her into it. Then, threading her fingers through his, he stepped out onto to the porch that surrounded the room, leaned against the wood railing, and looked out over the rainforest, training his eyes to the upper canopy and emergent far above.

When she looked up at him, questioning, he said, "Wait a moment."

She watched him, waiting, while he scanned the sky.

They stood in silence for several minutes. Then he saw it.

A harpy eagle.

His Gift was effective with any kind of bird, from hummer to parrot to toucan, but the harpy eagle was his favorite. The largest and most powerful of the raptors of the Americas, it was named after the harpies of ancient Greek mythology, the wind spirits that took the dead to Hades and were said to have the body of an eagle and the face of a woman.

In Portuguese, the eagle was called *gavião-real*. Royal hawk.

It soared far above, a black-and-white blur against vivid blue, hunting. Hawk wrapped his hand tightly around Jacqueline's. "Close your eyes."

She did. Then Hawk released himself from his body, and because their hands were grasped, he was able to take Jacqueline along for the ride.

A rushing; the sensation of gravity pulling in the wrong direction, a roaring in his ears, and then it was done.

The rainforest lay vast and sparkling beneath them, carpeting the landscape for mile upon endless emerald mile. He wheeled to the right, tucked his wings against his body and fell into a sharp dive, relishing the wind on his face, seeing every dewdrop on every leaf, the air scented of earth and rain and river. Jack was with him, tethered by the connection of their hands, flesh upon flesh, conducting magic through their veins, and he felt her exhilaration and shock as if it were his own.

She felt no fear. Only pure, astonished delight. With a cry of joy that pierced the morning sky, Hawk opened his wings and flew higher.

He rolled. He banked and wheeled and soared. He flew high and low, grazing the treetops, skimming the dark, serpentine Rio Negro—spotting the mirror flash of piranha and the pale ghosts of river dolphins below—then coasted higher on a warm updraft. On the other side of the rise, the Earth fell away abruptly, and there was only wind and air and sky, blinding blue. He flew higher still, and below the land curved gently away in either direction.

He'd never shared this with another living soul.

For another thirty minutes he played, showing her all his favorite spots—the small caves behind the waterfall, all the hidden grottos and pools and glens he haunted in his wild and lonely youth—until by the end of it, his wings ached and his hunger had grown to a sharp, gnawing thing, demanding to be sated.

He didn't think he'd subject Jacqueline to that particular activity, so he released the bird and came rushing back into his body, as did she into hers, both where they'd left them, standing empty and motionless on the porch in dappled morning sunlight.

Hawk turned to her after the final jolt of reconnection, just in time to watch her fall flat on her behind on the floor.

"Oh!" she said breathlessly, stunned and round-eyed, her legs sticking straight out in front of her and her hands pressed to either side of her head. "Oh!"

He knelt beside her, cupped his hand around the back of her neck. "Are you all right?"

In answer, she began to laugh.

"That was—*amazing*! Hawk! Oh my God!"

"I take it you enjoyed yourself," he said, feeling enormously happy and more than a little smug. She was staring at him in a way that made him want to stomp around the room, beating on his puffed-out chest with his fists.

"I can't believe it! How do you do it? What do you call it?"

"I do it just by concentrating, basically. I've always had this fascination with birds, and one day when I was twelve years old I was sitting in a fig tree, staring at this beautiful nighthawk on a branch above me, when suddenly I was . . . inside its mind. I saw through its eyes, like we just did with the harpy eagle. Only it shocked me so much I fell out of the tree and landed on my head.

Fortunately, my head has the consistency of a rock, so I wasn't hurt." He laughed, helping Jacqueline to her feet. "I ran back into the colony screaming, 'Hawk! Hawk!' because I couldn't think of anything else to say, and from then on everyone started calling me Hawk. After that, I learned to control it in secret, experimenting with every kind of bird. There isn't a name for it, or at least if there is I don't know it. There hasn't ever been another one who could do it in the tribe's history."

"In secret? Why?"

He brushed a lock of hair from her forehead. "Because I hate politics, that's why. If word got out that I had this unusual Gift, I'd be expected to challenge the Alpha for his position at the top of the food chain. It's bad enough I have to live this restricted life . . . I could never be in charge of forcing everyone else to. And that's what being an Alpha's all about. They put the 'dick' in dictator."

She studied his face for a moment, her big blue eyes shining with something like pride. "Melder," she pronounced. "That's what you should call it. You're a Melder."

"Melder." He tried it out, unsure.

"A Mind Melder! Yes!" She clapped and hopped in place, gleeful as a child on holiday. "Can you only do it with birds? What about other animals? What about with—" She broke off.

"What is it?"

"Does . . . does this mean you can get inside my mind?"

Strange, but she looked almost hopeful. He drew her into the circle of his arms and rested his chin atop her head. "No. I've tried it with different animals, and people, too, but I only have the connection with birds. Though I admit being able to read your mind is something I'd love to be able to do."

She tilted her head up and gazed at him, eyes wide. "You can ask me anything, Hawk," she said softly. "I'll tell you whatever you want to know."

A terrible thought took seed. It sank its roots deep into the darkest, most selfish parts of him, grabbing hold with greedy claws. He pushed it back, but it held on, stubborn as a case of hiccups.

She can't lie. Grow some balls and find out the truth. Ask the three most important questions that will ever pass your lips:

Do you love me? Will you be mine? Will you turn your back on everything you used to know, and run away with me?

What if she said no? Even more terrifying . . . what if she said *yes*?

Fighting himself, he turned his head away, stared out into the sea of restless green.

She rested her head on his bare chest. "Do you get tired, after?"

Hawk smiled. "After?"

"Not after that, gutter mind," she said, stifling a yawn. "After the flying thing. Melding."

"Oh." He thought about it. "Not particularly. Why? Do you feel tired?"

"Mmm. It's a side effect of adrenaline overloads. Afterward I get sleepy."

He whispered in her ear, "You sure it's adrenaline? I think maybe I'm just too hot for you to handle, Red. My charisma alone could suck all the energy from the sun, and that's not even getting into how much of a stud I am in the sack."

She bent down and nipped his nipple with her teeth.

"Ow!"

"Oh, did you feel that?" she said, looking up at him. "I thought maybe your giant ego would be in the way. "

"All right, you." He bent his knees, lifted her up in his arms, swung around, and carried her back to the bed. "Time for a nap. But don't think you're going to be sleeping for too long, because I have *plans*."

"Promises, promises," she said, yawning again.

He laid her gently down and crawled in beside her, not bothering with the covers, drawing her against his chest so she was facing away, their legs entangled.

"Who knew the big, bad, egomaniacal wolf would be such a *cuddler*?" she said, sighing with what he hoped was contentment.

"I think we've already established I'm a big, bad, egomaniacal *cat*."

"Hmmm." She wriggled her bottom against his pelvis. "Here, kitty kitty."

Had she not sounded on the verge of sleep, Hawk would have taken her up on that enticing proposition.

Another yawn, this one accompanied by a deep, rising *whoop*, akin to the mating call of a whale. "Why did the Alpha call you 'Lord Bastard' at the punishment tree? And why does he hate you so much?"

A pulse of surprise at the question, a rueful twist in his stomach, bittersweet, as he realized he was ashamed to answer. Of course he would tell her only the truth; even if he'd wanted to lie, his tongue wouldn't allow it. His entire body rebelled against his better judgment when it came to her.

"Do you remember what you called me in the forest, *Salsu Maru*? What Nando had called me?"

"Mmm."

"In our language it means 'Least Son.' That's what I am. Not the youngest of three, but the least important, because I was illegitimate. My brother has made an art form of rubbing it in my face, hence his amusing nicknames for me."

She'd fallen still, listening. "Your brother? The Alpha is your *brother*?"

"Half," he corrected. "So is Xander, Morgan's husband. Three different mothers, three different lives. And in answer to the second part of your question, why he hates me so much, well . . ."

How to explain the unexplainable? What words might properly convey the twisted logic that makes one sibling jealous of the attention given to another by a parent, even if that attention came in the form of vicious beatings for the smallest, most innocent offense? Their father had brutalized both him and Xander from the time they could walk, but for some unknown reason, to Alejandro he'd shown only supreme indifference, as if he didn't exist at all. He never even looked at Alejandro, never acknowledged his presence in a room. Hawk would have given his eyeteeth to avoid his father's fists, but to Alejandro, it seemed as if only he were invisible. As if he didn't even merit the energy required to throw a punch.

To the lonely and the longing, even negative attention is better than no attention at all.

Hawk thought it the worst kind of sickness and perversion that his brother hated him for being an outlet for their father's evil temper, and he'd never been able to find it in his heart to feel sorry for Alejandro, though he'd tried. Years of rancor had dug a chasm between them, a bottomless abyss that could no longer be bridged, and with the kind of cruel twist Fate so enjoys, Alejandro had turned out much like the man who sired him.

Aloud he only said, "I wasn't a good brother. Or a particularly good son."

"Are they still alive? Your parents?"

Hawk closed his eyes. "No."

Hawk's mother had suffered the same fate as Xander's; the scope of their father's murderous brutality wasn't limited to his two sons. By luck or cunning only Alejandro's mother had escaped her marriage to the Alpha alive. She'd lived a good life after her husband's demise—he died, finally, the day Xander decided to fight back—and only a few years ago, she had drowned in a flash flood during the Season of the Inundation, when she was swept away picking mushrooms before she could climb into the trees.

"I'm sorry," Jacqueline murmured. "I wish there were more people in your life who loved you. You deserve it."

His face warmed with pleasure. *Like you?* he wanted to ask. *Do you?*

She was silent a moment, then said, "Okay, since we're sharing stories and you're too chicken to ask—"

"Cat. I am a *cat*. Do I need to demonstrate my essential cat-ness and pounce on you like you're a ball of twine?" He hissed and lightly bit the back of her neck, eliciting a giggle.

"Excuse me. Since you're too *catty* to ask . . . I'll just go ahead and tell you."

Hawk froze, his hand on her arm. She burrowed down deeper into the pillow, sighing again.

"My mother had three nervous breakdowns by the time I was ten years old."

Feeling the invisible steel band that had seized his heart slightly loosen, Hawk slowly exhaled.

Not "I love you."

Idiot.

"The first time I was five. I remember it because it was my birthday. There were all these people in the house: cousins, friends, my father's military buddies. My dad was between wars then, so he was home with the family. He used to remember our birthdays by which war he was away fighting at the time we were born. Mine was Granada . . ." She faltered, her voice took on an odd, flat tone. "And . . . and Garrett's was Cambodia."

Garrett. Her older brother.

He's the reason I'm so messed up. He's the one who broke me.

The steel band around Hawk's heart began to tighten again.

"I was just about to blow out the candles on my birthday cake when we heard the scream."

Hawk held still, not even daring to breathe. The little hairs on his arms stood on end.

"Everyone turned. There was my mother, standing in the doorway of the kitchen in this beautiful, tailored yellow dress, her makeup flawless, holding a pair of sewing shears in one hand and all her hair in the other. She looked back at all the staring faces and said, 'Heavy. It's so heavy.' Then she opened her hand and her hair floated to the floor, forming this forlorn red drift around her feet. After that, after she'd been taken away to 'rest,' I used to lie in my bed at night and wonder what had been so heavy. I just knew she wasn't talking about her hair. I think I knew even at five years old that what she really meant was *life*. Life was just so goddamn heavy her mind couldn't hold up under the weight of it, and it just kind of collapsed like an origami bird under an angry fist."

Hawk slid his hand down Jacqueline's arm, slipped his fingers between hers, and squeezed.

"She came back after a while, and the family pretended everything was fine. It wasn't, of course, but we were polite and never talked about anything that mattered, which was the only way we knew how to love one another. Two years later, she cracked again. I can't remember why. But . . . another few years went by. And this time when she cracked, the final time, I remember the reason." Jacqueline's voice grew small. "Though God knows I wish I didn't."

Hawk drew her closer. The room had taken on a tension, a sense of anticipation, as if the air itself were waiting to hear what she would say next.

"She wasn't supposed to be home. It was her bridge night. My father was away on some stupid sortie or something, who knows, but we always knew how to contact him in case of an emergency.

I was ten by then, and Garrett was twenty-five, still living at home, still jobless, so he was supposed to be watching me. And he was. He was always, always watching me."

Something in her tone set off a warning bell in Hawk's mind. Every nerve in his body stood at high alert, shrieking a song of horror, so that when he finally heard it, he already knew.

"It had been going on for years, of course. The first time was right before that fateful birthday party. He was my brother, and I loved him, and I believed him when he said he loved me, that it was our secret and I couldn't tell anyone. I didn't understand . . . why . . . but I still loved him. Even though it hurt. Even though I always cried."

"No," Hawk said, choked, into her hair. "No."

"My mother came home. She found us. She found him, on top of me in my bed. She went and got my father's gun from the night-stand and told my brother to leave the room and then she pointed the gun at me and called me a little whore, and she pulled the trigger. She shot me three times in the stomach. And then she turned the gun on herself."

Her voice was totally devoid of emotion. Dead. Hawk's arms were around her, crushing tight. He couldn't breathe. He couldn't move. He couldn't see through the water in his eyes.

"She was in a coma for three months before she died. My brother went to prison; my father made sure of that. And I lived. If you could call it that. I survived. I became best friends with shame, and I grew to understand how fear never lets you go once it's sunk its hooks in you. Fear becomes a part of you, like a tumor that can never be cut out."

Hawk felt like he was drowning. He felt as if all the gravity in the universe had centered on a place in the middle of his chest.

"Garrett kept trying to kill himself in prison, so eventually they moved him to a psychiatric facility. He's still there. Still keeps trying to kill himself. Still calls my father every year on my birthday, asking if I've forgiven him yet."

There was a long, terrible silence. Hawk was trembling with horror, thinking of her face when she'd told him she could only look back on their first night together as another betrayal. He whispered her name.

In a quiet voice, she said, "You're the only one I've ever told that story. My girlfriend Nola knows part of it. And my father knows, of course. But other than that . . . you're the only one."

Hawk rolled her over and took her face in his hands. "I'm sorry. I'm so sorry." His voice shook.

She wiped away the moisture at the corners of his eyes. "I didn't tell you so you could feel sorry for me. I told you because I want you to know that all the broken things inside me feel less broken when I look at you."

He squeezed his eyes shut. "Now, you mean. Because of what I gave you. Because of the drugs. When they wear off—"

"If it means I'll feel differently than I do right now, I hope they never wear off. I've never felt this happy. This free. I want to feel like this forever."

Her smile was lovely and warm, but he saw the haze, the faint fog of the spirit vine dulling the normally crystalline sheen of her eyes.

A mad, mad idea seized him.

She *could* feel like this forever. He couldn't make the past go away, but he could take away its power to hurt her.

All he had to do was ask *kalum* to show him how to make the spirit vine brew.

He buried his face in her neck, hiding, shaking with the awful realization that he'd never wanted anything so much in his entire life.

And what kind of man did that make him, that he wanted to basically keep her enslaved, her free will devoured by psychoactive drugs that made her happy and malleable and . . . and . . .

Mine.

It came from some primeval place inside him, an ancient beast calling out, roused by the scent of blood. It began to whisper to him, coercive and sly.

There's nothing for you here, in this colony where you're only the Misbegotten, the lone wolf who lives like a hermit, misunderstood and unwanted except for the occasional, impersonal, tryst. Why shouldn't you take what you want? Why shouldn't you have a taste of happiness, after all these years of living in the dark? Why shouldn't you both? You can heal her. You can heal yourself.

Take her. Take her and run.

Hawk's shaking grew worse.

Jacqueline felt it. She wound her arms around his neck. "It's all right," she whispered into his ear as he crushed her against him. "Whatever you're thinking, it'll be all right. You'll see. No matter what happens, I promise everything is going to be all right. It has to be. Because I don't think anything else could ever compare to this."

She squeezed him when she said the word, "this," and in that moment, Hawk knew she was right.

And he knew exactly what he was going to do next.

He pressed a kiss to her forehead, smoothed her hair away from her face. She settled against him, warm and perfect, and within seconds fell asleep.

Hawk held her as the sun rose higher in the sky, held her as the minutes turned to hours and his mind spun with plans and possibilities. Then he rose from the bed as quietly as he could so as not to wake her, and slipped out of the room.

THIRTY-TWO

Monsters and Miracles

Olivia Sutherland was having a nightmare.

She was a strong woman, not prone to fear or flights of fancy, but ever since she and the rest of the final families had left Sommerley and begun the journey to the rainforest, she felt as if a malevolent specter had been lurking silently behind her, following every footstep, its bony hands reaching out for the back of her neck.

The feeling worsened the deeper they'd gone into the jungle. They were led by an eerily silent Leander and the colony guide. Tonight after she'd breastfed her own child and the Queen's twins and they'd been tucked into their snug pouches, she'd lain in a makeshift bed of bracken and leaves beside her snoring husband, staring up at the black tangle of branches above, feeling her skin crawl as if a cluster of tarantulas were using her body for a mating ground.

Wrong wrong wrong. Something was wrong—terribly so—but she couldn't put her finger on what it was.

She tried telling herself it was homesickness. She tried telling herself it was nerves. She tried making a thousand different logical arguments to convince herself she was overreacting, but something deep inside her belly argued back that she was in danger.

She'd fallen asleep with that thought in mind . . . and the feeling of doom had crept into her dream.

She was running. A highway stretched open in front of her, cutting through a landscape of floating ash and desolation. Buildings burned, smoke coated the sky, piles of rubble spat flames. Though she was running as fast as she could, the road began to tilt up, rising swiftly, and she had to scratch and claw at the asphalt to keep herself from sliding back, sliding down into what she knew awaited her:

Death.

The road reared too high, sheer as a cliff face. She screamed and dug her fingers and toes into it, but it wanted to shake her off. It wanted her to fall. She fought as long as she could, but the angle was too steep, and there were no footholds, just unforgiving black pavement, bisected by two mocking yellow lines.

Just before her fingers slipped, Olivia looked over her shoulder to see what awaited her at the bottom.

Two tiny babies looked up at her from far, far below with solemn, identical faces. They sat naked on a blanket the color of blood, surrounded by howling winds and firestorms but untouched and tranquil, as if floating inside the eye of a hurricane. Four small arms reached up, pale and pudgy, tiny hands opened, fingers spread wide. A sound came from everywhere and nowhere, an ancient and terrible intonation that resonated with such power everything quaked, including Olivia's soul.

Laughter. It was the laughter of children, warped into a babble of such force and shrieking frenzy Olivia opened her mouth and screamed in terror.

Then she let go.

Olivia bolted upright in blackness, the scream still on her lips. Grayson awoke, instantly on high alert, and shot to his feet from his position on the pallet beside her. He whirled around with a snarl, trying to locate the threat in the teeming dark jungle.

But Olivia knew now where the real threat lay. It wasn't in the darkness. It wasn't in whatever would greet them at the new colony, or in anything they might have left behind.

With trepidation, she turned her gaze to the small, snug pouches that held the twins, perhaps a dozen yards away, nestled beside Leander as he slept under the branches of another tree. He was awake now also, demanding to know what was wrong, but Olivia couldn't look at him.

She couldn't take her eyes away from the twins.

They were awake, too. They were looking directly at her. And though she was still half asleep and her heart was pounding so hard it made it difficult to hear anything above the rushing of blood through her veins, she was quite sure she heard the four-month-old girls speak in unison.

"Olivia."

Just her name, clear as a bell. Only their lips didn't move.

And they were infants; they couldn't speak.

No one else seemed to hear it. Leander and Grayson and the guide were focused on her, not on the twins. But she felt certain her ears weren't playing tricks on her . . . as certain as she now felt that these two children of the Queen and her Alpha were monsters.

Or miracles.

Or perhaps a bit of both.

THIRTY-THREE
Challenges

Hawk was intercepted on his way to *kalum*'s cave by a messenger, a lanky boy of sixteen named Zaca, who had unkempt hair, a long, loping gait, and a thousand-watt smile he flashed at regular intervals. He was barefoot and bare-chested, and wore only a loose pair of tan cargo shorts, which were slipping down his narrow hips. He ran up beside Hawk just as he jumped down from the rope.

"Big Daddy wants to see you."

Hawk tried not to smile at the ironic nickname for Alejandro. He liked the kid, who reminded him of himself at that age, wild and smart-alecky, though Zaca's easy smile earned him a lot more friends than Hawk's scowls ever had.

"The Alpha finds out you're calling him that, you're in a boatload of trouble, Z."

"It's not like anyone's gonna tell him!" Zaca scoffed.

"Really? Not even Big Daddy's big brother?"

Zaca went white. The smile dropped from his face. "I . . . uh . . . I didn't mean . . ."

Hawk put a hand on his shoulder. "It's all right, I was only trying to warn you to watch what you say. Things get around. And Big Daddy has a terminal case of PMS, if you know what I'm saying."

He winked, and Zaca breathed a sigh of relief. "Yeah. I guess so. I'll be more careful."

"Any idea why he wants to see me?"

"He's called an emergency meeting of the Assembly. It's about the girl."

His nerves immediately stood on end like a thousand exclamation points. Hawk studied Zaca's face. "What about her?"

Zaca hunched his shoulders up to his ears, spreading his hands open.

Right. As if Alejandro would ever tip his hand. Hawk decided his visit to *kalum* could wait a few more minutes.

"All right. Thanks for the heads-up. And remember what I told you." He gave Zaca a friendly shove, which Zaca returned, dancing on his toes with boxing fists, taking jabs. Hawk pulled him into a headlock just to show him who was boss.

"I give!" Zaca shouted to the ground. "I give!"

Hawk released him, and gave him a slap on the back of his head for good measure. Zaca loped away, smiling, but turned after a few paces. "I totally had you, old man. I just let you think you won because I feel sorry for how feeble you are."

"Old man! Feeble!" Hawk lunged forward, and Zaca darted off, laughing.

"Punk!" Hawk shouted after him. The smile he'd repressed before spread over his face as he watched Zaca run. *Good kid. His father must be proud of him.*

That errant thought momentarily paralyzed him, as did the ache that blossomed in his chest when he imagined having a son of his own, a son who smiled and made friends and breezed through life as if it were an all-you-can-eat buffet and he was the only one in line.

Real life sidled up beside him, sucker punching him right in the gut. Family? Future? Peace? Those things were for other people, better people. For the infamous Bastard there could be one thing only, and that was disgrace.

By the time Hawk arrived at the Assembly meeting place, his mood had sunk a shade below black.

Unlike his own home, the meeting place was easily accessible by ladders, and was linked to the rest of the colony by the network of suspension bridges through the trees. When he entered the room, Alejandro looked up at him over the rim of an overfull wineglass. Perched on his elaborate chair, he was flanked on both sides by the members of the Assembly, who were seated at the curved tables. The atmosphere in the room felt as warm as a morgue.

"You wanted to see me?"

Alejandro looked irritated by Hawk's abrupt greeting. "I see a few days alone with the human hasn't improved your manners."

"It hasn't been easy," he said, jaw tight.

"Understandable. You must be finding it excessively hard to have someone invading your privacy, having to actually hold *conversations*."

"We're not doing much talking." Hawk willed his face to show nothing, aware he was treading on thin ice. From the corner of his eye, he saw Alejandro's brows rise, and he thought a bit of obfuscation was in order. "She's still healing."

"Ah yes. I understand *kalum* gave you something for her pain?"

Hawk's gaze snapped back to Alejandro's face. He wore a tiny smile, the meaning of which Hawk couldn't guess.

How much did Alejandro know? Was he being played?

"Yes," he agreed carefully. "She's been sleeping a lot."

"Sleeping," Alejandro repeated tonelessly. Only his smile was wry.

"She's recovering from being beaten with a cane," Hawk snarled, unable to keep the anger from his voice. "So yes, she's been doing a lot of sleeping. She needs to heal!"

Alejandro swallowed a long draught from his glass, then lowered it and stared at Hawk with penetrating intensity. "As you can imagine, I'm anxious to get to know our new friend a little better. She's so . . ." He paused to lick his lips. "Interesting. Don't you agree?"

The words, the tone, and the lip smacking were all designed to nettle him . . . and they did. Hawk enjoyed a vivid vision of Alejandro on the floor beneath him, eyes popped wide, face red, thrashing and gagging as Hawk strangled him with his bare hands.

When he didn't react, Alejandro asked, "How long do you suppose this 'healing' will take?"

Hawk controlled his breathing. As best he could, he kept his posture relaxed, though a vein began to throb in his temple. "I can't be expected to know how long it takes a human to heal."

"Good point. They're unpredictable, these humans, aren't they?" Alejandro tapped his fingers against the wineglass. "For instance, her offer of *belu* for you. What on Earth do you think could have prompted such a magnanimous gesture?"

Alejandro's smile grew wider, his expression all wide-eyed innocence, and Hawk thought, *He knows.*

It wasn't forbidden for him to be with Jacqueline, not exactly. The Law explicitly forbade him from impregnating human females, but not bedding them. As long as he kept his secret and his silence, the occasional dalliance outside the tribe was frowned upon, but tolerated. Especially since he was unmated, basically unmarriageable.

But Jacqueline Dolan was a special circumstance. Brought to the colony at the Alpha's behest, an enemy combatant they were trying to turn to their side, use for their purposes, she existed in that intangible gray area between friend and foe, property and person . . .

Savior and sacrifice.

Any decisions regarding intangibility belonged to the Alpha, by default. For as long as she remained in the colony, her fate remained in Alejandro's hands.

Also, she'd been meant as a *punishment* for Hawk. Not a reward. The Alpha would *not* be pleased to find out they'd been doing anything other than irritating each other.

So when Hawk finally answered, he chose his words carefully.

"She offered *belu* for Nando as well."

Alejandro nodded. "Odd, don't you think? Though if I recall correctly, her exact words were, 'Even the reason he hit Nando was my fault.' Which leads me to believe . . ."

Alejandro took another long drink of his wine. Around the tables, nervous glances were shared.

"That she only did it for you."

The room was deathly silent. Morgan's eyes were burning holes in Hawk's skull. He realized there was only one direction this conversation was headed: down.

Alejandro stood, gazing down his nose at Hawk. He smoothed a hand over his shining dark hair and said, "I want to see what the two of you got up to in the city. I want to inspect our insurance that Jacqueline Dolan will write the article she was brought here to write."

He paused, and the room held a collective breath.

"I want to see the pictures. Bring the disc to me."

A command, a challenge, and a threat, all rolled into one. Hawk had endured it his entire life, these sneered directions, this total lack of respect. He'd endured it because he'd never had anything worth standing up for.

Any*one*.

There was no way in hell Alejandro or anyone else was ever going to set sight on those pictures. Those were for him, and him alone.

So was Jacqueline. She'd finally given him reason to stand up for himself.

Which Alejandro obviously knew.

So be it.

Hawk put his shoulders back, rose to his full height, looked Alejandro dead in the eye, and said, "No."

Alejandro had anticipated this answer, evidenced by the expression of smug satisfaction that appeared on his face. "One hundred lashes for your dis—"

"No," Hawk said again, louder. He took a step toward the dais, and Alejandro's eyes widened in surprise. "No lashes. Not ever again. I'm finished taking orders from you."

Alejandro's face flushed red. "Guards!"

Before Nando and his team could leap forward from their positions, where they stood stiff and blank-eyed in a line behind the dais, Hawk shouted, "*Naparqudu ana sepiya, ak kalbu!*"

Lie at my feet, weak dog!

They were ritual words, known by all but spoken only by a *sananu*.

A rival. A challenger to the Alpha's throne.

Everyone gasped. The guards froze. Morgan leapt to her feet, as did several other Assembly members, everyone horrified and bug-eyed, looking at him and each other in astonishment.

"You *dare!*" Alejandro shouted, lips drawn over his teeth in a vicious snarl.

"Oh, I do," said Hawk, his voice low and dark, blood boiling like black lava through his veins. "I definitely do. And mark my words, brother . . . you'll be sorry I did."

Chaos.

Shouting, chairs overturned, the crash of a vase as someone knocked it over in their rush from the room. Almost all the guards ran out, followed by several of the Assembly members, the wine boy, and the scribe, who abandoned his pen and paper on the table, all of them shoving and jostling, in a great hurry to spread the news.

Alejandro was panting, seething, wanting to kill him on the spot, but he couldn't. No one could, which gave Hawk great satisfaction. According to the Ancient Ways, the Alpha and the challenger had to meet at sunset on the day of the challenge to do battle, with the entire tribe as witness. Once the ritual words had been spoken, not even the Alpha could strike until the appointed time.

So for the moment, Hawk was untouchable. He sent Alejandro a bitter smile.

"The Arena at sunset, then," hissed Alejandro. "And then we'll finally see what the Bastard is made of." Flicking a lethal look at one of the remaining guards, he added, "Get a pyre ready at the Well of Souls." He looked back at Hawk, his green eyes glowing hatefully bright. "*Salsu Maru* is going to burn."

Since ancient days, cremation had been their preferred form of burial, and Hawk knew that win or lose, someone was going to be on that funeral pyre tomorrow morning.

Because the gauntlet he'd thrown down was a winner-takes-all proposition.

The challenge of a *sananu* was to the death.

"Sunset," said Hawk. Then he turned and strode out of the room.

Jack awoke with a hangover so colossal it felt as if her brain was using jackhammers and dynamite to make a break from her skull.

There was pounding, copious pounding, accompanied by dizziness, the urge to vomit, and a violent twitching of the skin beneath her left eye. She sat up—bed? Why was she in bed? Whose bed was it?—and looked around the room she found herself in.

It appeared to be some kind of tree house. Large and open and beautiful . . . she'd never seen it before in her life.

The urge to vomit became an irrefutable order, transmitted from her angry brain to her queasy stomach, which she immediately obeyed.

When the last of the heaves died, Jack looked down at the polished wood floor. It was splattered with the contents of her stomach, which seemed not so much disgusting as physically impossible. She couldn't remember the last time she'd eaten anything.

She was having trouble remembering much of anything at all.

Towel, she thought. In this situation, a rational person would go find a towel and clean up this mess. One couldn't be expected to think clearly when faced with such a large—weirdly green— mess on the floor. Whoever's floor it happened to be. She'd figure out what to do next after she'd cleaned up.

Satisfied with her plan in spite of the agony in her head, Jack wiped her mouth on the back of her hand, stood from the bed, and looked around the room.

Standing was a mediocre idea, at best. The room became a sideways slipping blur, and she sank back to the mattress on gelatinous legs, shaking, her skin covered in a cold sweat.

"Okay. Just take it easy for a minute. Just sit here for a minute, and get your bearings. Nooo rush."

Clearly, she was no longer in New York. But where on Earth was she?

"All right. You're functioning at ten percent physically and mentally, best-case scenario." She was going to ignore the fact that she was talking out loud to an empty room, and cut herself some slack. "What you need is a big glass of water. And Advil. And a towel. Let's just focus on those three things, and we'll go from there."

She tried standing again, and found it less challenging this time. She shuffled to an open door on the other side of the room, grateful that it turned out to be a bathroom. A bit primitive, sparse and masculine, but still a bathroom. She washed her face and rinsed her mouth in the sink, used the toilet, pulled a towel from a folded stack in a small cabinet, returned to the bedroom, and sopped up the mess.

When she was finished, she debated what to do with the towel. She settled on leaving it outside on the porch, because there didn't seem to be any hamper or proper laundry facilities in her immediate vicinity, and she certainly wasn't going to go looking.

There had been no medicine cabinet in the bathroom. No Advil. There didn't appear to be a kitchen where she could find a drinking glass. What kind of place *was* this?

A theory took root.

She was on assignment. Obviously, she was in the jungle; the rainforest loomed thick and misted beyond the tree house, exotic birds called through the canopy, a brown monkey hung upside down by its tail from a branch not ten yards away, eating fruit. She was on assignment in some tropical war zone, and had gotten food poisoning. Or been given drugs?

The thought of drugs made her pause. Something about the word filtered through her haze . . .

No. Nothing.

Okay. Don't panic. Think. Concentrate. Her last assignment had been . . . Manaus. That's right! Relieved, she clung to the memory. She was getting off a plane at the Manaus airport. She'd checked into a hotel—not here, wherever here was—she'd gone to check out the Mercado Municipal . . .

After that there was a big black hole where her memory used to be.

Thinking she might have fallen and hit her head, Jack carefully felt her skull. She found no telltale lumps or bumps. Other than her throbbing head and a general sense of illness, her body seemed to be unharmed, too. So *what happened*?

There was a sound from somewhere below. Downstairs? Yes, there were footsteps on stairs, definitely. Someone was coming. Someone else was here!

"You're awake."

Holy shit.

That was her first and only thought as she stared at the man who'd appeared out of nowhere, charging into the room as if he belonged here. He pulled up to an abrupt stop when he caught sight of her standing beneath the eaves on the narrow porch that ran around the house.

He was huge, rugged, and altogether beautiful, staring at her with a tender light in his eyes like she was something out of a dream. But maybe this was *her* dream. Maybe she was still asleep?

No. The sunshine on her shoulder was real. Her pounding heart was real. Her sense of terror and confusion were definitely real.

The man took a step toward her. She took a step back. A flicker of worry crossed his face. Taking another step forward he said, "Jacqueline?"

"Stay away from me," she said, beginning to shake.

He froze. His gaze, electric green, raked over her. The intimacy of it made her feel utterly exposed, as if he knew all her secrets. As if he'd seen straight down into the darkest corners of her soul. His eyes flicked back up to hers and now they were wide and horrified. His expression turned horrified, too. He whispered, "The spirit vine. It wore off, didn't it?"

He took another step toward her, hand outstretched, and Jack did the only thing she could think to do.

She screamed.

THIRTY-FOUR
Holes

"What do you mean, she doesn't remember anything?" said Xander, confused.

"Just what I said!" shouted Hawk, red-faced. "She doesn't remember a *thing*!"

"Inaccurate," said Jacqueline between gritted teeth. "I remember my name, my age, where I'm from, and what I do for a living. The pertinent facts are intact. I just don't remember"—she glanced around the Assembly room—"this." Her gaze flicked between Morgan, Xander, and Hawk. "*You*."

The three of them stood on one side of the room, in front of the long, curving tables where the members had been sitting when Hawk made his declaration of war, which now seemed lifetimes ago. Jack stood across from them in almost the exact spot Hawk had stood, her feet spread apart, still in the chemise she'd slept in. Her lips were pressed thin. Her eyes blazed blue fury. Her legs were long and bare. And because Hawk hadn't been able to get her out of his home any other way, her hands were tied behind her back.

She hadn't liked that at all.

In fact, it would be accurate to say she hated it.

"Bloody hell, she isn't a farm animal—untie the poor thing!" snapped Morgan, glaring at Hawk. "Are you off your trolley? Jesus H. Christ on a cross, this entire day has gone pear-shaped!"

Hawk looked at Xander, who shrugged and nodded.

Swallowing around the fist in his throat, he approached Jacqueline, his hands spread wide in a placating gesture. "Jacqueline, I'm going to untie your hands."

"About friggin' time!"

"So don't try to hit me or anything."

"Gee, why would I want to do that? It's not like you overpowered me, and *bound* me, and threw me over your shoulders like a sack of potatoes! It's not like you walked a mile while I was hanging upside down—"

"It wasn't nearly that far—"

"—and every person around stood and stared as we passed—"

"I think you're exaggerating a little—"

"—at my *ass*, which was on display like it was the Kmart blue light special!"

Hawk was an arm's length away. Jacqueline was breathing hard, looking at him as if she wished she were holding a bazooka. "I apologize. But you were screaming very loudly. And you were throwing things. I had to subdue you—"

"*Subdue* me?" He didn't think it possible, but she stiffened even more. Her face turned a deep crimson.

"So that you wouldn't hurt either of us, and so that I could bring you here, to get help."

She repeated acidly, "Help."

"Yes." Hawk nodded. "They're going to help us."

"Not that we have any idea *how*," said Xander mildly. Hawk threw him a murderous glance over his shoulder. Xander was standing there with his muscular arms crossed over his chest, obviously trying not to smile.

"All right. Fine. *Help*. Untie me." She presented Hawk with her bound wrists, still glaring at him.

Without allowing himself to stop and think about the insanity of the situation, or the possibility that she might never again recognize him, or the awful, throbbing pain in his chest, Hawk quickly untied the knot he'd made in the rope that secured her wrists, and pulled it off.

She whirled around and slapped him across the face.

He exhaled hard, and closed his eyes. "That never gets old."

His sarcastic tone was lost on Jacqueline. "I'm sure women do that to you all the time, don't they, Tarzan? What with you being so *charming* and all!"

Hawk opened his eyes and watched her rub her wrists, scowling. "No. Just you."

"Yeah, well just count yourself lucky there's not a blunt object within easy reach, buddy, or the side of your head would be getting intimately acquainted with it!"

Wishing he had something to crush between his hands, throw, or break over his knee, Hawk said, "Morgan. A little help, please."

Morgan approached. With the bearing of a general addressing her troops before sending them off into battle, she said, "Jacqueline. My name is Morgan Montgomery Luna. That"—she pointed at Xander—"is my husband, Alexander. That"—she pointed at Hawk—"is my brother-in-law, Hawk. This"—she indicated the room, the jungle beyond—"is our colony, which is located in the rainforest outside Manaus, Brazil—"

"Morgan!" snapped Xander, outraged.

In response to her husband's angry interruption, Morgan waved a dismissive hand.

"You were brought here to observe us—our ways, our life-style—in an effort to bring a better understanding of the *Ikati* to the outside world. Hopefully, to ultimately foster a friendship between our two species. Or at least start the discussions toward peace. I know you're upset, but let me assure you that you're in no danger. I'll answer any questions you have to the best of my ability, and hopefully we can figure out exactly what happened to your memory so we can get it back. Does that sound reasonable to you?"

There followed a long silence wherein Jacqueline processed what Morgan had said. She tilted her head, frowning. "Lucas," she said.

Hawk started. His heart surged inside his chest. "Yes? What?"

She looked at him. "I don't know. That just came to me when she was talking."

Hawk licked his lips, tried to swallow. His mouth was Sahara dry. "That's my name."

Her frown deepened. "She just said your name was Hawk."

His heart was beginning to burrow its way through his breast-bone. "It's a long story. But my real name is Lucas."

Her expression soured. That little tidbit didn't seem to please her.

"That's a good sign!" said Morgan, brightening. "Now, Jacqueline, why don't you and I have a seat and talk. I'm sure the boys have other important things to attend to." She glanced at Hawk, then at Xander, her look no longer so bright. "Don't you."

It wasn't a question.

"I'm not leaving her," said Hawk, staring at Jacqueline.

"Hawk."

He ignored Xander's warning tone. "I'm not leaving this room until I know she's safe."

Jacqueline wouldn't look at him. Morgan did, however, and her look was long and penetrating. She said, "You have a challenge to prepare for, my friend. You should go get some rest, go—"

"Not. Leaving. This. *Room*," he reiterated, almost hissing.

Morgan's gaze grew questioning, even more intense. She examined his face, the twitching muscle in his jaw, his posture, rigid and battle ready. Then her eyes cleared, and she looked for a moment as if she would break into song. But she simply shook her head, smiling, as if at a private joke. With a sidelong glance, she said, "Consider it a favor to me. A gift, if you will."

She'd put emphasis on the word "gift," as if there were special meaning in it.

Hawk cocked his head, thinking . . . and then he knew.

Not a gift . . . a *Gift*.

Hope flooded his body as if he'd been injected with it.

He turned on his heel, jerked his head for Xander to follow, and, without another word, left.

They sat at one of the long tables in the warm, silent room. Tinted luminous violet from the fabric hanging from the tall tree branches above, shafts of sunlight illuminated the floor. Jacqueline was pale as stone, stoic and straight-backed in the chair opposite her, but Morgan smelled her confusion and fear as bright as a handful of lemon zest tossed in the air.

Fear. That one thing was everything that was wrong in the world.

"My husband was assigned to kill me," she began, crossing her legs and settling back into her chair. "That's how we met. He was an assassin, I was his mark. Funny, isn't it, the strange ways love stories can begin?"

Jacqueline sent her an arch look. "Ever heard of Stockholm syndrome?"

Morgan ignored that. "I was a traitor, you see. A traitor to the tribe. I'd done the unforgivable: colluded with the enemy. They promised me freedom—something I'd never, ever had, mind you—and all I had to give them in return was a name. At the time it seemed like a grand idea. I was always an outsider, a square peg trying to fit into a round hole. I never once felt I belonged to the place or time or people I was born to. And I wanted . . . things." She sighed, remembering the girl she'd once been. That lonely, longing girl. "I wanted to be the kind of girl who devoured life. The kind of girl who knew how to dance a tango and speak exotic languages and roll her own cigarettes. The kind of girl who splashed naked in Paris fountains at midnight and jumped out of airplanes for fun and died in some beautiful, tragic way that would inspire poets to write works of great genius and crowds of people to weep over my flower-draped coffin, wailing my name.

"I wanted so many things. Frivolous things. Grand, ridiculous conceits. But there was only one thing I really *needed*, though it took me half a lifetime to discover it."

She had Jacqueline's attention now.

"Hope." The word lingered on her tongue, soft as a lover's name. "I never understood that a person can endure anything, any tragedy or hardship, as long as she has hope. It's the single most powerful force in the universe. More powerful, even, than love."

"Hope," repeated Jacqueline warily.

"It's what differentiates us from all the other creatures of the Earth. Most people might point to love, but even insects love their offspring. It's coded into the DNA of every living being to love, to protect those closest by blood or bond. It's how species continue to exist, continue to procreate. But hope . . . that's the thing that truly sets us apart."

Her audience looked more than a little dubious. "What about language? Music? Art?"

"You can teach a monkey language," Morgan scoffed. "Besides, every animal has a means of communication. Just because they're not speaking the King's English doesn't mean they don't have language. Music, too. And art, well! Most of what we call 'art' *isn't*. It's just a bunch of narcissists jerking each other off. Technically speaking, animals make art all the time. Have you ever seen a pod of dolphins racing over the open water? Art. Have you ever seen a honeycomb, or a spider's web, or the incredible architecture of a bird's nest? All art. It's everywhere in the natural world, only we don't call it 'art' because animals aren't navel-gazers; their art is always functional. It doesn't exist just to relieve their mommy issues, or stroke their egos, or satisfy their pathetic need for approval."

After a time, Jacqueline said, "You're sure your husband wasn't assigned to kill you because you're over-opinionated? Men generally can't stand that. In my experience, a woman with strong opinions affects a man's testicles in the same way as exposure to extreme cold."

That made her laugh. "I can see why he likes you. He's always had dreadful taste in women, but *you* . . . you're a keeper, duckie."

"He?" said Jacqueline pointedly.

Morgan studied her, the laughter fading. "It's a great gift, too, you know. Probably the greatest gift one soul can give another. It's what Xander gave me. It's the reason I ultimately returned here with him, when I could have lived anywhere in the world. Done all the things I ever wanted. He gave me what I needed in order to accept my past. To embrace it. To *transcend* it."

Jacqueline said, "This is beginning to sound like a 'Drink the Kool-Aid' speech."

"It's actually more of a warning speech," she shot back, staring Jacqueline dead in the eye.

To her credit, she didn't blink. She simply waited, tense yet controlled, her pulse beating fast in her throat.

"Hawk is a friend, and a good man, and whatever you remember or don't, you should know that you've changed him. I can see it. It's all over him like he's been dipped in honey. You've given him hope, and if you take it away . . . I think it will kill him. He's strong, but no man is invincible. For him, as it was for me, hope might mean the difference between life and death."

Jacqueline processed that, her expression severe yet contemplative, and Morgan felt the same admiration she'd felt when Jacqueline had offered *belu* at the punishment tree. Whatever her faults, this was a woman of strong convictions, serious thought, and more than a little self-control. She might be afraid, angry, and utterly confused, but she wasn't intimidated, she wasn't backing down, and she definitely wasn't allowing her fear to make the decisions.

They're a good match, Morgan thought, surprised and pleased.

Jacqueline asked guardedly, "What exactly do you mean by that?"

"I mean that in just a few hours Hawk is going to put his life on the line in a contest against the man who leads this little colony of ours . . . and only one of them is going to emerge from that contest alive."

Jacqueline blanched, but Morgan forged ahead. "It's our way. It might not be the best way, and it's definitely not the most enlightened, but there you are. This isn't a democracy. I can explain more later, but suffice it to say that I have no doubt that you're the flame that set that particular stick of dynamite alight, and whatever Hawk thinks is going on between you and him will affect the outcome of their battle." Her voice darkened. "And believe me when I say that it's in everyone's best interest if Hawk is the victor. Including yours."

Jacqueline's jaw worked. "So you're asking me to . . . what? Pretend?"

"No. I'm asking you to be patient. And understanding, even though you don't understand, and never will, because you're a different species from him." She smiled. "Just like every other woman who loves a man."

Jacqueline stared at her for a long time. Eventually, she huffed a soft laugh, then stood. She dragged a hand through her hair, paced a circle around the table, and stared out into the jungle. After several minutes of chewing her thumbnail, she said, "Okay. Walk me through this. How long have I been here?"

"A few days. Before that, I believe it took another ten in travel from New York."

Silence. Then: "And you say I was brought here to observe. To witness."

"Yes."

"Why me?"

Morgan said, "Do you remember writing an article for the *New York Times* about Shifters? 'The Enemy Among Us,' it was called."

Jacqueline turned to look at Morgan. "No."

"Very effective piece of propaganda, that. And extremely well written. You were nominated for the Pulitzer."

"Did I win?"

"No. But it was the reason you were chosen. You're a voice they listen to. You're a voice we need to win them over to our side."

Jacqueline studied her closely. "They?"

"Humans."

The word hung there between them in the air, until finally she came and sat across from Morgan again, shifting her weight restlessly in the seat.

Her expression conflicted, she said, "I remember that word you said before, *Ikati*. I do remember what that is. What you are."

"What about how you feel about us? Do you remember anything about that?"

Jack looked her over, lips pursed. She said drily, "Well . . . aside from being the lovechild of the Wolverine and Coco Chanel, *you* seem all right."

Morgan laughed, long and loudly. "I'm gratified to hear it. I'm sure under different circumstances we could have been good friends."

Jacqueline looked down at her hands, and Morgan noticed they were slightly shaking. She gathered herself, took a breath, and said, "There are holes. The past few days are a black wall, but before that it's all pretty clear. My job, my life, my friends. But there are these big, gaping holes, too, like something's been . . . censored. Blacked out. I can't get too close to my childhood, for instance. I remember bits and pieces, but I don't remember my parents. I don't remember where I grew up." Her voice grew quiet. "I don't remember if I have any siblings. Or if I was happy." She looked up, her eyes filled with trepidation. "What do you think that means?"

Morgan debated whether or not to head down this particular path. After a few cheek-chewing moments, she decided that if the roles were reversed, she'd definitely want to know.

"There's a way I might be able to help you. I don't know if it will work, but I'd like to try. If you're willing."

"Does it involve drilling holes in my skull?"

Morgan smiled, faint and wry. "No, no drilling. But it does involve something you might not be willing to give. And if not, I understand completely. I'm leaving this entirely up to you."

Jacqueline's expression grew pensive. "What would I have to give, exactly?"

"Your trust."

They sat staring at one another while a brilliant green hummingbird zipped around the table, in search of food. Finally it darted off with a muted *buzz* of its blazing wings.

"I assume if I wait long enough an explanation will be forthcoming," said Jacqueline.

Morgan held out her hands, palm up. "I have a Gift called Suggestion. It means that if I touch you with the intent to direct your behavior, I can. For instance, if I touched you now and said, 'Quack like a duck,' you would do so."

Jacqueline stared at her. "That doesn't engender much confidence, just so you know."

"Not that I would say that, of course, that's just an example. But if I said something like, 'Remember your past,' well, you get the idea."

With narrowed eyes, Jacqueline said, "How do I know you wouldn't say something like, 'Jump out of this tree,' instead?"

Still with her hands extended, Morgan said softly, "You don't. That's why it's called trust. But if it makes any difference, I give you my word the that only thing I will Suggest will be for you to remember your past."

Jacqueline crossed her arms over her chest and sat back in her chair. She looked away, letting her gaze travel slowly around the room, over the fabric flowing down from above, the dais with the Alpha's sumptuous throne, the flowers massed in vases. Morgan wondered if it looked like a fairy tale or a nightmare to her, and decided probably a little bit of both.

"Okay," Jacqueline said finally. She sat forward and held out her hands. "I don't know why, but I do feel like I can trust you."

Morgan beamed. "Smashing! Let's begin by—"

"Just in case this goes totally sideways and you accidentally wipe my brain like a crashed hard drive, I want you to tell him something for me."

Morgan was too intrigued to be insulted by the insinuation that she wasn't in perfect control of her Gift. "Who? What?"

Jacqueline glanced up at her, looking a bit sheepish. "Hawk."

Morgan drawled, "Oh?"

"Tell him I said . . . tell him I said . . ." She looked away, took a breath, and said, "That he seems like someone I would have wanted to know. That's all."

"Handsome as the devil, isn't he?" Morgan whispered conspiratorially. Jacqueline glanced back at her, surprised. "Not as handsome as my husband, of course, but then I'm biased. Most of the women in this colony think Hawk is nothing short of Adonis."

"He's . . . very . . ." Jacqueline cleared her throat, then waved her hands in front of Morgan's face. "Can we just get on with this, please?"

Morgan tried to press the satisfied smile from her lips. "All right. Give me your hands."

Jacqueline carefully rested her palms atop Morgan's. She grasped her hands lightly, noting the slight tremble. She looked up, into Jacqueline's eyes, and said forcefully, "You're not afraid of me."

Instantly, the trembling stopped. Jacqueline's face went slack. Her eyes hazed. All the tension went out of her body.

"Tell me your name."

"Jacqueline Anne Dolan." Her voice was faraway, to match the look in her eyes.

"And what is my name?"

"Morgan Montgomery Luna," she repeated dutifully.

"Correct. Very good. Now, Jacqueline, I want you to remember your life. I want you to remove any blocks you may have constructed around your memory, and tell me where you were born."

"Boston," said Jacqueline instantly.

Relief, warm and thorough. *Success!* "And where have you been for the past twenty-four hours?"

Silence. A blank, eerie stare. Then, "Nowhere."

"Oh bollocks!" muttered Morgan. "Jacqueline, do not suppress your memory. Access it. *Think.* Now: Where have you been for the past twenty-four hours?"

Jacqueline blinked. "Nowhere. But I . . ."

"Yes?"

"But . . . it was nice there. I felt safe." Some emotion flickered across her face, there then gone. "I felt free. But that's all. There isn't anything else."

Morgan closed her eyes and bowed her head. She whispered, "Remember your mother."

Like a robot: "I don't have a mother."

Morgan's throat was closing. It was becoming hard to breathe. "Remember your father."

"I don't have a father."

It wasn't working. Whatever had happened to her memory was beyond the reaches of Morgan's Gift. She'd failed.

Or have I?

A chill ran up Morgan's spine. She lifted her head and stared at Jacqueline.

She'd trained since childhood to control her Gift, to be careful around others, careful not to touch, not to think any thoughts that might hurt someone. Because she had so much power, she had to be more vigilant than anyone else. She had to use her Gift sparingly, and only for good.

For *good.*

Sitting here with this woman at this moment, Morgan had the opportunity to do more good in one fell swoop than she could in her entire life.

The words were right there. So beautiful, so terrible, they burned like acid on her tongue.

You love the Ikati. *Humans and* Ikati *should coexist in peace. You rescind everything you said in that article. You will work for peace between our races for the rest of your days.*

Her hands began to shake. All she had to do was say it, and it would be so. Everything they'd wanted by bringing her here could come true.

"But it would be a lie," she whispered to herself. A voice inside her head whispered back, *And it would save lives.*

"You are happy and comfortable. Stay seated in this spot," she directed Jacqueline. She released her hands and began to pace in a circle around the room, debating with herself, as Jacqueline sat blank and docile as a lamb, waiting.

Morgan saw the future stretched out bright as a new penny before her, all the possibilities for good shining like stars in the sky. She didn't know why this hadn't occurred to her before, possibly because she'd been so vigilant for so many years, so trained to limit her Gift, but this could be a miracle for them. She could visit every single major politician and religious figure in the world, and Suggest they love *Ikati*, too. She could simply walk through crowds, touching people as she passed, murmuring words of peace and brotherhood. She could transform the human race.

Morgan stood looking out over the rainforest through drapes that lifted and fell with the slight breeze, slipping against her legs. She thought, *I could change the world.*

Aloud she murmured, "Hitler thought the same thing."

So did Caesar. So did a lot of other lunatics with visions of grandeur and perverted ideas about how people should live, and who gets to be in charge of that.

"Absolute power corrupts absolutely." A certain Lord Acton said that, back in the nineteenth century, and Morgan had to admit she agreed with him.

She could change the world . . . but it would all be a lie. And only minutes ago, she'd made Jacqueline a promise. *I give you my word that the only thing I will Suggest will be for you to remember your past.*

Her hand went to her hip, to the place she'd had tattooed with the words "Live Free Or Die." It was her personal motto, because she held freedom as dear as hope. A life without those two things was simply not worth living.

And therein was her answer.

She couldn't take away even a single person's free will. To do so would make her no better than the other monsters throughout history, no matter how noble she thought the cause.

With a heavy sigh, she turned from the view and made her way back to Jacqueline. She sat across from her, and gathered Jacqueline's hands into her own once again. The urge was still there, strong and terrible, so Morgan did the only thing she could think to do.

"Jacqueline Dolan," she said, looking into her eyes, "no matter what I say to you from this moment forth, you are immune to my Gift of Suggestion, and will be forevermore. I release you."

Her heart felt like a dead fish lodged beneath her breastbone. She stood and walked away.

For a long while, there was a silence, only disturbed by the sound of bird calls and monkey screeches, far off in the forest. Then from behind her Jacqueline said, "I know that was hard for you."

Her voice was tight. Angry. The dead fish flopped over, and Morgan thought, *Caught.*

Morgan sighed, passed a hand over her face, pinched the bridge of her nose between two fingers. "It would have been so much more convenient if you weren't quite so clever."

"For us both," Jacqueline rejoined.

Morgan heard her stand, and turned to face her. Jacqueline's face looked carved from granite.

"I owe you an apology."

"Keep it. I hate sorries. They're meant to make things better but they inevitably make things worse." They looked at one another across the room. Jacqueline said, "I want to leave. I want to go home, to New York. Now."

Morgan had never felt claustrophobic. She'd never experienced a panic attack, or suffered a nervous breakdown, or even had a single nightmare, in spite of all the tragedy and loss and iron-fisted repression she'd suffered up to now. But staring at the livid woman who she'd once imagined was the possible solution to bridge the chasm between humanity and her own kind, she felt the horrifying, soul-freezing reality of all of them combined.

For the first time in her entire adult life, she was rendered speechless.

Then a voice, raspy and kind, spoke from the other side of the room.

"And go you shall."

Morgan turned. *Kalum* smiled at the two of them like the Cheshire cat as he pushed the cowl of his white robe off his head. It fell around his shoulders, revealing his face, his glittering green eyes. He looked at Jacqueline. "As shall we all. Just not quite yet, *Gibil.* There's yet work for you here, work that can only be completed by you. When that work is done you shall go back from where you came. And after that . . ." His smile deepened, grew vaguely melancholy. "You will have to decide where *home* truly is."

From outside there came a tumult. Voices shouted, rising up through the canopy, the beat of drums began. Morgan didn't have to look to know what was happening, and she shivered, cold in spite of the humidity.

The Alpha of Sommerley had finally arrived.

THIRTY-FIVE

The Most Important Thing

"Hawk! Xander!"

Morgan rushed across the room, throwing back the gauzy fabric that led to the suspension bridge outside. She seemed panicked, frantic, and it set Jack's already frayed nerves on edge.

As if they'd been waiting close by, the two men appeared quickly, wearing matching expressions of worry, tension radiating from their bodies. The three of them started talking over each other, the words tumbling out of their mouths.

"Leander's here—"

"Did you have any success?"

"But something's wrong, I can feel it—"

"She doesn't remember, it didn't work—"

"Alejandro's going out to meet him—"

"Nothing at all?"

"The Queen isn't with them."

Morgan stopped and stared at Xander. "What do you mean, the Queen isn't with them?"

"Just what I said. It's Leander, the children, the viscount and his family, a few others. But no Queen."

In a horrified whisper, Morgan said, "Oh my God. Do you think something happened to her?"

Jacqueline said, "What's going on here?"

Xander and Morgan looked at her, but Hawk had already been watching her, since the moment he stepped inside.

"It didn't work," he said dispassionately, glancing between her and Morgan. His voice was cool, his expression was neutral, but there was something strange in his eyes. Something that, if she hadn't known better, almost looked like . . . relief.

"No. It didn't. Now will you please tell me what's happening?"

"I have to go to him. He'll be expecting me," said Morgan, smoothing her hands over her hair. She'd turned pale in the past few moments. Xander stared at her, concerned.

"We'll both go. Don't worry, *amada*, it's going to be fine," he murmured, and pulled his wife into his arms.

Jacqueline looked away. Even that small gesture of affection felt too intimate, as if there were no one else in the room but the two of them.

Xander said, "Hawk," and jerked his chin at Jacqueline. Then he and Morgan left without another glance in her direction.

Hawk crossed the room quickly, holding out his hand to her. "We have to go."

Automatically, Jack backed away. He stopped dead in his tracks and lowered his hand.

"Do you think I'm going to hurt you?" he asked, voice gruff.

Jack's heart was pounding. She was confused, her brain felt addled, and having him near was short-circuiting what little logical thinking ability she had left. With him in it, the room felt too close and warm, decidedly uncomfortable.

"I'd prefer not to travel on your shoulder, if you don't mind," she answered, avoiding his question. He looked her over, his jaw tight, then nodded curtly.

"There isn't a bridge to my home from here, but there is one that leads to Morgan and Xander's. It would be . . . best . . . if you stayed there for now."

He didn't look as if he thought it would be best, but she nodded anyway, relieved yet also oddly disappointed she wouldn't be going back with him to his own spare, masculine space.

That's it. You've officially lost your damn mind!

"Follow me," he said, and turned to leave. Jack hesitated, but then did as he instructed, walking quickly to keep up with his long strides. Once outside, he took one of the four suspension bridges through the trees in the opposite direction they'd originally come from. Below on the forest floor, a steady stream of people was also moving in this direction, and Jack stared down at them, fascinated.

She asked, "Who is Leander? And why is Morgan afraid of him? And what's this about a Queen?"

She thought she heard an aggravated exhalation, but couldn't be sure. The throbbing beat of drums drowned it out.

"Leander is the Alpha from another colony. Most of the members of his colony in England have already relocated here due to the threats against us, but he and the Queen and a few final families were left. The Queen is exactly what she sounds like: a Queen. The most powerful one of all the *Ikati*. Who apparently is missing."

They were moving quickly through the trees, passing house after ingenious tree house, following the network of bridges deeper into the forest. Jack was too busy trying to keep up to spend too much time marveling at the beauty of it all. She jerked away from the left-hand guide rope with a strangled scream as a hairy brown spider as big as a crab crawled up from under it.

Hawk halted when he heard her. He blew out a breath when he caught sight of the spider. "It eats fruit," he said, then turned and walked on. Over his shoulder, he added, "As for Leander, you could say his relationship with Morgan is . . . complicated."

"Complicated?"

"He once ordered her killed for treason."

Jack sucked in a shocked breath.

That's how we met. He was an assassin, I was his mark. Funny, isn't it, the strange ways love stories can begin?

Oh God. This place was like one of those Korean melodramas her neighbor Mrs. Lee watched on TV, all murder plots and espionage and crazy royals. How on Earth had she ended up here?

"He's not going to hurt her now, though, right?" For some reason, the thought of that made Jack's stomach turn over.

Hawk muttered, "You can never predict what an Alpha will do." He stopped at the trunk of a tree where the bridges split in four directions. "That's it."

She stood there hesitantly, looking in the direction he was pointing. The house was a bi-level wood structure like his, covered in curling vines and lined with unlit iron lanterns along the walkway to the front door. It looked friendly and pretty, and not at all like somewhere she wanted to go.

"Can't . . . can't I just stay with you?" she asked, her voice small.

The question affected him, evidenced by the way his eyes flared, the way he sucked in a breath, leaning toward her. But he caught himself. He jerked away and looked off into the trees, swallowing.

"It's safer for you here," he said, his voice rough, not meeting her eyes. "At least for the time being. I don't think it would be wise for anyone else to find out about your . . . condition. There's someone who might have answers for me, and I'll go to him as soon as I can, but for right now . . . I'm sorry, but you're just going to have to trust me."

There was so much she didn't know. So much he wasn't telling her. Though he'd scared her when he appeared after she'd woken up, and angered her when he carried her over his shoulder to the Assembly room, he'd been nothing but gentle and patient with her. He'd been . . . caring.

Watching him, so obviously conflicted, so obviously trying not to show whatever emotions he was feeling, a snippet of her conversation with Morgan came back to her.

So you're asking me to . . . what? Pretend?

No. I'm asking you to be patient. And understanding, even though you don't understand, and never will, because you're a different species from him. Just like every other woman who loves a man.

It had seemed like an odd aside at the time, just one more bit of insanity. But now it hit her as if she'd been struck by a bolt of lightning.

Were they *in love*? Was that part of what she wasn't remembering? Was that the cause of all this sexual tension between them, sizzling like butter in a hot pan?

Hawk must have sensed her shock, because he looked at her sharply, his eyes dark. "What is it?"

Eyes wide, Jack stared at him. "Tell me one thing, Hawk."

He stared back at her, taut as a bowstring. Waiting.

Feeling terrified, electrified, fraught with the most exquisite thrill, she whispered, "What's the most important thing I've forgotten?"

She watched him fight. She watched the vein throb in his temple, the way his lips pressed hard together, the way his hands flexed. She watched as his eyes fluttered shut, and his breathing faltered.

And she watched as he opened his eyes and said roughly, "This."

He took her in his arms and kissed her.

It was hot and hard and delicious, edged with tangible desperation; his tongue invaded her mouth as his hands crushed her against him, tangled in her hair, wrapped around her bottom. She arched against him, feeling the heat and rightness of his body, a thrill running through her when she heard the sound of pleasure he made, low in his throat.

It lasted forever. Or at least it felt as if it did; time had lost all meaning. Finally he pulled away, holding her face in his hands, breathing hard.

She swayed, breathing just as hard as he was. He steadied her with his strong arm wrapped around her waist.

"That definitely seems important," she said, feeling as boneless as a rag doll. He was so large and male and gorgeous, and he tasted amazing, and Jack was having a hard time coming up with any reason she shouldn't kiss him again.

So she did.

He pushed her back against the tree, pressed the length of his body against hers, and Jack had the wild thought he would tear off all her clothes and take her right then and there, in the open.

But then he broke away, panting, his expression tortured. "Stay here," he commanded, taking a step back, then another. "Stay inside."

Jack couldn't speak. She was too overwhelmed. Too ambivalent. She didn't trust what would come out of her mouth.

"Promise me, Jacqueline. Please. I have to go. There's something I have to do, but I'll be back as soon as I can. I swear I'll tell you everything, you can ask me any question you want. But if I can't be sure you're going to be safe in the meantime, I won't be able to . . . I won't be able . . ."

More of Morgan's words came back to haunt her, and a chill ran over her skin.

Hawk is going to put his life on the line in a contest against the man who leads this little colony of ours . . . and only one of them is going to emerge from that contest alive.

"Yes," she whispered, "okay. I will."

His relief was palpable. He scrubbed his hands over his face. He took one long, last look at her, then turned to leave.

"Hawk."

He turned back, staring at her with an expression that was truly awful to behold. Pain and frustration and longing . . . and hope. Most of all—worst of all—hope.

You've given him hope, and if you take it away . . . I think it will kill him.

Jack took a breath. In a voice clear and unwavering, she said, "I want you to win."

It startled him. He stared at her, his eyes searching, until finally he nodded.

"I will." It was a promise, spoken in a voice reverberating with emotion. "For you, Jacqueline, I will."

Then he turned and walked away.

The meeting of two Alphas was never a simple affair, or one devoid of danger.

Their race was as old as the bones of the Earth, their ways just as fixed. Only one Alpha ruled a colony, and his word was Law. An Alpha was bred for one thing, and one thing only: domination.

So when two of them were forced into close proximity, animosity abounded. The potential for a violent eruption was never far off.

"Alejandro," said Leander. Though his tone and aspect were perfectly polite, his eyes were narrowed to slits. Tall and lean, cool and composed, he stood in front of his party, a commanding presence that had all the other males in the vicinity standing up a little straighter. An aura of power, both electric and dark, encircled him like a bubble.

In contrast, Alejandro seemed flustered. His eyes were bright. His face was flushed. Though he was flanked by his cadre of guards, as he stood at the head of his entire colony, he was fidgeting like a child during church.

"Leander," he snapped. His eyes moved beyond Leander, taking in the viscount, the others. "And where is our beautiful Queen?"

The crowd, jostling shoulder to shoulder to get a good look at the spectacle, hushed.

Where, indeed?

They stood in an open clearing at the forefront of the colony, where the jungle gave way to ordered beds of flowers and vegetable gardens, near the grotto and hidden pools used for bathing. It was hot. The air was still. Sweat trickled down the back of Morgan's neck.

Deadly soft, Leander asked, "She's not here?"

A ripple of tension ran through the crowd. Standing beside Xander, Morgan shivered with a premonition of doom.

"*Here*?" repeated Alejandro, blinking. "Why would she be here? I know nothing of this. I thought she traveled with you."

Leander's gaze moved over the gathering. Though his expression revealed exactly nothing, Morgan knew he was assessing. Calculating. His eyes found hers through the crowd, pierced her, and for a moment she was breathless with terror.

This was the first time she'd seen him in years. A lifetime ago, he'd ordered her dead. His Queen had intervened, and she'd been spared . . . but his Queen was not here at the moment.

The man Morgan had betrayed to the enemy—a man Morgan had hated her entire life because of his arrogance, because of his power over her fate—stood just behind Leander, glaring at her through his small, round spectacles, his mouth as pinched as a prune.

Viscount Weymouth was just as vile as she remembered. *I hope you rot in hell*, she thought, glaring back at him, then realized with a start Leander was still staring at her.

One corner of Leander's mouth quirked. He gave the barest of nods, then looked away, releasing her.

Morgan sagged against Xander's strong shoulder. He wound his arm around her, pulling her close. He bent and whispered in her ear, "There, you see? I told you he'd be fine."

The day's not over yet. She burrowed closer to him.

"Where's Bhojak? And LeBlanc?" said Leander to Alejandro. "I want to call a meeting of the Council of Alphas. As soon as possible."

Bhojak and LeBlanc were the Alphas from the Nepal colony and the Quebec colony, respectively. They'd arrived with their retinues months ago, and had retreated with them to far corners of the rainforest settlement, as far away from each other and Alejandro as possible. They rarely mingled with others, excluding themselves from the frequent rituals and ceremonies that took place. They and their families were refugees, and though they'd been welcomed with open arms, they had a refugee's sense of displacement, of longing for home. Of rage.

"I'll call them," Alejandro said.

"Maybe you should wait for that meeting until after we decide who the Alpha of *this* colony actually is."

Hawk stepped forward, shouldering through the crowd. Everyone fell back in silence to let him pass. He came to a halt in front of Leander, gave a respectful nod of his head, then turned to Alejandro. He said, "Don't you agree? Brother?"

A snarl of such hostility ripped from Alejandro's throat that all the tiny hairs on Morgan's body stood on end. Hawk, however, simply smiled.

"A challenger," said Leander with interest, eying Hawk. For some reason, he sounded not at all surprised by this turn of events.

"A good-for-nothing, illegitimate *bastard*!" spat Alejandro.

"'Illegitimate bastard' is redundant." Leander spoke to Alejandro, but his gaze, razor sharp, stayed on Hawk. "And I'm afraid he's correct, under the circumstances. The meeting will have to wait. When does it happen?"

When Alejandro didn't reply—too busy shaking in fury and biting his tongue—one of his guards spoke. "Sunset." He hesitated only a moment before adding, "My Lord."

"Then we'll have the meeting an hour after sunset," Leander said, still staring at Hawk. The two of them locked eyes. Neither moved, or said another word, but there was violence in the stillness and silence, and for the first time, Morgan felt real fear for Hawk.

Leander had, so far, killed three challengers to his own rule. He could easily make it four.

Tension rippled in a palpable wave through the crowd.

Still looking at Hawk, he called out, "Morgan. Alexander. Will you please show us to our quarters?"

They made their way forward, and it was only when they finally stood directly in front of him that Leander looked away from Hawk. He looked first at Xander, nodding, then at Morgan. She willed herself not to break eye contact with him.

"You look well," he said. "Jenna will be pleased to know the jungle hasn't wilted you."

That was all that he said, but with those neutral words, Morgan knew he meant her no harm. She released the breath she didn't realize she'd been holding. Xander squeezed her hand. "I can think of few things that could," she said, and, just for good measure, dropped a swift, graceful curtsy.

Leander pressed his lips together, his eyes dancing with mirth. So low it was almost inaudible, he said, "Agreed."

Xander said, "Shall we?"

"Lead the way."

Hand in hand, Xander and Morgan pushed through the whispering crowd, while Leander and his entourage followed.

As they walked, Morgan felt Viscount Weymouth's eyes burning into her back.

THIRTY-SIX
A White Dot

Years later, Jack would look back on the next twenty-four hours as the single most defining day of her life.

She'd never been good at waiting, she remembered that much about herself as she paced back and forth inside Morgan's elegant home as the shadows grew long on the floor, and the songs of the night creatures of the forest began to echo through the trees. She also knew she'd once excelled at hiding, at slipping unnoticed through spaces and melting into the background, though she didn't recall exactly why she might have cultivated that talent.

Combined with a growing sense of anxiety and the two aforementioned facts, Jack found it impossible to keep her promise to Hawk. At dusk, she crept from her assigned waiting spot, climbed silently down the planks affixed to the tree that formed a ladder to the ground, and followed the thrum of the drums into the jungle.

She didn't know what she'd been expecting, but what she encountered stole all the breath from her lungs.

In a clearing surrounded on three sides by towering trees, the fourth a sheer cliff wall of red clay, where a flock of hundreds of blue and scarlet macaws perched, preening and picking at it, was a massive depression in the ground, roughly the shape of an oval. Ringed at regular intervals with torches spitting flame, with sides that sloped down toward a flat, dirt floor, it was a naturally formed arena. A throng of people encircled it, and many more were perched in the branches of the trees all around, staring down, watching the two men who stood there, bare-chested and barefoot, facing one another.

The man facing her direction was Hawk.

She knew immediately this was the contest Morgan had told her about. This was the fight where only one victor could emerge.

Jack crept forward, careful to keep behind the trees, stifling a scream as a brilliant blue snake with a red-tipped tail slid silently down the trunk closest to her. She jumped back, her hand to her chest, and bumped into something solid.

"Well, well, what have we here?"

Jack whirled around. Standing there in the shadows was a man with iron-gray hair and small, round spectacles. He was older, paunchy, and had a menacing smile and freezing eyes.

He reached out and grabbed her.

It should have surprised him more than it did. But Edward had come to understand during his time on Earth to expect the unexpected . . . so the sight of a half-dressed human female creeping around in the jungle, obviously spying, was little more than another oddity of his already odd life.

She was strong for a human—a female human, at that—but she wasn't a match for him, though he was no longer young. Or even in shape, for that matter. He twisted her arm behind her back, so high she squealed in pain, lifting onto her toes. He yanked her head back with a hand in her hair and hissed an unmistakable warning in her ear, enforced by the presence of the stiletto he always carried, now pressed against her throat.

Whoever she was, he knew she wasn't Expurgari. They only recruited men. A bounty hunter? An environmentalist reporting on the destruction of the rainforest who took a wrong turn somewhere, and now was hopelessly lost? Doubtful, but anything was possible. Either way, this would earn him points with the powers that be.

Maybe they'd even let him kill her himself.

Smiling at that thought, and grateful he'd found a satellite phone in the Alpha's deserted quarters so he was finally able to make that important call he hadn't been able to make for days, Viscount Weymouth shoved the female forward, broke through the edge of the trees, and walked into the clearing.

Alejandro's fist caught Hawk square in the jaw and knocked him staggering back.

Regaining his balance quickly, Hawk snarled at him in the Old Language, a curse forbidden to speak to the Alpha—but as far as he was concerned, Alejandro was Alpha no longer. He lunged forward, teeth bared, and crashed headlong into his brother's chest. They went down onto the dirt with a heavy thud that shivered the ground and was audible all the way up into the trees.

Rolling and punching and howling like a pair of slavering wolves, they were a spectacle that sent the crowd into a frenzy.

They leapt to their feet and began to circle one another. Alejandro swung, Hawk feinted. Hawk swung, Alejandro Shifted to Vapor, and his hand punched through a cool cloud of mist. The linen drawstring trousers Alejandro had been wearing slipped empty to the ground with a sigh. Hawk froze as a black panther appeared before him, crouched to spring.

Hawk couldn't Shift. His hand was injured; he'd cut it when he'd crushed the jar of ointment in his hand. Trapped in human form, he'd have to fight at a serious disadvantage.

For a hair of a moment, Alejandro looked surprised, waiting for Hawk to Shift, also. When he didn't, the look in the panther's eyes changed to one of victory. Then one of deadly focus.

There was only a single rule that governed this contest.

The loser dies.

Just as Alejandro leapt into the air with a powerful thrust of his haunches, Hawk caught sight of a flash of red with his peripheral vision. Distracted, he turned his attention away from the panther for a split second, snapping his gaze to the right and finding Jacqueline's face, pale, grimacing in pain. The flash of metal beneath her jaw: a knife.

Then a pair of razor-sharp fangs sank into his shoulder, and he went down, blood spurting over his chest.

Morgan felt the disturbance in the air at the exact same moment she caught sight of Viscount Weymouth pushing Jacqueline through the crowd, which also happened to be the same moment Alejandro leapt on Hawk in the arena and tore a sizable chunk of flesh from his shoulder.

Deep in the marrow of her bones, she knew what was about to happen.

Time slowed to a snail's crawl. Her vision came into perfect, crystalline focus, and she saw everything unfold simultaneously. There was Hawk on the ground, executing a swift, precise roll that took him from beneath Alejandro so efficiently for a moment the panther was off-balance, his long tail cracking like a whip behind him as he hissed and spun around. There was Viscount Weymouth, shoving his way toward where she stood with Leander, Xander, and the other Assembly members to one side of the arena, the expression on his face one of smug satisfaction, the crowd parting in shock to let him pass. There was Leander, rigid and feral-eyed, no longer paying attention to the contest below, but staring with avid concentration at the sky above, twilight staining it mottled purple and blue like a bruise.

And there, far off in the evening sky, was a white dot, vivid as a star on the distant horizon. Only this star sported wings.

It was moving fast in their direction.

Together, Leander and Morgan whispered, "Jenna!"

Jack's heart was choking her.

She couldn't catch a breath with it in her throat, as it beat furiously in fear and horror. The man shoving her forward had the strength of a bear in spite of having the appearance of an elderly fop, and was sweating in his fitted white dress shirt and formal black slacks. He pushed her relentlessly on as she tried to twist out of his grip, stumbling, panting, trying not to let the knife on her jugular press too hard against her skin.

He threw her down. Morgan was there, and Xander, and others she didn't recognize, a mass of bodies pressing in to see, everyone gaping at her captor. But Jack was looking to her right and down, to the awful scene in the arena: a bleeding Hawk and a giant, spitting black cat, ears flattened against its head, muscles bunched beneath its glossy black coat, sinking into a crouch.

My God, it's going to eat him!

"No!" she screamed.

The panther flicked a look over its shoulder. Hawk took the window of opportunity and leapt on the animal, throwing his big arms around its neck, knocking it off balance. Then Jack was hauled to her feet roughly by a strong pair of hands, and she lost sight of Hawk altogether as bodies around her closed the gap in her view.

"My Lord," said the man who'd had the knife at her throat, bowing stiffly to Leander. He kept his hand fisted in her hair as he did so. "I found *this*"—he gave Jack a kick—"hiding in the shrubbery. Shall I slit its throat?"

Leander shouldered past him, ignoring him, looking up at the sky as if it were about to rain diamonds.

"You bloody duffer, Weymouth!" screeched Morgan. She hauled off, made a fist, and punched the man right in the nose.

He fell to his knees with a cry, clutching his face. Blood poured between his fingers.

Gasps went up all around them, loud and amazed, and for a moment Jack thought it was because of what Morgan had done. But then she realized no one was looking at Weymouth.

Everyone was looking up.

She stood. Her eyes rose to the heavens, and she squinted, searching . . .

Impossible! Impossible!

It repeated in her head like a record stuck in a groove, over and over. Her mouth dropped open. Her knees turned to Jell-O. Her heart took a swan dive toward her feet.

Sinuous, beautiful, gleaming white as a pearl, the creature had silver-tipped wings and barbs along its powerful tail, a mane like a horse's flowing down its long, elegant neck. It was moving at an incredible rate of speed, scoring the sky like an arrow shot from a bow, magnificent in the economy and grace of its every movement.

Even at this distance, Jack saw the curved talons that tipped the legs drawn up against its belly, the preternatural yellow eyes . . . and the muzzle full of razor-sharp teeth.

A dragon. Holy mother of God, she was looking at a *dragon*.

A gentle hand on her arm. "Magnificent, isn't she?" Morgan spoke in a soft tone of wonderment, as she shook out the hand she'd used to hit Weymouth.

Jack's mouth wouldn't form words.

"Jenna," Morgan clarified. "The Queen."

Behind them, Weymouth was sputtering curses, staggering to his feet. He entreated Leander to punish Morgan, to make an example of such a volatile female, but Leander had no time for him, because he was watching the Queen like a bloodhound, watching her speed and the slight, telling tremble in the tips of her wings.

"Too fast," Leander muttered, judging the speed of the dragon by her distance from where they stood. "She's coming in too fast!" He turned to the crowd and, waving his arms, roared at the top of his lungs, "MOVE!"

Panic erupted in the clearing. Everyone began shoving and pushing, directionless, shouting at one another while trying to get away. Jack was pushed along by a surge of bodies toward the trees. She desperately tried to look for Hawk, but the arena was obscured by a sea of bobbing dark heads. She stumbled and fell, and someone picked her up with a hand under her arm.

Jack looked up just in time to glimpse the dragon overhead— big as a starship, its vast shimmering wings beating furiously in a futile attempt to slow itself, thrashing the air all around so dust swirled up and her hair flew into her eyes—then the tops of the trees were sheared off as it hurtled past. Greenery exploded everywhere like confetti shot from a cannon.

A great, thunderous *boom* was heard as it landed, shuddering the earth beneath Jack's feet. It shook every branch in every tree for miles. Then came a deafening cacophony of shrieks and cries as thousands of birds took to wing, disturbed from their perches, rising in droves to darken the sky.

Then all went still. Jack looked up through the flurry of leaves drifting down from above to behold the great white dragon standing in the middle of the arena, chest heaving, smoke pluming from its nostrils, wings aloft. It stretched its scaled neck, looking around as if trying to locate something.

Or someone. Leander bounded through the crowd toward it, tearing off his shirt.

Hawk, thought Jack.

She pushed to the front of the crowd. Just as she reached the place where the bodies thinned to emptiness to reveal the open clearing, the long, ragged claw marks gouged deep into the earth, the dragon shimmered and lost shape. Seconds later, only a glittering plume of mist hovered above the ground where the creature had once been. Everyone around her took a sharp intake of breath.

Jack sensed it, too.

Power. Raw and elemental, a sizzling current passed over her skin, unlike anything she'd ever felt.

Then the plume of mist gathered in on itself, reforming to take the shape of a woman.

She was nude. Pale and blonde whereas all the others except Jack were dark and golden-skinned, she stood silently, her gaze trained on Leander. Jack suffered the fleeting thought that maybe this whole adventure was the result of a psychotic break. Maybe this all was happening inside her mind, because this couldn't be happening in real life. *It wasn't possible.* Then she spied Hawk and her poor heart gave such a painful throb she felt sure she was either crazy or dreaming, because she didn't know him at all, but her heart definitely did.

Somehow, he'd gained the advantage over the massive black panther. They were in one corner of the arena, and Hawk was on the animal's back, an arm around its neck, the other squeezing his opposite fist, his muscles bulging as he bore all his weight down on its throat.

He was choking it. Quite successfully, it appeared. It listed and fell sideways, and Hawk squeezed harder.

Leander reached Jenna. He slung his shirt around her shoulders, quickly buttoned it to cover her nudity, then crushed her to his chest. They shared a passionate kiss, ignoring everyone, then the Queen buried her face in his neck.

After a moment she raised her head. Over Leander's shoulder, she locked eyes with Jack, and it took everything Jack had not to take a step backward.

The Queen turned and looked behind her. She shouted, "Stop!" and Hawk froze. He looked up, and his face hardened.

Could it be possible he hadn't noticed her? No, Jack realized, as Hawk released the panther and straightened, putting his shoulders back. He'd seen her all right. He'd just chosen to ignore her.

A hysterical giggle threatened to burst from Jack's throat. He'd chosen to ignore the arrival of a white dragon, in order to continue his fight to the death with a black panther. The world had gone entirely mad.

There was utter silence in the clearing, so she was able to hear with perfect clarity what the Queen said next.

"Tell me," she said to Leander, looking at the two men.

Leander, even in profile, looked as if he'd had better days. His relief was palpable. "A challenger to the Alpha," he said, sounding out of breath. He spread his hand over the small of Jenna's back, as if to reassure himself she was really standing there.

The Queen cursed, and Jack decided she liked her.

"What's your name?" she said to Hawk, ignoring the panther, who had crawled several feet away, and was shaking. It shook its head, coughed, and sprawled over the ground.

"I'm called Hawk," he replied, in a tone of impatient disrespect.

Leander growled, but the Queen simply held up her hand, staring at Hawk. She flicked a glance to the panther. "Stand down, Hawk. This contest is over."

He snarled, "I'll never stand down to the man who hurt my woman." His eyes met Jack's.

My woman. Dear God.

The Queen turned to look at her. From somewhere in the crowd, Morgan's voice rang out. "I can explain everything!"

The Queen's gaze found Morgan, and a faint smile crossed her face. She nodded, said, "I can hardly wait to hear it." Then she looked back at Jack and her voice turned hard. "But not just yet. First I have business to attend to."

Leander bent his head to her ear, murmuring, "You're exhausted. You look pale, and you're shaking. Whatever it is can wait until after you've res—"

She broke from his arms without waiting for him to finish, and made a beeline toward Jack.

Jack took one horrified step back, then another, until she realized the Queen wasn't looking at her, but at something right behind her. Weak with relief, Jack pressed to one side and let her pass, and then the Queen stood before Weymouth.

He was still bleeding. Red splatters decorated the front of his shirt in an erratic pattern, lurid against the white. He bowed, sniveling, his hand covering his nose. "Welcome, Your Highness!" he said nasally. "*So* wonderful to see you. And please don't worry about me, it's just a little—"

The Queen's hand shot out, and she grabbed him around the throat. "Traitor!" she hissed. Then the woman disappeared in a flash of glittering mist, power blasted through the clearing in a heated wave, her white shirt was shredded to confetti, and the dragon was there again, looming over them all.

Weymouth was clutched in one of its powerful claws.

His scream was high and piercing. The dragon flung him to the ground and he lay there, gasping, blood flowering through his shirt where the points of five sharp talons had punctured his skin.

He tried to scramble away. His glasses fell off, as did one shoe. The dragon reared high above him, inhaled a breath, and opened its muzzle, revealing row upon row of gleaming, pointed teeth.

Weymouth looked over his shoulder. Comprehending what was about to happen, he rolled to his back, pulled the same blade from his pocket he'd held to Jack's throat, grasped it with both hands, and plunged it, hilt deep, into his chest. He made a gurgling sound, hideous and wet, which was summarily drowned out when the dragon stretched its neck and exhaled.

A molten stream of fire roared from its mouth.

Weymouth was incinerated.

It was over within seconds. When the smoke cleared, a charred husk lay unmoving on the ground, the earth all around it scorched black.

The dragon turned back to woman, who delicately burped a tiny flame. She covered her mouth and said, "Excuse me." Then her eyes fluttered closed and she slumped to her knees, caught before falling all the way by Leander, who ran up to gather her in his arms.

Jack didn't see anything else after that because the ground came up hard to catch her, and the world faded to darkness.

THIRTY-SEVEN

Soul-Eating Demon

The rage inside Caesar felt like a nuclear bomb detonating in his bowels. He'd been staring at the satellite phone in his hands for long blank minutes, shaking with fury, needing to beat something bloody, thinking the same two words over and over.

That. *Bitch*!

This Queen of theirs was craftier than he'd given her credit for.

With a curse, he threw the phone at the wall, whereupon it immediately shattered with a satisfactory crash, spraying bits of plastic and metal over the dusty stone floor. He began to pace, seething.

"Filthy spy! You think you can come here and sneak around? You think there won't be consequences? You think you can outsmart *me*?".

He knew it was her now, that night when the desert air felt alive. Weymouth had just warned him in his hushed, hurried call that she wasn't with their party in the jungle, and was probably headed his way.

He wished he'd known earlier to watch out for anything *white*.

"Fucking falcon!" he shouted to the empty room. "Fucking SPIDER!"

She'd heard everything. She knew everything. Now there was only one thing left for him to do.

"Marcell!" Caesar roared. In moments he appeared, bowing, in the doorway of Caesar's chambers.

"Sire?"

"We're going into Marrakech. Tonight. You, me, that mercenary friend of yours who's such a good tracker. And the big bald one, the deserter from the Nepal colony who recently joined us."

"The Firestarter?"

"That's him."

Marcell's brows lifted.

Caesar said, "There's been a change of plans. We need an airplane." His eyes met Marcell's and his lips, cold and red, curved to a smile. "We're going to make a little unscheduled visit to Brazil."

Hawk had a lot of experience repressing his feelings. Before he met Jacqueline, he was profoundly uncomfortable even admitting he *had* feelings, and went to great lengths to smother, bury, or otherwise ignore them out of existence. Feelings were for the weak. Specifically, *tears* were for the weak.

He never cried. Never. Even as a boy, when his father gave him a vicious beating for some infraction, imagined or real, he bit his tongue and endured it, dry-eyed as a marble statue adorning a grave.

Only now, listening to the Queen speak, he thought he would.

". . . as soon as possible. I understand why you did it, Morgan, I know your heart was in the right place, but it's not for us to make a believer from a critic with kidnapping and coercion. She leaves first thing tomorrow morning."

Morgan stood in front of Jenna, head lowered, looking appropriately cowed.

Directing her fierce gaze in Hawk's direction, the Queen quietly added, "And those pictures will be destroyed. Immediately. *Tonight.*"

Her tone indicated exactly how despicable she considered him for his part in the whole wretched operation . . . an opinion with which he wholeheartedly agreed.

"It's already been done." He felt as though he'd been swallowing rocks. His voice sounded like it emanated from the depths of a well. *Pull yourself together!* he screamed silently to himself. *You knew Jacqueline would be leaving! You knew this would come!*

He just didn't think it would be happening quite so soon. He began a serious discussion with himself about the merits of slitting his wrists versus saying or doing something to make the Queen turn him into a charcoal briquette, as she had with Weymouth, eventually deciding he deserved nothing more than to live a long and healthy life, alone, wallowing in his own misery.

He deserved to suffer. How he could've gone along with the plan in the first place was making him too sick to even consider.

Along with him and Morgan, all the other Assembly members and the Alphas from each colony had gathered in the Queen's lavish new home. The tri-level structure was built around the trunk of a Brazil nut tree so large it would take ten men with outstretched arms to encircle its massive girth, and the tree grew right up through the center. Hawk and Morgan stood before Leander and Jenna, who were seated together on a cushioned settee in the main living area on the second floor.

Though it was upward of eighty degrees, Jenna was wrapped in a thick blanket. The occasional shiver wracked her body, and Leander, beside her, looked tense and unhappy, as he watched her with a frown.

As they were rocked listlessly by Olivia Sutherland, whose haunted eyes stared out of a wan face, the twins cooed happily in a bassinette nearby.

"That's what prompted his challenge against the Alpha." Morgan shot Hawk a sympathetic look. "He refused to turn over the pictures to Alejandro when ordered to do so. He's become very . . . fond of Jacqueline."

Fond.

Hawk closed his eyes. He wasn't fond of her. He was balls-out, soul searingly, madly in love with her. And she didn't even remember him. And she was leaving tomorrow.

What a bitch Fate turned out to be.

He opened his eyes to find the Queen staring wide-eyed at him. "Your challenge was prompted by your *fondness* for a woman who argued we should all be exterminated?"

Put that way, it did sound less than reasonable. "Given enough evidence that their prejudice is unfounded, people can change."

She studied him. "True enough. And you think you changed her?"

He said gruffly, "We changed each other. She wasn't the only one with stupid ideas."

There was a long, weighted pause while the Queen examined his face. "When I asked you to stand down, you said that you'd never stand down to the man who hurt your woman. I'd like you to explain that. How did Alejandro hurt her? How did you grow to become so . . . protective of her?"

So Hawk told the story. He began at the very beginning and told it through to the end, leaving nothing out, including Jacqueline's memory loss.

When he finished speaking, the Queen closed her eyes and exhaled a long, heavy breath. "So you're in love."

Scoffs and chuckles and gasps of horror rose from around the room. Hawk went rigid with anger. He said between clenched teeth, "I don't care that it's forbidden! You can give me as many lashes as you want and it won't change my—"

"Forbidden! Oh for God's sake, that stupid rule has caused more misery!" she interrupted, cross. She pointed at her chest. "Did you know that my *mother* was human? And my father was Alpha—and he was put to death for loving her?"

Everyone knew that. Her father was the most powerful Alpha ever, the Skinwalker himself. His treason was the stuff of legend. Hawk nodded.

"And did you know that I grew up on the run, hiding, hunted, until the day my father was taken away—and after that my mother drank herself to death? And after *that* I was alone and scared and even more miserable than before?"

Hawk opened his mouth, then shut it again. The room had become very quiet.

"And my unborn nephew is a half-Blood, like me—should I sentence him to a lifetime of running and hiding? Of eventually watching one or both of his parents die, as I did?"

"Nephew?" Hawk held very still, sure that whatever would next be spoken would have a monumental impact on them all.

With an unhappy look as if this was a secret he'd rather not share, Leander explained, "My brother, Christian. He lives in Barcelona with his wife. His *human* wife. They're expecting their first child."

Several soft gasps arose from behind Hawk. Clearly he wasn't the only one floored by this information.

Drawing herself tall, the Queen said, "Love is *never* forbidden, not as long as I'm in charge. I don't care if you're in love with a human woman or an *Ikati* male or a damn goat—love is love. The Law of single species mating is hereby abolished."

The silence that followed this statement was so profound Hawk's heartbeat sounded like thunder in his ears.

"And another thing. This whole Alpha business of fighting to the death—that's so dumb it gives me a migraine! Why does everything have to be life or death? Where's the common sense? Where's the middle ground? Here's an idea we've been far too slow to adopt: democracy. From now on, these contests will be decided by a vote from all the colony members. No one will be ruled without his or her consent."

A jolt of such shock went through Hawk that he felt as if he'd been electrocuted. Tension began to mount in the room. Men exchanged glances, there was a restless shuffling of feet. But the Queen wasn't done yet.

"And I'm abolishing corporal punishment. What you described about the punishment tree is . . . well, it's disgusting, honestly. We're done with all of that."

Amid the obvious shock this declaration caused, Leander drawled, "How do you propose we punish traitors and deserters, then, love? Shall we roast them alive instead?"

A flush of color rose in her pale cheeks. "We won't have to," she said quietly. "Because there won't *be* any more traitors and deserters. From now on everyone is free to go."

Into the stunned hush, LeBlanc, the Alpha from Quebec, said politely, "Excuse me, Your Highness?"

Jenna rose. She looked around the room, her gaze settling on each person in turn. In a strong, clear voice, she said, "Anyone who wants to leave this colony, can. They won't be apprehended, or punished. There will be no retaliation for leaving, or living among humans, or breeding with them. All the old Laws designed to keep us safe and hidden have failed. We don't need them anymore. If we're going to survive, we need to adapt." She paused, took a deep breath, and said, "We're not going to hide anymore. We're going to fight."

"Fight?" Leander jolted to his feet, radiating tension.

Jenna turned to him. Her eyes were vivid with anger, the set of her jaw was hard. "They know we're here, the Expurgari and Section Thirty, most likely the rest of the world. Caesar clued them in because Weymouth clued *him* in. I don't know how soon they'll strike, but I know one thing . . . I'm not running away from them. In fact, I'm in the mood to kick some serious *ass*."

Hearing this, Hawk endured a moment of scalding fury, chased by a sense of loss so deep it felt bottomless. All the years, all the long centuries of hiding, all the sacrifices made in the name of safety, undone by a single weak link in the chain. By one traitor, whispering words into the ear of the enemy.

The room erupted into cries of disbelief and anger, shock prickling the air, but Hawk could only stare at the floor, dumb with hate. He was sorry now the Queen had roasted Weymouth; the need for revenge was a pulse of heat in his palms, a drumbeat in his blood.

Eventually the tumult died. The Queen assured everyone she'd hold a proper meeting in the morning, after they'd all rested, and plans would be made. When the last of the crowd had filed from the room, he was still standing in his posture of defeat, staring blankly at nothing.

He heard a gentle voice say his name. He looked up to find Jenna staring at him from across the room with something like concern. "You'll want to leave with the reporter, I suppose."

In a voice low and dangerous, Leander said, "This is *madness*, Jenna."

She lifted a shoulder. "Such is life. If our end is here, if that's what's meant to happen, so be it. We're all on a ticking clock, and life in a cage isn't a life worth living."

"You sound like Morgan!" he exploded, but his wife remained calm as morning.

"Thank you."

"It wasn't a compliment! This isn't only about us! About *our* safety, *our* future! What about the girls?"

She sent him a look that would have had Hawk's testicles shrinking up into his abdomen. But Leander was apparently a stronger man than he; he didn't even flinch.

"This *is* for the girls. For their future. So they don't have to grow up like I did."

"But how in God's name are we supposed to protect them from—"

"The children can protect themselves."

Hawk looked up, arrested by the odd note in the voice that had spoken.

It was Olivia Sutherland; she hadn't left with the others. She stared down into the bassinette by her side with the strangest combination of awe, affection, and fear. She glanced up, looked between Jenna and Leander, and finally let her haunted gaze rest on Jenna. She whispered, "You know that."

Leander looked confused. Jenna stood, walked slowly to the waist-high railing that spanned the perimeter of the room, brushed aside a gauzy curtain, and stared off silently into the starry, humid night.

"What do you mean?" demanded Leander, striding to the bassinette. Two pairs of small white arms waved in the air as the twins reached for their father. He lowered his hand into the crib and stroked their faces, cupped four tiny hands within the broad expanse of his palm.

Without turning from the view, Jenna said, "They took your Gifts."

Olivia answered, "Yes."

"What?" said Hawk and Leander in unison.

Jenna passed a hand over her face, inhaled a heavy breath, then squared her shoulders. She turned to face them. "I think it's one of their Gifts. They can absorb the Gifts of others, at least while they're in close contact. Physical contact. During the pregnancy . . . then breastfeeding . . ." her gaze flicked to Olivia, who nodded.

Slowly, Leander withdrew his hand from the bassinette and let it fall to his side. He lifted his gaze to Jenna, his body still as stone. "They can *feed* on us? Like . . ." He swallowed, leaving the word unsaid.

Vampires.

Jenna walked toward him with a muted rustle of fabric, trailing the blanket behind her like the train of a wedding gown. "I realized tonight that my Gift of Sight was back. When I touched Weymouth, I Saw all his plans, all his lies. I knew them already from my visit to Caesar, what they'd been up to, but . . ." she trailed off to silence. After a moment, she said, "And the only difference was that I hadn't breastfed the twins for days."

"Why haven't they done it with me?" Leander murmured, looking back at the girls.

Jenna said, "I don't know. Maybe we should ask them."

"Do they speak to you, too?"

Olivia spoke in a tone of such hushed fervor it raised all the hair on the back of Hawk's neck.

Speak? he thought, horrified. *Infants? Babies? Speak?*

He and Leander stared at Olivia in shock, while Jenna remained silent, her gaze on the bassinette.

"They also go into my dreams," Olivia continued, her eyes glazed with fatigue. Her hands had begun to shake, and as she wrung them together, her gaze darted around the room as if she were looking for something lurking in the shadows. Past his horror, Hawk wondered how long it had been since she'd slept.

Leander whispered, "Dreamwalkers?"

"I think they've been trying to tell me that something bad is coming. Something catastrophic. And they . . . and they're going to . . ." Olivia faltered, glancing back to the bassinette. She wrapped her arms around her body, closed her eyes, and began to rock back and forth as if trying to comfort herself. As if deeply frightened.

Jenna touched Leander's arm, watching Olivia. She said, "We're all tired. This can wait until morning. Grayson left with the others; will you see she gets home safely?" Her husband looked shell-shocked as he glanced down into the crib then back at Jenna in mute dismay.

"Please," she said, when he still hesitated. "I'd like to talk to Hawk alone. Just for a moment."

Leander's expression transformed from dismayed to murderous. He sent Hawk a stare that could have frozen molten lava. It was crystal clear what he thought of this idea.

Jenna lifted a hand and stroked her fingers lightly down Leander's cheek. He turned his attention back to her and she smiled up at him. "I missed you, too," she murmured, then rose on her toes and pressed a kiss to his lips. He grabbed her around the waist and pulled her into a tight hug.

Hawk looked away, but heard what Leander whispered into his wife's ear.

"Five minutes, woman. When I get back, you'd better be waiting in bed. And you've got a lot of explaining to do."

He released her, crossed to Olivia, and took her gently by the arm. He led her from the room, stopping briefly at the top of the curved stairway to give Jenna a last, lingering look before leaving.

He sent Hawk a last look, too, this one not nearly as nice.

When he was gone, Jenna collapsed onto the settee. She crumpled boneless to the cushions as if it had taken all her strength to remain standing until now, and her knees could no longer support her weight.

Hawk leapt into motion and went to her. "Your Highness—"

"I'm fine," she said, waving him away. Unconvinced, he squatted on the floor in front of her, ready to assist in any way he could. Her head was in her hands, and through her fingers and a curtain of golden hair, she peeked at him. "And you don't have to call me that. In fact, I insist you don't. It's so . . . pretentious." She sighed, a heavy exhalation accompanied by a shudder, and Hawk thought he'd never seen anyone so weighted, her thoughts and responsibilities and the looming threat of war wrapped around her shoulders like a mantle made of stone.

"What would you like me to call you, then?"

She sat up, and pushed her hair out of her face. "She Who Must Be Obeyed."

Though her expression was solemn, her green eyes twinkled as she spoke, and Hawk realized she was teasing him.

"I know several bossy females who'd appreciate being called that," he said in utter seriousness, and the Queen's lips curled.

"Bossy?" she said with arched brows. "Aren't you the brave one?"

"No, just exceptionally stupid."

She laughed at that, and for a moment the weight seemed to lift from her shoulders. "Yes, that's the testosterone. But we 'females' have to deal with estrogen, which makes us a little crazy."

"Actually I think it makes you tough," he replied, all humor gone. "Tougher than we are because you feel things even more deeply than we do, and if I had to feel anything more deeply than I already do, I'd probably throw myself off a cliff. Strike that—I *would* throw myself off a cliff. I don't know how you handle it."

She peered at him, trying to ascertain if he was mocking her. Apparently satisfied he wasn't, she patted the cushion beside her, inviting him to sit.

He did. They sat in awkward silence for a moment, staring at one another. When the silence grew too uncomfortable, Hawk said, "I hope you're not trying to debate whether to take your dragon form and bite off my head. I could probably survive without it, seeing how I hardly ever use it, but I've gotten used to having it around. I'm sentimental that way."

"Humor," she said, "is something I've really missed. Consider your head safe." She amended, "For the moment."

Unsure whether she was now teasing him or not, Hawk simply inclined his head.

After another uncomfortable pause wherein she examined his face in such a way that made him feel almost naked, she said quietly, "It's not easy, is it?"

"Life?"

"Love."

He looked away, dragging a hand through his hair. Not easy. That might be the understatement of the century. He didn't want her to think him a coward, but he also didn't have the energy to lie. And he didn't think anything he said would make a damn bit of difference one way or another, so he just went with the truth.

"I think . . . I think it might be the most terrible thing in the world."

"No. There's something else that's worse. But love is a close second."

He looked back at her to find her smiling at him, her eyes soft. She said, "Love is the most difficult journey you'll ever embark upon, but the destination is worth all the horrible things you'll experience during the trip. Don't let the bumps and pitfalls scare you away from where you need to go. Hang in there until the bitter end. Believe me, I know from experience it's worth every second of torture. One day you'll look back and be glad for all you suffered, because the pain made the eventual joy all the more sweet."

Hawk looked away, his throat tight. She was wrong; there would be only suffering. There would be no joy, no sweetness, not for him and Jacqueline. "This is what you wanted to talk to me about? War is coming, extinction is looming over us, your babies are—whatever they are—and you'd like to hear about my personal life?"

From the corner of his eye, he saw her sphinxlike smile. "I'm sentimental that way. So stop avoiding the subject and tell me why you're so upset."

Upset didn't begin to cover it. He closed his eyes, exhaled, and in a voice that cracked several times as he spoke said, "She doesn't remember me. There is no destination anymore. There's only a bridge that got burned down, and no way to rebuild it."

"There's always a way," Jenna said enigmatically, but Hawk was already shaking his head.

"Morgan already tried. Jacqueline's memory is gone; the spirit vine eroded it. She'll never remember *us*." He looked down at his hands, not entirely surprised to see them trembling. "And even if she somehow did remember, I can't offer her a future. What chance of happiness could we have? All we have ahead of us now is war. Bloodshed. Death. Even if she wanted to stay, I wouldn't allow it. I would never put her in harm's way. And I can't leave, especially now; it's my duty to stay and fight. And think of how we started—what I did to her!"

Growing more and more agitated, Hawk stood and began to pace to and fro across the room while Jenna watched him, expressionless. "What woman in her right mind would trust me after a thing like that? I don't deserve her trust. I don't deserve *her*! I have nothing to give her, nothing worthwhile, not even my name! I'm a bastard, the illegitimate son of one of the worst men I've ever known—I'm nothing!"

Jenna cleared her throat. He pulled up short, breathing hard, anguish lashing him like a thousand steel-tipped whips, and stared at her.

"Are you done?"

She was looking at him with raised brows, waiting. He sent her a curt nod.

"I wish we knew one another better," she said evenly, "because I'd love to smack you a good one upside your thick head right about now."

Before he could formulate an appropriate response, she continued. "So you have a conscience. You feel bad about the plan. Congratulations. But let's not forget you were operating *under pain of death* if you didn't comply with Alejandro's commands."

Hawk stood stiffly, lips pinched, heat suffusing his face. "That's no excuse—"

"Shut up," she said mildly.

He did.

"Let's also not forget you destroyed the pictures, and opted to challenge Alejandro in a fight to the death instead of showing them to him. Which means you'd rather risk your life than see her hurt, or disrespected, no matter how you might have felt about her at the beginning. With me so far?"

Reluctantly, he nodded.

"I applaud you for your loyalty to the colony, for thinking you need to stay and fight. And if I'm being perfectly honest, I hope that's what you'll do, because we're going to need every man we can get. But, again if I'm being honest, I'm not sure if one person will make a bit of difference." She glanced at the bassinette, then back at him, her green eyes dark and troubled. "I have . . . I have the oddest feeling that this fight and its outcome have already been determined."

Seeing his look, she sighed another of her weighted sighs, lifted a hand to her forehead. "I could be wrong. These things I feel and dream . . . who knows." She dropped her hand and raised her gaze to his. "The only thing I know for sure is that life happens one day at a time, one second at a time, and everything you think you know can change"—she snapped her fingers—"in the space of one instant to the next. So my advice to you is this: Forget the past. Take all that baggage you've been carrying around forever and just set it down. Then take a good hard look inside yourself, and decide what you really want, regardless of what you think you *should* want or do or be. And then go after it. With every bit of focus and determination, with absolutely no holds barred, go after what you want. Even if it doesn't work out, you can still respect yourself, knowing you tried."

Jenna pushed off the settee and rose to face him, the blanket pooling around her feet. "We're all going to die one day, Hawk. Maybe one day very soon. So make the most of your life, before it's too late. Find your happiness, and hold on to it. To hell with everything else."

Hawk stared at her with his mouth hanging open, astonished.

One side of her mouth quirked. "Yeah. I get that a lot."

Leander's footsteps echoed on the lower-level stairs. He hadn't even been *three* minutes, let alone five.

Jenna turned her head toward the sound. "I'd love to talk with you more, but I can't guarantee my husband isn't going to start breaking things the minute he sets foot back in this room. You know how Alphas are." She glanced back at him and winked, leaving him speechless once again.

Leander was taking the steps three at a time, pounding up them like a man possessed. Jenna urged Hawk, "Go," and gestured toward the opposite side of the room, and another flight of stairs, narrow and winding.

He went, befuddled, stopping just before passing to the lower level. When he looked over, she was still watching him, holding the blanket tight against her body.

"Just out of curiosity, what's the other thing? The thing that's worse than love?"

Her smile was beautiful, and incredibly sad. "Regret," she said softly. "Love can be painful, sometimes cruel, but regret will devour you, bite by bite, until there's nothing left at all. If love is a tyrant, regret is a soul-eating demon. Be careful it doesn't eat yours."

Then she turned and walked away.

THIRTY-EIGHT
Free to Go

The blade sliced deeply and cleanly through the pilot's neck, severing his internal, anterior, and external jugular veins, exposing the muscles of his throat straight down to his spinal cord in the process.

Caesar laughed in glee at the spectacular arc of blood that sprayed across the instrument panel, dripping down the windshield and rounded walls of the cockpit. The pilot, choking on his own blood, coughed—a strangled, animal sound—and thrashed in his seat. Still strapped in, he struggled but it didn't yield much result.

"Shh," Caesar whispered into his ear, holding tight to the man's head as his struggles grew weaker, the blood arcing lower and lower with each pulse of his heart. In mere moments it was over. The pilot slumped to one side, dead, and Caesar was left with nothing but a slippery red cockpit and a raging hard-on throbbing against the zipper of his trousers.

Too fast. It's always over too fast. What he wouldn't give for a woman right now. A chained and screaming one, preferably.

Marcell popped his head into the cockpit, surveyed the scene without batting an eye, then said, "All clear, Sire." Just as quickly, he was gone.

With a sigh of regret, Caesar released the limp pilot and stepped back, adjusting his crotch. *"Paenitet, amicus."* Sorry friend. He spoke in Latin, the language of his youth, a dead language that perfectly matched the landscape of his heart. "But I do appreciate the flight."

He turned and exited the cockpit. He had to crouch a bit as he made his way through the cabin to the open door because the plane was a smallish one, but it suited their purposes. It was fast, and there had been no pesky security checks or identification required on the way out of Morocco. Cash was still king in certain parts of the world.

Which reminded him.

Caesar returned to the cockpit, removed the wad of cash from the pilot's flight bag, stuffed it into the small backpack he carried, then left the plane for good. Once outside on the tarmac, he showed Marcell's tracker friend the GPS coordinates logged from Weymouth's call on his satellite phone.

The tracker, a hunter and mercenary named Badr who Marcell had met in the souks of Marrakech, had a face like a slab of meat, adorned with a filthy black beard. Inspecting the blood on Caesar's hands, he grinned. In a faux British accent he said, "Easy peasy, guv'nuh," then turned and ambled away, whistling.

Caesar sent Marcell a sidelong glance. Marcell pursed his lips. "Perhaps wait until after he leads us back out of the jungle, Sire," he suggested, and Caesar sighed, knowing it was good advice.

In the meantime, he, Marcell, and the silent, twitchy male known only as the Firestarter followed the tracker in a line, straight off the tarmac of the Manaus airport and into the warm Brazilian night.

Jack awoke in warm darkness to the sound of gently falling rain.

She bolted upright. She was in a room, open and spacious, in a bed . . . Oh yes. This was the same room she'd woken up in earlier. But something was different . . .

Someone was standing across the room, leaning against the wood railing, his broad back facing her, his gaze trained far off into the night.

Hawk.

She realized she'd spoken his name aloud when he turned, pushing off the railing to stare at her. In the darkness, his eyes glinted silver like a cat's.

"You're awake." His voice sounded different. Flat, somehow. Empty.

"What happened? I remember you, fighting. I remember . . ." she hesitated to say it aloud, it sounded so insane. "A dragon?"

He looked at her for a long, silent moment, then turned back to the railing. "You leave in the morning. Try to get some sleep."

Leave? Her heart leapt into her throat. When he began to move away, Jack said, "Did I faint? Did . . . did you win?"

"Yes. And no. At least, I don't know for sure. It remains to be seen if I won." He paused, and there was something unsettling in his short silence. His voice grew deeper. Rougher. "Not that it matters either way."

"Why? What do you mean?" Her mouth dry, Jack slipped from the bed and stood waiting for him to answer.

But he wouldn't even look at her. Her eyes had adjusted to the darkness, and now she saw the tension in the line of his shoulders, the hard, clenched edges of his jaw. "Just . . . try to rest. You'll be back home in New York tomorrow, Jacqueline. This will all be over tomorrow."

The way he said the word "this," the swift, pained glance he sent in her direction as he spoke that one word, made her wonder again what exactly had occurred between them, what lurked unseen in the black holes in her memory.

She needed to know. If she really was leaving tomorrow, she needed to know what she was leaving behind.

She moved toward him slowly, then stopped just a few feet away, aware of how his breathing had changed as she'd stepped closer. Aware of how his body had stiffened. Her voice came low. "And is that . . . good? Is that what you want?"

He moistened his lips. "That's what's best."

"That's not what I asked."

There was a pause in which the only sound was the rain on the roof, dripping with a melancholy sigh through the canopy of leaves. "Yes. It's good. It's . . . what I want."

The lie was so blatant she didn't even bother to offer a retort. She simply walked in front of him, stopped a foot away, and looked up into his face. He refused to look at her, so she turned his head with her fingers on his chin. When his gaze met hers, his eyes were black.

She whispered, "I'm so sorry that I can't remember whatever happened between us. Maybe eventually I will . . . or maybe you could just tell me."

His eyes were tortured. He swallowed, then gently removed her hand from his face. He stepped back, out of arms' reach. "Some things are better forgotten, Jacqueline. Sometimes . . . forgetting can be a gift." He drew his brows together, closing his eyes just longer than a blink. When he opened them again, there was a new coldness there, a hardness that made her heart hurt.

"Hawk—"

"Sleep," he said abruptly, turning to go. "I'll be back just after dawn."

Then he vanished, silent as smoke, leaving Jack alone with nothing but the sound of the rain. After a few minutes of listening hard into the darkness, Jack went back to the bed, crawled under the sheets, and lay there, staring up at the ceiling, until the first golden rays of dawn slipped through the canopy, and the birds awoke to sing their morning songs into the trees.

As was their custom, the tribe gathered at dawn at the Well of Souls for the burning.

Shrouded in white linen, Weymouth's charred corpse lay atop a hollow rectangular altar of stone that had been built across a deep, ragged fissure in the ground, which opened, far below, to a cave with an underground river. The altar had two levels: one for the body, one for the kindling strewn beneath. Both levels were slatted with metal bars so that as the pyre burned, the ash would fall directly into the well, and eventually be swept out to sea.

Kalum stepped forward. Though Weymouth was a traitor, he was of the Blood; therefore the Rites of Fire would be read in accordance with the ancient ways, so his soul could be purged by the flames that devoured his body, and he could pass through *Kadingir*, the Gateway of the Gods, and reunite with *Ama-gi*.

After the proper words were spoken, the kindling was lit. The flame sputtered and smoked a moment, then caught in a burst of heat and produced a flash of yellow so bright it was nearly white.

The blaze burned greedily, high and hot, sending a plume of black smoke into the dewy morning sky. It didn't take long for Weymouth's remains to be reduced to ash; a dragon had already done most of the work. Hawk looked on from his spot alone in the rear of the vast, silent gathering, watching Weymouth's widow weep at the front, flanked by her stiff-backed, white-lipped sons.

Hawk watched a feather of orange ash twirl lazily on the breeze, lifting high above the grove, and felt nothing but a brief flicker of jealousy. He wished in some dark, twisted part of his heart that it was he on that funeral pyre. That it was he who burned.

He whispered, *"Ana harrani sa alaktasa la tarat."*

The road that does not turn back.

How much easier to be done with it all than to face the long, lonely years of emptiness ahead.

A small figure approached the barren hill where the pyre still smoked. Robed in black, she turned to face the gathering, her long, pale hair held back from her face with a pair of matching gold combs. She was slight and somber in the gray light, a wisp of a thing, a changeling of great power and ancient magic disguised as a mortal woman.

The woman raised her voice and said into the waiting silence, *"Im ana simtim alaku, mala sihirtu."*

Gasps and shocked whispers rippled through the crowd. The Diamond Queen, half human, raised as an outsider in the human world, had just spoken in the Old Language.

A language no one outside this colony knew. Had *ever* known, for thousands upon thousands of years.

What she'd said was: "He goes to his fate, as must we all."

Hawk stood in frozen stupor, unable to tear his gaze from her face. Even *kalum* looked surprised: he stood off to the side of the pyre, leaning on his cane, his eyes widening.

In English, the Queen continued. "This day is a dark one. The man who passes from this world to the next was a friend to me once. I've come to believe that our friendship was doomed not because of hatred or ignorance, but because the rules of our world were set up so long ago, in such a different time, that they do nothing but strangle us today. If we continue to abide by the old ways, we guarantee our extinction, whether by friend or foe. Everything must evolve to survive. I've lost too many people because of our outdated ways . . . I refuse to lose another one."

She paused, looking into the crowd.

"You're my family, not my subjects. You're not beholden to me. Your lives are your own. From this moment on, you're free to live your lives any way you see fit. You're free to leave this colony if you choose. If you do so, you won't be punished or chased. But you will be on your own. And from what I know of the world . . . you won't be welcome. Not yet."

A crushing silence followed this declaration, a hush of such weight it seemed to affect gravity, deepening it, so that Hawk felt himself sink down further into the ground beneath his feet.

"I say this not as a threat, but as a call to arms. If you decide to stay, as I dearly hope you will, you'll be faced with a test. A dire one, and immediate. Our enemies know where we are, and they're ready to strike. War is coming. Soon. Anyone who chooses to stay must be willing to fight. There's no guarantee we'll win, but if we don't fight, we're guaranteed to perish. So I'll leave it to you. I'll fight until I'm dead to defend my home and my people. With you or without you, I'll fight. But with all the gods, old and new, as my witness, I pray it's with you." Her voice broke. "Because *you* are what I fight for. What I live for. What I would gladly die for. Every single one of *you*."

A beat of silence. A breath of wind. A lone bird call in the trees. Then the sound of a thousand voices rising as one, a scream of support and euphoria.

A rallying cry.

Hawk looked around at all the faces as if he were in a dream. The open mouths, the raised arms, the expressions of elated astonishment, people jumping and hugging and shouting in glee as if they hadn't just been told their lives were in danger and they might all soon be dead.

Hawk knew why there was such an outpouring of happiness. The danger didn't matter. Not compared to what they'd just been given, something not a single soul present had ever had in their lives.

Freedom.

Hawk looked back at the Queen, marveling at her. In one fell swoop, she had crushed thousands of years of draconian Law, and gained the loyalty and love of an entire army of supernatural beasts.

They would stay. Judging by the roar that had overtaken the crowd, every one of them would stay. A single word rose above the noise, a word repeated with growing volume until it had become deafening, shaking the foundations of the Earth.

"*Ta-hu! Ta-hu! Ta-hu!*"

Fight. Fight. Fight.

Hawk raised his arms overhead, opened his mouth, and lent his own voice to the multitude.

Jack heard the cry that went up far off into the forest, and jerked upright in bed.

She listened, a rash of goose bumps covering her arms, the hair on the back of her neck prickling. She listened as the cry rose to a crescendo, distant and eerie, listened as it changed from shapeless babble to the rhythm of two syllables, chanted over and over again.

She rose from the bed, crossed quickly to the dresser, and donned the jeans, T-shirt, and jacket she found there, all freshly washed and folded in a neat pile atop the wood. She assumed they were hers, they fit her, though she didn't recognize them. A pair of boots were beside the dresser, and she tugged those on, too, still listening to the cry of voices echoing over the tops of the trees.

What could it mean?

She didn't know, but of one thing she was certain: it was something important.

She went down to the lower level—astonished by the stacks of fruit piled haphazardly throughout the tree house, the jumbled mounds of jewelry and pottery and trinkets adorning every flat surface—and shimmied down the rope that hung from the bottom floor to the ground below.

Then she stood waiting.

It didn't take long until she saw them, approaching en masse from the opposite end of the colony. Led by a woman in black, the throng of people chattered in English and Portuguese and a language she didn't know, mellifluous and sensual. They were an agitated bunch, except for that woman in front, and the man who walked beside her.

Jenna. Leander. They were headed her way.

By the time the group reached her, the ranks had considerably thinned. Many had ascended into the trees, while others had dropped back to form small groups, talking, and still others turned into massive black animals and disappeared into the forest. Jack got the distinct impression whatever had happened to cause such an outcry was still happening.

A group of perhaps two hundred surrounded her. Everyone except Jenna and Leander gave her a small, respectful bow, shocking her, and evidently Jenna and Leander as well, who shared a look. Unsure of the correct way to acknowledge such a thing, Jack simply nodded back, murmuring a confused, "Hello."

Then the Queen said, "I can take you as far as the clear-cut near Moura, but you'll have to walk into town from there. They have a small airport, so you should be able to make your way to Manaus and find an American consulate, but it's too dangerous for me to fly any closer."

"Fly?" Dear God, she didn't mean . . . she *couldn't* mean—

"It's the fastest way to get you home. And it's far too dangerous for you to stay here any longer. Are you ready?"

Jack said, "Please tell me you don't expect me to *fly* on the *back* of a *dragon*."

"Why not?"

"I could . . . I could fall, that's why not! As in, to my death! And—*a dragon*? Seriously?"

The Queen was looking at her as if her concerns were ridiculous. "I'd catch you. Just hold onto my mane, you'll be perfectly fine. Haven't you ever ridden a horse?"

There were no words. Jack just stared at her, open-mouthed. Beside the Queen, a red-faced Leander had rolled his eyes heavenward and looked to be silently counting to ten.

"We'll give you money, water, and a gun." She nodded to a young man in the crowd, and Jack recognized him as the boy who'd helped her up when she'd fallen yesterday during the Queen's impressive arrival. "In something she doesn't have to use her hands to carry," Jenna added to the boy. He nodded, turned, and dashed away. Turning back to Jack, Jenna said, "Hopefully you won't need the gun, but I think safe is always better than sorry."

Jack was having a problem with her tongue. It didn't seem to be connected in any meaningful way to her brain.

"We'll have to walk out to the arena. I need a bit more space than this for takeoff," she said, looking thoughtfully at the trees.

"But . . . I'm . . . I can't-this is insane!" Jack craned her neck, looking over the crowd.

The Queen gave her a sympathetic look. "He isn't coming, Jacqueline," she said, and everything inside Jack came to a stop.

She stared at the Queen in silence. After a moment, Jenna said, "Believe me when I say this is much harder for him than it is for you. It's better this way. A goodbye will only drive the knife deeper."

Jack didn't know what to do, or say, or think. She desperately wanted to go home, but she was full to bursting with so many unanswered questions—for Jenna, for Morgan, but especially for Hawk. Everything was happening too fast. It was all too confusing, too strange, and to top it off, she couldn't remember the last few weeks of her life . . . or much of the beginning of it.

Lost, she looked around at the gathered faces, the beautiful strangers she'd been told she once hated but for whom she now felt nothing but curiosity and awe and, okay, a little fear.

Jenna said, "It will all work out exactly how it's meant to, I truly believe that. And sometimes . . . sometimes distance can give you more clarity than when you're seeing things up close."

Jenna seemed conflicted—it was as if there was so much more she wanted to say—but she left it at that. Then the young man returned, pushing his way to the front of the group with a small nylon backpack in his hands. Jenna murmured her thanks and held it out toward Jack.

She took it and stared down at it, filled with apprehension and a cold, painful lump in her chest she recognized as grief.

"Wait!"

The voice came from the tree. Everyone looked up, and there was Morgan, leaning over the porch railing of Hawk's home. Branches filtered down light from above, haloing her head in a gossamer cloud. "Don't forget this!"

She held out her arm and dropped a small bundle over the side.

It was caught, passed forward through the crowd, then held out. Jack took it. Lightweight, folded in a rectangle of blue fabric tied with a white ribbon, it fit easily inside the backpack, nestled between a bottle of water and the shiny metal barrel of a revolver. Seeing the gun gave Jack a small sense of relief; she remembered she knew how to shoot, at least.

Jack craned her neck, gazing upward, then held out a hand in farewell to Morgan. She returned the gesture, her face grave, and her words echoed in Jack's mind, words spoken only yesterday, though they seemed a lifetime ago.

I'm sure under different circumstances we could have been good friends.

They looked at each other a moment longer, then Morgan stood up and disappeared.

"All right," Jack said quietly, turning back to Jenna and Leander. "Let's do it."

The Queen nodded and walked forward. Seething with such a storm of emotions she could barely discern left from right, Jack fell into step beside her.

Neither one spoke again.

THIRTY-NINE
Comings And Goings

Riding a dragon turned out to be exactly nothing like riding a horse.

For starters, there was the issue of mounting.

There was no saddle or bridle or stirrups, nothing to clasp onto but miles of diamond-hard, slippery scales. The creature crouched low on its belly on the arena floor. After several awkward attempts, Jack resorted to grabbing a fistful of silky white mane, bracing a foot against the leathery joint of a wing where it met the body, and hauling herself up. The wing curved around her like a cloak, supporting her, until she was seated, straddled atop the beast, her calves gripping its ribs, both feet resting above its wings.

It radiated heat. The skin on her inner thighs smarted from it.

The dragon curved its neck and looked back at her with brilliant emerald eyes, a long, assessing look. Feeling reckless, Jack said, "Sure. Why the hell not?" and before she could say another word, the dragon jerked its head forward. She just had time to wrap her other hand in its mane before it launched into the sky.

That was the main difference between a horse and a dragon. Horses didn't fly.

The dragon took to the heavens—circling once so Jack saw the gathered figures below growing smaller, faces upturned to the sky—and exhilaration, hot and vivid as sunlight, flooded her.

The air was warm and humid, redolent with the sweet perfume of flowers, heavy with clouds. The dragon sliced through them as neatly as a scythe. She climbed higher, breaking free of the clouds, then tipped to the left, following an updraft of heated wind. The earth below peeked through in patches of glistening emerald through the fluffy cloudscape. The horizon was aflame with the rising sun, bleeding scarlet into infinity.

Jack wanted to cry at the beauty of it. Instead she laughed, and screamed with exhilaration. The dragon turned back to look at her—grinning, its muzzle and lashes beaded with moisture—then surged forward with a powerful thrust of its wings and climbed higher still, until the air was so thin it was hard to breathe.

Her hair snapping out behind her, the morning sun blinding her eyes, the wind a deafening roar in her ears, Jack thought, *If I die at this moment, I'll die happy.*

But she didn't die. The white dragon flew steady and straight, leading them farther and farther from the colony, careful not to let Jack tip from its back.

Jenna slowed and banked right, maneuvering carefully through the narrow break in the upper canopy. She was much better at taking off than landing, so she approached the small square of cleared forest where a large tree had fallen, taking out several other trees, with apprehension.

One wrong move and she and her passenger would both be in a world of hurt.

Luckily, her fears turned out to be unfounded, and soon she and Jacqueline were safely aground. Jacqueline slid off her back, landing on her feet with a huff, and Jenna Shifted back to woman. Without further ado, she began walking south through the small clearing, headed for the abrupt end to the forest several hundred yards ahead.

Jacqueline followed silently. After several minutes of walking, she said wryly, "Too bad you couldn't manage to keep some clothes on during all these costume changes of yours."

Jenna smiled. Costume changes. She'd never heard the Shift described quite like that. "Sorry. After a while you get used to going around naked." She stopped and looked back at Jacqueline. "Why don't you go ahead? Just keep going straight. That way you won't have to stare at my . . ." she jerked a thumb toward her rear end.

This suggestion was met with a grateful smile. Jacqueline went ahead, and Jenna followed.

Finally they stood on the edge of the forest, looking out.

The clear-cut was exactly that: a total absence of trees, vegetation, or even a single leaf. Emerging from the lush, moist dimness of the forest was a harsh assault on the senses.

In pursuit of such prized, exotic woods as mahogany, teak, and rosewood, loggers had brutally razed this section of the rainforest in an enormous, perfect square. Shorn trunks stuck up like brown stubble for as far as she could see. It was as dead and silent as a graveyard, an ugly scar on the land.

Jenna pointed. "Go straight toward that hill, you see it? On the other side is a small road that leads to a highway, and if you follow that, it'll take you into town. From there you can hire a car to take you to the airport. You probably won't need a passport or ID—there's enough money in your pack to bribe a local pilot three times over—but a commercial flight's a different story. Once you get to Manaus you'll have to find a government office and declare yourself. An American embassy would be best. If there is one."

When she finished, Jacqueline was studying her face. She said, "What *are* you?"

"I'm a woman. Just like you."

This statement was met with a short, disbelieving laugh. "You're nothing like me."

Jenna answered softly, "You're wrong. I'm exactly like you. In all the ways that matter, we're exactly the same."

Jacqueline swallowed, turning away. In profile she was stern and remote, her hair a vivid flame atop her head. Jenna touched her arm. Jacqueline met her gaze head-on, unflinching, the confusion clear in her eyes.

"Everyone has Gifts, not only my kind. In fact, you have one of the most powerful Gifts I've ever seen."

Jacqueline waited, silently watching her.

"You have the ability to shape people's thoughts with your words. What you write, the way you communicate ideas so they make sense, gives you the ability to *change people's minds*. To open their eyes to a different way of thinking." She shrugged. "So I can change my form. So can a caterpillar, or a seed. But *you* . . . you can change the world."

They stared at each other. After a while, Jacqueline said, "If I had a choice, I'd take the dragon."

They stood there awkwardly another moment longer until Jenna said, "I'm sorry about all this."

Jacqueline sent her a small, melancholy smile. "Well, life is funny that way. One day you're riding the subway in New York

City, the next you're waking up in the jungle with a man you've never seen before in your life, and the one after that you're riding around on the back of a dragon. If nothing else, it'll make for a good story."

"Yes," said Jenna. "I imagine it will."

They both knew Jacqueline would have to tell her story, what would be waiting for her upon her return to her old life. Jacqueline looked at Jenna, not quite sure how to respond, so Jenna said, "Just tell them the truth. Whatever you remember. I know you'll be fair."

Jacqueline shook her head, frowning at her. "I don't understand. I was told I was brought here to observe you in hopes of gaining a better understanding of your kind because I hated you, and spread it around like a bad case of the flu. Why are you being so nice to me? Why not roast me like you did with that other guy? This doesn't make sense."

Hawk had told Jenna that he changed Jacqueline, that they'd changed each other, and even though Jacqueline couldn't remember what had happened between them, Jenna knew the heart had a funny way of remembering what the mind pushed aside.

Love can't lie. There was still hope.

"For one thing, that other guy deserved it. You don't. And like you said, life is funny. You never know how things will turn out."

Now Jacqueline looked angry. "What does that mean?"

Jenna began to slowly back away into the trees. "It means it was my pleasure to meet you, Jacqueline Dolan. I wish you the best. Maybe someday we'll meet again. Goodbye."

Without another word, Jenna Shifted to Vapor and drifted upward into the trees, a soft coil of mist floating higher and higher among the branches, until Jacqueline was a small shape far below.

Jack stood looking up for long moments, searching the canopy, silent. After a while she sighed, adjusted the backpack on her shoulders, and turned and walked out of the forest.

She didn't look back.

With all his heart, Hawk wished he could Shift to Vapor.

As Vapor, emotions were quelled. There was no pounding heart, no rushing blood, no sickness in the pit of his stomach. There was only lovely and calming mist, total tranquility. Peace.

But he'd been injured by Alejandro's claws, and peace was out of his reach.

He'd watched Jenna and Jacqueline take to the skies from the cover of the trees, away from the colony because he couldn't bear to speak to anyone. Not now. Maybe not ever. And as the two of them shrank to nothing but a brilliant spot of white on the distant horizon, Hawk wondered if this was what hell felt like. The pain was so intense he thought his heart might actually explode inside his chest.

It didn't. Unlucky for him, it didn't.

Blind, deaf, mute, he made his way back through the forest to his home. He climbed the rope, the wound in his shoulder breaking open again, leaking blood down his chest. Then he lay down on his back in his bed, pulled the pillow over his face, smelled the lingering, lovely scent of jasmine and honey that was Jacqueline, and, for the first time in his entire life, wept.

When Hawk could bear the weight of the empty rooms no longer, he went to the forest and started walking with no direction in mind, unsure if he'd ever turn back.

By the time Jenna made it back to the colony, the sun was high overhead, but the cloud cover below her had thickened to the point of visual impenetrability. She was in dragon form again, and again was exhausted, having only slept one night since her journey from Morocco.

She began her descent, angling sharply toward the clouds, and that was when she felt it.

Correction: him. She felt him.

As unmistakable as a slap across the face, the energy Caesar exuded was curdled and violent, the same crackling current that had set her nerves on edge when she'd first seen him standing on that crenellated turret at the kasbah outside Marrakech.

No!

She went to Vapor, funneled herself into a narrow channel of wind, and shot down through the cloud cover, punching through to the other side just in time to feel the first pinpricks of rain slice through her.

Rain was good. Rain would dampen her scent, muffle her energy.

She slowed her speed and edged toward the colony, trying to appear as just one more wisp of misted air steaming above the treetops. She didn't take the time to wonder at his motives or his appearance here, when he was supposed to be on the other side of the world, because her thoughts had winnowed to three words, shrieking like banshees inside her skull.

Leander. The children.

If any of them were hurt, Jenna would rain down hell of such biblical proportion Caesar would be wishing for all eternity that he'd been Gifted with anything other than immortality.

It had been almost too easy. Hell, it *had* been too easy. Where was the security? Where were the lookouts?

Most important, where was the Queen?

Their tracker, Badr, had brought them right to the edge of the colony without incident, and Caesar was actually quite disappointed he hadn't been able to use the Firestarter yet to scare away any potential assailants. He'd been looking forward to seeing a few roasted kitties, but it was probably for the best; this was supposed to be a covert operation, and giant balls of fire were anything but covert.

His plan was simply this: get in, kill the Queen, let Weymouth handle the logistics from there. He didn't care how many members of this godforsaken jungle colony wanted to join him . . . he only cared about gutting that spying bitch with his own hands. The rest was gravy.

With the help of the GPS, they'd found the locale from where Weymouth's call had originated. Judging by the size of the structure in relation to the other dwellings suspended through the trees, it was clear they'd come to the home of the Queen, or at the very least the Alpha of this colony who, if properly motivated, could point them in the Queen's direction. But it was eerily quiet, the forest deserted, and Caesar sensed the Queen wasn't there.

So the four of them settled in beneath the dense cover of a stand of mammoth ferns to wait.

"They'll have to come by air," Leander said, pacing in front of the dais in the Assembly room where Alejandro normally held court. "Planes are the most logical choice. They won't be hindered by the terrain, and they'll be much safer flying than on foot." His voice darkened. "And they can bring a much bigger force that way."

The Assembly members were all present, but today the elaborate throne stood empty. Alejandro hadn't been seen since the interrupted contest with Hawk, and there had been no time to organize a vote to decide which of the two would be Alpha.

Voting for the Alpha, thought Leander, his lips quirking with mirth in spite of the seriousness of the current situation. If nothing else, his wife never failed to surprise him.

Everyone was on edge. LeBlanc and Bhojak were glowering at each other from opposite sides of the room. The Assembly members were agitated, fidgeting in their chairs, the tension palpable because no one knew when the Expurgari and Section Thirty might strike. It could be one hour, one day, one week. And no one knew how best to prepare.

Even the twins seemed restless. Tucked into an open drawer in a sideboard that acted as a makeshift bassinette, they fretted beneath a white blanket knitted by their mother, squirming like a pair of hatchlings.

Leander hadn't wanted to leave them alone to come to this meeting. As things stood, he didn't want to leave them alone for a second.

Xander said, "We can't defend ourselves if they come by air. Our only chance is if we can somehow draw them to the ground, engage them in hand-to-hand combat."

Leander said, "Or figure out a way to crash the planes." He stared at Xander, the kernel of an idea forming. He was just about to open his mouth again, when a zephyr blasted through the sheer curtains on the far side of the platform, lifting them to a billowing bell before they settled back against the polished floor.

The zephyr was Jenna. She took shape as woman, and her first words were, *"He's here!"*

"What? Who?" In a moment of blind panic, Leander thought she meant Jahad, the leader of the Expurgari. Had they arrived already? But the name she growled with hatred belonged to someone else.

"Caesar!"

Instant pandemonium. Everyone leapt to their feet and started shouting.

"That's not possible!"

"Where? How?"

"What do we do?"

"Did you see him?"

"Is he alone?"

Jenna glimpsed the twins in the sideboard and all the blood drained from her face, leaving it the color of chalk. "Leander, get the children out of here! Get them into the caves—get everyone to the caves—I'm the only one who has a chance against him—"

"I'm not leaving you here! He can't overpower all of us!"

A voice, slick and full of malice, rang out from the other side of the room.

"Oh dear. I'm not interrupting anything, am I?"

Everyone turned and there was Caesar, flanked by three men, standing by the curtains to the suspended bridge. Caesar was smiling, grimly, without an ounce of warmth. The other three—a hulking, black-eyed male with a cool, menacing beauty; a skinny male with darting eyes and twitchy hands; and a human with a bushy, filthy beard—stood still and silent.

"Son of a bitch," Leander breathed, pushing Jenna behind him.

Fools, all of them. They'd been so intent on making plans for war they hadn't noticed the wolves circling the henhouse. A snapping sensation started in his spine, shooting outward, ratcheting higher when he saw Caesar's grim smile grow wider.

"Son of an Alpha, actually." Caesar's gaze cut to Jenna. "And you're wrong about what you said before. I *can* overpower all of you. Quite easily, as it turns out. Allow me to demonstrate."

He snapped his fingers, and the male with the twitchy hands lifted them, palms out, and pointed them right at Leander and Jenna.

Caesar said, "Nighty-night, kitty cats."

And that's when the air became fire.

FORTY

Good Girls

In the infinitesimal moment before the wall of flame consumed them, Jenna put her hand on Leander's shoulder and Shifted to a form she'd never taken before.

Ice.

It was instant and unthinking, a visceral reaction that required no thought or exertion save a small focus of will, and then she was transformed. Leander was encased in a block of solid ice, entirely surrounded.

The wall of fire passed right over them, leaving them unharmed.

As soon as it passed, Jenna Shifted to Vapor, then back to woman, a flash of mist that coalesced in an instant to flesh and bone. Now she stood in front of Leander, facing Caesar, watching an expression of pure fury twist his face, watching his minions go rigid with shock.

She shouted, "That's right, assholes! How d'you like me now?"

Behind her, Leander made a small, wordless noise. Smoke and the smell of charred fabric hung acrid in the air; the fireball had singed the drapery on two sides of the room, leaving it waving in charred tatters from the branches far above, dripping rain.

From everywhere and nowhere arose the screams.

They were eerie and otherworldly, the most frightening sounds she'd ever heard. She didn't have time to consider the source, because Caesar was shouting at his flame-throwing companion to go again, throwing his arms wide to indicate a wall of fire not only for Jenna and Leander, but for the entire room with everyone in it.

Several members of the Assembly had the presence of mind to Shift to panther. Bursts of heated power rippled through the room as they transformed. With lashing tails, bulging muscles, deadly claws and fangs, they sank into pounce positions, roars of rage ripping from their chests.

The flamethrower stepped to one side. Jenna inhaled a breath that felt like snow. Her pulse slowed with the minute focus of her attention. In the space of a heartbeat, a million thoughts flashed through her mind at the speed of light, a million possible calculations and transformations.

Rain, lightning, bullet, steel, cage, stop, wall, box, kill that piece of—

But instead of throwing another stream of fire in her direction, he turned around in a whip-crack move, bent over, and turned back again.

In his fists, held out at arms' length, were the twins. It was they who were screaming, screaming with such deafening volume Jenna's eyes watered. They stared straight at her, holding perfectly still with wide, wide eyes . . . and closed mouths.

Their screams were in her head. Only she could hear them.

Jenna jolted forward, every nerve in her body flayed raw, protective instinct pummeling her mercilessly, flooding her cells with adrenaline. Before she took two full steps, Caesar yanked Hope from the flamethrower's left hand, and crushed her to his chest.

"Stop!" commanded Caesar. Abruptly, she and everyone else did.

"Jenna." Leander's voice was hoarse, beseeching, but Jenna couldn't look away.

Hope's tiny white arm flailed up. Her fingers gripped his shirt, bunching the fabric. Her little legs kicked out beneath his arm for a moment, frantic, then she fell completely still.

Hurting my baby! Oh my God, he's hurting my—

"You and I," Caesar said to Jenna, lowering his head and looking at her with eyes so black they reflected back not a single flicker of light, "have unfinished business. Send everyone else away and I'll let the little brats live."

A lie. She smelled it. She saw it in his eyes. But for a moment she clung to it, hoping she could somehow still turn this to her advantage. If she agreed, she'd at least save the Assembly members, she'd at least gain a few more minutes so she could—

Mama.

Jenna froze. She looked at Honor. Dangling at the end of the flamethrower's fist, her baby stared back at her with total, unblinking concentration, her green eyes brilliantly, chillingly, alive in her small, angelic face.

Then her infant child smiled at her, and the world ground to a standstill.

To Jenna it was as if a switch had been thrown, and a room that had once been dead black was flooded with drenching golden sunlight. She felt it in her muscles, her cells, the atoms of her body, a mother's recognition that transcended words or logic, a thing only those joined by flesh and blood can know. She had the urge to laugh and cry at once, as those experiencing transcendent moments often do, but she only exhaled, all the tension draining from her body as if a plug had been pulled.

She was no longer afraid. She didn't have to be.

"Yes, Honor," Jenna whispered. "Good girl."

Honor laughed.

First the flamethrower stiffened, his eyes bulging wide. He tried to speak, but the only sound that passed his lips was a choked, hacking cough, cut off abruptly when his tongue caught on fire. His hair burst into flame next.

Someone screamed.

At the end of his arm, Honor gurgled another sweet laugh, happily kicking her little feet.

The flamethrower shrieked and stumbled back, letting go of Honor, but Jenna had anticipated it. She was Vapor, darting in, then woman, catching the precious bundle an instant before she hit the ground. She slid sideways on her knees over the bare wood until she collided hard with the side of a divan, shielding Honor in her arms. She looked up and froze.

The flamethrower was engulfed in a roaring blaze of fire. He staggered around the room, arms flailing, bumping into furniture as everyone scrambled to get out of his way. Caesar was still standing with Hope in his arms near the doorway, his expression of horror identical to the one worn by his companion.

Leander took advantage of their shocked distraction to leap on Caesar.

They went down in a tangle of limbs, Hope caught between them. They hit the floor hard. Leander rolled onto his back and Jenna went weak with relief when she saw he'd snatched Hope from Caesar's grip. Leander leapt up and away from Caesar before Caesar could even get to his feet, and then Leander was beside Jenna, crouching over her, placing Hope in her arms.

He straightened just as the flamethrower collapsed atop the dais, and lay unmoving at the foot of the Alpha's throne. The noise of his body burning was a terrible thing, the crackling and snapping and ugly, loud pops. And the *smell* . . .

From the corner of her eye, she saw movement.

The human with the bushy beard had been taken down by four large, black animals, and was being ripped to shreds as he tried in vain to fight them off. All she could see were his two feet kicking beneath the muscled bodies of the panthers, that and the widening circle of blood that had begun to pool beneath him.

A few feet away, Caesar knelt on the floor, gripping his head in both hands. His expression was one of surprise, disbelief, and confusion; it was clear he wasn't quite sure what was happening. He lifted his eyes and looked right into hers, his gaze searching. Then he dropped his gaze to the babies in her arms, and his mouth formed a small, horrified O.

In her arms, Hope and Honor were both reaching out to him, their tiny, dimpled fingers stretching, flexing wide. Honor gurgled a little laugh, and just like that, Jenna knew.

With a grim smile, she whispered, "Mommy loves you, girls."

Caesar burst into flame.

It was like a detonation: the explosion of heat and pressure slammed through the room, blowing her hair back from her face. Jenna squinted against it, lowering her head to shield the babies from the blast. She heard a high, keening scream that wavered, sustained on a single note for what seemed an eternity, but then it cut off and the only sound was that of licking flames and the rain that was falling harder now through the trees.

Jenna looked up. Where Caesar had been kneeling, there now appeared a pile of bone and ash, the floor all around it scorched in a perfect circle, as if the fire had been contained to only the space of Caesar's body, enclosed and superheated.

The third male who had accompanied Caesar had Shifted to Vapor and had vanished, leaving a jumbled pile of clothing and weapons on the floor near the exit to the bridge.

She only realized when Hope and Honor began to squirm that she'd tightened her arms around them so hard they ached.

Leander gripped her shoulder, sinking his fingers hard into her flesh. She glanced up at him and he was staring down at her and the twins, his eyes shadowed and endless. "But Caesar's immortal," he said, struggling, his handsome face blanched, his voice harsh and low.

Jenna said, "Not anymore."

Leander bent and took Honor from Jenna's arms. He held the baby out at arms' length, staring at her with unflagging intensity. "They . . . they took the flamethrower's Gift?"

The others were beginning to gather around them, stepping past the smoking body on the dais, moving carefully around the circle of ash and bone on the floor. Morgan and Xander gaped at them, as did the rest of the Assembly, everyone visibly shaken.

Jenna said, "Yes."

"Which means . . ." Leander's gaze went to the pile of ash that used to be Caesar.

Jenna whispered, "I think so."

She saw it in all of their faces, reflected back in every pair of eyes that gazed down at her and the twins.

Awe.

Dread.

Fear.

Jenna had a terrible premonition that this was the way her children would be looked at for the rest of their lives. This would set them apart from even their own kind, a breed already so apart from the rest of the world. They would be worshipped but they would be feared, objects of suspicion and distrust.

Outcasts among outcasts.

She and Leander stood. As they did, the gathered group took a step back.

"Is anyone hurt?" Jenna asked into the hush.

They shook their heads and exchanged glances, but no one spoke.

"Good." She gathered herself, drawing a fortifying breath, trying to steady her shaking hands. Beside her, Leander was a warm, strong presence. She turned her attention to Xander and said, "Have the remains removed. Put them in a box and bury them somewhere they'll never be found, or disturbed. No rites, no headstone. Only you are to know the location."

Xander nodded. He had the Gift of Passage, so he could walk right into a wall of rock with the box and embed it there, if he wanted, leaving the box behind, emerging unchanged. Jenna hoped he would do exactly that.

"Everyone else, let's . . . let's just . . ." Jenna faltered, finding it more and more difficult to breathe.

"Sutherland, get the security detail back out there," Leander cut in, stepping closer to her so his chest pressed against her back, offering support. She sagged against him, and he snaked an arm around her waist. "There may have been more in his party. And see if you can find any trace of that one." He jerked his chin to the pile of clothes on the floor.

"Right away, My Lord." Grayson bowed, and left at a trot.

"Everyone else, go home for now. We'll send word when this mess has been cleaned up and we can refocus, but in the meantime, stay sharp."

The group obeyed, swiftly and silently, a few of the men staying behind to assist Xander.

Then, his arm still around her waist, Leander led Jenna away, the twins cooing happily in her arms while fear hatched ugly and huge inside her, a carrion bird circling and cawing inside her gut.

God only knew what was coming next.

FORTY-ONE

The Los Angeles Times, *Friday, October 11, 20—*

MISSING JOURNALIST FOUND ALIVE

In a recent development, missing *New York Times* journalist Jacqueline Dolan was found alive and apparently unharmed after disappearing from New York more than two weeks ago.

Paulo Varela, a soybean farmer in the small municipality of Rolim de Moura, in the state of Rodônia, Brazil, first saw Ms. Dolan Thursday morning, walking down the center of a two-lane highway used primarily by logging trucks. With the assistance of his English-speaking niece, Natália, the farmer learned Ms. Dolan was looking for transportation to the airport, which he provided himself. It was only after he returned home and his niece told him she believed his passenger was a missing American journalist that the farmer called the local police.

Sources say Ms. Dolan is calm and coherent, but has so far refused to speak with the New York Police Department or the press about the details of her disappearance. A press conference has been scheduled for Monday morning at 9 a.m., and it is anticipated she will make a statement regarding her whereabouts at that time.

Calls to her residence and family have not been returned.

FORTY-TWO

Not Knowing

So far, life at home had been a nightmare.

From the moment she stepped off the plane at JFK three days ago, accosted by a throng of shouting reporters with cameras shoved in her face, Jack had been hunted.

She'd never been famous before. She'd been a name on a byline, a writer more at home in Kevlar and war zones than mingling among the glittering dignitaries and slick politicians she had occasion to interview. Now she was a story with a capital S, and it was hell.

Someone had unearthed the picture of her taken at that cocktail party she'd attended with Nola at the White House, and it had become the one all the news outlets used. In it, she was striding toward a waiting limousine, dressed in a gown the color of raspberries, her hair upswept, her neck, ears, and wrists in borrowed jewels, a glimpse of leg revealed by a slit in the skirt, which billowed as she moved.

She looked feminine and glamorous and nothing at all like herself. Jack remembered that at the moment that picture was snapped, she'd been thinking how wonderful it was going to be to rip off that stupid dress, take her hair down, and sit in her bathtub neck-deep in hot water with a cold beer.

But the picture was selling the story of the mysterious vanishing act of the veteran reporter, and everyone and their brother wanted a piece of it.

Of her.

Somehow her unlisted phone number was now in the hands of dozens of aggressive magazine editors, newspaper reporters, and talk show hosts. Her answering machine had stopped recording new messages because it was full.

Her building had doormen, and electronic security fobs to operate the elevator, so she'd been spared from having people knocking directly on her door so far. But it was coming. The doormen didn't make enough money to buy loyalty, and sooner or later one of them was going to have a greasy palm. Or maybe the superintendent would be the one to give her up; she'd had to get a spare fob and key from him when she'd first come home, and the entire time she was in his small office, he slid long, assessing glances in her direction, thoughtfully chewing a toothpick.

The worst thing, though, was the phone messages. Not the ones from the hyenas in the press. Not the ones from Nola, though she grew increasingly frantic as the days wore on, and Jack hated to hear her so worried.

The worst were from the father she didn't remember.

"Jackie. Baby. Why won't you pick up the phone? Your work called . . . what's going on? Please call me to let me know you're okay."

That was the first one, two days after her disappearance.

Then: "Jackie. I hope this isn't about your birthday. Please call me. I-I love you."

Snuffling, then a click, and Jack was left to wonder what the hell happened on her birthday. And why this man sounded so wracked with guilt.

There were more, and they got worse. As she listened to these messages, dozens of them, each one more gruff and weepy than the next, it occurred to Jack that what Hawk had told her may have had more meaning than what she first assumed.

Some things are better forgotten, Jacqueline. Sometimes . . . forgetting can be a gift.

Because she could remember only bits and pieces of her early life, and nothing at all of the past weeks, with the exception of a few recent days, she'd become obsessed with those words. She dug through her apartment, hunting for anything personal, a diary, photo albums, any kind of mementos that might trigger her memory or offer some insight into the person she'd once been—and what had happened to her—but there was nothing. Her apartment was utterly barren of clues that would have given her a glimpse into her past life. Or her current life, for that matter.

With the exception of the clothes in the closet, the toothbrush in the jar in the bathroom, a few cosmetics in a vanity drawer, and a handful of take-out menus in the kitchen, it was almost as if no one had ever lived there at all.

Jack found that telling. Sad, and telling. She also wondered about that look on Hawk's face when Morgan tried to access her memory and failed. Beyond his disappointment, the glimpse of relief, swiftly erased.

It made her think Hawk knew something. Something she'd forgotten. Something that didn't have anything to do with him.

Something bad.

But there was nothing to be done about it. She looked up hypnotherapists in the yellow pages, eventually deciding that if she couldn't regain her memory with the assistance of a woman who could make you quack like a duck with only a word, a hypnotherapist was probably a complete waste of time.

And . . . did she really want to know?

That question continued to simmer on the back burner of her mind as she tried to piece her life back together, going through the motions in a daze. Though she didn't remember leaving it there or even having one, a cell phone lay on the kitchen counter, next to a gleaming stainless-steel toaster that had obviously never been used. When she scrolled through it, a list of numbers appeared, only some of which she recognized.

"Dad" was there. So was "Work," "Nola," and someone named "Asshat," among dozens of others. She stared at the names, her hands shaking, her eyes welling with tears, wanting to break something, wanting to run.

She scrolled to the *H*s, but there was no "Hawk." And why would there be? He wasn't from her world. He was someone she knew for a few weeks . . . who she just happened to have the awful, impossible feeling might be her soul mate.

"Idiot," she whispered as the tears slid down her cheeks. And then, "Fuck."

The minute she said it, she wanted to take it back. It felt wrong, though she didn't know why. Which made her cry even harder; stupid, useless tears that did nothing to quell the ache of longing or the crushing despair caused by the certainty that she'd never feel right again.

"You ready for this?"

Nola, dressed in an elegant black pantsuit, her hair scraped back severely from her face and gathered into a low knot, was watching Jack with worried eyes, just as she had been watching her for the past two days. Nola had appeared at Jack's door the morning after her return, and had only left the apartment on forays for fresh clothes and food.

And booze. Jack wasn't sure the exact quantity of alcohol one had to consume before being involuntarily admitted to rehab, damaging the liver beyond repair, or falling into a coma from which one would never awake, but she was well on her way to finding out.

Now it was Monday morning, and they were standing in Jack's kitchen, preparing to leave for a press conference she was looking forward to about as much as standing naked in line at the DMV.

"Not even close," Jack admitted, shoving a loose strand of hair behind her ear. "But if I don't give them something, the vultures will never stop circling." She gulped down the last of her coffee and set the mug in the sink. She was wearing a black suit, too, and between the two of them they looked like part of a funeral procession, which seemed apropos.

"You have your speech ready?"

Jack nodded. She'd spent hours working on it, and though it wasn't long, it said everything she wanted to say. After this morning, she was determined never to speak of her lost weeks again.

She still hadn't called her father. She didn't know what she could possibly say that wouldn't sound insane. "Hi, it's your daughter, I have no idea who you are?" That wasn't a phone call she could imagine making. Instead she'd had Nola call him to let him know she was fine, just not ready to talk yet.

She'd asked Nola to leave out the part about not remembering him.

She was scheduled to go back to work first thing the following morning. Work was the only thing she could think of that might help her keep her ever-loosening grip on her sanity, and her boss, though proffering half-hearted protests that it was too early, quickly agreed. It would be great PR for the paper, and, in fact, it had been his idea to hold the press conference at the *Times*'s offices. She wouldn't be able to go out on assignment for a while—she'd attract too much attention—but there was always work to be done around the office, and once the circus and its attendant carnies had left town, she'd be able to return to the only thing she was one hundred percent sure about: reporting.

Though she knew she'd forever have the bloated ghost of notoriety hanging over her head, cackling like a crone stirring a bubbling cauldron of newt eyes and frog toes.

Some demons, once summoned, can never be exorcized.

"Okay, before we go, I'm just going to put this out there."

Jack looked at Nola, her eyes narrowing in suspicion at the tone in her voice. "What?"

Nola began to fiddle with the small gold hoop earring in her left ear. Fiddling was uncharacteristic for her, and it amplified Jack's nervousness like a dial had been cranked.

"I know you don't want to talk about what happened to you yet . . . or maybe ever."

Jack's face flushed. "I'm just . . . not ready, No. It's too . . . strange. I can hardly get my own head around it. I'm only doing this to get the press off my back, and then I'm going to crawl back into my shell."

"I get it," she said softly. "And I know you. You're the most private person I've ever met. So I'm only going to say this once, and then we'll consider the subject closed forever."

Jack's heart began to flutter. "Why does that sound so ominous?"

Nola looked at her with big, dark eyes, her expression pained. "You've said you don't remember most of the past few weeks, and there are holes in your memory . . . from other times." She glanced away for a moment, hesitating, then met her gaze again. "You're my best friend. You know that, right? There's nothing I wouldn't do for you."

All the little hairs on Jack's arms lifted. With a sinking feeling in her stomach, she whispered, "You know, don't you? You know what I don't remember about my father? About my childhood?"

Slowly, Nola nodded.

Jack whispered hoarsely, "Do I want to know?"

The answer was immediate, blunt, as hard as two fingers snapping. "No."

Jack closed her eyes.

Nola said, "And that's why I'm not going to tell you. Because you and I have the same set of monsters, and there's nothing in this world I wouldn't do to escape mine. Even for a single day. Even for a minute."

Jack opened her eyes to find Nola staring at her with fierce intensity, her dark eyes blazing wild-thing bright. "But you *should* know that your father is a good man. Flawed, but good. He never hurt you. Ever. And he never will. He loves you more than anything in the world. You can trust him."

Jack put her face into her hands, her tentative façade of equilibrium riven with cracks. She whispered a curse, and Nola pulled her into a hug.

"I know. I'm sorry. This sucks. But you're a tough cookie, Dolan. You're going to be fine." She pulled away and swiped at the tear that had begun to track down Jack's cheek. "Okay. One other thing and then I'm shutting up."

"Oh dear God. I don't think I can take 'one other thing.'"

"This guy you met in Brazil."

Jack stiffened. She'd never told Nola about Hawk. How could she possibly know?

"Guy?"

"Yeah, the one you thought I bought you for your birthday. You know, the supermodel assassin rock-star sex god."

Sex god? Birthday? She remembered the date of her birthday, she knew that it was a few days before she disappeared, when she was on assignment in . . . Manaus.

A picture flashed before her eyes. A burning building. The figure of a man, large and leonine, standing motionless across a cobbled street. Staring at her as if nothing else in the world existed.

A wave of heat flashed over her. Jack made an incoherent noise, which Nola took as an invitation to continue.

"When the police questioned me when you first disappeared, they wanted to know if anything unusual had happened to you within the last few weeks or months. So I told them about the guy you said you hooked up with. They looked into it, but I'm not sure if they found anything. Did . . . did he have anything to do with it? Your disappearance?"

Another picture, vivid as daylight. Jack on her back on a mattress in a hotel room, moaning, Hawk's dark head moving between her spread thighs.

You like that, don't you, Red?

All the breath left her body as if a giant, invisible hand had pressed down on her chest.

"Jack? Are you okay?"

She hadn't realized she'd closed her eyes, hadn't known she'd sunk into the wood chair at the small kitchen table. Her hand was cupped over her mouth, and she was fighting for air.

"I'm . . . I'm . . ." Jack swallowed, feeling as if the earth had just collapsed under her feet.

Hawk is a friend, and a good man, and whatever you remember or don't, you should know that you've changed him.

Why hadn't she asked Morgan who it was who'd brought her to the rainforest colony? Who she'd spent more than a week traveling with? How the whole thing had begun?

Funny, isn't it, the strange ways love stories can begin?

Why hadn't she thought to ask Hawk why she was staying in his home while she was there?

Did he have anything to do with your disappearance?

"Jack?"

She looked up to find Nola staring at her in obvious concern. "Your face is as white as a sheet. What's going on?"

I don't know what's real anymore, she wanted to say. *I think I don't know anything at all.*

But instead she said, "Just . . . just nervous. I'll be fine. This is all . . . it's all just a little overwhelming." She stood, gripping the edge of the table for support, and offered Nola a shaky smile, which didn't appear to convince her.

She crossed her arms over her chest, lowered her head, and said in her most lawyerly, intimidating way, "Jack. What's. Going. *On?*"

Jack said, "Nola . . . have you ever been in love?"

"That's it," she said flatly. "We're cancelling this press conference." She pulled a cell phone from her jacket pocket.

"No, wait, no!"

Nola cocked a brow at her, waiting.

Jack began to pace back and forth over the kitchen floor, wringing her hands, knowing she had to give Nola something good—something convincing—or else she absolutely would cancel the press conference, which Jack didn't want to happen. She wanted to get this over with, as soon as possible, and move on with her so-called life.

"It's just driving me crazy, this . . . *not knowing*. And it's not only my father, my mother, my childhood, it's . . ." she swung around and stared at her friend, her anguish like a gnawing thing inside her. "It's that I think I might have forgotten the most important thing I ever knew."

"Which is?"

Jack's face crumpled. She said, "Love."

For a long, silent moment, Nola studied her face. Then she looked at her watch. She crossed to the cabinets, took out two glasses, crossed to the other counter, and filled the glasses with a shot from the bottle of Patrón that Jack's neighbor, Mr. Flores, had given Jack when she came home. Nola, handed Jack a glass, and raised her own in a toast.

"The advantage of a bad memory is that one enjoys several times the same good things for the first time."

"That's a good toast," Jack said, her voice weak.

"Nietzsche. Drink up."

Jack did. When she finished, Nola set the glasses on the counter. She turned back to Jack and said, "I don't know what happened to you, and maybe you don't either. And even though I've spent my life in pursuit of logical things, rational things, things that are concrete, and can be measured, I know deep down that nothing worth knowing can be grasped with the rational mind." She touched Jack's chest. "Everything you need to know is in here. Just trust that, no matter what happens."

She stared at her friend, her eyes welling with tears. "Damn. You're smart."

"Of course I'm smart. I'm an attorney. We're the smartest people in the world. Just ask us." She gave Jack a swift, hard hug, then released her.

"All right, kiddo, let's get this show on the road."

Jack exhaled, nodding. Then she grabbed her handbag from the counter, and, with one final deep breath, followed Nola out the door.

FORTY-THREE
Lost and Found

Jack knew the press conference would be bad. She was expecting bad.

What she wasn't expecting was a riot.

The New York Times Building was a massive skyscraper in the heart of midtown, built only a few years prior, a masterpiece of contemporary design with 1.6 million square feet of retail and office space. It also sported a 400-seat auditorium that was annexed to the lobby, complete with a stunning view of a glassed-in aspen grove and moss garden, open to the sky.

It was in front of the lovely garden view, on a riser in the auditorium, that Jack was scheduled to speak.

Her first clue that something was amiss was the traffic being redirected off forty-first Street. The limousine she and Nola were riding in, however, was waved through the line of orange cones and barricades by a white-gloved traffic cop, who closely examined the *Times* pass on the dashboard, then nodded at the driver.

After attempting to peer through the windshield into the back seat to get a look at Jack.

Too bad for him, the tinted divider window between the driver's seat and the back seats was up. Sitting beside her, Nola took her hand, muttering, "This should be interesting."

It was when the car pulled to a stop at the curb outside the main lobby entrance that Jack understood the reality of the situation.

"You can't be serious." She recoiled in horror as a flock of reporters with cameras and microphones surrounded the car, shouting and jostling, clamoring over each other to get close. There were no fewer than six television news vans parked along the curb, their satellite dishes sprung in the air like mushrooms, and a crowd of pedestrians and onlookers had gathered beyond the cordoned-off entrance to the building.

Nola sent her a sympathetic glance. "I know you haven't been watching TV, but, sweetie, you're the chum in the shark tank at the moment."

Jack made a small, choked noise in her throat.

"Veteran reporter, Pulitzer nominee, notorious for all her anti-Shifter rhetoric, vanishes without a trace from New York then reappears from the Amazon jungle weeks later without a scratch . . . think about it."

Jack closed her eyes and tried not to hyperventilate.

Nola added, "And it doesn't help that you're young and pretty and Ivy League . . . and regarded as kind of a bitch."

Jack moaned and slumped farther down in the seat, hiding behind her hands.

"Hey." Nola pried Jack's hands from her face and stared into her eyes. "We bitches have to stick together, okay? Maybe we'll form a union," she joked.

Another random memory popped into Jack's head.

The bitch is back, remember?

She'd been talking to Hawk. Yelling at him, actually. What about? When?

Nola was carefully watching her face. "Jack. You don't have to do this. You don't have to tell anyone anything."

Just tell them the truth. Whatever you remember. I know you'll be fair.

Jack's hands were shaking. She stared down at them, feeling on the verge of something vast and black and inescapable, a worm hole about to suck her straight into oblivion. Was she losing her mind? Is that what had happened to her out there in the jungle? She'd lost all semblance of sanity?

"No ... I ... I have something I want to say. Something that needs to be heard."

Nola sighed. Gazing at the crowd out the window she said, "Okay. But afterward you might want to get on the next flight to Canada."

Or Antarctica, Jack thought, bracing herself for the onslaught as the limousine driver got out to open her door.

It's funny how the sound of a camera shutter shooting rapid-fire can sound completely innocent or like a machine gun, depending on where you're standing.

That was one of two dozen haphazard thoughts crossing Jack's mind as Nola, acting as defense, guided her by the arm through the crowd of reporters who were shouting questions and shoving microphones in her face.

Their attention felt carnivorous. She kept her head down, concentrating on getting inside as quickly as possible without being mauled.

Security rescued them as soon as they were inside the glass lobby doors. Surrounded by a team of uniformed men, burly and formidable enough to get the most aggressive of the reporters to back off, they made their way in a tight knot toward the amphitheater and were ushered into a small antechamber adjacent to the main room. It was calmer there, quieter, but Jack's heart pounded so hard it felt like it might claw its way right out of her chest.

Security left, and then it was just Nola and Jack in the room. She flattened her back against the closed door, panting.

"Where's Ed?" she asked Nola, lifting a shaking hand to her forehead. "I thought he'd be here already."

"He is. He's out front, holding court with the mob. You didn't see him on his soapbox?"

She should have known her boss would be front and center of this madhouse. Ed O'Malley, Executive Editor, was an old-school, tough-as-nails journalist who closely resembled a circus ringleader both in appearance and personality. He thrived on this kind of chaos.

Nola checked her watch. "Ten minutes, babe. Can I get you anything? Water? Advil? Cyanide?"

Jack smiled weakly at her joke and pushed away from the door. "Maybe just a few minutes alone."

Nola squeezed her arm, understanding as she always had that Jack needed solitude like other people needed air.

"Okay. I'll be right on the other side of that door. I'll knock when it's time, if Ed hasn't come to get you yet." Nola blew her a kiss, and left through another door that opened directly to the amphitheater. The murmuring of the gathered crowd swelled, then disappeared once the door swung shut.

A carafe of water stood on a small side table in the corner. Jack set her handbag down, then poured herself a glass, wishing instead for another shot of Patrón. She guzzled it, then lowered herself into an uncomfortable plastic chair to wait.

The sound of the clock ticking on the wall grew louder and louder, until she couldn't stand it anymore. She leapt to her feet and began to pace.

Someone rapped sharply on the door. She jumped, nerves screaming, then crossed the room. She reached for the knob but before she could grab it, the door swung open forcefully, slamming Jack right in the face.

Fireworks exploded behind her eyes. Pain sliced through her head. The room tilted, narrowed, and went black.

The next thing she knew, she was lying on her back on the floor, blinking up into Ed O'Malley's florid, worried face.

"Dolan! *Dolan!* Are you all right?"

Warped and echoing, his voice sounded as if it were broadcast from underwater. There was a watery aspect to his face, too, and the room behind him, everything wavering and slipping, the colors faint and blurred.

Crouching beside her, Ed helped her sit up. He pulled a handkerchief from his coat pocket, shook it out, and pressed it against her face. "Jesus, Dolan, you're bleedin' like a stuck pig. Is your nose broken? How d'you feel, darlin'; talk to me!"

Dazed, Jack was unable to speak. Her eyes couldn't focus. Her brain was fuzzy, her thoughts amorphous as smoke. Beyond the ringing in her ears and the throbbing in her nose, she remembered she was in the New York Times Building. She remembered she was here for a press conference. She remembered . . .

"Oh God," Jack breathed, going ice cold.

She remembered everything.

Like a sharp kick that shakes the fruit from a tree, the blow to her head had knocked all the stuck memories loose. They flooded her, mercilessly lashing her with sound and color and scent and taste. Everything she'd forgotten came back in one huge fireball of recall, exploding in her brain like a supernova.

Her father.

Her mother.

Her brother.

Her childhood.

The article.

The pictures.

The lost weeks . . .

Hawk.

She burst into body-wracking sobs and collapsed into Ed's arms.

"Jesus, Mary, and Joseph," he muttered, patting her on the back. "I'm glad I never saw you cry before this, Dolan. It's downright disturbin'. You never would've got that last promotion."

Nola arrived and started barking at Ed like a rabid dog. "What the hell did you do to her? Did you break her nose? There's so much blood!"

"I opened the door into her face."

"What?"

"It was an accident!"

"Christ, Ed!"

"C'mon, help me get her to her feet. There's a restroom in there." He jerked his head to another door on the opposite side of the room. "Get her cleaned up, let me know if you need me to call an ambulance. Otherwise the limo can take her to the emergency room. I'll reschedule the press conference—"

"No!" Jack choked between sobs. "We're having the goddamn press conference!"

"Dolan, you can't go on television lookin' like you went twelve rounds with Mayweather!" Ed slung an arm around her waist, Nola took the other side, and they lifted her as she held onto their shoulders. She wobbled a moment, then shook her head to clear it, and wrenched herself out of their arms.

"Five minutes!" she cried, hysterical. "Don't cancel it!"

Nola and Ed exchanged a glance, but didn't contradict her. They'd seen her in this mode too many times, knew it was useless to try to talk her out of something once she had her mind made up. She knew she had to pull herself together, however, or Ed would never let her go in front of the cameras, no matter how vehemently she argued she could.

She stumbled to the restroom, locked the door behind her, crossed to the enamel sink, and sagged against it, breathing as if she'd run a sprint. Tears streamed down her cheeks. She stared at her reflection in the mirror, at her bloody face and haunted eyes, thinking one word over and over again.

Hawk.

She lowered her head and closed her eyes. Blood from her nose dripped with a soft, regular *plash* into the sink.

She *did* love him. He was the man she loved, the only man she'd ever loved, and she'd left him behind in a jungle on another continent, with no way to contact him, no way to let him know she remembered everything, including *them*.

Especially them.

She suddenly realized he'd been relieved she didn't remember her past because he'd rather have her forget him than remember all the pain, all the sickness she'd forgotten. Even though it must have killed him to have her forget, he preferred that than seeing her in pain.

That seemed like the most beautiful and the most awful thing in the world.

Shaking violently, she turned on the faucet, splashed water onto her hot face. She washed away the blood, feeling for a break in her nose but not finding one, not that it mattered if she did; she didn't give a damn how she looked. Suddenly all she cared about was an enchanted man who lived in a rainforest thousands of miles away with his enchanted rainforest family, hiding from the rest of the world.

Hiding because of people like her. People like she'd once been. People full of so much anger and hate even their ignorance had a hard time carving out space for itself.

Jack pinched her nostrils between two fingers and ripped a wad of paper towels from the wall dispenser. When the blood flow stopped, she tossed the towels into the trash, then slowly removed her jacket, slung it over the top of the toilet stall, and unbuttoned her shirt.

She turned around and looked over her shoulder.

Pink and white and distinct, the raised welts stared back at her almost accusingly, every ripple and pucker blatant evidence of all she had lost and gained and lost again, that fragile, magical *hope* that had filled her full to bursting in those lazy, loving hours in Hawk's arms. He'd given her hope, and so much more. He'd given her a dream so huge it was at once terrible and beautiful, a thing so precious and bright it outshone all the horror and hopelessness of her life.

Peace. He'd given her a taste of peace, and she thought that even one small sip was a gift of immeasurable value, because at any moment in the long years that would come, she could remember that feeling. She could take it out and hold it in her hands and cherish it, and remind herself that once, however fleetingly, she had been loved.

Jack re-buttoned her shirt, her fingers trembling, a roar like a thousand wing beats in her ears. She donned her jacket, wiped away the rest of her tears, smoothed her hands over her hair, and stood there for a moment longer, looking at herself in the mirror.

"What am I supposed to do now?" Jack whispered hoarsely to her reflection.

Just tell them the truth. Whatever you remember. I know you'll be fair.

The truth.

She nodded, hearing Jenna's ghost-like voice in her head. "All right then, dragon lady. Fuck it. That's exactly what I'll do."

Then she turned away from the mirror, withdrew her prepared speech from her jacket pocket, tore the sheets of paper in two and threw them in the trash, and went out to meet the press.

"Hawk!"

Someone was calling his name, but Hawk couldn't be bothered to find out who, or why. He couldn't be bothered with much of anything at all, as he'd determined he was going to spend the rest of his life right here in this room, on this bed, staring up at this ceiling, while the world and everything in it passed him by until one day he'd die and be done with it all.

Or, as he'd realized during his trek through the jungle, he might get lucky and be killed in the invasion. The thought of death in battle—where he could, at least, take down as many of the colony's enemies as possible before forfeiting his own life—was the one thing that had ultimately made him turn back. He could use a few people to kill right about now.

He was aware that his reaction to Jacqueline's leaving had blown far past Shakespearean levels of melodrama into the ridiculous, but he didn't give a damn. She was gone. His life was over. Whether he eventually died of a broken heart or at the business end of a gun was just splitting hairs.

So whoever was calling his name could go right on doing so until his tongue fell out. Hawk wasn't moving from this spot. A rock sailed over the edge of the porch railing, bounced off the mattress, and landed in the middle of his chest with a painful *thud*.

He leapt up with a muttered oath, rock in hand, and went to the railing, snarling in fury. He leaned over, arm cocked back to retaliate, but restrained himself when he saw who it was.

"The Queen wants to see you," said Zaca, peering up at him from the forest floor below. "Says it's important."

The Queen. Another strategic planning meeting, no doubt. He didn't know why their enemies hadn't attacked yet, but when they got here, they were in for a big bloody surprise, he knew that.

The story of what Hope and Honor had done to Caesar had spread like wildfire through the colony. People were talking about them as if they were weapons of mass destruction, which Hawk thought they probably were. When he wasn't thinking about Jacqueline, he was thinking about Olivia Sutherland's face when she said "The children can take care of themselves."

Gave him the willies. Didn't matter, though. Everything that mattered had walked out of his life. And didn't even remember him, anyway.

Zaca waved his hands overhead. "Hey—you listening to me, old man?"

Hawk didn't even have the energy to return the playful insult with one of his own. He nodded and withdrew, leaving Zaca to stare up with a worried look, until he wandered off, hands stuffed into the pockets of his shorts.

Hawk dressed in no particular hurry, then headed out.

When he arrived at the Queen's residence, he was welcomed by Morgan. "Has your shoulder healed yet?" she asked, her expression revealing nothing.

He nodded. "Why?"

"Oh, just wondering. C'mon in." He followed her through the house to the living room, where Leander was standing with his arms crossed, behind Jenna, on the settee. Both of them were staring at a satellite television screen.

The image on the screen was frozen. It was Jacqueline.

She stood behind a Plexiglas podium in front of a large crowd of seated people. A view of trees and greenery loomed open behind her, light reflected off wide expanses of glass. A title at the bottom of the screen read, "Live from the *New York Times* offices, reporter Jacqueline Dolan."

A press conference.

His heart seized. His stomach clenched. He wanted to say something but all that came out of his mouth was a choked noise of shock.

"You'll want to see this," Jenna said without turning around. "It was recorded just an hour ago."

Leander looked at him, gestured to a chair. The expression in his eyes, Hawk noted, was one of faint amusement.

He sank into the chair, grateful he no longer had to stand because his knees had started to shake.

Jenna pushed a button on the remote control in her hand, and the image sprang to life. Jacqueline's soft voice filled the room.

"Thank you all for coming. I won't take up too much of your time, and I won't be taking questions. After today, this is the last time I'll speak publicly on this subject."

She paused and gazed down at the podium, her hands gripping tightly on either side, her chest rising and falling erratically. She looked wan and exhausted, with purple bruises of sleeplessness beneath her eyes. He drank in the sight of her like one who's gone too long without water, gasping and gulping it down, until something made him blink.

Were those drops of *blood* on the collar of her white blouse? Stomach in knots, he leaned forward in his chair.

She looked up, stared slowly around the room at the gathered faces, then focused her gaze directly into the camera. "Someone recently accused me of being a bigot. And . . . he was right."

The clicking of camera shutters. The lights on her face, searingly bright.

"There are few things in life more difficult than seeing yourself objectively, especially when what you might see if you look too closely is something ugly, or painful, or small. I thought I knew everything about myself. I thought I was a good person. But it took forgetting everything to remember that I *wasn't* a good person. In fact . . ." She swallowed, blinking into the glare. "I'm ashamed of myself. The things I've said and done have spread misunderstanding and distrust, prejudice and hatred, and if I could take them all back, I would."

The silence in the amphitheater was deafening. Hawk's heart was clenching and twisting, and he put his hand over his chest, pressing hard against his sternum as if it could help.

"I owe an apology to those I've harmed with my ignorance. The op-ed I wrote—"The Enemy Among Us," for which I was nominated for a Pulitzer Prize—is so filled with ugliness it disgusts me now to read it. The people it maligns are not deserving of such a thing. In fact, I think it safe to say they're deserving of nothing less than our utmost respect and admiration. They're different from us, yes. Their ways are foreign and their culture strange, but that only means we should work harder to understand them, and find ways to bridge our differences so we can live together in peace."

Hawk closed his eyes, struggling for air, sick and aching and so swamped with longing he wanted to scream.

DARKNESS BOUND

"This planet doesn't only belong to the human race. It belongs to every living creature on it. Equality isn't an ideal that can be applied according to the whim of popularity, or toward one race or gender or species in lieu of another. We either believe in equality for all—*all*—and strive toward that . . . or we're nothing but a bunch of hypocrites."

There was another beat of silence after she stopped speaking. Then the room erupted into noise, everyone shouted at once, questions were volleyed, cameras clicked furiously.

"There's one last thing I'd like to say." Jack held up a hand and the roar slowly dulled to a restless murmur.

The cameras zoomed in tight on her face so it filled the screen. Pale skin, dusted with freckles. Bloodshot eyes fringed in a curve of brown lashes. Her mouth, the lower lip full and trembling. She inhaled a long, deep breath, nostrils flaring, and for a gut-wrenching moment Hawk thought she might cry.

Instead she said in a steady, soft voice, those blue eyes burning, "Lucas Eduardo Tavares Castelo Luna, you underhanded son of a dung beetle . . . I love you. With all my heart and soul, I love you. I'm not a religious person, but because of you, I believe in miracles. You taught me how to be loved. I never knew what that meant before, I was too busy feeling terrible and hating myself and thinking that's the way things were always going to be, but you gave me the gift of yourself and a glimpse of happiness, and for that I want to say thank you."

She bit her lower lip. Her eyes filled with tears. Her voice breaking, she said, "Knowing you made me a better person. I'll always be grateful I met you. And I'll always be yours."

She turned and ran off the stage.

The room leapt to its feet, the reporters shouting questions, shooting pictures, surging toward the stage to get one last, final

405

picture of her before she disappeared through a side door. A team of newscasters behind a desk came on to comment on the broadcast, and Jenna pushed a button on the remote, plunging the television screen into darkness. She rose, turned to look at Hawk, and smiled. "So, what did you think? Interesting speech, wasn't it?"

He stood unsteadily. His chest felt constricted, as if an invisible winch was tightening around it, and he couldn't catch his breath. He thought for one wild, deranged moment he was having a heart attack.

Jacqueline remembered. She remembered everything.

And she loved him.

He stammered, "I . . . I . . ."

"I know," said the Queen, moving to the other side of the room. She stopped beside Leander, glancing up at him with a smile. When she looked back at Hawk, her whole face was alight. "Go," she urged softly, resting her head on Leander's chest. "If you catch a good tailwind, you'll be in New York by nightfall."

Hawk made a noise that was somewhere between a sob and a laugh, then put his hand to his face, rubbing his jaw. He nodded, looking between Jenna, Leander, and Morgan, who was grinning mischievously.

Without another word, he Shifted to Vapor and surged out of the room and into the sky, leaving his clothes behind in a pile on the Queen's living room floor.

FORTY-FOUR
Home

The carton of noodles with spicy garlic sauce was empty, as was the carton of curry dumplings, the box of veggie rolls, and the container of pad thai, which Jack normally didn't order because it tasted vaguely of pork. She suspected those small, meaty chunks Mr. Hsu at her favorite Chinese place always claimed were fried tofu were, in fact, of animal origin.

Tonight, consuming things of animal origin seemed like a perfectly rational idea. Right up there with ruining your career, conducting a weepy confessional on national television, becoming the laughingstock of everyone you ever knew, and realizing you'd lost the love of your life because you were, one: suffering from amnesia, and two: a complete jerk.

"Maybe no one will recognize me in Iceland," Jack muttered, looking up at the moon hanging in the night sky. Cold and remote, it stared balefully back through her apartment windows. "Or . . . Costa Rica."

Yes. Costa Rica. Better than Iceland. Less ice.

She'd finally convinced Nola she'd spent enough time away from her own life and should return to it, and that *no*, she was in no danger of slitting her wrists. Nola had gone grudgingly, threatening to call first thing in the morning, though she'd already texted her three times in the past three hours.

Instead of walking to China Palace as Jack normally would have, she'd asked the restaurant to deliver the food because there were still two news vans parked outside her apartment building, filled with reporters waiting to pounce. And now she was sitting on the floor in the living room, with her back against the wall, surrounded by empty food containers, wondering why she'd never had the sense to buy more furniture.

"Because you didn't need it, that's why," she said aloud to the empty room. "You were never home."

Home. Now there was a concept. For the first time in her life she knew where home really was.

The same place her heart was. With Hawk.

Just thinking his name hurt. She squeezed her eyes shut, took a few deep breaths, then pushed herself up to her feet, leaving the cartons behind. She wandered through the dim, silent apartment, went to stand at the tall windows to look out into the night. Lights in windows and streams of traffic and a skyline forested with skyscrapers . . . New York City was about as different from the rainforest as it was from the moon.

She'd finally called her father. The conversation was awkward. At the end, Jack told him she loved him, and that if he ever again uttered racist, sexist, hateful things about people in her presence that would be the last time he'd see her. He'd gone quiet when she said that; then he'd said, "Okay, Jackie," and Jack had felt such a surge of relief she wished she'd demanded it years ago.

Then he told her Garrett had finally succeeded in killing himself.

She'd sunk to her knees as he spoke, clutching the phone so hard she thought it might break, every muscle in her body shaking.

"Made himself a rope of thread he'd been pulling from his clothes. Took him over a year to make it, they think. Guess he was determined."

There was an exposed metal pipe along the ceiling in the communal shower at the mental institution. They'd found him swinging from it, with the rope he'd fashioned with his own hands tight around his neck.

She'd thought she would cry then. Emotion rolled through her, there was an awful constriction in her throat, but the tears wouldn't come. Finally she'd just said goodbye to her father and ended the call, exhausted.

She'd napped. She'd ordered food. And now she was staring out the window, trying to decide what to do with the rest of her life.

"Hawaii could be good," she said to the glaring moon. Then, "No, not far enough. But definitely somewhere tropical. Maybe . . . the Caribbean."

From behind her a low voice said, "What about Brazil?"

She whirled around and there he was, a shadowed presence against the open rectangle of her bedroom door, cat's eyes shining silver through the dark.

Light coursed through her, pure and blinding bright, and for a moment it was all she could do to stand still and breathe, feeling blood pound in her temples and a happiness so profound she thought it might leak through her pores in drops of sunbeam gold.

"I . . . you . . ." Astonishment was wreaking havoc with her ability to string a sentence together, and she stood there staring at him stupidly, gaping, her body taut with hope and disbelief. "You're here. You're *here*."

"I was in the neighborhood. If a continent south could be considered the neighborhood."

The sound she made was a weak approximation of a laugh, gutted by shock, and it made his cat eyes flash mercury bright.

"Interesting speech you gave."

"Oh, you know," she said, failing to match his offhand tone, "those silly speech writers. Anything for the ratings."

He stepped away from the door, his gaze scorching the air between them like a lit fuse.

He was nude, and glorious. Had she ever seen a thing so beautiful as him, drenched in moonlight, moving toward her with that predatory gleam in his eye?

She closed her eyes just as he reached her, terrified he might be a dream. But then his hand brushed her cheek, his thumb traced the curve of her lower lip, and everywhere he touched it felt like he left a trail of fire.

He was no dream. He was here. Her rigid disbelief gave way and she was wracked with trembling.

"Yes. I'm sure the ratings were amazing," he murmured, moving closer. "That was quite a show, Red. About-face of the century." He radiated heat, standing so close now she felt his warmth straight through her clothes, burning her chest and stomach. He put his lips to her ear and in a thick voice said, "I especially liked the end part."

"I thought that would be a good touch," she whispered. His hands came around her waist. She wound her arms up around his shoulders, broad and bare and strong. "More dramatic, you know."

He angled his head, gazing down at her with a scant smile, fire burning in his eyes. "For the ratings."

His hands tightened around her waist and she said his name, a catch in her throat. Her pulse was a jagged throb in her neck.

He dipped his head and pressed his lips against the throbbing vein. "Say it again, Jacqueline," he whispered, his lips moving against her skin. "I want to hear you say it again."

Her head fell back. Her eyes slid shut. He pressed his mouth against her neck, teeth and tongue and wonderful sucking, and she felt a jolt of electricity straight down to the soles of her feet. Gasping, she said, "I'm yours."

He chuckled, a sound with an edge to it like a purr. An arm snaked around her waist, pulling her hard against him, a hand tightened in her hair.

"No, that wasn't quite it." Lips, velvet soft and teasing, brushed against hers. "Try again."

He slid his tongue across her lower lip, that hand still tight in her hair, holding her head, and for a moment she thought her knees might give way altogether, so intense was the pleasure and emotion. She tried to speak, but all that came out was the smallest of sounds, a low, choked sob.

He took her face in his hands and demanded, "Jacqueline. *Say it again.*"

With the first of the tears burning her eyes, she whispered, "I'll *always* be yours."

Then he kissed her, hard, until her breath was short and she was clinging to him, shaking so badly she was shaking him, too. He broke away, panting.

"That's right," he growled, lifting her up in his arms in one swift, smooth motion, one arm supporting her back, the other hooked under her knees. "I lay claim to you, woman. You're mine, and you always will be, and there's nothing in this world that's ever going to separate us again."

Jack buried her face into his neck and sobbed. He swung around and carried her into the bedroom, laid her on the bed, tore off her clothes, and kissed her everywhere until her sobs turned to moans. Still the tears didn't stop, even when he came between her legs and pushed inside her, even as he told her everything he felt for her, how much he loved her, how he'd thought he would die when she'd left, his eyes rapt on her face, his body moving inside hers.

When finally the culmination burst over her in a blazing white flare, she cried out his name, her body bowed with a pleasure so acute it was almost agony.

He pumped deep, hard and rough, letting his hips take over as she met his every thrust with her hips, coaxing him to where she wanted him to go. Then he stilled, his entire body flexed, and he moaned, his head thrown back, eyes closed.

She felt it deep inside her—throbbing, a spreading heat—then he shuddered.

"Say it again," he begged, his voice broken. "Please—Jacqueline—"

"Always, only yours," she wept, pulling him down with her hands on his face so they were staring into each other's eyes as he twitched and groaned, his beautiful face flushed, dark hair falling over his forehead, down his cheeks. "Forever."

He collapsed against her, wrapped his arms so hard around her she wondered briefly if there would be bruises. He kissed her wet face, her mouth, her eyes, turned his face against her so her tears dampened his cheeks, too. He said hoarsely into her ear, "You're the only woman I've ever loved, or ever will."

And her heart, her poor hummingbird heart that had been broken so long ago and kept in a dark little box behind a thousand locked doors, was finally free.

Hawk had set her heart free, and it was soaring.

Jacqueline woke as the horizon was turning faintly pale in the east, and shifted her head on his arm. When she opened her eyes there was a moment of confusion, then recognition, and then they blazed with a heat that made his soul sing.

"I was having the most wonderful dream." She burrowed closer to him beneath the blankets, and he pressed a kiss to her forehead, stroking his hand over the smooth satin curve of her hip.

"Hmm." He nuzzled his nose into her neck, inhaling the sweet, soft scent that rose from her skin. Though he was tired from his flight, and hours of lovemaking, he couldn't fall asleep; instead had just watched her all night, marveling.

Love. It burned hot as a swallowed sun within him.

"We were on a sailboat, out in the open sea. It was sunny and warm and the water was this amazing, crystal blue, and we were sailing right into the most beautiful sunset, all crimson and orange and purple and gold. You were feeding me figs, sips of wine, little bites of cheese—"

"A picnic on a sailboat at sunset. I had no idea you were so romantic," he teased.

She blinked up at him, coy. "I'm super romantic, buddy. You're going to have to invest in some poetry writing classes and guitar lessons, because I have high expectations. I mean, you can't just throw me over your shoulder and toss me into bed every time the mood hits."

He said, "Watch me."

She pretended to pout. "I need some wooing, cave man! I deserve to be wooed!"

He rose up on one elbow and stared down into her face. He said quietly, "I want to spend every second of every day for the rest of my life with you, finding out what makes you happy, and doing it. I want you to have my children, and grow old with me, and love me until the day you die. I want to protect you from harm, and I will kill anyone or anything that ever hurts you. I want to shower you in love and worship you and I promise there won't be a day that goes by that I won't tell you how much you mean to me. I want you to be my wife. Will you marry me?"

She breathed, "Oh," and her eyes went wide.

He raised his brows, waiting for her answer. She nodded. He said, "Good. Consider yourself wooed."

He kissed her, feeling the curve of her smile against his mouth. Then he rolled over and pulled her atop him, cradling her to his chest.

After a while, she whispered, "Okay, I admit that was some pretty great wooing."

He stroked her hair off her face and shoulders, smoothed it down her back. They lay in silence for a while, watching the streetlights wink out with the first rays of dawn, until his gaze settled on an embroidered square of fabric hung in a frame on the wall. It was the only thing on any of the walls in her apartment, which suggested it held sentimental value. Which made him curious.

"You a big fan of Edgar Allan Poe?"

Her laugh was sweet and low. "I am now." She lifted her head and looked at him. "But I wasn't before. Morgan gave that to me. Remember, the present with the white bow? I think she made it herself, but I can't be sure. She didn't say."

He looked again at the patch of fabric, stitched with a quote.

The ninety and nine are with dreams,
content but the hope of the world made new,
is the hundredth man who is grimly bent
on making those dreams come true.

"He was a smart man, ahead of his time," Hawk murmured, trailing his fingers up the gentle bumps of her spine. "'Hope of the world made new,' indeed."

"Wait—you're not telling me he was one of you . . . are you?"

He smiled at her. "One of these days I'll make you a complete list. But in the meantime, we're going to have to decide where to live."

"Oh. Well . . . why not the colony?"

His hand on her skin stilled. "You would live there with me? Leave your life here behind?"

She gazed up at him, smiling, her eyes soft. "Did we not just establish that I was properly wooed? Home is wherever you are, Hawk." She spread her hand over his chest, above his heart. "Home is this, right here."

He closed his eyes briefly, gratitude rising up in a wave that overwhelmed him, along with a flare of love so violent he felt burned. "Things aren't safe at the colony for you. In fact, they're not safe for any of us. If I hadn't been voted the new Alpha, I'd probably—"

"Alpha! Voted! What happened to fighting to the death?" She'd jerked upright, was staring at him with unblinking eyes.

"Oh? You'd rather that than a nice, civilized vote?"

"Of course not!" she huffed, shoving his chest. "But—how—"

"I'll give you one guess. It involves a dragon."

Jack stared at him, the light of comprehension dawning in her eyes. "The Queen."

He nodded. "Looks like democracy finally made it to the jungle. Our new Queen is proving herself quite the reformist. So far she's overturned pretty much every Law we ever had."

Jack smiled. "I knew I liked her."

He drew her down against his chest again, combing his fingers through her hair. "And she likes you. God help us if the two of you ever put your heads together: we'll end up living on the moon."

Jacqueline grew solemn as she trailed her fingers over his arm. "Is that the only place that will be safe for us, you think? The moon? Do you think your species and mine will ever be able to live together in harmony?"

He thought about it for a long time, looking out into the sky. He finally said, "I don't know. I just don't know."

Hearing her dark sigh, he teased, "Look at the lengths I had to go to just to change your mind about us. Seducing you was a hell of a lot of work, sweetheart. I don't know any other male who would be up to the challenge."

"Oh, *really*?" She bit his nipple, and he yelped in outrage, throwing her onto her back. "And by the way," she said as he returned the favor but with fewer teeth and a lot more tongue, making her arch her back and her voice go breathy, "if I recall correctly, it was *I* who seduced *you*."

He lifted his head and gazed down at his love, her face flushed, her smile so beautiful. He said, "We seduced each other. That's what happens when you fall in love."

"Hmm. So it's a fairy-tale ending, then?"

Hawk slowly shook his head. "It's not a fairy tale, but it's real, and it's good. And it's everything I could possibly hope for. It's more than I deserve."

Her smile grew dazzling. "Look at you, an expert in wooing already. You just earned yourself a gold star, buddy."

He smiled back at her. "I see a lot of those in my future."

She whispered, "Me, too." Then she drew him down and kissed him, and he forgot about gold stars and democracy and fights to the death, and just let himself fall deeper and deeper into her.

The only place in the world he ever wanted to be.

EPILOGUE

Jenna bolted upright in bed.

Her heart raced. Her hands shook. She was sweating, gulping deep breaths as if she'd been running. It was very late, or very early, only an hour or so before first light. Beside her in bed, Leander sat up, and cupped her bare shoulder in his hand.

"What is it?" he asked, his voice low.

Jenna looked around the shadowed bedroom, watched the sheer white curtains that enclosed their bed billow and shift in the night breeze. In the air hung an unpleasant smell, sour as a rat's nest.

"The comet," Jenna whispered. She sat still upon the bedcovers, listening hard into the darkness. "I dreamt about the red comet. And everything . . . everything everywhere was on fire. The whole world was fire. There was nothing left."

She looked at Leander, saw the fear in his eyes, the same fear he undoubtedly saw in hers. He pulled her against him, wrapped his arms around her, and didn't say a word.

There was nothing to say. They both knew what her dream meant. *Mama.*

From the darkness beyond the bed, Jenna's babies called to her.

She rose quickly, donned the robe left on a chair beside the nightstand, glanced at Leander as he rose and pulled on a pair of loose drawstring trousers, watching her all the while. His expression registered his knowledge that she heard what he could not, and he simply followed silently behind her as she made her way across the room to the bassinette.

In it, the twins were standing up. Waiting.

Tottering on unsteady legs, Hope and Honor cooed happily when they saw her. They raised their arms, wanting to be picked up. Jenna moistened her lips, felt her heartbeat flutter, her hands grow clammy. Inside her head, their voices murmured in the Old Language, the latest addition to their burgeoning Gifts. She wondered what unlucky soul had recently lost his ability to speak his native tongue.

"They want to go outside," she said quietly to Leander as she lifted Hope from the bassinette. He lifted Honor, tucking her into the crook of one strong arm.

"Why?" In the darkness, his eyes shone vivid emerald, intense with emotion.

Jenna whispered, "Because it's time."

Above the babies' heads, their gazes locked. She thought she'd never seen him look so beautiful, bare-chested and tense, holding their child, his hair an inky mess around his shoulders, those eyes so full of love and anguish.

He said her name, a low, fervid entreaty, but she only shook her head, her eyes filling with moisture. "Don't wake anyone else. There's no need."

She turned and made her way quickly through the dark house, slipping from room to room as she listened to the sound of his footsteps close behind. The night air was soft and fragrant on her heated skin when they crossed the suspension bridge that led away from the massive Brazil nut tree, the wood planks smooth beneath her bare feet.

Finally the four of them stood on the rise of the bare rock at the Well of Souls, the stone funeral pyre a hulking black shape in the moonlight.

Jenna stood still a moment, watching the sky, her robe shifting around her ankles as a warm draft caught in its folds. Then Leander pulled her hard against him with one arm, his hand wrapped around the back of her neck, and kissed her.

It was hard, passionate, and desperate. It felt like a goodbye.

The tears she'd been holding back broke free and streamed down her cheeks. She pulled away and they stood with their foreheads pressed together, breathing hard, looking down at Hope and Honor who stared up at them solemnly, quiet in their arms.

"Don't say anything," Jenna begged, her voice breaking. "Please."

"Only that I love you. And I always will."

Jenna heard the shaking he couldn't control in his voice, and when she looked up into his eyes, his were wet, too.

"I love you, too," she whispered. "And I wouldn't change a thing. Not a single thing, Leander."

They stared into each other's eyes until finally he nodded, swallowing.

In Jenna's arms, Hope made a small sound. Jenna looked down at her to find her arm outstretched, her little pudgy finger pointing at the horizon. She and Leander lifted their heads, and saw far, far away in the early dawn sky, the glimmer of lights. A long, wavering line of pinprick white danced above the black outline of the treetops. Just as she felt the first, faint tremors run through the ground beneath her feet, a whiff of something sharply antiseptic hit her nose.

Jet fuel.

"All right, you sons of bitches," Jenna muttered. "You want to play? Let's play."

Leander took her hand, clasping it firmly in his. She allowed herself one last look at his profile, handsome and hard, then she turned her attention back to the sky, not bothering to wipe the tears from her cheeks. The two of them stood there shoulder to shoulder on the bare rock, their children tucked into the crooks of their arms, holding hands, waiting.

As the lights came closer, Leander said in a horrified whisper, "There are a thousand of them!"

"More," was Jenna's grim reply.

A gust of wind whipped her hair into her eyes, swirling it wildly around her shoulders. Leander's grip on her hand tightened. Far off in the forest, a flock of birds took flight from a tree with a haunting cry.

Then Honor lifted both her arms, reaching out to the horizon. Hope mimicked the motion, and Jenna felt a fear unlike she'd ever known sink with cold, serpentine darkness down into her soul.

When the first of the military planes were close enough for Jenna to glimpse the white helmets of the pilots inside, Honor let out a loud, delighted squeal of laughter.

Over the roar of a thousand jet engines, Jenna screamed, "Mommy loves you, girls!"

And so it began.

ACKNOWLEDGMENTS

This is the part where I always get weepy, because it means I've come to the end of the story. Also because I take a moment to breathe—the first moment in months—and recognize how many people producing a novel involves. How many people are necessary to helping me get to the final page, and to whom I owe thanks.

As always, I thank my team at Montlake Romance and Amazon Publishing for their support and professionalism. You make it look so easy! Maria Gomez, my editor, my dear, you are wonderful. The copyediting and proofreading teams deserve shout-outs, as do the merchandising and PR teams. Thank you for your hard work. And special mention goes to the Duke of Montlake and the Dude (who, of course, abides) for just being cool.

I am eternally grateful to Marlene Stringer for picking me out of her ginormous slush pile, and advocating for me. I'm also eternally grateful to Eleni Caminis, for many reasons, none of which can be mentioned here.

Melody Guy. You. *Rock*. Thank you for always making my books better.

To my Street Team, I'm so happy you have decided to join me on this journey and help spread the word about my work. It means so much to me. Thank you also to the many book bloggers who have been incredibly supportive, and said such kind things about the Night Prowler world. I so appreciate it. To my readers, I owe a special debt of thanks because without you, there wouldn't be any Night Prowler world!

Thanks to Shannon and Scott Smith of SS Media Co. for being web designer geniuses. It's been over ten years we've worked together, can you believe it?

Thank you to my book club "ladies," who give me more entertainment in one evening than most people do in one year. Here's to decades more of drunken debauchery . . . oh, and reading, of course.

To my parents, Jean and Jim, thank you for believing in me even during those hellish teenage years, and for your general greatness. I love you.

And last but never least, thank you to my own personal Alpha, Jay. I can't believe married people are allowed to have so much fun together. (I won't tell if you don't.)

ABOUT THE AUTHOR

 J.T. Geissinger's debut novel, *Shadow's Edge*, was published in 2012 and was a #1 Amazon US and UK bestseller in both fantasy romance and romance series, and won the PRISM award for Best First Book. Her second book in the Night Prowler series, *Edge of Oblivion*, was a finalist for the prestigious RITA® award for Best Paranormal Romance from the Romance Writers of America. She lives in Los Angeles with her family and is currently at work on book six in the series. Visit her online at jtgeissinger.com